Edith Pargeter is a distinguished author of historical fiction. Her work includes the *Brothers of Gwynedd* quartet and *A Bloody Field by Shrewsbury* as well as the *Heaven Tree* trilogy. Under the pseudonym Ellis Peters she writes best-selling medieval whodunnits featuring Brother Cadfael as the sleuthing monk. She lives in Shropshire.

EDITH PARGETER

The Heaven Tree

Futura

A Futura Book

First published in Great Britain in 1960
by William Heinemann Ltd

This edition published in 1986
by Futura Publications, a Division of
Macdonald & Co (Publishers) Ltd
London & Sydney

ISBN 0 7088 3056 0

Reproduced, printed and bound in Great Britain by
Hazell Watson & Viney Limited,
Member of the BPCC Group,
Aylesbury, Bucks

Futura Publications
A Division of
Macdonald & Co (Publishers) Ltd
Greater London House
Hampstead Road
London NW1 7QX
A BPCC plc Company

PART ONE

THE WELSH MARCHES

1200

CHAPTER ONE

The angel, eternally alighting with arched wings and delicate, stretched feet, spread his hands palms outwards towards the radiance, and bowed in ceremonious humility the youthful, narrow head, with its long gold hair still erect and quivering from his flight. The shuddering hum of his great wings hung perpetually upon the astonished air, for ever stilling and never stilled. His eyes, half-averted from the unbearable brightness, had themselves a brilliance not to be borne, and his face was as taut and fierce as the body arrested for ever in the instant of alighting, straining downwards from breast to loin to thigh to instep, silver sinews braced and quivering under the frozen turmoil of the gilded robe. He touched the earth with long, naked, shapely feet, and the earth gave forth a brazen cry, and the tremulous air vibrated like a bowstring along the descending arc of his passage from heaven.

In the shadowy spaces above him the creator bent his head to look upon his work, and saw that it was good.

Ebrard came to fetch them home from Shrewsbury on a green morning some days after Easter, with his fledgling knighthood glossy and stiff upon him like new clothes, and three armed grooms at his back to keep him in good conceit of himself. They waited at the gatehouse to salute him dutifully as he dismounted, Harry with a brotherly kiss, Adam with a deep reverence. And Abbot Hugh de Lacy came limping through the bustle of the great court to bless their departing. He was lame of the left leg from a certain hunting affray in his youth, when a wounded boar had brought down both him and his horse, and the moist spring season always gnawed hard at the place where his bones had knit awry. He had taken boar and wolf and deer in his time, and not always with license; but that was before he donned the cowl and fixed his sights upon the mitre.

He held them before him by the shoulders, and: 'Well, boys,' said he, 'you are in a fair way to be men. Keep fast what you have learned here among us, and make good use of it in the stations to which you are called, and you will do well. You have both Latin and French, have you not?'

'Yes, Father.'

'And some knowledge and skill in music?'

'Yes, Father.'

'And of your gifts in the carving of wood and stone we have good reason to be glad, for they have enriched our house.' Better, perhaps, not to dwell on that. Harry was going to miss his chisels and punches all too sorely, he needed no reminders. And yet Hugh de Lacy could not forbear from smiling with pleasure at the thought of the little wooden angel on the Virgin's altar, fifteen inches tall and browed like his creator, with the same deep-arched eyelids, the same half-hidden glitter of brilliant eyes, the same narrow, fiery face. Every maker, when he first sets his hands to work, makes an image of himself, whether he will or no. God made man in his own image; Harry was in good company. Plagued by the likeness without recognising the source of his unease, the subprior had never liked that angel. To his orderly mind it seemed proper, no doubt, that only demons, not ministers of grace, should be thus abrupt and terrible.

'All these are of God's giving, and faithfully to be used and valued. And I trust you have as good a grounding in the courses of the spirit, and will hold fast to that learning above all.'

'Yes, Father,' piped the dark boy and the fair boy in amiable unison. They were listening to him with no more than one ear between them, and he knew it. What boy of fifteen can be bothered with homilies on the day of his escape from school?

They stood before him side by side, Harry swart and wiry and small, with the bold chin and jutting bones and straight, adventurous mouth of his line, Adam gay and fair, half a head taller than his lord, with blue, merry eyes in a face like a wide-open flower. He saw their hands linked in the shelter of their bodies, and the swift exchange of their glances, so eloquent that they had little need of words between them. Separating them, even for an hour, was like wrenching apart one flesh. Yet the one was son to a villein craftsman, and the other distant kin to the great earl himself, the founder of the house, who lay under his massy stone in the Lady Chapel, mouldering in the kirtle of Saint Hugh.

The Talvaces of Sleapford were descended from a bastard half-brother of Earl Roger's first countess, who had attached himself to the earl's fortunes at the invasion of England, and established himself in a comfortable manor within the honour of Montgomery, with the status of a knight, rights of warren over the forest land he held, and a Saxon wife who commanded the allegiance of two villages, and gave him a measure of security. The family were still proud of reproducing in every generation his face, as well as his name, and traced with care every stage of their relationship with the lords of Belesme, Ponthieu and Alençon.

Ebrard had the name, but Harry had the face. Only his eyes, so often veiled under heavily-lashed lids, and so startling when he raised them, set him apart. The lashes and brows were almost black, but the eyes, when they looked up, were between blue and green like the mid sea, flecked with grey and golden lights, restless and changing, the eyes of the dowerless girl from Brittany who had given birth to the founder of his line.

'Be obedient to your elder, Harry, as is due, deal faithfully for him when you come into your office, and you will do well.'

'Yes, Father,' said the meek voice patiently.

The spring and the century were new, and the sparkling morning was made for new beginnings; and Harry, to do him justice, had shown some sense of the occasion, for his best cotte was well brushed, and his person so combed and washed that Ebrard might justifiably have failed to recognise the reluctant urchin who had been despatched to the abbey of Shrewsbury five years ago, with a smarting tail but with his foster-brother by the hand as the dual reward of his tears and obstinacy. And the more fool Eudo for letting him have his way, but how many wiser men, before and since, had fallen exhausted into the same error?

'And you, Adam, work diligently at your trade, and doubt not that God values the honest mason as he values the honourable knight and the learned clerk, for his offices are legion.'

Better not to have made so pointed a distinction between them; what did it achieve but to make Harry cling ever more stubbornly to his breast-brother? The abbot smoothed his lean, patrician cheek, and wished from his heart that the boy had never been allowed to run wild in Boteler's yard, and discover the dexterity of his hands and the audacity of his imagination. From this day he was to make his future in keeping the manor rolls of Sleapford, exacting from his father's free tenants their due rents, and from his villeins their three days of labour weekly, and their five days in the harvest, and their merchets and heriots and tallages. What better could be done for him, younger son as he was, and born to an estate too circumscribed to be worth dividing? At least he had gained by an education which was thought unnecessary for his father's heir, who could barely write his aristocratic name. If there was to be no knighthood for Harry, neither was there Latin for Ebrard.

'There, I have done! I know you have good sense in you. Only bear it in mind that you have here a friend to whom you may come in your need, at whatever time. Be gentle and patient with your charges, Ebrard, authority has its obligations, too.'

Ebrard stooped to the extended hand a head fair as flax. At nineteen he was already touching six feet, with his pretty mother's blooming rose-and-white complexion and long, fine bones. His knighthood was only a few months old, and still fitted uneasily. Hugh de Lacy still remembered the solemnities in the hall of Shrewsbury castle at the Christmas feast, and the loud guffaw which had risen from the rear ranks of the young gentlemen attendant when Ebrard, pale and exalted, had stepped on the hem of his robe in rising, and almost fallen on his face before the king's castellan. Sir Eudo Talvace, luckily, had not identified the voice of his younger son, but the abbot had, and so had poor Ebrard, withdrawing from the hall with a face like a peony. Rumour had it that the first act of his knighthood had been to beat his brother soundly for it, and small blame to him. Those two were eternally at odds. The abbot had not failed to remark the hard blue glance that swept Harry from crown to shoe when they met, expecting defiance, or the aggressive way the boy instantly jutted his chin at his elder. He wondered which had come first, the defiance or the expectation. There was no dislike in it; they would both have been astonished had anyone ventured to doubt that they loved each other as brothers should. Oil and water bear each other no ill-will. Nevertheless, it was touch and go whether they would get as far as Sleapford without coming to blows.

'God be with you, children. I wish you the pleasantest of journeys. When next you come to Shrewsbury, I look to see you at my table.'

Harry rode without any of his brother's graces, but his loose, inattentive ease would outlast Ebrard's erect, self-conscious gallantry. That comes of not being apprenticed to the trade of arms, thought the abbot, looking them over. To Harry a horse is a convenient means of moving from place to place, and he feels no more exalted in mounting it, and no more disgraced should he fall off it, than does a travelling journeyman. To Ebrard a horse is the symbol of his status. Fall off that, and he falls off his own self-esteem; which would be a dangerous fall.

He watched them file through the gateway, Ebrard in the lead, Harry and Adam already jostling and laughing behind him. The villein's boy was the handsomest of the three, with his ready smile, and the hood of his capuchon pushed back to uncover his yellow hair and sturdy brown neck. And a nature, into the bargain, as sunny and candid as his face. No wonder Harry clung to him.

Time will take care of all, the abbot told himself; and yet he was not comforted. Time had had long enough to ease them apart without pain, and had but bound them more stubbornly into one. Why, he thought with exasperation, as he turned back towards the cloister, could not Eudo's wife have been a lusty creature like Boteler's, able to suckle her own child? Or why must Eudo be such a fool with him afterwards? The time to coax them away from each other was long ago, as soon as they could ride or run, and that old dotard was too engrossed in his heir to see the need for care with this one. Had he but cast a father's eye on Harry in time, and sent some other body-servant here with him in Adam's place, maugre his tears and tantrums, he might have spared both himself and the boy God knows what of trouble to come.

Or why, since they were so made as to love each other out of all reason, could not those two young creatures have been born true brothers, predestined alike to the mason's bench? What, and both unfree?

What is freedom? thought the abbot, turning to cast a last look after the twins who were no twins. Tell me, if you know, which of those two is bond, and which is free?

They passed by the mill, where the outlet of the abbey pool fell back into the brook, and the brook curved and leaped the last few paces to the river. The heavy wains passed in and out, lumbering down from the town over the stone bridge. The abbey mills had a monopoly of the multure for the whole town, and the prior saw to it that their rights were not infringed, for they brought in more money than all the rents on this side of the river.

Severn's flood was high but placid, pale, silvery blue under the open sky, grey-brown beneath the bushy banks. Its level had dropped a yard within the last day, and the time of the spring spate was already passing. Beyond the bridge the hill of Shrewsbury rose, double-girdled with rolling water and towered wall, and to the right, where the river left a neck of land unprotected, the broad, squat shape of Earl Roger's castle straddled the promontory, its crenellated towers gnawing at the sky. Between the castle and the bridge all the slope outside the wall nursed the terraces of the abbot's vineyard. Gnarled and black, as yet hardly budding, the vines showed like thorns.

'You and your angel!' Adam said cheerfully, as they turned south on the near side of the bridge, and crossed the brook. 'What is there so wonderful about it? I believe you'd steal it back if you could. All the angel, and not a word of the rest of the work. Don't you like the capitals you carved?'

'They're well enough, I suppose, but they're only copies. No, not copies, exactly. You remember Master Robert's drawings from Canterbury? I had those in mind when I made my designs. I didn't copy, but I made nothing new. Myself I knew it only when they were lifted into place. Anyone could have made them.'

'Oh, you're too nice! Don't you think every man who carves makes use of what other men have carved before him? Must everything *you* do be the first of its kind? Though it's true,' said Adam wickedly, 'that you found quite a new way with the quintain last Shrove Tuesday. Man, that was alone of its kind, if you like! I never saw a fellow clouted so far across the green – '

It had not been the first and would not be the last of Harry's spectacular failures in the field of manly exercise, and he had no strong feelings about his downfall, but he felt obliged to lean across and take Adam round the neck at this, and haul him sidelong off-balance. Adam clawed one-handed at the pommel of his saddle to keep his seat, and with the other arm clipped Harry about the body. They wrestled together precariously, panting and giggling, and the horses, accustomed to this kind of foolery, sidled to a stop, and stood gently nuzzling. Like Adam, they accepted without comprehending. Adam threw his weight back in the saddle, and tried to heave his lighter opponent bodily from his mount, but Harry dug the fingers of his free hand into the brown tunic and the straining ribs under it, and tickled him until he was writhing in a helpless agony of laughter and distress.

'No! Stop! Harry, you'll have me down!'

'I will have you down, and no mercy! Beg my pardon! Do you ask pardon? Do you?'

Ebrard had turned in the saddle, and cried to them peremptorily to come on and stop their antics. His voice had such a ring of displeasure that it split them apart sharply. Even at that distance they could see how blackly he frowned. They shook themselves hastily into some semblance of order, and spurred forward to overtake him, still muttering breathless recriminations, still giggling.

'For God's sake, must you always be fooling? Have you not had long enough time for play?' Ebrard waited for them with a curling lip and an irascible eye. 'Before I was fifteen I was in my second year of service with FitzAlan, and expected to behave like a man, and not like a brawling brat of seven or eight years. And you had better learn the trick of it, young Harry, for your soft years among the good brothers are over. I wonder father kept you there so long, frolicking away your time to so little purpose. I've heard of your stone-cutting and your wood-carving, and your other antics, and even something of your verses, but little enough of any sensible accomplishments. Do you think father put you to school, and spared you the rigours of a man's life, so that you could tussle like a mongrel puppy, and whittle wood?'

'Here's a sermon over a few minutes' fooling!' said Harry, with a mild face and a conciliatory voice, falling in meekly at his brother's elbow. 'I promise you my Latin will be a match for old Edric's, and I can reckon well enough to keep abreast of all your debtors. I haven't wasted all my time.'

'It's hard to believe you've hoarded much of it, or you'd have outgrown your childish ways by now. Does it speak well for your masters or you when a son of the Talvaces is seen romping on the high road like a village hind? And you, Master Adam, let me counsel you not to abet him so readily. You are too free with these hands of yours.'

As he spoke he flicked the short riding-whip he carried so that the tip of it slapped lightly across the back of Adam's bridle-hand. It was a gesture rather than a blow, and only sheer surprise caused Adam to clap the palm of his other hand to the sting. Harry was the one who started and caught his breath, Harry was the one who blanched with rage and lunged forward in the saddle as though he would fly at his brother's throat. Ebrard was between his two charges, and Adam could not even reach to pluck at the raised arm, or kick exasperatedly at an ankle to recall Harry to sense. He leaned forward, frowning and shaking his head vehemently to silence the threatened outburst. For a moment they hung close together all three, in a tension which made the horses toss and quiver uneasily; then it was all over.

Harry dropped his hands, and sat back in the saddle. The flesh round his mouth and nostrils was lividly pale; the line of his jaw stood out whitely, and for a moment he dared not unclench it for fear of what would burst forth. Then he swallowed the bitter residue of his rage, and said with arduous calm: 'That's unfair! It was I first laid hands on him, he did no more than take hold of me to keep his balance.'

'I can well believe it was you began it. But it's high time he showed some sense of his own, since you have none. You allow him too much familiarity with you, and he takes it too easily for granted. You had better not let father see how little you prize yourself, to play the fool with him in this fashion.' Ebrard spurred from between them and rode ahead, looking back for a moment over his shoulder. 'Now come on! We're losing time.'

Adam, who had long ago learned to bend before these passing storms, waited resignedly for Harry to provoke fate by shouting some furious last word after his elder, and marvelled that no words came. It was something new if Harry was learning sense enough to hold his tongue. They drew together in silence for comfort, and rode side by side, subdued by a chagrin which seemed to them both far too great for the occasion. Adam felt Harry's angry grief heavy upon his heart. Why must he always make so much of such slight things?

A year ago Adam would have shaken him by the shoulder without a second thought, and told him roundly not to be a fool. Even now, though with an unaccustomed timidity, he reached out a hand to touch Harry's arm, and then, hesitating with his eyes on Ebrard's irate back, withdrew again wretchedly before his fingers brushed the green homespun sleeve. He had already been warned that he took too many liberties, the last thing he wanted was to give Ebrard even the slenderest of reasons to elaborate on the same text.

Harry glimpsed the uncompleted gesture out of the tail of his eye, and turning violently but silently, caught at the hand as it drew away, and held it hard, all the harder when Adam, jerking his head warningly towards Ebrard, sought to free himself from the convulsive grip. The print of the whip, a mere snake-tongue of red, had already almost faded from sight, but Harry stared at it as at a mortal wound, and would not let him go.

By the quarry of Rotesay, in mid-afternoon, a dray with a team of horses was slowly straining out of the cutting on to the road, laden with the dove-grey stone. Almost axle-deep in the mud which peeled away from the iron shoes coloured smoothly grey as the rock, it groaned round the difficult curve with a shoving shoulder at every wheel, and came up on to sounder ground with a great sucking sigh. Ebrard slowed up to pass by, and just as the boys drew alongside the dray it pulled slowly out of the shadow of trees into the sunlight. The stone flushed and fired into an over-glow of pale, creamy gold, like a halo round its soft greyness.

Harry's face took fire with it. He reached for Adam's sleeve, forgetting all resolutions of discretion. 'Look at it! Did you ever see such a beautiful colour? Oh, this is what I should like to build in! Think of a church built in a stone like that, think of it on a spring day, half sunshine and half cloudy – a face changing like a woman's, every moment new. It would come to life afresh every morning.'

'It's a good stone,' allowed Adam, studying it with a craftsman's eye as his father would have done. 'It works well, too. Not too hard for carving, but hard; they say it weathers like granite. There's another quarry that has a like stone, and freer working, but it's too near the Welsh border to be safe. I was there once with father, I remember the play of light on the cut face, it was like a mine of sunshine.'

'As big a quarry as this?'

'Three times as big!'

'Keep it in mind for when we build our church. I shall need an assured supply.' He clenched his fingers on Adam's arm, and shook it in his excitement. 'I know now – I'm just beginning to know – how I would have a church look.' Not like the abbey church, he thought, for the first time consciously rejecting that heavy, impregnable splendour. Those great round arches led his eyes upwards only to turn them downwards again like the trajectory of a stone. A church ought not to feel like a sealed grave, or look like the motionless leaden landscape of an eternal frost.

'Do you know, Adam, what I was thinking in the Lady Chapel this morning? I was thinking that if I had my way I would have Earl Roger's tomb out of there. I stood looking at it, and it made me so angry. There it stands where space should be, so that the lines of the aisle could bring a man straight to the altar –'

'– and to your angel,' said Adam gaily.

'Leave my angel be, I'm serious! – and the lines of the arches could enclose a body of light. And instead, there's that ugly thing that breaks up all the planes and puts an encumbrance where space should be, and darkness where light should be. I would throw it out, and never hesitate.'

'As well you didn't say so. Even Father Hugh would have been shocked.' Adam picked his way past the slow-moving team, and kept his voice low, for Ebrard, so much more susceptible to shock from such sacrilege than the abbot, was only a few yards ahead. 'Remember you once told Father Subprior as much about the crucifix above the rood-screen? You said it spoiled the lines of the roof, and ought to come down. My soul, but he did his best to spoil the lines of you!'

'I was too honest, but I was right. And I never took it back, either.' He looked back lovingly over his shoulder, caressing the smooth, honey-coloured faces of the stone with his eyes.

'Oh, Adam, I tell you, stone is the thing! Wood is beautiful, but stone is better! Stone is best of all!'

CHAPTER TWO

After the long, parched day in the harvest fields it was warm and drowsy in the corner of the hall next to the staircase, and Harry's head nodded over the manor survey.

'In the village of Sleapford there are 28 full villeins, and in the hamlet of Teyne 13, each holding one yardland. Sleapford has 12 half villeins, and Teyne has 5, each holding one half yardland. The full villeins work 3 days a week until the feast of Saint Peter, and 5 days thence until Michaelmas, the half villeins in proportion with their tenures. Sleapford has 14 cottagers, and Teyne has 5 –'

He knew it almost by heart, down to the number of pigs and sheep and draught oxen on the manor farm, and the smallest penny rents from the hill intakes, hewn out of the waste above Teyne by enterprising younger sons, who, like Harry himself, had no inheritance to look forward to. He thought it waste of time to copy it out afresh, for it was some years old, and he could as easily have been writing down for them a new and up-to-date survey. But it was not policy to reveal just how well he knew his father's business, or his father's tenants and villeins. So he copied laboriously but good-humouredly, and let them congratulate themselves that he was learning his trade. Soon the light would fail, and he would be let off for the evening. And the day had been beautiful. He had only to close his eyes to see again the bright gold, shimmering selions of still standing corn, curving gently in their S-bends over the vast sunlit field, and the dusty, trampled green headlands between, and the bristling pallor of the stubble where the grain had already been reaped and carted. And Adam, doing day-labour on his father's behalf, brown and ruddy and bare-legged, laughing and whistling as he swung his sickle. He could still feel the dry prickling of the new stubble against his ankles, and see the languid flight of butterflies low among the straw, and in the baked headlands the tiny scarlet and black harvest moths fluttering in colonies, like flowers in a fresh wind, and the vetches and the pimpernels dimmed with the golden dust of summer. The taste of the field ale was still in his mouth, and the ticklish, warm grain-scent in his nostrils.

Old Edric, his father's clerk for thirty years, peered and grimaced and shook his head over his pupil's round, boyish hand. It was the end of Harry's first week of keeping the rolls, and it was the master, not the apprentice, who would be answerable to his lord for the accuracy of the records.

'Here is an error, Harry. You have written Lambert among the villeins at work today in the gore by the meadows. He was not there. I remarked his absence.'

The devil! thought Harry, who knew very well where Lambert had spent his day, with his two dun greyhounds and his bow, while every other man in the shire was absorbed in the harvest. There was no better poaching month than August. 'But surely he was there? Did we not meet him with the ox-wain on his way back to the field? Surely you remember?'

'It was Leofric leading the oxen,' said the old man, but somewhat shaken by the boy's conviction.

'There were two men with the wain, sir. Lambert was walking behind with the goad. He was singing. You can't have forgotten!' He saw, with some astonishment, that he had the advantage. Was it possible that the old fool was beginning to doubt his own memory? 'Let it stand,' he said quickly, seeing his father's bulky body rolling ponderously down the staircase from the solar, 'and in the morning I'll ask the reeve to confirm what I've written, and correct it if it need correction. But you will find I am not mistaken.' That was a prevarication of which he felt ashamed, but he could not have Lambert betrayed to the foresters. He would have to be out early in the morning, and warn both Lambert and the reeve what their story was to be; and not without extracting a promise that the truant would put in his day-labour faithfully for the rest of the harvest. If he had salted away the venison from even one beast, he owed that much thanks for it.

'Well, well, let it stand, then, and do you see to it in the morning. You have made very few errors, child, that I will allow.' And mercifully he closed the roll, as Sir Eudo lumbered down the last steps of the stairs, and rustled through the rushes to their corner. Ebrard was with him, flushed with fresh sunburn to the cap-mark on his brow, his fair hair bleached still whiter by the sun. He had been out all the afternoon flying a half-trained merlin on a creance, and the reel of cord was still in his gloved hand. A warmth of content came into the hall with him, and a smell of the stable and the mews.

Sir Eudo hooked a stool rustling through the rushes with one booted foot, and sat down with the vast, satisfied sigh of a fat, ageing but healthy man. 'Well, how is our clerk shaping?'

'He has made strides, Sir Eudo, strides. This week past he has kept the rolls himself, unaided, and I have but very little fault to find with him, unless it be in his hand, and time and practice will mend that.'

'So he gets his accounts right,' said Sir Eudo bluntly, scrubbing in his thick, grizzled beard with hard fingers, with a sound that reminded Harry of the stubble in the fields whispering against his shoes. 'I care not if he write the crabbedest fist that ever marred vellum.' He looked at his younger son over the bristling hairiness of his cheeks with twinkling brown eyes, a little reddened about the rims with old ale and sack, a little shrunken with the enclosing fat of age and good living, but very bright and shrewd.

'Speak up, Harry, what is there needing my attention about the place? Did Walter Wace send me his idiot son again to do his day-labour for him? I'll have his hide if he try it but once more, and he with four great lads in their wits.'

'No, sir, he sent Michael, and I think you had the best of the four. He could not in any case send you Nicholas, for the poor fellow's sick. You know he was always a weakly soul –'

'I know he would not work,' said Sir Eudo smartly; 'not reeve nor bailiff nor steward could make him stir his stumps.'

'To my mind, sir, Nicholas has ailed since he was born, and it was shame that Walter should send him to the fields at all.' Harry reached for the roll and opened it before him, to give himself time to quench the jealous tremor in his voice when he spoke of the gentle, uncomplaining imbecile. Wace would be glad if Nicholas died, and so removed from his household one hungry mouth and two unprofitable hands. But Harry, when he was a four-year-old tumbling about the meadows with Adam, had learned the names of the flowers in the grass from that same mouth, and been tenderly restrained from the brook and the marlhole by those same hands. He frowned over the tally, and said slowly, because this was an opportunity and he must make a quick assessment of how best to use it: 'There are only a few matters needing your eye, Father.

First, in the matter of Thomas Harnett's rent, which is still overdue. You remember he had an accident, and has been unable to tend to his craft, and you allowed him extra time to pay his debt. It is still unpaid, but if – '

'But if!' said Ebrard lazily, making fast the end of his reel. 'Where's the need of "but ifs"? If he does not pay, he has a fine horse that would pay the score for him handsomely. What does a wheelwright want with a beast like that?'

'If I may speak, sir – I would not distrain on him. If you would extend his time by two months, I think you would gain by it, for his wife and the girl have near killed themselves ploughing and sowing and harrowing his few acres, and have brought him in the best crop for years. It is still standing. If you distrain,' said Harry trying not to sound triumphant too soon, 'they will be slower getting in the grain, and who knows how long this weather will hold? They may lose all, and you the full payment – for he'll be a less profitable tenant if he lacks a horse.'

The old knight peered hard at him, but he kept his eyes on the roll, and his face impartial. Sir Eudo grunted, and eased up the sleeve of his cotte above a massy arm. 'Well, well, I'll not close on him until the harvest's in. Let him have his two months. What next?'

'There is a debt outstanding from Giles of Teyne, who has not paid his Easter tribute of eggs this year, nor his two shillings at St Peter's feast.'

'Nor ever will,' said Ebrard, 'if you distrain on every poor pot in his hovel. He does nothing but drink and fish. The whole of his yardland would not bring him in a penny if it rested with him to work it, it's the boy who makes shift to get a crop from it. Has he presented himself for the harvest?'

'Giles? Not he! He sent poor Wat to do that for him, too. He was dropping on his feet with weariness, for he'd worked as long as the light held last night on his father's land, after leaving ours. And so he will tonight, I know. Father, may I speak to the reeve, and have him send the boy back if he come tomorrow? He is not yet fourteen; we have a good legal case to refuse him as not fulfilling the terms, not being of age.'

'And let Giles off his dues? No, not for all Salop, boy! What sort of fool's talk is that?'

'No, sir, I never meant it so. Giles would then be legally responsible for his own default. Charge him with it, take it from him in whatever goods he has –'

'He has nothing worth the taking, and you know it. As shiftless a lout as ever tickled trout in the brook yonder. I should never get my dues.'

'He has a big body and a rogue's smile,' said Ebrard, 'plausible properties. Sell him. Or give him to the oratory, if no buyer offers. It would be worth it to get rid of him.'

'And his yardland with him? They would not thank me for him without it, I promise you.'

'If I may venture, Sir Eudo,' said old Edric, 'I would advise rather that you sell the boy Wat. He is a bright, well-grown lad, and the abbey at Shrewsbury would have him gladly to train for their company of archers, without any question of land, since he holds none. As soon as he turns fourteen the sale may be made. You would get a fair price for him, and they a fair property for their price. And as for the boy, it would be the making of him. Then you may hale up Giles for labour, and if he do not come you may have justice on him, for he'll have no other to send in his place.'

Sir Eudo threw back his grizzled head, as round as a horse-chestnut, and sent a bellowing laugh up into the smoke-stained roof of the hall. 'That's well thought of, old fellow. I'll do it! Make a note of it, Harry, make a note of it!'

Harry sat staring at him with eyes very wide in a startled face. 'Sell him? Sell Wat? But his mother – ! Father, you'll not do it! He'll break his heart.' This had gone hideously wrong where he had thought there was nothing to go wrong. What did he care, what would the boy and his mother care, if their lord tossed that profitless husband and father into prison for his defaults? He had thought nothing worse than that could happen, and now Edric, of all people, had launched this dreadful alternative upon him. 'Sell – !' The word stuck in his throat. He saw the sleepy boy rubbing his eyes with the back of the hand in which he held the sickle, and again, in his memory, reached over the naked shoulder and took the blade from him. 'Go into the rickyard and find a quiet corner, and sleep. You hear me? I'll call you at noon for your dinner, never fear!' The hay made him a better bed than he enjoyed at home, and the bread and pork and ale was such plenty as he seldom tasted. 'Sell Wat!' How often had he know this happen, and thought nothing of it!

'God's life, boy, what are you babbling about now? If I choose to transfer one of my villeins to the abbey, why should I not? Have

I the right to do it, or have I not?'

'Yes, Father, I know you have, and I know you mean it kindly for Wat, too. But – '

But *sell* him! Like a bolt of cloth, or a bushel of flour, or a side of flesh in a butcher's shop. The same transaction, the money passes and the goods pass.

'But, but, but – ' Sir Eudo's colour was rising, and he had begun to bawl. 'What's amiss with you, Harry? Will the child be the better off, or not? Will he eat better and more regularly than ever in his life, and get a good coat to his back, and more kindness than ever he knew at home? Tell me that!'

'Yes, Father, I know he will. But what will his mother do without him?'

'Thank God and me for putting him out of his father's reach, if she has a fondness for him.'

And that was probably true, too, for indeed she had a fondness, and she would think first of that safe, well-fed, well-clothed, justly used life opening before him, and the word 'sell' would not stick in her throat. But Harry could not get it down, though for the life of him he could not have said why it so suddenly offended and repelled him. He said no more. He himself had a notion that he was being a fool. He looked down at his own hands, folded rather nervously on the roll. This right one had held the sickle when he took it from the boy. The two hands on the haft had lain side by side, like as two blades of grass, browned by the sun, rippling with the constant motion of life, which even in stillness is never utterly still. One hand could be sold, the other could not. Free and unfree. Adam – !

'You are surely right, sir,' he said in a low voice. 'I am new to this, I pray you pardon me.' All the same, he protested within himself, food, clean bed, clothes, gentleness and all, he will not want to go. Before you send him away he'll weep all night. Foolishly, but has he no right to be foolish, just because he is unfree?

'Well, well, you have much to learn, Harry,' said Sir Eudo gruffly, almost as rapidly mollified as roused. 'That matter is settled. What else?'

'Arnulf wants to marry off his daughter.' This was the most ticklish business of all, but now he was too deeply shaken for subtlety, and could only blurt it out baldly and hope for a happy issue.

'Does he so? Well, so he may, if he can pay his merchet for her.'

'He is in some difficulty, Father, and he begs that you will remit a part of the merchet until he can pay it after the harvest. And since it rests with you to fix the amount, and he has been always a good man to you, I venture to ask it of you on his behalf that you will abate the fine as much as may be fair.'

'Well, you are forward to bargain for him. I hope you may be as assiduous for your brother when you come to be in office. But Arnulf is a good fellow, I grant you that. Which daughter is it he wants to marry?'

'The elder, Father. Hawis.'

'What, the girl that weaves mother's homespuns?' put in Ebrard, pushing away with his foot the two greyhound puppies that rolled and played in the rushes. 'You'd better content her, Father, she'll take out her price in good woollens if need be, and mother would be pleased to gratify her.'

Harry flashed him a look whose startled gratitude he did not bestir himself to understand. 'Yes, Hawis is the webster, she wove the cloth you are wearing, sir.'

'Why, then, for so useful a lass – Wait a moment, not too fast! Who is the bridegroom? Is he our man?'

No help for it now. If he hoped to maintain any pretence of innocence and detachment he could do no other than answer the question promptly, though it was the very inquiry he had most wished to avoid. As smoothly as he could he replied: 'No, sir, he is from Hunyate, Stephen Mortmain by name. Arnulf gives him a good report for a sober, hardworking fellow who will make Hawis a good husband.'

'Hunyate?' A spark of calculation kindled in Sir Eudo's small, bright eyes. 'So he's le Tourneur's man, is he?'

Harry frowned over the roll and held his breath. Keep silence now, and let him think so, and he'll not stand in their way. He'll even deprive mother of her cloths if he can make a virtual present of an expert webster to Sir Roger le Tourneur. Villein wife goes with villein husband, and he sees Sir Roger's lady sweetened with Hawis's homespuns, and urging her husband to come to terms with his neighbour, and be friends.

Two years Sir Eudo had spent in wooing his old rival and enemy so that they might join forces to palisade their two territories against the growing encroachments of the Welsh of Powis, and two years Sir Roger had fended him off dourly, and avoided discussing the matter. His forest land stood higher and was less vulnerable than the soft valley of Sleapford under its flank, which was the reason Sir Eudo had such need of his goodwill. The transfer of Hawis, valuable property as she was, might well turn the scale. Harry feigned preoccupation with his own scrawled figures, held his peace, and waited in a chilly sweat for his father to rumble on.

'Are you deaf, boy?' roared the old knight irascibly. 'Answer my question! Is he Tourneur's man?'

'I'm sorry, Father, I have been remiss, I made no note of that, and I am not sure – '

'Harry, Harry!' Old Edric leaned forward across the table and shook him kindly by the arm. 'Have you forgotten? We spoke of this same matter, and I told you.' He looked up placatingly at his master, and said gently: 'He has worked a long day, Sir Eudo, and he does himself less than justice, for indeed he did take up that point.'

If Harry could have reached him he would have kicked him under the table, but now it was already too late. The kind old fool had blurted out the truth: 'Stephen Mortmain is a free man.'

'Free? Free, is he?' Sir Eudo lumbered to his feet with an ominous roar, and jerked up Harry's face by the chin. 'What are you about, you rogue? Do you dare try and gull me? You knew, none so well, that he was free! Did you not, eh?' He released him with a shake, and by way of admonition fetched him a blow on the ear that almost swept him from his stool. 'Try and deceive me again, and I'll teach you better sense.'

'Father, I wasn't – I can't keep everything clear in my mind yet, the work's new to me – '

'Very well, let us leave it so. But mind me, Harry, never be subtle with me, or you'll rue it. In whose interest, for God's sake, have I set you down to make your surveys and scratch your ciphers – mine, or theirs?'

Harry said sullenly: 'I conceive, sir, that there should be no conflict. Master and men should be as one, and have one interest. If they are content and well-provided, they are of the more value to you, and serve you with the better will.'

'You talk like a priest and a fool rolled in one, boy. Keep a shut mouth until you have lived a few years more and got a little common sense. And leave the judgements to me. All I want of you is true accounting. True, I said! Not this juggling with truth and lies. Well, so we have it now! This Stephen is a free man, is he? And wants to take from me one of my best chattels, for nine of your judges out of ten will swear a free man makes a free wife and free issue. And Arnulf wants me to abet the theft of my maid by remitting the merchet for her, does he? No, by God! I would have let her pass into Tourneur's hands. But give us both the slip? Not unless Arnulf pay for it handsomely! Thirty shillings is my price and let him be thankful I set it no higher. You may tell him so!'

'But, Father, he has only two-thirds of a yardland, and no son, and the two girls and their grandam to feed – where should he get thirty shillings, or twenty, either? If he sold all the gear he owns he could not raise so much.'

'Then the girl remains unmarried. I have named my price for her, it is for him to meet it. I have done!'

'Father, give me leave – and don't be angry!' He himself was so sick with nervous rage that he could hardly speak, and the voice came out of him muffled and breathless round the gall that choked his throat. If I could coax and beg, he thought despairingly, I could win him; he is not so hard, not even wilfully unkind. 'Father, if you knew what a great fondness they have for each other – '

Ebrard sprawled out his feet among the rushes with a great shout of laughter. The bellow that came out of the old man might have been of mirth or of rage, or of both together; it startled the pups helter-skelter for the doorway, and made Harry's spirit shrivel in him, but he stood his ground with a pale, mortified, earnest face.

'A great fondness, the brat says! Why, you green babe, what the devil has a fondness to do with marrying? Her duty is to take the husband her father and her lord please to give her, and that's all there is to it. Now let me hear no more of your foolishness.'

'But, Father, there is something more – '

'Enough, I said!'

'Hawis is with child!' shouted Harry, scarlet and trembling.

He had succeeded at least in arresting their merriment. They both turned their heads and stared at him in ludicrous astonishment, mouths gaping.

'God's life, child,' gasped Sir Eudo, 'where do you get your gossip? A man would think they took you to bed with them! There's no such fine, detailed reports ever reach me of what goes on in my own manor. How do you know this?'

'He gets his news in Boteler's yard,' said Ebrard scornfully, 'where he's for ever hanging about the family and their cronies. Did you not know it, sir? He spends more time there than he does with us, and has a punch in his hand oftener than a pen. He was there this morning before the dew was off the ground.'

'Were you so, Harry?'

'I was there but half an hour, and on your business, sir. The wall of the big barn and the gatepost need repair, I pointed out both to you a week ago. I went to bid him come and see to them.' He had all this ready, and when there was need of the next excuse he would have another one tucked in his sleeve, ready to palm and produce before them with the same facility. Necessity had forced upon him a cunning of which he was not even aware. 'It was Arnulf told me about Hawis. He is in great distress. It was because they knew he was afraid to ask you for leave to marry her – because he could not find the price, and would keep putting them off – that they did what they did.'

'Thinking to force my hand, eh? Thinking the old dotard would turn soft and give her to the lad out of pity? They were never more mistaken!'

'No, Father, thinking to compel him to ask you. They had confidence that you would deal generously with them, if he would but speak to you.'

'I deal justly. I name my price, and he may pay it or leave it, but it stands. That's the end of it.'

'But Hawis will have the child, and everyone will miscall her – '

'She should have thought of that before. Am I to pull her chestnuts out of the fire for her? No, no more! Not a word!'

'Father, you can't mean to be so hard on her – '

'Not a word, I said!' roared his father, thumping the table.

Harry shrank, and was silent. The old man stared him out until he lowered his eyes, and sat mute but not submissive, his black lashes shadowing his cheeks.

'That's better!' He stood over him for a full minute, studying him with diminishing irritation and growing bewilderment, even with some baffled tenderness, though Harry did not feel it. Sir Eudo had contracted a second marriage in middle age to get an heir, and once that was achieved he had settled all his thoughts and affections on Ebrard, and rested content. This one had slipped into the world almost unnoticed, except as the occasion of his mother's long fever and his own banishment to a wet-nurse's care, so that there were times when it surprised and puzzled his father to encounter him in head-on collision, and find himself staring into a fierce face and a stubborn spirit which were strangely familiar to him, though he could never quite recognise them. He looked over the boy's averted head at the clerk, and said in a mollified growl: 'Mewed too long, Edric. Let him fly!' And to Harry, in a gruffer tone: 'Get you gone, boy! Enough scratching for tonight, and tomorrow you shall have a holiday from your books for once. There, be off with you! Go to your mother.'

In the window embrasure of the solar the fading evening light, pale luminous green from the afterglow, shone on Lady Talvace's rounded, youthful face, finding no wrinkles there and leaving no shadows. She had laid aside the embroidery with which she occasionally amused herself when no other entertainment offered. A son fawning upon her, either son, diverted her more agreeably.

'Mother, he would listen to *you*. Dear Mother, you see that we must do something to help them. Stephen wants only Hawis, and she wants to be his wife. I've talked to her, Mother, I know her well. She used to take care of Adam and me sometimes, when we were little. She's so unhappy.'

He sat on a stool at her feet, her hand clasped between his, and poured out the whole story into her lap. With her free hand, white and soft and growing plump, she stroked his hair, and his forehead, and his palpitating cheek.

'Harry, your father is a just man, he exacts no more than his due. You must not think yourself wiser than he. Why do you cross him so? You are a froward child!' Her voice, which was mellow and vague as the summer night's quickening wind, turned scolding into a caress, but like the wind she breathed sweetness on him and yet slipped through his fingers. He turned and wound his arms about her waist, nuzzling her breast. Her sensuous pleasure in endearments could always release him from his shyness; only with her was he able to be demonstrative.

'I don't mean to be,' he said in muffled tones out of the green brocade of her bliaut. 'I try not to be.'

'Then why do you vex him so? Is it not froward in you to try to tell him what he must do with his own? Truly, I am sorry for the girl, but she has made her own bed. Sir Eudo does her no wrong in this matter. If the price is paid, she may marry.'

'But it cannot be paid! He set it so high that he knows it cannot be paid.'

'Harry, mind what you say! This is a bad, rebellious spirit in you. Do you dare accuse your father of unfair dealings?'

'Oh, Mother, I never said unfair. I know he has the right, but it does seem hard on them – on Hawis and Stephen – '

'It is according to law, is it not?'

'Yes, it is, I know it is – ' He was not capable of showing her the gulf which was opening before his eyes between law and justice, and he felt his helplessness in argument, and resorted to the blandishments of the body, smoothing his cheek against her breast, kissing the hollow of her neck where the bliaut ended in a narrow stitching of gold thread. 'Please, please, Mother, speak to him for them! Think how terrible it will be for her if she has the child, and they can't marry! If she had no skills, father would have let her go for a few shillings. Ten at most – they might manage ten. But thirty! Oh, Mother, you must speak to him! I can't bear it!'

'What a silly child you are! Naturally he sets a high value on her, since she is valuable. How do you think these ordinary affairs of business ought to be conducted? Does one lower the price when the merchandise is better worth? Really, my poor Hal, you have some babyish notions in that head of yours.'

'She is not merchandise,' said Harry furiously, raising a ruffled head to glare at her, 'she is a *woman*. She is *Hawis*. She laughs and weeps and sings, just like you. If I did *that* to her it would hurt – just as it hurts you – '

He pinched her arm, with a sudden impulse of spite more smartly than he had intended, and she gave a tiny scream of surprise and slapped him hard across the cheek.

'You dare! Vicious little wretch! You go too far!'

Her occasional blows, too, had something of sensuous enjoyment about them, and excited and moved him much as her caresses did. Trembling and stammering, he caught at her hand. 'Mother, forgive me! I didn't mean to do that – I'm sorry, I'm sorry!' He hid his face in her lap, and shed a few despairing tears of remorse and bewilderment, knowing that he had lost every throw. She put her arm round his shoulders and rocked him serenely, complimented both by his cruelty and his remorse, and contented as a purring cat.

'There, Harry, there! Why should you care so much about Hawis? What is she to you, that you torment yourself and everyone else like this for her sake?'

She felt him shuddering under her stroking hands, and suddenly she was shaken by the fear that the intensity of suffering to which her palms quivered might not, after all, be on her account. She gripped him by the shoulders, and raised him so that she could look into his face.

'Harry, why are you so anxious that she should marry? What's your concern that her child should be fathered? Harry, look at me!' He was already gazing at her wide-eyed, in absolute bewilderment, unable even to guess where her thoughts were tending. 'Tell me the truth, Harry! You need not be afraid that I shall be angry with you. These matters can be arranged. But I must know the truth.'

'I don't understand,' he said, staring open-mouthed, and a little frightened now in good earnest. 'I have told you the truth, I've told you everything I know.'

'Everything, Harry? Come, I think not. You have had to do with this girl, have you not? Was it you got the child on her? Is that why you are so urgent – '

'Mother! *No!*' He burst into a peal of laughter, and then as suddenly his face flamed, and he recoiled from between her hands in indescribable offence. '*No!* How could you think it?' Hawis was twenty years old, and had seemed to him, in the days when she used to mind the children for Alison Boteler, already an adult, a generation advanced from him. He had not even liked her very much, because she had carried out her duties in a conscientious fashion which he felt to be tyrannical, though he had long since forgiven her for that. But he had lived in such close proximity to her, and taken her so companionably for granted, that his mother's suggestion outraged him deeply. 'I've *never* – ' he said stiffly. 'Not Hawis nor anyone.'

'Poor ruffled chick!' said his mother, and laughed to see him burn crimson to the hair. 'Don't be so angry with me, Hal, even if I have misjudged you. Indeed I'm glad if you have not that on your conscience, but you must trust me these things can happen, yes, even to your modest lordship some day. But if I am so clean off the mark, then *why* – why does it mean so much to you that she should marry her Stephen?'

'It is simply that I feel they have rights – a right to marriage, a right to the child, since they cared enough to – to brave all of us – '

'Your father will not rob any man of his rights in law.'

'Oh, in law!' He laid his cheek, on which the mark of her fingers burned dully, against her knee. 'Mother, help them! If you ask him, he'll let her go.'

'No, Harry, I cannot interfere. It is for your father to do as he thinks fit. And it is unbecoming in you to doubt that he will do right.' She brushed back the dark hair absently from his forehead, and saw how wearily his eyelids hung. 'They've worked you too hard, no wonder you're tired and fretful. You should go to bed.'

'Yes, Mother,' he said in a dull voice, and began to straighten up slowly from the low stool.

'And have you not been looking at this matter somewhat inconsiderately?' she added feelingly, as she held up her face for his goodnight kiss. 'If we part with Hawis, who is to weave wool cloths for me and make up my dresses?'

Sleapford manor had a low, squat stone keep, built on forty years later than the hall, and topped with a slitted watch-turret. In the upper room under the crenellated roof the two brothers had slept together until Ebrard had departed to take service under Fitz-Alan, and on his return, almost a knight and tenderly alive to his budding dignity, he had asked and obtained permission to take over one of the small rooms opening from the solar. Without recognising the source of his joy, or at least without admitting it, even to himself, Harry had put away that day in his memory as one of the radiant turning-points of his life.

Alone in the stony, six-sided room, with shot-windows all round him, stretching out his toes and his fingers into every corner of the rustling straw bed, he had a kingdom of his own, waiting for his imagination to populate it. In the night he looked towards the hills of Wales, and thought of raids and alarms gone by, and new ones threatening, of Gwenwynwyn harrying the border like a brush fire from end to end of Powis, and the sudden young prince of Gwynedd, Llewellyn, burning up in the north as a comet rises, until he blazed into the castle of Mold and alerted Chester to a new and splendid enemy.

Because of these uneasy neighbours there was always a watchman in the turret on top of the tower, and though he had all the valley spread like a silver bowl in his sight, he spent most of the hours of his watch staring towards Wales. It had taken Harry only a few weeks to discover how simple it was to slip down the staircase with his shoes in his hand, work his way round to the old water-gate in the shelter of the wall, and let himself out on the English side, while the watchman faithfully gazed at the Welsh hills. The tower had an outer staircase to the ground, so no one else in the house was ever likely to hear or see him, and the constant chance that the guard would choose the wrong moment to turn towards that side of the house, and catch him in the act of lifting the wooden bar, only added a particular sweetness to these nocturnal excursions. It had never happened, and he had been sparing in his use of his freedom, to avoid out-running his luck.

In the sleeping village an occasional dog stirred and barked, but he knew them all by name, and they grew quiet at his voice. The stonemason's yard lay at one end of the undulating street, screened at the back by a copse of birch trees. The house was only a low undercroft and one room above, and a loft in the roof, with a shuttered opening in the gable. There the three boys slept, tangled together in their piled bed of dried bracken and straw. Harry had only to whistle beneath the gable, and Adam put his head out from the window, which was left unshuttered through all the soft summer nights. In a moment he swung himself out by his hands and dropped into the turf.

They went to earth in the copse, and lay on their bellies in the warm, sweet-smelling grass.

'Adam, I'm let off work tomorrow. Can you get Ranald to go to the harvest instead of you, and come with me? There's something I must do.'

'I'll come,' said Adam without hesitation. 'Where are we going?'

'To Hunyate. But roundabout, because no one must know I've gone there. We'll take our bows, and start out through our own woods to the gores beyond the mill. They'll be cutting there, and there'll be plenty of hares and conies breaking cover. We'll take a few, and hide them in the wood to pick up on our way back. That's what they'll expect of us when we have a day's holiday.'

'From there to Hunyate we shall have to go through Tourneur land,' said Adam dubiously. He had never yet taken a deer, but like all the boys in the village he felt himself identified in loyalty with those who played that risky game, and approached the private chase of the king's verderer only with considerable trepidation.

'That's no crime, we want none of his venison. And we'll keep out of sight. But we must go that way, for I mustn't be seen to set out towards Hunyate.'

'Why not? What are you about, Harry?'

Harry hoisted himself nearer in the grass, and told him. Adam, chin on fist, listened large-eyed. 'But what do you mean to do?'

'I'm going to tell Stephen Mortmain what my father intends, before word reaches Arnulf. I can do no more. He is my father, and I'll not take active part against him, but what he purposes Stephen has a right to know. Then it's for him to act, and quickly.'

'But what can he do? If he can't help Arnulf to raise the merchet – and how can he?'

'He has a craft he can carry with him, and no land to leave, for he's still in his father's house. I know what I would do if I were Stephen. I'd take Hawis by night, and have her away to some charter town where a good shoemaker can get more work than he can do, and hire himself journeyman to a decent master, and marry his sweetheart there. And I think him man enough to do it, too, and her woman enough to get up at his call and go with him. No one can pursue him, he's a free man. And for a villein woman my father won't raise the hue and cry he would for a man. If they get safe out of Salop they can set up house where they will. And if they're hard pressed to run far enough before the hunt is up, well, the Welsh wear shoes, too.'

'Not all,' said Adam contentiously. 'Andrew Miller says when they came raiding two years ago, out Wyndhoe way – '

'Who listens to Andrew Miller! To hear him talk he was at every border raid in six shires these last two years, and we all know he runs if a dog barks. I must go, Adam. In the morning I'll come at eight, but we'll leave the horses with Wilfred at the mill, and go afoot. And no hounds. I'll not take a dog in the verderer's chase, not even leashed. But don't forget your bow. We'll make a day of it.'

Adam clambered to his feet, and brushed away the ripe dry grass-seeds from the short drawers of coarse linen which were his only garment. The hand-cart from his father's yard, braced shafts-upwards against the door of the undercroft, was his ladder to the narrow lintel-ledge above, and from there his brothers would be ready to reach out their arms and draw him back into the garret. It was a service they had done for him many times, and he for them. He had already hauled himself up to the front board of the cart when he turned and scrambled down again.

'Harry – '

Harry halted and looked back. 'Well?'

'If your father finds out it was you put this idea into Stephen's head – '

'Who said I meant to put any idea in his head? He must do as he thinks best.'

'Do you take me for a fool? I know you too well to be cozened. Harry, if he finds out he'll just about kill you.'

'He won't find out. He won't know I've been near Hunyate.'

'You don't know that. Something could go wrong. You go and shoot your hares in the cornfields tomorrow, and I'll go to Hunyate.'

'No!' said Harry shortly and arrogantly. 'I do my own errands. I was in two minds even about asking you to go with me, but you were asked to go and help me pick off the conies, mind that! You know nothing, if anyone asks you, about Stephen Mortmain or Hunyate. I have not mentioned them.'

'Oh, if you're going to climb on your high horse, I say no more. But, Harry, have you not thought – could not your mother persuade him – '

The Talvace brows drew together in a formidable scowl, and the Talvace nose sniffed the air with quivering nostrils. 'My mother would have her private sympathies, but she could do no other than support my father. It is her duty.' And Harry turned and stalked away through the birches upon trembling legs, before Adam could get out a word of either challenge or apology. It might have been either, but for shame Harry dared not wait to hear it; either would have discomfited him to the point of tears.

He hated himself for what he had just said. He wanted to turn back and fling himself into Adam's ready arms, and blurt out: 'I'm a liar! I did ask her. She won't help, she doesn't even care.' Instead, he walked the faster away from the memory that shamed him; and when he reached the road he broke into a run, but he could not outrun his own desolation.

CHAPTER THREE

The private chase of Sir Roger le Tourneur, the senior member of the four royal verderers for the shire, was enclosed and strictly kept, but several village paths passed through it, and by these it was legal for local folk to move at will, provided they committed no offence against forest law. The Talvaces with their rights of warren might hunt fox, wolf, hare and coney, badger and cat upon their own land, but could not touch the deer without a special dispensation; but le Tourneur's enclosure from the royal forest had been granted to him with all its rights intact. Here in the thick coverts the fallow and the roe belonged not to the king, but to Sir Roger, and he had the same powers to deal with those who encroached on his rights as had the king himself elsewhere. To do him justice, he felt the weight of his office so heavy upon him that he would not be judge in his own cause, and regularly produced whatever charges he had to make at the forest attachment courts, instead of proceeding to summary punishment in his own court. But that said, he insisted on the full penalty at law. He was respected but hated; he might almost have been liked if he had not been the king's verderer. But who could like a verderer?

'Man,' said Adam, kicking his heels blithely among the sweet, rustling bed of leaves from many summers, 'but he keeps his woods well! These coverts are full of game. Did you see the buck that crashed away from us among the beeches there? Lambert brought in a buck last night, as soon as it was dark. He swears he winged a doe, too, but he lost her.' He gave a hitch to the thong of the crossbow that swung behind his shoulder, and reached up to put back a branch from his face.

It had been like one of the summer days of their childhood. They had climbed to the beacon on the Hunyate hills, where the small, lively, short-woolled sheep grazed among the tussocky grass and heather, and the last harebells quivered on their thin green stems. And after they had eaten their bread and bacon and little summer apples, lying in the sun-warmed mosses that smelled of birth and baking, they had bathed and swum in the pool set in the lee of the hill, and then lain naked in the sun upon the grassy shore until the afternoon blaze mellowed into the golden serenity of early evening. Saturated with summer and leisure and content, they made their way homeward without haste to reclaim their horses and their conies from the miller's boy at Teyne.

'Do you think they'll go?' asked Adam suddenly.

'They'll go.' He was sure of himself. Stephen's broad, deliberate countenance had cleared magically when the seed was let fall into his mind, and Harry had felt its germination like a bursting of the tension that had confined and restricted him.

'Tonight, do you think?'

'I don't know. It's better we shouldn't know. We have the less to deny. And see here, Adam, we must not let fall a word of where we've been, or they might still be intercepted.'

'You need not tell me that.' Adam looked along the green ride, dappled with the filigree sun. They had withdrawn from the most frequented path, to reach the fence and Sleapford and their supper by the shortest route; and here the coverts were thick and deep, and the silence and dimness closed over them green and sombre, drawing on the night. The forest was full of sounds, of wings fluttering and feet scurrying, but the sum of the sounds was still silence. Adam began to whistle, but the notes sank into the muffling quietness and were lost.

Then suddenly there was a sound softer than all the rest, but which could not be swallowed up. It touched their ears just audibly, but with so desolate a vibration that they halted instantly, clutching at each other.

'Christ aid, what was that? Did you hear it? Something's hurt – or someone. Listen!'

Faint, distant, inexpressibly sad and forlorn, something between a human moan and the last almost voiceless bellow of a beast too weak to rise or call. It came from the deep woods on their left hand, and Adam was off the path and thrashing through the bushes towards it before the sound died, panting back over his shoulder as he elbowed off thorns: 'Something hurt – deer, I think. Was he here? He wouldn't say where he got his buck.'

'Don't go!' Harry clutched at him in sudden agitation. 'Don't touch it!' But Adam did not even hear him, and he himself did not stop, but blundered headlong after the anguished sound, paying no heed to the noise they made.

They tumbled out into a small clearing, close-turfed and rimmed with densely-growing bushes. One green wall threshed feebly while the rest were still. Adam went forward with steps suddenly piteously soft and gentle, and thrust his arms into the thicket, parting the branches and leaning inward upon darkness. Something pallid and dappled like the filigree sward of the clearing heaved and sighed faintly. A silvery-white face with great eyes of motionless terror and despair stared up at them. Low in the rounded side, towards the silver belly, the head of a crossbow quarrel stood out like a clove from a pasty. Ribbons of blood laced her delicate flanks and folded legs. The smell of blood and the disturbed buzzing of flies turned Harry sick.

'Lambert's doe!' said Adam in a quavering whisper. 'Oh, God, there's been something at her – a fox, maybe – she was too feeble – ' He stretched a hand backwards without looking round. 'Give me your knife! Quick, man, your knife!'

Harry fumbled his hunting knife out of its sheath with shaking fingers, and thrust the haft into the outstretched hand. Adam laid his left palm gently and slowly upon the blood-crusted muzzle, and smoothed it upwards until it covered the anguished eyes. The knife's tip felt for the place. It was something he had never done before, but he had to do it well. He saw nothing but the light shudder that passed along the speckled hide, felt nothing but the one convulsive jerk of the torn body, and then its great quietness, heard nothing at all. Harry, leaning intently over him, was as blind and deaf as he.

Branches thrashed suddenly as though the wind had risen, on this side of them, on that, all round them. A voice among the trees bellowed: 'Stand! Come out of that and show yourselves! We have you caged!' And another voice, close, and in the air above them: 'In the act, by God, in the act! Lads, lay hold!'

Harry felt the earth shake to the horse's hooves, and flung himself round in confusion and panic, throwing up his arms instinctively to protect his head. The whip curled round head and arms together, and threw him backwards into Adam. He groped for his friend's arm, screaming: 'Run!' and caught one glimpse of Adam's face, a pale mask of incredulity, not yet even frightened. He had the knife in his hand. The gush of blood had run down his wrist and was dripping from his sleeve.

'Redhanded, boys!' The man on horseback let the whip hang from his wrist, and swung himself down beside them. The walking foresters, two, three, half a dozen of them, boiled out of the bushes and filled the clearing. Large hands plucked Harry round and dragged his arms behind him. Without consideration, in pure rage and terror, he fought the grip, and tore himself clear. A corner of his mind, still alert, recognised that they could not both get away, and knew only too well which of them was in the more desperate case.

'Run! Get home!' he screamed into Adam's stunned face, and flung himself at the tall horseman. The face for which he reached with frantic fists was nothing but a blur to him, black of beard and brows and white of flesh, without identity. He touched neither face nor throat, though he did his best. The man made a rapid step aside, caught him by one arm as he hurled himself forward and, swinging him about in a circle, flung him face downwards on the grass and pinned him there with a booted foot between his shoulderblades. The whip slashed across his legs.

'Ah, would you! You'll pay dear for that!'

He clenched his arm over his face and set his teeth, trying to strain his head round to console himself that Adam had taken his chance. The next blow left a red weal across his chin and neck, it dragged a moan of pain out of him.

It was that blow that brought Adam out of his daze. He saw Harry pinned to the ground and writhing away from the whip, and with a shout of rage he leaped clear of the hands that clutched at him, and flung himself like a fury at the horseman. The knife was still in his hand, though he had forgotten that he held it. His weight struck the man in shoulder and side, and threw him off-balance, and down they went together in the turf, Adam battering at the bearded face. The knife slashed through surcoat and sleeve into the arm below. Then two of the walking foresters pinned Adam by the arms and hauled him off, and two more pulled Harry to his feet and held him panting and sobbing between them.

As suddenly as the chaos fell the quietness. The tall horseman got to his feet, clutching together the tatters of his sleeve over the knife-slash, and shaking off a thin trickle of blood from his finger-tips with a cold deliberation which was terrifying to see. The face he turned upon them, long and weather-beaten and beaked like a hawk, was all too recognisable now that they were compelled to stand and look upon it. Not, as they had supposed, one of the riding foresters; that would have been bad enough in all conscience: but the king's verderer himself, Sir Roger le Tourneur, in all the dreadful majesty of his office.

He squeezed together the lips of his wound, put off with an impatient frown the forester who would have made a move to offer help, and motioned towards the thicket.

'What are you waiting for? Have out the beast, let me see their kill.'

Two men dragged forth the mangled carcass of the doe, leaving fresh smears of her blood across the trampled grass.

'A crossbow bolt in her, Sir Roger – and worried by a hound. I heard some beast leave her, I swear, when the lads came near. Her throat newly cut – you need not look far for the knife that did it.'

'He's well blooded,' said one of the two who held Adam quaking between them, and presented the knife they had wrested out of his hand.

Harry moistened his dry lips with a tongue almost as dry, and croaked hoarsely: 'We never hunted her.'

'Will you say so? Nor cut her throat, neither? Her fresh blood on you both, and the knife in your fellow's hand, but you did her no harm!'

'We did kill her – '

'*I* killed her,' said Adam in a trembling voice.

' – but we never hunted her. We heard her crying, and found her mangled. What could we do but put her out of her pain?'

'So say all poachers taken in the act. And in the same spirit of pure charity you designed to do as much for me? It's no light matter to offer violence to the king's verderer, as you shall find. You may well wish you had no more than a murdered deer to answer for.'

'We didn't know!' Harry looked from Adam's fixed face, grey as chalk, to the slow drops Sir Roger wrung from his fingers. 'I was at fault – it was my folly. He wanted only to help me.'

'With the knife! You may make your pleas to the attachment court, not to me.'

'I forgot I had the knife,' whispered Adam. 'I ask pardon, sir, I didn't know you – '

'What signifies whether you knew me? I'll have no officer of mine, not the meanest, mishandled more lightly than myself. Your names!' They stood mute with misery and despair, unwilling to contemplate the consequences of speaking. 'Your names, I said! Speak up!' He had drawn a kerchief from the breast of his cotte, and was knotting it one-handed about his arm over the slit in the sleeve, and now he bent his head and drew the knot tight with great white teeth that bit viciously into the linen. Still unanswered when his attention was again free, he swung the butt of the whip purposefully into his palm. 'Will you speak, or have I to cut it out of your hides?'

'By your leave, Sir Roger,' said one of the foresters, lugging Harry a step forward. 'I fancy this sprig here is Sir Eudo Talvace's boy, from Sleapford. The younger, he that came home from Shrewsbury at Eastertide.'

'What? A Talvace?' The thick black brows knit above a terrifying star. 'Come here, boy, show yourself!' They thrust him forward, and Sir Roger plucked him round to face the light. 'God's life, if you're right! He has the face on him. Speak up, boy, are you a Talvace or no?'

Harry admitted his lineage like a felon confessing to theft and outrage.

'The more shame on you. What says your father to these cantrips of yours?'

'My father knows nothing of it, sir, he – '

'I had not supposed even Talvace would send his own brat poaching in broad daylight in his neighbour's chase.'

'We were not poaching, sir, I swear we were not. We were no more than walking through the forest, until we heard the doe crying, and – '

'So, and this you carry with you for the pleasure of its weight?' He dragged the slung crossbow over Harry's shoulder and thrust it in his face. 'And these – and this – to pick your teeth with?' The short quiver full of quarrels and the bloody knife were brandished under his nose. 'You always take the air armed like this, do you, boy?'

'We spent the morning in the cornfields, shooting at coney and hare – '

'And the afternoon in my woods, harrying my deer.'

'No, sir, I swear we did not! Look, she has bled for hours, and lain there in the covert so long the blood is dried black, and, on my head, we have not been in the forest above an hour.'

'Where, then? Come, speak! Make account of yourself! If not here on my land, where have you been until this last hour? If you were elsewhere upon honest business, someone will be able to bear you out.'

Harry stared into the pit he had dug for himself, and it seemed to him a bottomless blackness. How could they tell where they had spent their day, without causing Sir Eudo to prick up his ears as soon as the name Hunyate came back to him, as most surely it must before night? Then goodbye to Stephen's chance of getting clear away from Sleapford with his Hawis. No, it was unthinkable to risk that betrayal. And even if they could have told a measure of truth without taking that risk, who could have confirmed it but Stephen himself, on whom they could never call? On the hill among the earthworks of their ancestors, with the sheep and the heather, they had seen no one, been seen by no one. Ever since they left the mill they had taken pains to be inconspicuous, because of the secrecy of their errand. And now this gulf opened under their feet, and they had no means of filling in the lost hours of time. Harry opened his mouth, dredging his mind desperately for some other place he might name without treason, some attraction for boys on holiday which might be reached through these woods.

'If you cannot lie faster than that,' said Sir Roger grimly, 'better not try it at all. You have been here most of the day, and harried and lost her some hours, and found her now in a very ill moment for you. Admit it! Before God, I'd think better of you if you stood to your ventures, lose or win. This is a poor part for a Talvace. I suppose you will tell me next who did course the poor beast, since you are so insistent it was not you?'

That was but one more thing they could not tell, though they knew the answer. Better go to the flayers themselves than give away Lambert. Wherever they turned there was a wall of silence, and they could do nothing but shut their mouths and abide whatever must come.

'Bring them to the hall,' said Sir Roger abruptly, reaching for his bridle with his good hand. 'I must ride ahead and get this slash dressed. And faith, I must consider what can be done between neighbours to amend this sorry business. I had rather it had been any man's son but Talvace's.'

He hoisted himself into the saddle and disposed his left hand and forearm within the breast of his cotte. 'Keep them apart on the way, or they'll compound in a lie and be perfect in their story before you get them home to me.'

With that he wheeled his horse, and, dipping his head low beneath the branches of the trees, threaded his way into the green gloom towards the open ride, and was lost to sight; and in a moment they heard the soft thudding of hooves as he reached the pathway and spurred into a canter. Too broken to look at each other, they followed between their guards, in the silence of despair.

It was middle evening, and the time of the pale golden calm just before set of sun, when the sorry little cavalcade entered the courtyard at Sleapford. The gateman, gaping to see his lord's younger child come home under escort, crumpled and crestfallen and bearing whip-marks on cheek and neck, sent an archer running to inform Sir Eudo, while he himself admitted the party cautiously into the courtyard and delayed them there with wary civilities until the master of the house appeared, rolling hastily out from his supper, bundling on his surcoat as he bustled through the doorway from his great hall. Ebrard was at his heels, quivering with curiosity and ready to bristle in defence of his name. Half the household caught the stir of excitement in the air, and crept unobtrusively forth from buttery and stables and kitchen and armoury, to stare and listen as the riding forester dismounted and uncovered.

Behind him two of his subordinates, also mounted, brought the two boys ignominiously before them on their saddle bows, and lighting down, gave them a hand to dismount after, not unkindly. They had been rough-handled enough in the first encounter, and sunk through enough slow torments of suspense and anxiety since, to excite a faint stirring of sympathy even in their captors. Two hours they had spent in the guardroom by Sir Roger's gate-house, constantly watched and held apart, while Sir Roger had debated how best to handle the business, and had his clerk write to his neighbour the letter the forester was now about delivering. No one had told them what was in it, no one had been able to offer them a crumb of comfort about the fate that awaited them; and no one had fed them, which in the state of stunned resignation to which they had been reduced ought to have been a small matter, but which in fact had gradually grown into the greatest grievance of all, for felons or not, they were still fifteen, and had not eaten since noon, and courage and dignity would have come a little easier if they had not been quite so hungry. They stood now side by side, and silently followed the verderer's letter with their eyes as it passed from hand to hand.

The very fact of being thus sent home to their father and master at once encouraged and depressed them. Surely it meant that Sir Roger did not intend to proceed to the attachment court – not out of any love to Sir Eudo, but out of solidarity with his own estate, and reluctance to hold them up to the scorn of the commonalty.

If the affair could be compounded in private, Sir Eudo might be less irreconcilable, and in time the storm would blow over. So they were tempted to think, until they remembered the new causes for rage and suspicion likely to confront him before the week was out. And at best, these next hours would be the extreme of discomfort.

They watched the foresters hand over their bows and bolts, and the knife and its sheath. Once, only once, they stole a disconsolate glance at each other, and pledged each other to silence and endurance. Sir Eudo, literate but no scholar, was fingering his way laboriously through Sir Roger's letter, and the lightnings were about to fall.

Harry had thought his heart could sink no farther, but it lurched downwards sickeningly as his father bore down upon him with a suffused face, and the open scroll in his hand.

'So, Master Harry, you have done finely for yourself and for me, and worse yet for this fellow of yours. I hope you know how well you have undone two years of work for me, and by God, I hope you are in good heart to pay for what you have done. Bring my name into common rebuke, would you? Poach my neighbour's deer in my despite and his, would you, and drag this luckless fool to ruin in your wake! You shall answer for all – you hear me? – in full!'

Harry knew the signs too well, the purple cheek-bones, the eyes sunk so far into swollen, angry flesh that he saw them as two sparks in a smothered fire, the great fist clenched so hard on the vellum that the veins swelled and pulsed. He expected to be felled to the ground, and shut his eyes for one instant of terror. He was not afraid, not more than any sensible man must be, of pain or violence, but he was desperately afraid of his father's anger. It lay too near to his own affections, cut too deeply and viciously at the roots of his life. Some day it would sever them.

'Father,' he began quaveringly, 'I swear to you we did not hunt the doe. By my honour, we did not! If we have done anything foolishly – indeed, I know we did, because we were frightened – I am very sorry. But we did not hunt or wound the doe.'

It was a miracle that he was heard out to the end, but perhaps it was only that Sir Eudo could not choke down his fury in time to become articulate and cut him off earlier. He did not really listen; he had never listened.

'Did not hunt her! Did not hunt her! And half a dozen foresters and the king's verderer himself saw your lad cut her throat! Is this blood on your knife? Do you tell me I am blind, or cannot smell? What did you there with bows on your backs? Not hunt her! Do you not know he might have laid a charge against you even for carrying the bow? Two years of peace-making, and you must ruin all with this stupendous folly! Not hunt her! Read, boy, read what he writes to me! Do you talk to me of the doe, as though she were the measure of your roguery? And I suppose you did not offer violence to the king's verderer? Do you know he could have your liberty for that, if he chose to attach you? Read, and see what irretrievable mischief you have made!'

Harry, through his daze, found himself reading stupidly, hardly grasping words or sense. Yet the letter was very much to the point.

'To the noble Sir Eudo Talvace, Knight, of Sleapford, with respect, these:

'These, taken in arms and in the act of killing a deer in my chase this day, in my presence and in the presence of six of my foresters, all witnesses to the killing of the said deer, namely a doe, before wounded by a crossbow bolt, I find to be yours. And in courtesy, the offences being committed against my game, and not the game of the King's Grace, I return them to you, and desire you will deal with them according to my judgement of what is just, and indeed merciful. To which if you consent, out of consideration to the good name of knight, which dearly concerns us both, I purpose not to proceed to the forest attachment court with the charges to which your son and your villein have laid themselves open, and to which, seeing the nature of the case, they have no defence.

'Touching the matter of the deer, since the act was committed, I say, to my injury, and not to the injury of the King's Grace, I can and do remit the severity of the law, which would have submitted your son to a ruinous fine, and his fellow to death by flaying, as you well know. I am content that you should beat into them both that degree of good sense and respect for property that might have been bred into them long since in more able hands.

'Touching the assaults made upon my person by both of them, to which six witnesses will stand, and which the culprits, I think, will not deny, as they were affronts to me I can and do excuse them; but as they were affronts to my office I have no right to do so, and in duty to my fellow officers of the King's Grace in his forests I have no choice but to exact justice. The assault made by your boy, as being unarmed and committed in the first astonishment, may be compounded in the severity of his punishment for the deer. But that of the boy Boteler, being made with a knife and in despite of my life, though by God's grace the wound was taken in the upper arm, may not be so compounded. If you so send word by my man who brings this, my officers shall attend you tomorrow and execute upon him that penalty which you know the law demands, he being of age and a villein, namely, the lopping of his right hand. Until which time I hold you responsible for the delivery of his person.

'If you be not content with this my judgement, I shall proceed with all charges in due order to the attachment court, and look to it that you surrender both the accused upon demand to the court – '

He felt his cheeks burn with shame at the tone used to his father before he could grasp the terrible thing threatened against Adam. He, being free and noble, might have got clear even in court with a fine, at the worst with the loss of his liberty. But Adam had no liberty to lose, and must be deprived of something even the unfree possess. He had always known these academic items of law, these niceties of selection between culprit and culprit. How could he have guessed the terror they would let fall on him when they ceased to be academic?

He looked up at his father over the trembling hands that held the scroll, and cried: 'No! Father, you can't, you mustn't! Let it go to the court! Let him charge us! We killed the doe, but only because she was mortally hurt, and not by us. We'll tell them, they must believe us. Father, it's the truth! Let it go to the court, I beg you!'

'Let it go to the court, and my name be dragged through the dust, you fool? Pay a heavy fine for you, and risk his skin as well as hand? How would that help him? Can you read? Have you his sense? You know well he is coming off lightly, and you far lighter than you deserve.'

'My hand?' whispered Adam, and blanched to the grey pallor of clay, staring at them with terrified eyes. He looked round him in one wild, hunted glance, and the forester who stood beside him laid hold of his arm and held him hard.

'But I struck him, too! I struck him first! It was only to help me that Adam attacked him.'

'With a knife?'

'It was ill-luck that he had the knife in his hand, he never meant to use it. And we did not know it was Sir Roger. I was the first to strike him, I – '

'How will it help him if you lop yourself of a hand to match? Have done! You have made a pretty cauldron of trouble for us all. We must be thankful to get clear of it thus cheaply.'

He turned and marched upon the waiting foresters. 'You may thank your lord for his courtesy, and tell him I approve his judgement, and will see it faithfully executed. Let his officers wait on me tomorrow at what hour they will.' And with a motion of his hand he committed Adam to the staring, whispering archers, who closed in upon him with still faces and blank eyes, and laid hands upon him almost gently. He started at the touch, and began to struggle hopelessly, turning his terrified face wildly round upon them all, though he made not a sound. They held him fast as the foresters withdrew, but they held him as though he might break in their hands.

'Tie him up,' said Sir Eudo, 'and in God's name let's make an end!'

They had the tunic stripped from Adam's back, and his wrists bound to the iron loops of the whipping-post, before Harry could make his numbed legs move. The brown hands – tomorrow night he would have but one – were strained rather high, because the shackles were set for a man, and for all his handsome growth Adam was not yet a man. He was no longer struggling; what was the use? Even in this there had to be nice differences; even punishment had its hierarchies. Harry could smart in private and without ceremony, but Adam must suffer this violation of his beauty and his humanity in public and with circumstance.

Harry ran blindly, and flung himself on his knees before his father, clutching at his hand and sobbing drily: 'No, Father, I beg you! I implore you! I'll make amends, I'll do anything, anything, but don't let them take Adam's hand. Beat me, do what you like to me, but don't maim him! Oh, Father, for God's sake, let us be treated alike – the same fault, the very same! It's unjust!'

'Fool, would you have villeins treated like free men? Is not his presumption more monstrous than yours? It's the law,' said Sir Eudo violently, and thrust him off. 'Get up, child, you shame me. Go in! You hear me? Go into the house!'

'It's a vile law,' shouted Harry, bursting into an uncontrollable storm of weeping. 'It ought not to be the law! It's unjust!'

The old man struck him heavily on the side of the head, but

Harry clung to him still, and when he would have drawn free and passed on, fell on his face in a frenzy of tears, and wound his arms about his father's ankles, still gasping out inarticulate pleas and reproaches. With a bellow of fury the old man took him by the collar and dragged him to his feet. 'Devil take the boy, will you be silent! You make me ashamed of my stock. Ebrard! Ebrard, I say, take this crazed fool out of my sight, he sickens me. Shut him in the mews till we are done with this one.'

Ebrard received him willingly, and bundled him out of sight with the same relief, slightly pitying, infinitely scornful and impatient, with which his father saw him go. All this unseemly fuss over a villein, and one who had no more than his due! The roughness of Ebrard's handling of his brother reflected the degree of embarrassment and shame he felt for him. No such distasteful exhibition had ever been made by a Talvace before. Where he got his bad blood, from what distant, dark ancestor, Ebrard could not guess. He bent the boy's arms competently behind his back, and ran him into the mews, where the disturbed hawks were shifting and barking uneasily on their perches; but as soon as he was loosed Harry turned and fought to reach the doorway again and break free. Ebrard had much ado to shut the door on him, and drop the wooden bar into place, and even then the boy beat frenziedly on the door with his fists, and screamed for release like an hysterical girl.

When he was exhausted he slid down the door to his knees, and lay for a while against the boards with his arms clenched over his ears. Even so, he heard Adam cry.

With the first cry it seemed to him that something which had always contained and generally confined him was broken, that he was loosed from it for ever; but whether he came forth into freedom or exile was something he could not determine. Whichever it might be, it was a desolation more extreme than any cold or darkness he had ever known. And in it everything familiar had become his enemy. He thought he would have liked to destroy all that he could see and touch here, everything which had first turned traitor to him and then expelled him. Ebrard's merlin, the new one that was not yet trained, muttered like a spitting cat on her perch above him, and turned her hooded, plumed head to stare blindly. He thought he would kill her, but in his heart he knew he could not do it. But the hoods and the jesses, the perches and leashes, and the fine cage Ebrard was making for his mother's linnets, and all the material things that had been in a sense his, these he would destroy.

In a calm more frenzied than frenzy itself he did what he could to smash and bend and tear all that offered itself to his hands. The birds spat and screamed, but them he let alone. When Ebrard unbarred the door at last, and came to fetch him out of his prison, the floor was littered with shredded gloves, and slashed harness, and Harry, with his dagger in his hand, was cutting the tooled jesses into bits. Peering into the dimness within, Ebrard did not at first distinguish the details of chaos, and waded unawares into the tangle of leather thongs and unravelled creances. He let out a bellow of rage, and seized his brother by the shoulder; and Harry, turning to meet the assault, launched himself like a fury at the angry face looming over him. Adam had struck out with the knife unintentionally; Harry struck wittingly, and with all his weight behind the dagger, utterly reckless of consequences.

'Ah, would you?' Ebrard caught at the thrusting wrist, and twisted it without mercy. 'Draw on me, would you, you devil! Draw on your brother! I'll teach you better manners.'

The dagger clattered to the floor, and Harry was tossed after it by a swinging blow on the ear. Ebrard taught him nothing, for he was past learning, but he did his best to beat him into a proper appreciation of the enormity of declaring war on his kind. When Harry had given up the unequal struggle, and lay hunched and still under the blows, they ceased at once. To tell the truth, Ebrard, outraged as he was, felt sorry for this creature he did not understand. He stood over him, frowning down at the soiled and crumpled figure that seemed now so small and helpless, and yet contained such a daunting reserve of obstinacy and defiance.

'Get up! I'll not touch you – get up! Father wants you in the solar. If you have any sense left, you'll come quickly and behave yourself meekly. No need to make bad even worse.'

Harry picked himself up stiffly, and brushed himself down without a word. He would go to his father, but he had nothing now to say to him and nothing left to ask of him. All that was over.

A hush of curiosity, sympathy and almost pleasurable excitement followed him through the hall. The men-at-arms paused over their dice as he threaded his way through the romping dogs in the rushes, and climbed the stairs to the solar. He looked at no one. Only a little while ago their knowing sympathy would have galled him to the quick, but now it had ceased to be of any importance.

'Wipe your face,' whispered Ebrard at the door. 'You're no sight for mother's eyes.' He thrust his own kerchief into Harry's hand, and waited for him to scrub the filth of dust and tears from his cheeks. That started a quivering nerve of affection and regret, but it did not ache for long.

Sir Eudo was straddling the empty hearth with his hands linked behind him in the wide sleeves of his surcoat. Lady Talvace sat in a straight-backed chair a discreet yard away from him, so that she could pluck gently at his arm if he needed the restraint of her touch.

'Here he is,' said Ebrard, and closed the door. He pushed Harry forward to stand before his father, and clattered the dagger down upon the table. 'He drew on me! And he's played the merry devil in the mews. I should have stayed with him.'

That flourish, in its turn, eased Harry's heart of that one dragging thread of regret. He stood and looked at his judges, still soiled and tear-stained, and a miserable object enough, but stonily calm.

'Drew on you? Drew on his brother? It shall be remembered in the account,' the old man promised grimly, and fixed his bloodshot eyes upon his younger son. 'Come here, you! Come nearer! You're quiet enough now, are you? Are you in your right senses yet? Drew on your brother, did you? – a thing a very savage would not do. You shall ask his pardon for it here and now, before you pay the rest of your score. On your knees! Do it, I say!'

Harry did not move.

'I ordered you to ask your brother's pardon. Instantly!'

Harry shook his head a little, and maintained his stony regard, not even glancing in Ebrard's direction. The blow his father aimed at him laid him flat, and he was dragged bodily across the floor and forced to his knees before his brother, who had contemplated this flurry of violence with an uneasy and unhappy face. Looking up through his disordered hair, Harry kept his bruised lips tightly shut, and would not say one word.

'It was done in a temper,' said Ebrard shortly, 'he didn't know what he was doing. Let him be, sir.'

Sir Eudo flung him down in a passion of helpless rage, and stamped away from him. Lady Talvace went and laid her plump, pretty hands upon the boy's shoulders.

'Come now, Harry, this is no good part,' said the soft, caressing voice in his ear. 'It is human to commit a fault, but like a beast to persist so in one. I know that temper of yours, I know you think we are all against you, but indeed we're not. You have only to submit yourself like a dutiful son, take your punishment and purge your rebellion, and it will all be forgiven.'

She raised him tenderly, and kept her arm about him while she smoothed the hair back from his forehead and wiped a few specks of blood from a graze beneath his eye. Her demands, it seemed, were the same as his father's, except that she had a more insinuating way of presenting them. He listened to her, and was moved to a distant pleasure and a sharp and agonising pain, but not moved to submit himself or purge his rebellion.

'There, now you will be my dear boy, and make amends of your own free will, I know. You have grieved us all very much, and caused a great deal of trouble, you have need of grace. But you have only to ask, and it will be granted. Come, now, first to your father, against whom you have offended most deeply. Go to him, Harry, tell him you are sorry for your faults, and ask his pardon.' She coaxed him forward in her arm. 'It's not so difficult, and I'll help you. Only a few words, and your peace is made.'

And indeed it sounded tempting to him, at this last moment. He was tired and hungry and sore, and he had still to pay his part of the doe's price; and it would have been so simple to surrender himself to the will of his family, and say the few magical words that would readmit him into its ranks, where at least he knew the worst that could be done to him, and need only obey, and not think any more.

'Do it, Harry, with a good will, and then you shall have your supper, and – who knows? – perhaps you may even be let off your punishment if you promise amendment.'

He had to pluck himself violently away from her, or he would have let her persuade him to his knees, and everything, his honour, his integrity, even his new, bleak freedom, would have been lost.

'I can't!' he cried, and stiffened defiantly, pushing her away. 'I am sorry for nothing! I have nothing to be sorry for, except that I haven't the courage to cut off my right hand, too. I'm not sorry I called the law vile and unjust, for so it is.'

'You see, my lady,' said Sir Eudo grimly, 'how you lose your pains with him. There's nothing to be done with one that will not bend, except break him, and by God we'll see if it cannot be done. We have time enough for it.'

'Eudo, you'll not be too hard on him!'

'Too hard? Have we not been soft with him long enough, and

to no purpose? I swear I don't know the boy for my son. But we'll amend that,' said Sir Eudo blackly, halting before Harry and fixing upon him a formidable, glittering stare. 'We'll try which of us is to be master and call the tune here. You'll not set foot among us here or in hall again, or eat, either, until you're in your right senses again, and ready to kneel and pray our mercy. Go to your room, and wait there until I come to you. Go, get out of my sight! And strip!' he said through his teeth into Harry's face, and thrust him neck-and-crop out of the door.

She came, as he had hoped and prayed she would. He was no longer afraid of her, she could not drag him back now, he had gone too far away from them all, even from her. She could hurt him still, and delight him still, but she could not influence him to modify any part of his intention. It was for something quite different he needed her now; she was the only one of them all whom he could hope to influence.

He was lying naked on his bed when she lifted the latch of the door and softly drew it open. He knew her touch and her step, and lifted his head from his arms to watch the movements of her shadowy figure as she came in. He turned over and sat up, wincing at every movement, and drew up the skin coverlet to his loins.

'Mother!'

'Harry, my poor, stubborn, wicked boy! Oh, how am I to touch you without hurting you? Harry, why have you brought this on yourself? I tried to help you, indeed I did. But you won't be helped! Did you *want* to be beaten? One might well have thought it, you went so far to invite it, and to drive him to extremes, too. And yet he does love you, Harry, if you would not make him so angry. There, now, I've brought something to ease you a little. Let me look at you. Lie down again – ah, let me help you turn!'

'It's not as bad as that, Mother,' he said, feeling on his cheek her easy, sparkling tears that came and passed like spring rain.

'Oh, he was cruel! Poor Harry, poor child! Lie still, now, it's only my herbal lotion, it's cooling and healing. And it would have cost you only a few easy words to spare yourself this! Oh, I could beat you myself for being so stupid! Does that feel good?'

'Wonderful, Mother!' It was cold and fragrant on his smarting shoulders, even the sting of it was good. 'Mother!'

'Yes?'

'Is Adam worse than this?'

She was silent for a moment. She drew down the cover to his hips and went on bathing him gently. 'I don't know, I was not a witness. Afterwards you must eat something, and then try to sleep. I've brought you some barley cakes and bread, but you must mind that your father doesn't get to know of it.'

'Did they give Adam anything to eat? He hasn't eaten since noon.'

'Yes,' she said, after another momentary hesitation, 'I sent one of the scullions with some bread and meat for him.' She did not say that Adam had eaten none of it when last the porter had looked in upon him, but was still lying face-down in the straw, half-conscious. 'So now, I suppose, you will not refuse to eat something yourself! Oh, Harry, what obstinacy is this? Is it your fault if the law's penalties fall heavier on him than on you?'

'What he did, I did, and did it first. Mother, if you could have seen how he flew to help me – '

'I will do what can be done for him,' she said, grieved, but not deeply. 'He shall not want for a home afterwards, and some simple work, fit for – ' She did not end it, but he heard her thoughts: ' – for a one-handed man.'

'Has he a bed, Mother?'

'Stop this!' she said, half angry. 'I will not play this game with you any longer. Do you want me to go down to the stables and tend him, instead of you? You'd have me carry wine across the bailey, I suppose, all that way in the dark – '

'Oh, is it in the empty stable in the corner of the bailey they've put him?' asked Harry, mumbling out of the pillow to hide the trembling of his voice. Such clues as she had let fall he had put together eagerly: the stables, across the bailey, all that way in the dark. 'Isn't father afraid to leave him in a stall with no lock? What, only a six-inch bar of oak between him and liberty? I expect he can still crawl, if he can't walk. But I suppose he has half a dozen men-at-arms to guard him – such a desperate felon!'

'Harry, I shall leave you if you speak so bitterly of your father. I begin to see how you could drive him to use you so. No, of course the boy is not guarded. Nobody is like y to lift the bar, but if they did he would not get far, he's in no case – ' She bit off the words guiltily, feeling Harry shrink and gasp. 'Ah, I've hurt you!' She had, and shrewdly, but not with her touch. He pressed his face into the pillow, and fought back the tears which might have disarmed his father had he shed them for himself. She stooped and kissed him on the ear, and he turned towards her, and wound one arm about her neck, drawing her down to him.

'There, there, Harry, it will pass! In the morning it will be better.'

He turned on his side, and held her tightly with both arms. 'Yes, it will! Yes, Mother, it will!' It cost him an effort to hold back the tears. 'I think I could sleep now.'

'Shall I stay with you a little while?'

'No, Mother, you must rest, too. I shall sleep, I promise you.'

'And tomorrow, Harry, you won't provoke your father any more, will you?'

'I won't say a word amiss to him, Mother. Oh, Mother, don't think ill of me!' He was crying now; he wished she would go, and yet he could not bear to let her go. He kissed her warm cheek, and took away his arms almost roughly, dropping into the pillow again with a great sigh. When she stooped over him, peering at him closely, he kept his eyelids half-closed, and breathed long and softly, as though he were already slipping into drowsiness. Satisfied, she kissed his brow, and withdrew with the lamp, closing the door gently after her.

As soon as she was gone he opened his eyes again, and they were dry and bright and wide-awake. He waited a few minutes, lying still, in case she should come back. Then he slid stiffly and awkwardly from his bed, and began to pull on his clothes.

The iron peg which lifted the latch of his door his father had removed and taken away with him, so that the door could be opened only from outside; but it was not the first time he had been thus confined, and he had long ago made provision for such a case. The smith in the village had made him another peg, smaller and lighter, and capable of being drawn out on either side. When he was dressed, an operation which took him longer than usual because every movement and every touch of cloth hurt him, he ferreted out his treasure from its hiding-place in the straw of his bed, and inserted it into the hole in the door. The heavy latch lifted, and he pushed the door open gingerly and stood listening. Nothing. The steps of the watchman in the turret never carried so far, and below there was nothing stirring. He was taking with him only the clothes he wore, a cloak, and such money as he had of his own, which was little enough. Long ago he had remembered and kept to himself the blessed chance that the horses were still in the paddock at the mill. They were his, not his father's, both the grey he rode himself and the cob he had provided for Adam, and they would be fresh and ready for exercise.

He pushed the door to after him, and eased the great latch soundlessly into place. The peg – Matthew Smith had never realised what manner of illicit tool he was providing – he drew out and pocketed, for the sight of it protruding would have been enough to launch the hounds after him, and how did he know the watchman had not been given orders to keep an eye on his room? It would be his father who first came to visit him in exile in the morning, he was quite sure of that; somewhat uneasy in mind after sleeping on his rage, inclined to regret that he had carried execution to such lengths, and firmly resolved this time to be gentle and patient with the obdurate boy, but he would end up by beating him again, of course. Only the boy would not be there to be either cajoled or beaten, on that or any other morning.

He did not know what time it was, but judged it must be after midnight. His mother would not have ventured to come to him until his father was deep asleep; moreover, the early moon was already almost down, and there was only starlight to contend with as he crept down the outer staircase and set foot on the warm, baked soil of the bailey. The shadow of the wall provided him with cover until he reached the extreme corner of the great hall; then there was open ground to cross to the huddle of sheds, armouries, stables and stores built along the lee of the curtain wall. He braced himself, and crossed at a run in the narrowest spot, and dropped under the lean-to roof of the fletcher's store. The night continued silent and indifferent. After a moment, satisfied, he got up and went on, slipping from shelter to shelter along the line, until he reached the remotest corner by the water-gate.

Adam's prison lay not far from the gate, and in deep shadow. By the complete stillness about it he was encouraged to believe that his mother had been right, and the captive was unguarded. No one, least of all Adam himself, had considered the possibility of rescue.

He braced his shoulder under the heavy oak bar that bolted the door, and drew it cautiously back in its socket, and pulling the door open slid inside, and pulled it to again behind him.

'Adam!' he whispered, standing quite still until his eyes should have accustomed themselves to the darkness.

A sharp rustle of straw answered him, and that was all. He groped forward inch by inch along the floor with cautious toes, shaken at every step by the thunderous beating of his heart.

'Adam – it's Harry!'

A square of pallor before him, low towards the floor, stirred slightly, and the straw rustled again. He put down his shoes and the rolled cloak, and went down on his knees, feeling his way forward into the fringes of the heap of straw that filled half the stable. His fingers encountered a foot, and instantly, in a violent recoil, it kicked him away and withdrew, shuffling along the floor. He followed, whispering reassurances and promises, not knowing himself what he said; and he found a naked arm, a body lying breast-down, a head that resolutely buried its face from him. Someone, probably one of the archers, who had hated their task to a man, had wrung out a linen cloth in cold water and spread it over the boy's back; but when Harry touched it now, inadvertently, it steamed warmly, and he felt the flesh through it hot as fever.

'Adam!' He lay down in the straw beside him, shaking him gently by the arm, where at least he was not afraid to touch him, and bending his cheek close to the averted head. 'It's me; Harry. Won't you speak to me? How is it with you, Adam? Can you rise and go, if I help you? Oh, Adam, look up! You frighten me! Don't you know me?' He began to tremble, and then to cry, and for the life of him could not stop, but went on straining out the words through the ugly, obliterating sobs that convulsed him, until Adam, turning at last, struck at him viciously with a clenched fist.

'Get away from me!' he spat feebly. 'I should have known better than count on friendship with a Talvace.'

'Adam, I came to you as soon as I could – '

'Why?' asked Adam harshly. 'I'm none of your kin nor kind Get back to your own!'

He pressed closer, and caught the flailing fist between his hands, and drawing it into his breast held it fast to him and dropped helpless tears over it. 'I *have* come back to my own. Don't send me away! I'm not going back there, Adam, I'm going with you, away from here. We must make haste! Can you rise? Lean on me! Try! Put your arm round my neck!'

Adam lifted his head and stared distrustfully through the darkness. 'What do you mean? Is this true? You'll let me go?'

'I'm coming with you. We'll go together. No one shall rob you of your hand, Adam, no one who could wish to is any kin of mine. Lean on me, and see if you can stand and go. Only a little way, only safely out of here, then you can rest while I go for the horses. Thanks be to God we left them at the mill, I could never have got them out of here undiscovered, and we couldn't get far afoot.'

'My mother,' whispered Adam, breaking into tears of relief and hope and regret all desperately mingled, 'she'll grieve – '

'Within a day she'll hear that we're gone, and she'll know we're together. Come, your arm round my neck, lean on me – put all your weight on me. She'll know you still have your hand, she'll know why we went, and that we'll always stay together. There, you see, you can do it.' Still streaming with tears and stammering with eagerness, he got Adam to his feet and held him up, breast to breast. 'Your cotte – is it here? And your capuchon, that I'll roll in my cloak, you won't need it now. Can you bear the cotte?'

The linen cloth was stuck to the bloody weals it covered. Harry eased shirt and cotte down over it, flinching to see how Adam flinched. But he was coming to life again, he was beginning to believe. He took a step away from the supporting arm, and stood alone.

'Where are we going? Where can we go?'

'To Shrewsbury, to Father Hugh. He'll not give us up, we shall find sanctuary there until you're able to travel. Can you ride so far tonight?'

'But Harry, your family,' said Adam, shaking.

'What family? My father is a stone-mason, and my mother – ' That was too dangerous a line of thought, he turned from it passionately. 'You have always been my brother to me, and now you and yours are the only brothers I have. I'm never going back. Even without you I should have to go. Come, stay close to me, cling to me if you like. Only a little way, to the water-gate. We should be seen if we took to the boat, it's a pity.'

'Harry, I'm sorry I struck you – I'm bitterly sorry – '

'Don't think of it, I didn't mind it. I knew how it was with you. Now, gently – '

He opened the door and slipped through the narrow space, one hand stretched back ready to hold Adam if he foundered. 'Close to me, put your arm over my shoulders, lean on my back.'

'I can go, indeed I can. Hush!'

He was fully alive now, even in his weakness and pain. He leaned forward eagerly to the soft coolness of the night, and trod more steadily with every yard of shadow that slid away behind them. In the deep archway of the water-gate they were covered from sight. Harry unbarred the wicket, and they stepped through into the grass of the meadow. From the gate to the copse along the river bank was not far, and the bailey wall screened them. They drew the first breath of freedom warily, knowing how tenuous was their hold upon it; and eagerly, with linked arms, they began to hobble towards the shelter of the trees.

CHAPTER FOUR

Towards seven in the morning, when the bell was ringing for Prime, the lay porter at the gate-house of the abbey heard hoofbeats approaching along the dusty road, and marked how oddly they came, sidling and halting as though undirected, until they came to a stop outside the gate. He looked out to see what manner of horsemen these might be, and saw two boys, the one slumped in his saddle as though in a faint, or near it, the other holding him up with one arm while the two horses, long understanding companions, sidled along flank to flank in a patient, delicate walk, shifting and steadying under their precarious load at every change of balance. The second boy was not in much better case than his friend. It seemed he had got his convoy where he wished to bring it, but now he had not the strength to transfer his companion's weight while he dismounted.

The porter, without asking questions, went round to the other side of the anxious horses, and hoisted the unconscious boy gently out of his saddle, gathering him into his arms like a baby. Through the tunic and shirt and the stiffened cloth beneath he felt and knew the harsh encrustations of dried blood.

'Wait but a moment, lad,' he said to the other, who was trying with stiff, painful movements to free his feet from the stirrups. 'I'll help you down. Sit quiet.' And when he had bestowed his burden on his own bed in the gatehouse he stretched up his arms and took Harry, too, beneath the armpits like a child, and lifted him down. When he set him on his feet the boy's numbed legs would not bear him up, and he clung to the porter's large, steady arm for support, and, looking up, showed him a face he knew.

'Master Talvace, what's this? What are you doing here, and in such a case? Here, hold to my arm, and come your ways in.' He knew now who the other must be, though he had not yet looked at his face. 'What has befallen you? Have you been attacked? Where was your sense to ride that road by night, with all the footpads there are loose along the borders these days?'

'No footpads,' said Harry with a crooked grin. 'We got our injuries in quite another quarter. Edmund, I must see the abbot. Soon, as soon as he can receive me.'

'Well, and so you shall, at his convenience, but it won't be till after chapter, at earliest, and by the look of you you've need of rest, the pair of you. Is young Adam injured – beyond what I know? Or is this only a swoon?' He bent over the limp body, and listened to the lengthening, steadying breath, and smiled, reassured. 'What it is to be young! It was a swoon a minute ago, and with the first touch of a bed it's sleep. He'll do well so. Nothing better could be done for him.'

'He stood it like a Trojan till beyond the ford,' said Harry, his voice quavering with exhaustion. 'Then he began to flag, and we had to take it more easily. A walk hurt him less. But the last mile or so I know not how I kept him in the saddle, or myself, either. Edmund, have the horses looked to, would you? I could not unsaddle if my life hung on it, I'm so stiff. Without you I should have had to fall off – no other way.'

'They shall be taken care of. First I'm going to find the infirmarer, and have this one carried to bed, and you, too. Time enough when you've had your sleep out to ask you what ailed you to come stravaging through the night like this. Stay with him till I come again.'

Harry would not have stirred a step away from the bedside for any lure. Not until safe sanctuary or many more miles of alien land separated Adam from the king's verderer would Harry be willing to let him out of his sight. He sat propping up his sagging eyelids and staring at the soiled, drained face now relaxing into natural sleep, until the infirmarer came hurrying in with two of his nursing brothers, and swept both boys before him into the clean, cool, narrow cubicles of the infirmary. Harry began an arduous explanation to which no one listened, and which soon subsided into incoherent mumbling, and thence into acquiescent silence. He surrendered the responsibility for himself gratefully, and allowed himself to be undressed and washed and filled up with warm milk and bread like a baby. The last half-conscious thought he had as he was settled gently on his breast in a hard but fragrant bed, was that Adam was blessedly too sound asleep to feel the pain as the brothers patiently cut and bathed the linen cloth from his back and dressed his weals. When he awoke it would be to a kind of ease, in an enclave of safety. With tears of gratitude filling his eyelids he fell asleep in his turn, and left his own pain behind, the last sloughed skin of the old life which was over.

In the abbot's parlour in his private lodging the infirmarer reported the arrivals. Hugh de Lacy pushed away pen and inkhorn along the polished table, and sat for a long minute gazing before him into his walled garden, moist and radiant in the fresh morning.

'So soon!' he said. And after a moment, with a sigh: 'Poor Harry!' He thrust back his chair, and got to his feet. 'I'll come with you and see these truants, Brother Denis.'

'They are fast asleep, Father. It was what they most needed. They have been barbarously used.' The infirmarer was old and gentle, and disapproved even of the extent to which the subprior used the discipline on his novices and pupils.

'We'll not disturb them. But I must see for myself.' If he was to have a difficult mediation on his hands he must have his facts pat. Brother Denis's indignation he discounted; nevertheless there were ugly possibilities. Harry knew only too well how to provoke ferocity, an unlucky characteristic in the young who have so few means of defending themselves.

He limped across the great court beside the infirmarer, and entered the cell where the boys lay sleeping, their two narrow beds drawn close together.

'Harry would have it so,' said Brother Denis. 'It was all we could do to make him leave go of Adam while we stripped him. I thought it best to humour him. If his fellow lay out of reach of his hand he would be restless, and, poor lad, he has need of rest.'

Flushed and moist-lipped, Harry lay with one smooth naked arm stretched across on to Adam's bed, his curled fingers close to his brother's brown wrist. Brother Denis lifted the coverlet and exposed his back to the thighs, and after a moment as gently replaced the linen.

'The other one is worse.'

Adam's back was covered with a compress steeped in a decoction of snakeweed and centaury to cool and heal the open wounds, and he lay uneasily, brokenly upon his face, but so dead asleep that he never stirred or checked in his deep, heavy breathing when the infirmarer turned back a corner of the cloth and showed the purple-striped corrosion of his flesh. 'How they rode so far in such a case I cannot tell. Motion and weariness and the rubbing of their garments have aggravated their ills, but, praise God they're both strong, healthy boys, and a few days of proper care will mend all.'

'It argues,' said the abbot, looking down at them with a frowning face and shadowed eyes, 'a degree of desperation in them. Since they were not running to escape this, what else pursues them?'

The infirmarer, smoothing his compress lightly into place, shook his head forebodingly. 'If they had been felons convicted they could not have been used much worse. What more could there be threatening two mere boys? They have not been questioned at all yet, of course, but it is evident the household of Sleapford cannot know they have ridden here to us. I have taken no steps to send them word. As Harry has asked for an audience with you, Father, I thought it best that any action should wait for your considered judgement.'

'You were wise, Denis. We may take it, I suppose, that if they are being sought the search will stay close at home for a day or two. For Eudo will certainly not be unaware,' he said very drily, 'that they were in no case to travel far.'

'When they begin to look farther afield,' said Brother Denis candidly, 'we shall be among the first refuges to come to mind. But they will not look for them here until they have combed the valley and their own woods. Surely that should give us two or three days' grace.'

'Good! By then at least I shall know what lies behind this escapade. When Harry is awake and fed and clear in mind, send him to me. If he sleeps till tomorrow, why, let him sleep. We are surely to be left in peace until then; and I cannot well be expected to pass on information which I do not yet possess myself, can I?'

A fly settled for an instant upon Harry's flushed cheek, and Hugh de Lacy stooped to brush it away. The boy shivered and gave a soft, frightened cry in his sleep, and the outflung hand groped distressfully for a moment and touched only the cool, rustling mattress. His lashes fluttered wildly, and his parted lips formed Adam's name, though they uttered only a little animal whimper. Then Hugh de Lacy took the questing hand in his own, and folded the trembling fingers upon Adam's wrist. They fastened eagerly, and clung, and were calm; he sighed away again tranquilly into sleep.

The abbot went back to his own apartments with a heavy heart. On the slender wrist now so lovingly circled he had seen a fading blue bracelet, the bruise left by the iron loop of the whipping-post.

Harry tapped at the door of the abbot's parlour during the hour of the first Mass next morning, while the servants and labourers and lay officials were in the church, and the great court was quiet. He had no fear of the abbot, but he approached this room with a kind of reminiscent trepidation, left over from the days when he had, on rare occasions, been sent here to receive a more than usually solemn reprimand for his casual boyish sins. The feeling discomfited him now, because he felt so strongly that he was innocent of sin. Sometimes in the old days he had entered here in that same conviction, and gone out subdued and near to tears of penitence over faults newly-recognised. And all this Father Hugh had been able to achieve without so much as raising his voice.

Bidden to enter, Harry did so almost timidly. The abbot turned from his table at the window, and smiled at him, though with some anxiety still shadowing his brows.

'Come in, Harry! Have you breakfasted?'

'Yes, Father, I thank you.' Harry went forward and kissed the hand Hugh de Lacy held out to him. 'I wanted to come to you when I awoke, last night, but Brother Denis said it was too late and you were busy. I have been remiss, to have enjoyed your grace a whole day already without waiting upon you, but – '

'Say no more, Harry, I know you were very tired, I was glad that you should sleep. And how is Adam this morning? He is not up, I suppose?'

'Not yet, but Brother Denis said that perhaps he may get up during the morning for a little while. He is wonderfully restored.' He looked doubtfully at the abbot's calm face, and said with some embarrassment: 'I am not sure, Father, if you know – '

'I visited you,' said the abbot, 'while you were both sleeping. I know. Come, sit down here by me, and tell me what brings you here in such a case.'

The boy pulled up the low chair the abbot indicated, and sat down within touch of the long, thin, muscular hand that lay on the crossed knees.

'Father Hugh, Adam and I are come to throw ourselves on your mercy. When I left you, you said that I might come to you in my need, at whatever time, and you would stand my friend. Father, we are in great need of that friendship now.'

'So I had supposed, my child. Tell me the story.'

'On the day before yesterday I had a holiday from the rolls, and Adam and I took our crossbows and went shooting at hares and conies in the fields that were just being reaped. You know there is always good sport when they break cover as the reapers close in. When we had taken several and were tired of that, we rode on to the mill and left our horses there, and went on afoot into the forest. It is Sir Roger le Tourneur's chase there. We stayed out all day, and as we were coming back through the forest in the early evening – '

Thus far he had gone slowly, feeling his way past the need for mentioning Hunyate and their secret errand there. The record sounded satisfactorily complete; he went on with growing confidence to tell all the rest of the story truthfully, even to his own hysterical fit of temper in the mews, of which he was not proud. His voice gathered angry way, pouring out the passionate grievance he had against the injustice of Adam's sentence. The abbot heard him to the end in courteous silence, and with a grave face. It was worse than he had feared.

'And so you took Adam from his prison, and brought him here to me. I see.'

'I knew that the church could not fail to protect him from injustice.'

'Injustice! You are in love with that word, are you not, Harry? Don't be angry with me, my dear child, and don't leap to the conclusion that I am withdrawing the assurance of my friendship if I put some questions to you: the questions you have failed to ask yourself.'

Harry looked up sharply, and the sunlight burning in from the walled garden struck gold from his bright, disconcerting eyes. 'I shall answer them if I can, Father.'

'First, then, imagine yourself to be one of the king's verderers. You, with your foresters, have come upon two young fellows, armed with bows – itself an indictable offence within forest precincts – in the act of cutting the throat of a wounded doe. They deny hunting her, and say they did but find her hurt and put her from her pain. They say in support of this that they have been in the forest only an hour, whereas the doe has clearly bled several hours since she took the bolt in her side. But they will cite no witness to say they have been elsewhere during those hours, nor will they themselves say where they have been. Tell me, verderer, would you believe them or your own eyes?'

'It was a reasonable suspicion, I know it. But I swear to you, as I swore to him, that we did not hunt her.'

'And I accept your word without question. But I am in a position to do so, and Sir Roger was not. He is in a situation of trust and responsibility where he must proceed only upon the weight of evidence.'

'I have said, Father, that it was a reasonable suspicion. But we have been sentenced and punished without trial!'

'You were taken in a private chase. Though Sir Roger makes it his habit to send all charges to the attachment court – and that is a good and scrupulous quality in him – he is not obliged to do so. He could bring you up at his own manor court and be judge in his own cause, and he would be within his rights. Do you think you would in either case have fared any better?'

'It might at least have given us time to find witnesses who had seen us – ' He broke off just in time, and flashed upwards a brilliant glance of doubt and uncertainty.

'I am not trying to trap you, my child. If you can tell me what you would not tell him, where you had been that day, well; if not – '

'I cannot, Father, because it is not my secret, and it is important to someone else that I should not betray it. But in a little while, even a few days, I might have been free to speak.'

'That is unfortunate, but scarcely Sir Roger's fault, or your father's either. Well, so! You deny the charge of hunting the doe, but agree that circumstances made it eminently reasonable you should be thus charged – and certain, Harry, that in a court, upon such evidence as exists up to now, you would have been convicted. Will you go so far with me?'

Reluctantly but honestly, the boy said: 'Yes, Father.'

'Now as to the second charge, of assaulting Sir Roger's person. Do you deny that?'

'No, Father. I did attack him. I was frightened, I knew we should never be believed. But I didn't know it was he – '

'Folly is no defence. Do you deny that Adam also attacked him?'

'No, Father, but he did it because – '

'He did it. The reason would not, I fear, extenuate the crime. To this charge you both plead guilty. Of what, then, do you complain?'

Harry's head jerked up fiercely: 'I don't understand you, Father. They would have cut off Adam's hand!'

'Harry, Harry, when will you learn to accept realities? You know forest law as well as I do. You admit to a crime of the highest gravity, for so the law holds it to be. What does forest law say of the penalties for offering violence to the king's verderer?'

' "If he be a free man, he shall lose his freedom and all that he has." '

'And if he be a villein?'

' " – he shall lose his right hand." Yes, but – '

'No buts! There you read your sentence and Adam's if the charge had gone forward to the attachment court. How would he be helped by your losing your freedom to keep company with his hand? And if the charge referring to the deer had been brought to a verdict – God forbid innocent men should be so beset, but God He knows it must happen sometimes! – you know the penalties for that, too. For you, being free and noble, a heavy fine, but for Adam, being a villein, death under the knife of the flayer. Do you tell me the verderer was not merciful in commuting that to a whipping? He has not exacted his full rights, he has gone out of his way to spare you, as he sees the case. Yet you complain of him.'

Harry was on his feet, quivering before the abbot's chair. 'Are you telling me that it is right and good that they should take Adam's hand?'

'Whether I think it so or not is beside the point. I am telling you that it is *legal*.'

'Legal!' said the boy with an upward jerk of his head and a curl of his lip. 'You insist on talking of law. I am talking about justice. It may be legal for him to spare my freedom, if he please, and yet not spare Adam's hand, but it is not *just*, even if you approve the law. And I do not! It is a vile law that makes distinction between hand and hand. You talk of accepting realities! If my hand and Adam's lay severed before you, would you know which was the free, and which the unfree? What respect can I have for a law which pretends there are differences where I *know* there are none?'

'So it comes to this,' said the abbot mildly, 'that you are venturing to set up your own judgement against the law of this land.'

'Father, if I have a mind, if I have that faculty of measuring which you call judgement, is it not the gift of God? Am I to bury it in the ground and let it rot? For God's sake, what can I do with it in conscience and duty but use it as best I can?'

'That is very well said, Harry! And let me tell you this, law is a compromise, a makeshift, a best that can be done with the material at hand, never finished. Human minds, though – forgive me! – older and wiser and greater minds than yours, compounded it, and I think none who had a hand in it will ever claim that it cannot be bettered. And you are right to speak out where you think it fails of its purpose, which is justice, though you must beware of thinking that your criticisms are therefore invariably justified. There are doubtless some laws which are bad – though to be plain with you I do not think this is among them – and in time they will be changed. It is a good part to work for such amendment. But while the law is as it is, you are bound by it, and so am I, and we must conform. It is no cure for a bad law to trample it underfoot.'

'Father, what choice had we? In a year, or two years, or ten, this penalty which I find vile may be done away. But Adam would have lost his hand yesterday if I had not taken him and run to you.' He stood breathing heavily, staring at the abbot's still and rueful face, and his eyes widened into green ovals of horror. 'I see! That's one of the realities you are willing to accept. Well, I am not! Never!' His voice sank to a flat, cold tone that dropped like icy rain on the abbot's listening heart. 'What do you purpose to do? Give us up?'

'Sit down again, Harry, and listen to me. You are too hasty.'

'I have need to be hasty, I am but one pace ahead of the axe,' said Harry in the same bleak voice; but he sat down obediently, and waited with a composed and wary face.

'I shall not give you up, Harry, because you will make it unnecessary. No, let me speak! You were at fault, my poor child, in running away, and a fault, however understandable, must be expiated. I cannot and will not abet a son's revolt against his father, or a villein's flight from his lord. I am bound by the law, and I owe a duty to authority. I can and will intervene on your behalf, and try if I cannot get Sir Roger to stretch his clemency yet again and spare Adam's hand, and your father to forgive your rebellion against him. But if they stand on their full rights I cannot withhold from Sir Eudo either his son or his villein, nor restrain him from exacting the full penalties from you both. I'll stretch every eloquence and every art I know to beg you both off, Harry, but upon one condition – that you submit and deliver yourselves up voluntarily, and throw yourselves on Sir Eudo's mercy.'

'I thank you,' said Harry, on his feet, 'I have experienced my father's mercy. I had thought I was confiding myself to yours.'

'You must listen to me, child, and trust me to use all the influence I have in your behalf. But I can do nothing while you are in revolt. The law is the law, and must be respected. Your father's authority is sacred, and I cannot assist you to flout it.'

The boy stood drawn back a little from him, the sea-green eyes fixed steadily upon his face. All the warmth which had reached out to him when Harry entered the room had withdrawn into the erect, alert body, and left him shivering with cold in the summer sunlight. He had expected an outburst, but none came. Harry was done with tears and entreaties. Neither law nor church would protect the weak. It remained only to find some means of ceasing to be weak, and protect himself and his own.

'I cannot argue with you, Father. I only know that I am right and you are wrong, and I will abide by that as long as I live. I will never again ask you for anything. I pray you will not involve yourself for me, I will make shift alone. And now, if you have said all you have to say to me – ' He waited for dismissal with his mouth shut tight like a straight sword-cut, and his nostrils quivering, so perfectly a Talvace, so dauntingly a man, that the abbot looked in vain for the boy he had welcomed so short a while ago.

Hugh de Lacy got up from his chair and crossed to the window, turning his back upon the room. He stood for a long moment with his eyes shut against the sun, trying to comprehend the dread and anxiety he felt for this fiery creature who flew his pennant into the teeth of so irresistible a wind. What could be done to control him? What can be done to divert the launched arrow, or turn downward the mounting flame? Not argue with me, he thought, oh child, if you but knew! It is I who am being driven back by the storm, not you.

'Have I your leave to go, sir?' asked the cold voice that had in it all the heritage he was denying, all the steel and arrogance of Belesme and Ponthieu and Alençon.

'Harry, for God's sake and for your own, bend that neck of yours before life bend it for you or tear your head from your shoulders. It is not possible to live as you want to live; every man must give way sooner or later, kings, popes, all who live yield some step backwards on occasion to remain upright and draw breath. Learn humility, while there's yet time, before life teach you with harsher beatings than ever you suffered yet. Bow yourself now, and you will find it less difficult and less shaming than you think. You shall not kneel alone, Harry, I shall be a suppliant with you. And I swear to you that I will find some means to obtain Adam's pardon, though I must follow your father and Tourneur across the shire on my knees – '

He halted there, feeling the room grown cold at his back. He turned and saw the door already closed, and heard the boy's steps receding steadily in the distance along the flagged corridor, until silence washed over his footfalls like the incoming sea.

In the dimness within doors he went like one dazed from a blow, and felt that the heart in him was broken; and when he came out into the air, and the morning sunshine leaped and clasped him like a warm hand, and the surge of colour and brightness clashed like cymbals and pealed like bells about him in the bustle of the great court, it seemed to him at first that he was only being mocked and tormented with a cruel illusion of summer and life and gaiety. But he walked between the abbey villeins, arguing and laughing over their preparations for the day's field labour, and the beggars sunning themselves under the wall of the almonry, and the merchants waiting to bargain with the prior over pots and cloth and stock and timber before chapter, and the free tenants come to pay dues or air grievances; and in spite of himself he was warmed, and in spite of his conviction of outrage and betrayal his senses reached out hungrily, and fed and enjoyed. The world was busy and beautiful and diverse, no less now that the abbot had failed him; and for the life of him he could not help delighting in it.

Nevertheless, their situation was desperate. They were now utterly forsaken. 'Learn humility, while there's yet time – ': those were the last of the abbot's words he had waited to hear. All very well, he thought, to be humble in accepting one's own pain and deprivation, perhaps, but what right have I, what right has he, to make a virtue of meekness when it will be Adam who suffers? I call that a cheap humility. And he thought, well, now we have no one to lean on but each other. So much the better, now there will be no one to let us fall.

He stopped for a moment to watch the travellers from the guest-house making ready for the road; two packmen, a ragged jongleur, and a nomad tinsmith with his trade on his back, from the humbler quarters; then a very young knight, probably as new as Ebrard, very pert and pretty in a brocaded cotte trimmed shorter than the fashion to display a fine leg in a well-cut riding boot. He drew in his rein short and tight as he mounted, to make his chestnut horse arch his neck and sidle and dance, so that he might show his skill, and Harry suffered a momentary temptation to slap unexpectedly under the glossy belly as he went by, and start a livelier measure. But he resisted it manfully. He had grown up to some tune, or so he considered, since he had delighted in Ebrard's disaster at the

Christmas festivities in Shrewsbury castle. It was beneath his own dignity, now, publicly to upset the dignity of another, even when provoked. Though he would not undertake to guarantee his good behaviour too long where this ineffable lordling was concerned. Now he had wheeled the beast on his hind legs in a quite unnecessary circle, and caused one or two elderly merchants and the jongleur to scuttle hurriedly out of his way. People who used the spur to make a show of their horsemanship in a crowded court should be well rowelled themselves.

A little girl of ten or eleven, who had been tossing a bright needlework ball against the wall of the refectory, dropped her toy and squeezed herself into the angle of a buttress from the dancing hooves. Harry plucked her out of her corner and swept her away in his arm, to put her down well out of range as the horseman cantered out of the court. Her ball had rolled away under a wagon which was drawn up beneath the refectory windows; he retrieved it and tossed it back to her with a smile.

'Fools on horseback need a deal of room,' he said.

She clasped the ball to her breast, and looked at him consideringly with large dark eyes, exceedingly grave and intent. She wore a cotte of blue linen, and a flowered bliaut over it, and the toes of little pointed blue cloth shoes, planted formally side by side, peeped from under her skirt. In her two short braids of black hair there was a gilt thread wound. Her mouth was like two tightly folded petals of a red rose.

'I am not afraid of horses,' she said loftily. 'We have fifteen horses, besides the ones the archers ride.'

'You are fortunate,' said Harry, impressed. 'I have only two.'

She turned her head a little, sidewise, and looked at him from beneath her lashes, and arched a foot from under her gown, drawing negligent half-circles in the dust. She was more than halfway to being a woman, and he was not an ill-looking boy.

'But *I* ride in the cart, because all the horses are too big for me. At home I have a little one. Will you show me your horses, if I show you ours?'

'I would, gladly,' said Harry, preoccupied with other thoughts, 'but I have a friend who is sick, and I must go and see him in the infirmary.'

'Afterwards!' said the child, calling after him. 'We shall be a long time yet, loading and harnessing. Come back afterwards, boy!'

'Yes, afterwards,' he laughed over his shoulder, and passed on, threading his way between the hurrying servants who were carrying bales of cloth from the guesthouse and loading them into the standing cart. A second wain was just being man-handled out of the stableyard, and the lively stamping of horses, fresh from their stalls, followed it across the cobbles. He halted abruptly and turned towards the sound, reminded how brief a time he might have to extricate himself and Adam from this place which had become now so dangerous to them, and how precious were the two mounts which were their only means of escape. He was suddenly desperate to look once again upon the horses and unreasonably afraid that they would no longer be there, and he ran into the yard and began to hunt through it from stall to stall.

They were not there! There was no doubt of it. He searched the stables from end to end, and back again to the gate, but his flecked grey was nowhere to be found, nor the fat brown cob Adam had ridden. As soon as he had assured himself of their loss he turned furiously to rush to the gate-house and demand of Edmund what he had done with them; and then, before he had gone a dozen yards, he checked equally sharply, knowing beyond question in whose private, walled courtyard they were now stabled. He turned to march back to the abbot's lodging and challenge the thief directly. Father Hugh had been wonderfully quick in taking measures to ensure that his truants should not get away again. The last and logical treason!

But if he bearded him and demanded his property, how would they be helped? It would most surely be withheld, and what means had he of forcing its return? No, that was not the way. One angry word to the abbot, and he would be watched narrowly at every move, and goodbye to all chance of getting Adam away. No, he must not approach either the abbot or the gate-house, or do anything to warn them that he was making new plans for escape. The need was to go, without warning, without detection; and how was it to be done?

His rapid walk had slowed, and he was again beside the guesthouse. Three carts stood waiting now, the first already loaded and tied down with a coarse cloth coated with pitch for protection against rain. The third was covered with an awning of the same cloth, and had at the front a cushioned seat prepared. The awning was merely a span from side to side of the wain, stretched upon wooden struts, open at front and back. The cart was agreeably deep, and if the load was cloth it would be reasonably soft lying. His eyes began to brighten, and shone with flecks of gold.

'Those are our carts,' said an insinuating voice at his shoulder. The child with the ball had a doll, too, now, a small wooden copy of herself, down to the blue shoes. She looked up at him speculatingly through her long lashes, and when he smiled she smiled also. 'And our horses,' she said.

'You must be very rich,' said Harry respectfully, 'to have all those horses, and all those bales of cloth. Where are they all going?'

'Home,' she said practically, as if that should have been self-evident.

'And where is home?'

'London. My father has a shop there, and he comes to Shrewsbury once a year to buy wool cloths from all the border websters, and the Welsh ones, too, and now we're taking what we've bought back to London, except we shall sell some bolts of it on the way. My father says it is as good cloth as any comes from the north. My father says the merchants of the Staple can preen themselves as much as they please, but finished goods, piece goods, is the coming trade. We deal only in piece goods. What do you deal in?'

'Nothing as yet,' said Harry. 'How soon are you leaving with the carts? Do you travel far in one day?'

'We shall be ready within the hour. Sometimes we can do more than twenty miles a day in the summer. We shall today, because from here there is a good road. What does your father do?'

No need to publish his name or estate, where they were already too well-known. 'He is a stone-mason,' said Harry.

'And shall you become one, too?'

She had the freshest and most honest of voices, for all her sidelong glances, and the artful, artless movements with which she sought to engage his attention; and if her lips were the firm, folded convolutions of the budding rose, her cheeks were the round, smooth fullness of the ripe bloom. He looked down at her, and broke into a dazzled smile.

'Yes,' he said, 'surely I shall! That's very well thought of, and you are a clever lass.'

'Would you like to play ball with me?' she offered, encouraged by this success, and made an inviting gesture towards him with the many-coloured ball and a dancing step or two away from him.

'I should like it very much, but there are some duties I have to do before I may play. Perhaps before you leave I shall have completed them.'

'Then you'll come back?' she asked, her face clouding slightly, but her eyes hopeful.

'If I'm ready in time, yes, I'll come back.'

She watched him go, her brows knit, her small white teeth biting thoughtfully at the end of one of her black braids. She reached up, without taking her eyes from Harry's receding figure, and dropped the doll over the tailboard of the cart, and the ball after it. She had no more interest in them.

Harry went into the infirmary and sought out Brother Denis, who was preparing to attend the second Mass and the chapter which would follow it. He accosted him with a drooping head and a disconsolate face.

'Father Infirmarer, if Adam may get up and dress, I should like him to come with me into the church after Mass. You won't mind? While it's very quiet, during chapter, I want to pray – ' he cast down his eyes and compressed his lips for a moment ' – for a happy issue out of our trouble.' If it would give them a moment's pleasure to see him submissive, that satisfaction at any rate they might have, and welcome. They would be the more likely to let him alone during that vital half-hour of chapter, while every one of the brothers was safely accounted for, and only the lay servants were left to notice his movements.

He felt a tremor of shame, none the less, when Brother Denis, instead of giving him a hurried glance and a word of commendation, took him gently by the shoulders and embraced him, kissing his forehead. 'God bless you, Harry! I have prayed, too. Never fear but you shall find grace. But will it not suffice if you make use of the infirmary chapel?'

'No, I have a desire to ask specially for Our Lady's intercession. Since I gave her my angel I have a fondness for that altar most of all.'

'Very well, you shall not be disturbed. I will mention it to Father Prior, it will rejoice his heart. Be gentle with Adam, don't let him kneel too long. Afterwards he may sit in the sun in the garden.'

Gentle, solicitous and happy, the father of great numbers of adopted sons, from the youngest schoolboy tearful with toothache to the aged and dying turned children again, he looked round his clean, bare kingdom with one loving glance, and bustled away to Mass. No wonder the novices had many times been known to feign illness in order to creep into the haven of his care for a little while, as a respite from the subprior's iron rule. One youngster, homesick and lonely, had even eaten noxious berries once to ensure for himself a long stay in the infirmarer's beneficent shadow, and never grudged the sickness and misery it cost him at the outset. And Brother Denis had seen to it that he was not disciplined for his act when he was well again, though everyone knew that the kind old man's story of an honest mistake was a gracious fiction. They said he missed every one of his patients sorely when they left him. Looking after him with rueful eyes, Harry wondered if even he, unworthy though not ungrateful, would cost Brother Denis another small pang of loss.

Adam, with his scars newly dressed and his stomach comfortably filled, was whistling as he lay on his bed, his chin propped on his fists to lift his face into the small patch of sunlight that found its way in through the window of the cell. His bare toes drummed the mattress in time to the tune. His eyes were closed against the radiance, and his easy eyelids and every line of his face smiled contentedly. He was quite without fear, and did not mind what was left of the pain. His confidence in the abbot was as implicit as Harry's had been an hour ago.

Harry sat down on the edge of the bed. 'Get up and dress. You have Brother Denis's permission to come into the church with me after Mass and pray for safe deliverance.'

Adam opened one astonished blue eye at him, and pondered a flippant reply; and then very rapidly opened the second eye to look more attentively, and was confirmed in his impression that this was no time for fooling. He raised himself stiffly and swung his feet to the floor, searching Harry's face with eyes alert and anxious. 'What has happened? What did he say to you?' He kept his voice very low, in case one of the nursing brothers should be passing within earshot.

'You shall hear later. Hurry! I'll help you dress. How do you feel? Can you walk without pain?'

'I'm well enough, only stiff as an old man. I need exercise.' Adam stood stamping his feet experimentally as he drew his shirt over his head. Harry eased it down gingerly over the laced and puckered scars already beginning to fade into livid blue from their blackened crimson. The open wounds had healed over already, for his flesh was as clean as a flower, but the worst among them were covered only by a thin film, and would break again only too easily.

'It hurts you! Badly? Can you bear it so?'

'Bear it, yes, and well! I've nursed myself a whole day and a night, what more could I ask? And if we're going far,' said Adam in a very low voice, 'you had better remember your cloak.'

'Yes, well thought of!' He was wildly grateful for the understanding they had between them, which rendered words so significant and enabled them to be spent so sparingly.

'I can't stand the touch of homespun yet,' said Adam, smiling at him, 'and it's cold in the church after this sunshine. Will you lend me your cloak to put round my shoulders?'

Harry rolled up their capuchons and Adam's discarded tunic into a tight bundle, and thrust it within his own more ample cotte, under his armpit and clasped against his side. Upon that arm Adam leaned to steady himself as they went slowly out and crossed the great court to the church. The cloak, which would have been too bulky to be hidden so, hung loosely from Adam's shoulders by its neck-chain, and in the porch he drew a fold of it round him.

'Where are we really going?' he asked in a whisper, beneath the last chanting of the Mass.

'Out of here. They intend to force us to give ourselves up.'

'Father Hugh?' asked Adam, drawing an incredulous breath.

'Himself he gave it to me. I am to kneel and submit to my father, for you and for me. If I will abase myself and pray mercy, he will graciously intercede for us.'

'Waste of breath!' muttered Adam, large-eyed in the dimness of the nave, and shivered.

'So I think!'

Mass was ending. From the parochial part of the church, at their backs, a few townsfolk withdrew quietly. The brethren filed away into the cloister on their way to chapter. The two boys kept their places, kneeling side by side, until they were alone and the door to the cloister had clashed to softly for the last time.

'Watch the parish door for me,' said Harry, leaping up.

'What are you going to do?' But Adam rose hastily and took station beside one of the great round columns close to the porch. Harry was at the almsboxes; Adam heard wood part with a splintering crack, and stared horrified. 'For God's sake, what are you about?'

'I'm about getting what I can for my property.' Harry's dagger, fellow to the one Ebrard had taken from him two nights ago, prised up the lid of the box and raised it intact. Pence rattled hurriedly through his fingers. 'Nothing near their value. Let's see if the other can do better.'

'Harry, it's sacrilege!' Adam was shivering.

'Let him pursue me for it if he choose, and I will charge him with the theft of my horses. What right had he to impound them? I owe him nothing.' He thrust the blade beneath the lid of the second box, and levered upwards viciously, and the joints parted. He emptied that box, too, carefully counting the coins he had taken, and then set the lids back into position so that to the passing view they looked undisturbed. 'Eleven shillings and seven pence – I'm leaving him still in my debt.'

'Harry, some poor devil will be thrown into prison for suspicion of this.'

'No, by God, he shall not!' said Harry, brought up short against this idea. 'I'll leave his lordship a message that shall let him know to whom he must come if he wants to recover his alms. I'll not let anyone else suffer for what I've done.'

He took Adam by the arm, and drew him into the western cloister. In one of the alcoves flanking the garth, which had the sun on this side through the morning, there would surely be someone's copying left, complete with pens and inkhorn, waiting for the labourer's return from chapter. In fact there were three desks thus left vacant. Harry helped himself to the most insignificant piece of parchment he could find, already imperfectly cleaned at least once of a previous text, and wrote hurriedly:

'To the Lord Abbot Hugh de Lacy, with respect, these:

'Since it has pleased your lordship to impound my horses, thereby denying me their use who alone have the right to it, I have been compelled to avail myself of your lordship's loan of eleven shillings and seven pence, hereby acknowledged. The sum is less than the value of my beasts, but perforce I leave them as security. And I charge your lordship look well to them, for the time shall come when the money shall be repaid in full, and the horses shall again be required of you.

'Touching the nice question of ownership, let your lordship take note that the horses are undoubtedly mine, and not the property of my father or my brother, or any other soever, and should they be given up to any man but me I will require of you their price in full.

'That your lordship may continue in health until my debt and your undertaking be discharged, is the prayer of your lordship's most humble servant'

'Henry Talvace.'

'He'll be struck dumb by your impudence,' said Adam, torn between horror and admiration as he read over the writer's shoulder.

'I think not,' said Harry, remembering the scene which had already passed between them that morning. 'Sit here in the sun, Adam, and wait for me, I'll be but a moment. And let me take back my cloak.' He bundled it under his arm, and ran back into the church. The rolled-up parchment he thrust into one of the empty almsboxes. Then he went into the Lady Chapel.

On the altar the lamp with its small red flame flushed to the warmth of life the vivid face of the angel. Harry knelt upon the steps, looking up at the ancient stone Virgin whose worn features and thick body yet seemed to him to possess so much monumental beauty, and into whose capacious lap he had sometimes made believe he could climb for comfort when he was wretched.

'Holy Virgin, forgive me for taking back a gift once given, and trust me it shall be restored some day. But you know how much I need it, since I have no other work of my own to show. I do but borrow it back until I come again. Holy Virgin, don't be angry with me! Help me to turn it to good account.'

There was no time for more. He climbed the steps and caught up the angel, and the bright being turned impetuously in his grasp and embraced him with slender, outstretched arms. He wrapped the cloak about it, and ran, clasping it tenderly under his arm. As soon as he emerged into the cloister Adam rose from his place on the stone bench, large-eyed and nervous.

'What is it? What have you done? Harry, this will end badly!'

'Hush! Come, now, quickly! Afterwards I'll tell you.'

Adam, at least, had done nothing this time. If the worst befell, and the carts were already gone, if they were recaptured before they could get clear, at least he could ensure that the penalties fell where they were due. As well be flayed for a buck as a fawn. This time he understood fully his relationship with law; this time he would not lament if it exacted from him every last farthing of his debt, since he had incurred it with open eyes.

But the three carts were still there when they crept out from the cloister into the great court, and the horses were just being put to the foremost one. Harry slipped into the deep doorway of the refectory, drawing Adam after him, and watched from the shadow as the team were backed into place with encouraging words and a busy clicking of tongues. All eyes were on them, even the lay servants and the dogs had gathered to watch. A tall, portly fellow, large-voiced and merry and brisk, marshalled his men to the task with the easy good-humour of long custom. The third cart, a coarse cover thrown loosely over its bales of cloth, stood close to the doorway, its open back not three yards from where the boys stood, its bulk sheltering them from sight.

'Quickly!' said Harry. 'Into the cart, and cover yourself!'

Adam hauled himself up without one questioning look, and vanished with a convulsive heave beneath the loose cloth. Harry stood quite still in the shadow until the ripple of movement had ceased, and then lifted the swathed angel and dropped him over one rear corner of the cart. The team of four horses was already coupled; they thrust forward into the harness and drew the first cart away towards the gate-house, there to wait for its fellows. The cluster of archers and grooms stood back placidly while the second team was brought forth from the stable-yard; and in the moment when the horses were again the centre of attention Harry made a leap, and hauled himself aboard the cart.

Beneath the sackcloth it was hot, and smelled of hairy fibres and woven wool. He drew the angel into cover with him, and parting the bales of cloth with his arms, dug a place for it beneath them, and bestowed it there out of sight. Close beside him Adam, breathing heavily and painfully, was hoisting up bales to make a hollow for himself. Harry dragged aside the bolt that lay heavy against his brother's shoulders, and eased him down gently on his side. They lay together, quivering, between the hot stuffs, and Harry tugged at the bales above until they leaned together and touched over their panting bodies. Then they lay still, sweating with the weight of their covering and the want of air, but utterly buried from sight.

Some three minutes later Sir Eudo Talvace himself rode in at the gate, with Ebrard beside him and four archers of Sleapford at his back, and bawled for immediate audience with my lord abbot.

Chapter was not yet over when a lay servant brought word to the abbot. He closed his book, and pushed back his chair, and sat for a moment pondering. He had not expected them quite so soon; it was lucky he had already talked with the boy.

'Very well,' he said, 'admit them. And find Harry and bring him here to me. Mark me, Harry only! Keep the other one out of sight until I send for him. Tell Brother Infirmarer I wish it so. And Harry is to come straight to me, you understand? No one is to lay hand on him.'

'Yes, Father!' And the messenger went tranquilly to the infirmary to find his charge, and from there no less placidly to the church. Even when he failed to find them there he thought no wrong, but inquired yet again at the infirmary, in case they had gone back through the cloisters. They could not be far away. He knew, as everyone knew by now, that earlier this morning the gatekeeper had received orders to set watch for them at the gate, and have a servant ready outside the parochial door of the church, and to turn them back if they attempted to leave. It was only a matter of finding them. He went from gate-house to garden, from the pool to the stables, from the meadows to the guest-house, and back to the infirmary again, hurrying now, and in a sweat, for the abbot did not like to be kept waiting. Brother Denis met him at the door with an anxious, almost an accusing face.

'His cloak is gone Why should he need his cloak? What can have become of them?'

It was high time to report the disappearance. Brother Denis dismissed the servant and undertook the embassage himself. The face he brought into the abbot's parlour, silencing voices which had been raised in some choler a moment before, was a reproach to them all. 'Between you,' it said indignantly, 'you have driven them to the end of their tether, and you must answer for the consequences.'

What he said was: 'I am sorry to say it, Father, but Harry is vanished, and cannot be found. We have looked for them everywhere, but both the boys are gone.'

'Gone? How can they be gone? The gates are guarded.' The abbot's temper was ruffled, for Sir Eudo was in no mood to defer to any man, or to deal leniently with a son who had cost him so much trouble and annoyance.

'Nevertheless, gone they are. I have sent half a dozen men to search along the brook and in the pool,' said Brother Denis, as near to malice as he had ever been in his gentle life, 'and have ordered the millers to keep watch at the mill-race.'

'Spare your trouble,' said Sir Eudo, purple in the face, 'that lad of mine was never born to drown.' But his very fury was a measure of his uneasiness, and Ebrard looked far from happy. 'They're hiding somewhere, the rogues. Give me leave, Hugh, and I'll have them out of their holes in no time. If the gates are watched, they must be somewhere close. And whether you are in the right of it or I, found they must be.'

'They shall be,' said the abbot grimly. 'Understand me, Eudo, while they are within our precincts they are in my charge, and to me they must be delivered when they are found, until we have taken counsel with cooler heads what is to be done with them. Agreed? Then lend me your four archers, and, Brother Denis, have Edmund find us half a dozen reliable men, and we'll comb this household, every building in it, from attic to cellar.'

'And first,' roared Sir Eudo after Brother Denis's ruffled tonsure and irate back, 'close the gate on any who may be about leaving. I'll not lose my rascal for want of looking under a hood.' And he billowed forth from the abbot's lodging like a purple thunder-cloud swollen to bursting with lightnings, and himself rolled away to the gate to ensure its efficient sealing.

The abbot followed, limping more noticeably than usual, as always when he was angry. The boy was really impossible, he would not be helped. Talk of the brook and the mill-race did not fool Hugh de Lacy; Harry's bent was for life at all costs. But short of dying there was not much he would not do to win his battle, and who could tell what folly he might not have committed by now?

The hubbub at the gate penetrated beneath the smothering weight of cloth in the covered cart. Harry lay straining his ears, in a scalding sweat of dread, but he could see nothing except a faint filtering of air and light from the front of the carts, between the ends of the rolls of cloth. If he tilted back his head as far as he could, he could see through this aperture an irregular star of blue sky and a corner of the almonry roof; and occasionally the dark passing of some nearer bulk cut off for a moment the clear gold light. Someone was riding in the cushioned nest in the front of the cart.

All the rest came to him merely as sound, and the dominant sound was the bellowing voice of his father, demanding that the gates be shut. On hearing that overbearing roar again his inside liquefied into such molten terror and desperation that he could hardly notice or recognise anything else. A new kind of terror, not of punishment for himself, not even chiefly for Adam's hand any longer, but simply of being dragged back and confined again into the stone circle which had broken and let him go. Tears burst out of his eyes because of his helplessness.

'Boys?' cried the great voice that had coaxed the horses merrily into their traces. 'You'll find no boys with us but the ones you see honestly mounted here. And hark you, my masters, mind you ruffle not my little lass, back there, or I'll give you boys! Make haste and look, if look you must. Waste your own time as you will, but forbear from wasting mine. I have a long journey ahead of me.'

Sir Eudo was not accustomed to being addressed in such a tone, and roared the expected challenge: 'Fellow, I think you do not know who I am!'

'Why, by all I hear you must be Sir Eudo Talvace. Never fear, the tale's gone round ahead of you. I'm on reputable business, I have no need to mind who you are. Come, look in the cart and have done. And take care how you prod among my bolts of cloth, or I'll have the worth of it out of you at law.' And all this with so much good-humour that in effect it was all the more formidable. None the less, this independent cloth merchant in his innocence was casting them back into the fire from which they had tried desperately to escape. It could be only a matter of moments now, and they would be dragged forth like dug badgers.

The shadow passed across the little space of light, again and again, seeming to cut off sound as well as sight, so that the strident voices, the stamping of the horses, the clambering of the archers mounting the hubs of the first cart, were all cut off by fits and snatches. Harry craned his head back and saw something round and brightly-coloured that danced in the air; and then two small hands that came up and caught it as it fell, and tossed it again.

'Not here, Sir Eudo – '

'Did I not tell you you were losing your labour? I've no runaways aboard, we've been loading this hour past, we should have seen them.'

'The other carts, too! I don't doubt you, fellow. Nevertheless, by your leave – '

Harry strained his shaking lips as near as he could to the opening, and whispered hoarsely: 'Mistress!'

She started and tossed the ball awry, and it fell over the back of her nest and rolled between the bales of cloth. Reaching for it, she knocked it farther from her, and it slipped into the hollow and lay close to Harry's face. She touched a hot, quivering cheek, and uttered a barely audible cry, and would have snatched her hand back, but Harry caught at it and clung. Startled and wild, with great black eyes round as moons, and soft, bold mouth fallen open, he saw her face flower against his stifling darkness; and she, leaning to look more closely, caught a glimpse of flushed cheeks, lips dewed with sweat, agitated blue-green eyes that implored her silence and her pity. She knew him. She hung over him for a second, holding her breath, and with an instinct more cruelly cunning than he knew he pressed her hand to his lips.

For an instant she was quite still, then she drew away her hand, and with a finger to her mouth motioned them to lie quiet. Her eyes were sparkling, the startled lips had folded into a single resolute bud. One more conspiratorial glance, wild with excitement, then she propped up her cushions over the gap that let in light upon them, and leaned over them to straighten the cloth that covered them. Over it she spread the skin rug on which she had been sitting, to make a bed for her doll, and whipped off the square of white linen she wore as a wimple, to make a coverlet. By the time the archers reached the third cart she was perched up on the bales of cloth, her skirts spread out about her as widely as they would go, rocking the doll with a plump little hand, and singing a nursery lullaby in a gusty undertone.

'By your leave, little mistress,' said one of the archers, smiling at her, and set foot on the hub of the wheel and reached in between the rolls at the rear of the cart.

She stopped singing and stared at him wide-eyed, keeping her place like an outraged princess and spreading a protective arm above her doll. 'What do you want? You mustn't come here, you'll make a noise.'

'Have you been long in your place, sweetheart?' asked the archer gently. 'Have you seen ought of a pair of lads we're looking for? You'd speak out to your father, would you not, if any stranger tried to climb into the cart?'

'I would so,' she said, eyeing him distrustfully and sitting up very straight, 'and I will, if you don't go away. I've seen no boys. No one has bothered me until now, or I should have called my father. I don't let anyone touch my father's goods. I am in charge of this cart.'

She jutted an uncertain underlip, and when the second archer swung a leg over into the cart and prodded farther between the bales she opened her dewy mouth and let out an indignant shriek: 'Father, they're trying to steal our cloth! *Father!*'

The probing hand touched Harry's sleeve, but touched only cloth where cloth was in any case to be expected; and the next moment the man had withdrawn hastily before the child's possessive rage, and the merchant was striding purposefully back to see what was offending his daughter.

'Oh, let be!' said the first man, dropping to the ground. 'How could they be here, with such a game little lass minding the cart? Sure, she'd bring the whole household down on them if they laid a finger on her bolts of stuff.'

The voices receded. They heard the merchant's great, warm laughter: 'That's my own bird! And now, master and my lord abbot, if you're satisfied we're not harbouring your runaways, we'll be on our way.'

Hugh de Lacy's voice, clear and thin with fastidious irritation said: 'Open the gate!'

Hooves stamped the cobbles, and the wheels creaked forward. In a few moments they knew, as the carts swung round in a great turn to the right, that they had passed through the gate and were out on the highroad.

CHAPTER FIVE

A shaft of summer sky looked in upon their hot, heavy darkness. 'Boy!' whispered the breathless little voice. 'You may come out from under the load now. Only keep beneath the cover, in case someone should glance into the cart. *I* will tell you if there's danger.'

She had settled herself and her doll in the front of the cart again, as soon as they were well away from the monastery gates. Now even the last corner of the boundary wall was left behind, and the lofty shape of Shrewsbury, a garlanded hill within its silver moat, was dwindling lower and lower into the green bowl of water-meadows.

They hoisted themselves gratefully out of the stifling trough beneath the bales of woollens, and lay panting on the top of them, bathed in sweat and still trembling. Harry raised the canvas sheet upon his arm, and helped Adam to settle himself comfortable before he stretched himself out beside him. Two or three of the scars on his back had broken again and slashed his shirt with thin stains of blood. The little girl's bright, knowing eyes marked their laborious wallowings beneath the sheet, and did not fail to observe Harry's solicitude and trace it to its cause.

'He's hurt!' she said with indignant sympathy. 'Who has done that to him?' And with round eyes, not waiting for an answer: 'Is that why you were hiding from that cross old man? But I heard them say that he was father to one of you!'

'He's father to me,' said Harry, wiping his sticky face and drawing great breaths of the clean, radiant air.

'And lord to me,' owned Adam, lying limp with relief beside him.

Through the arched opening of the cart they looked out cautiously upon the heaving rumps of the horses, and the steady, grinding rear wheels of the cart ahead. Two men walked with the team, the long, furled lash of a whip nodding in air above the shoulder of one of them. Four more, well mounted, rode alongside at leisure, ready to spur forward or back as they were needed. The merchant was at the head of the cavalcade, they caught a glimpse of his hat-plume dancing beside the leading cart.

'*I* would not run from *my* father,' said the child, studying them as ardently as they studied the opening world of freedom and wonder before them. 'You must have done something very bad to anger him so.' The great eyes were brilliant with greedy curiosity, but she was unwilling to ask. They owed her their confidence, and she waited for it proudly.

'On my word,' said Harry, 'we have not done anything that should make you regret helping us to escape capture. And indeed we haven't thanked you yet, and want words enough to do it properly. If you had not been the boldest and quickest-witted lass that ever was born, we should surely have been dragged out of our holes and whipped back to Sleapford, to another judgement worse than the last. Adam here would have lost a hand, and I should have been locked up and beaten and starved until I crawled on my knees and begged for mercy. Lady, my name is Harry Talvace, and I am your devoted servant while I live. And this is my foster-brother, Adam Boteler, and I dare say as much for him. Will you not tell us your name, too?'

'My name is Gilleis Otley. My father is Nicholas Otley, and an alderman of London,' she said with conscious pride.

'Well, Mistress Gilleis, you have the best right in the world to know the worst of us and decide for yourself whether you repent of helping us to go free.'

He spread his arms comfortably along the bales of woollens, and laid his cheek upon them, and in a soft undertone, in case one of the outriders should pass too near, he told her the whole story, even to the secret meeting with Stephen Mortmain in Hunyate.

'My soul!' said Adam, lifting his head at mention of the name. 'I have been all this while so bothered about myself, I had forgotten about them. Harry, if there's one thing sure, it is that we've let Stephen and Hawis safe out of the shire. Lord, with this to-do about us, they could have taken hands and walked out of Sleapford in broad daylight, and no one would have marked them. Every hound in the place has been hard on our trail, there'll be no hunt for them till our scent's lost for good.'

'I have been thinking of it, too. There's nothing surer than that they're safely away by now. Maybe we haven't spent our pains for nothing, after all.'

'I'd rather it had been done more cheaply,' owned Adam, grinning ruefully. 'But I don't grudge them a few strips of my skin.'

The shadow had passed from over him before Shrewsbury was out of sight. He looked at the broad green fringes of the road, on which the hoofmarks were like darker green dapples in the drying dew, and at the Wrekin's bulk stretched along the sky like a sleeping beast in the sun, and he began the soft whistling which was the measure of his wellbeing.

Harry took up the tale where he had left it. Only when he reached the incident of the almsboxes did he hesitate. He was not ashamed of what he had done, but this child might have superstitious scruples about such behaviour, and he did not want either to prejudice his own case or to offend her. It was easy to omit the dangerous confession, and say simply that they had made use of the church to assure themselves an undisturbed passage through the cloisters to the carts. He told it so, not without a chafing sense of humiliation in the deception, and met her bright, intelligent stare at the end of his recital with a heightened colour.

'I should have run away, too!' she said, shivering as she looked down at her own small, childish right hand. 'I was frightened of that old man, he shouted so. If he had come to look in my cart I should have cried. He was very cruel to you.'

Now that the terror of defeat and recapture had ebbed out of his very bones, however prematurely, Harry felt a fleeting desire to defend his father. Justice, after all, was due to those who kept the law, as well as to those who broke it, however inadvertently.

'He would be aghast if he heard you say so. He never means to be so, but he has a hot temper – and it's been well drummed into me he had the law on his side. Law! On my word, I'm glad we are clear of it.'

'And what will you do now?' asked Gilleis practically.

'Why, first, put the length of England between us and Sleapford, and then find work with some mason and go on learning our trade. We're already well grounded, for we've been helping Adam's father ever since we were big enough to handle tools. We shall not be unprofitable workmen. In some charter borough we can work for a year and a day, and then Adam will be free. Then my father could not hale him back home even if he found him.'

'The best plan,' said the child briskly, tugging at her short, fat black braids of hair, one in either hand, 'would be to come with us to London. London is the finest place to hide in, because it is the biggest and the busiest city in the land, and good workmen are always wanted there.'

They lay side by side, the cover pushed back to their shoulders, peeping over the cushioned barrier along the straight, dusty ribbon of road. They felt light as air, wanting the weight that had fallen from them with the life they had shaken off. The squat, square tower of Atcham church came in sight, with the low village roofs clustered about it. Looking beyond, into the pale blue sky above the road, they saw other prospects opening to invite them, and like an emanation of dreams at the end, the fabulous city, with King William's great tower at the eastern end of it, and the two strong fortresses of Baynard's Castle and Montfichet's Tower to westward, and London Wall stretching between, with seven double gates in it and towers along the north side. They saw the Thames teeming with ships, and the thriving suburbs spilling over outside the city wall in gardens and pleasances right to the king's royal palace of Westminster, on the river bank. They saw a great and powerful place, rooted like a tree and budding prolifically all the year round with new houses, churches, shops and mansions for its multiplying thousands. Where better could a mason go?

'We have money,' said Harry. 'Not a great sum, but enough to pay our way. If we should deliver ourselves to your father tonight and ask him to let us travel south with him, do you think he would consent? We could work, if he would have us. We know how to manage horses, and we're strong.'

She shook her head emphatically. 'No, not tonight, it's too soon, you could still be sent back. I'll tell you what you must do, it will be quite easy. Tonight we shall lie at the hospice of Lilleshall Abbey, at Dunnington. That is too near to Shrewsbury, the abbot may have received word of your flight. But I can bring you food, and you can sleep in the woods for tonight. You *could* sleep here in the cart, for it won't be unloaded, we shall be selling nothing until we reach St Albans. But if they should send to inquire after you – '

'You are in the right of it, we're still too near home to take risks,' said Harry. 'The woods will suit us very well.'

'But tomorrow you'll join us again, won't you?' She watched his face anxiously. 'I shall be looking for you. I'll help you – tonight I'll show you where to wait for the carts, in the wood just beyond Dunnington. And tomorrow night we shall lie at Lichfield, then I think it would be safe for you to come to my father. You need not tell him who you are. You'll come to him during the evening, as though you were boys from the town, and tell him you want to travel to London to hire yourselves to a master there. And it would be better for you to take another name.' She drew back a little from them in sudden doubt, seeing how they looked at her sparkling-eyed, and then at each other, their cheeks quivering into uncontrollable mirth. A little of it was the pure hysterical joy of being free and launched upon a new course, but most of it was astonished delight in her shameless cunning. She sat red-cheeked in mortification and offence, her lips trembling. 'Why are you laughing? What have I said?'

'Oh, Gilleis, Gilleis, how old are you?' asked Harry in a splutter of laughter.

'Ten years – nearly eleven,' she said, stiffening her slender back and jutting her rounded underlip to keep it from drooping.

'And where did you learn to be such a little she-fox in only ten years? Have you had so much practice in conspiracy? Do you deceive your father so frequently?'

'Oh,' crowed Adam into his sheltering arms, 'I see the city is the place to learn all the tricks of the trade. Here in Salop we're but simpletons to her.'

The smallest of muffled sounds brought Harry's head up sharply, and struck the mirth from his face. Gilleis had turned her back on them. Her arms were pressed against the side of the cart, and her forehead upon them, and the two thick, short braids of black hair jutted pathetically, one on either side of the tender, pale hollow of her nape, with its single delicate curl. Under the blue cotte and the flowered over-tunic the small shoulders, hunched against them in outrage, heaved silently.

'Gilleis!' He was suddenly overwhelmed with shame and dismay. 'Lady!' She would not turn, even for that. He forgot caution, and scrambled forward to reach over the cushioned partition and take her by the shoulders, trying to draw her round to face him. 'I am an unkind, uncivil wretch, and it would serve me right if you boxed my ears. God forbid I should laugh at you, indeed it was not quite such a gross offence as that. Will you not look on me any more? I'm ashamed! Pray pardon me!'

She shrugged him off fiercely, and sobbed out of her muffling arms: 'Go away! I don't like you!'

'And you're in the right of it, for I don't like myself. You see how much I have to learn.'

'I wanted to help you,' she sobbed almost inarticulately. 'I don't deceive my father! Never, never, never! All because of you

I've told lies, and I shall be damned, and all you can do is make game of me. I never did such things before. It was all for you.'

'I don't deserve it. Nor Adam nor I was worth your trouble. But indeed no one would ever have the heart to damn you, though you should tell more lies than there are blades of grass in a meadow. And besides, you never told even one! You said no one had bothered you – well, we were not bothering you, were we? You said you would call your father if you saw someone climb into the cart – and so you would have done, but you did not see us, did you? So where's the lie?'

'Much to learn, have you?' murmured Adam, still shaking with suppressed laughter. 'You learn fast!'

Gilleis had stopped crying, and was listening intently, but still she would not look round. Harry tried to turn her about, and she resisted him obstinately, her face still buried from view.

'Come, then, if you won't forgive me, call the archers and have me hauled back to Shrewsbury. Or shall I give myself up, to prove to you how sorry I am for my unkindness?'

'On my soul,' remarked Adam admiringly, 'when it comes to low cunning there's not a pin to choose between you.' He could say what he liked, it was not to him she was listening. Harry's dishonest offer was all she heard, and she turned on him with flashing eyes, her small jaw set in fury, and struck at him with a clenched fist.

'Get down! Hide yourself, quickly! The bridge!'

He let go of her, and dropped back meekly into cover, and she thumped at him vengefully until he had drawn the canvas over his head and vanished from sight. She enjoyed hitting him, because he had wounded her, and she was woman enough to want to make him pay for it; but she would not have him betrayed to any ill-usage but her own.

In his anxiety to placate her he had forgotten the river crossing at Atcham. The leading cart was rattling ponderously on to the unfinished stone arches of the bridge, where the tollman of the abbot of Lilleshall waited to collect his dues. There were always people lingering to talk here, and always there might be disputes over the pence due for the loaded carts, since the abbot's exactions were a standing grievance to the villagers and to many regular travellers. He, for his part, maintained that his rates were unprofitable to him, and would do no more than finance the completion of the bridge; they, for theirs, pointed out that the last arch was still but a makeshift structure of wood, and had been so now for a year or more without a hand's turn being put into it, though every loaded cart during that time had been expected to pay its penny, and every empty one its halfpenny. They said openly that their tolls were building the fine new extensions to the abbey at Lilleshall, instead of their bridge. But what could they expect of those foreigners brought north from Dorchester?

In the darkness of their hiding-place the boys followed with straining ears all the small sounds of the crossing, the new note of the wheels as they ground from solid land on to the first stone arch, the hollow ring beneath them, the lapping of low summer water against the piers; then the halt, which seemed to them, as they held their breath with the last tension of fear, hours long. The horses stamped and twitched off flies, cheerful voices exchanged the casual gossip of Shrewsbury market for news of the traffic on the highroad, and money passed. The grooms chirruped, hooves bit willingly at the dusty road again and clopped hollowly on to wood. They were through and over, and soon the long, straight, impetuous road the Romans had made opened out to receive them.

'Gilleis!' Harry lifted the canvas to put out his head.

'Not yet!' she hissed, and beat him back with one hand, so roughly that he knew she was still angry. But he caught the little fist before it could withdraw, and drew it under the cover with him; and in a moment her fingers relaxed from their tight bunch, and folded and settled confidingly into his. He rolled over on to his back, and lay smiling, cradling her hand against his cheek.

Nicholas Otley had dined well, and was still sitting at table over his ale in the small guest-chamber when they presented themselves before him, cap in hand, with their request. Adam did the talking, for Adam it was who could the more confidently stand up and proclaim his parentage and training in the craft. All he had to do was name a village in this district, and remember that his family name was Lestrange instead of Boteler, and for the rest he had no need even to watch his tongue. Trippingly he told over the accomplishments he had from his father, and the modest works in which he had helped him about the village. Besides, Adam had a winning way with him, stood the taller and looked the elder, though in fact there was but a day between their births. If they were to be brothers, the elder must be the spokesman.

'And my brother Harry here can also carve exceedingly well, both in wood and stone. I can a little myself, but he excels me. We purpose, sir, to travel to London, and go on learning our trade there. If you will agree to our joining your company we shall be greatly obliged. We will gladly work for you on the journey, if you have work for us to do. Or if you have hands enough by you and can make no use of us, we can pay our way on the road, if we may have the protection of going with you. It's a long journey to make alone, and they say none too safe in places, even on the king's highway. We've never yet been so far as London.'

The merchant looked them over with gay black eyes very like his daughter's. He was nearing fifty, and in the pride of his life, a tall man so charged with vigour that his every movement had a neat, controlled violence, and every turn of his head or change of expression was quick and pert as a bird's flight. He stroked his well-trimmed brown beard, and spread his long legs amply; and Gilleis, who had already twice been told to go to bed, sidled up to him as he considered them, and slipped her arm round his neck. He smiled, without looking at her, and encircled her waist, drawing her close against his side. She was his only child, and his wife had died in bearing her.

'Sweetheart, did I not bid you go and sleep? We are on men's business, it's time the children were abed.' But she pressed close to him, and made no move to go, and his embracing arm hugged her warmly. 'Tell me, pigeon, how like you these two lads? Shall they go with us to London?'

'If it please you, Father,' she said demurely, and looked at them as if she saw them for the first time, and deeply wise, looked longer at Adam. 'It speaks well for their wit,' she said very sagely, 'that they wish to go to London.' He laughed and hugged her again, for she was quoting him, and it was an open secret between them that he liked nothing better.

'I see they don't displease you. Come nearer, boys, let me see you side by side. Brothers, are you? And you the elder, what was your name – Adam?'

Adam said truthfully that he was, but turned his day's advantage into a year.

'And which of you features your mother? For two brothers more unlike in the face I never saw.'

'Mother is fair,' said Harry, truthfully.

'And father?' The merchant's smile had sharpened, the merry

eyes had narrowed a little. Harry should have kept his mouth shut.

'Father is dead,' he said, a shade too quickly, and paled at the sound of the words.

'A sudden loss! He sounded very much alive, to my mind – at the abbey of Shrewsbury, yesterday.'

They stared him steadily in the eyes with faces of blank incomprehension, and furrowed their brows in pursuit of his meaning, though they trembled inwardly.

'I don't understand you, sir,' Adam began slowly.

'You understand me very well, lad. Never lie to me, I have a nose for it. Come here to me!' And when Adam approached dubiously, the merchant reached forward and clapped a hand on his shoulder, and suddenly ground hard fingers into his back. Adam flinched and drew breath sharply, twisting away from the pain. Otley shifted his grip to the boy's arm, and put him off from him by a pace, quite gently. 'Your pardon, Adam, that was no fair trick, but you must remember, before you lie to a man with wits in his head, that you bear marks of identification not yet faded. Your tale's too well known this day to any who come from Shrewsbury, they know where to read your name – Master Lestrange!' His voice was hard, but not angry, and he looked at them so thoughtfully that they began to take heart again.

'You should not hurt him,' Gilleis said reproachfully. 'I don't think they are bad boys.'

'I'll not hurt the boy, pigeon, never fear. I wanted only the answer to a question, and I have it. And as for you, my bird, run to bed, and let me deal with the lads my own way. There, I mean it! Trot!' He turned her about and gave her a gentle push towards the door, and a pat to start her on her way; and whether she recognised the third warning which must be obeyed, or whether she heard in his voice a note which reassured her that her presence was no longer necessary, she did indeed trot, with a last flashing smile at the two silent boys out of the corner of her eye before she skipped through the door.

'There, now we are rid of the women, now come and sit by me, and begin to tell me again, from the beginning, who you are and what you want of me. You're newly come into the hospice asking for me. Here I am. Now start fair.'

They told him all that they had told his daughter; what else was there to be done with such a man? There was one difficulty to be faced, however; they could do no other than end their story still captive within the closed circle of the abbey wall, since it was impossible to involve the child, and might be impolitic to confess that they had made use of this masterful man to cover their flight, even without the connivance of his daughter. Men of the world, with a healthy opinion of themselves, do not take kindly to being hoodwinked.

'We have made shift,' said Adam, leaping the gap boldly, 'to break out and follow you thus far, as you see. And if you will let us continue of your company from here to London, you shall find for yourself whether we mean honestly.'

They waited with held breath for him to probe where he could hardly choose but feel curiosity; but he remained thoughtfully silent for a moment, looking from one to the other of them with a small curl to his mouth within the brown beard, and a quiet gleam in his eye. But he answered gravely enough after his pause for consideration.

'I am an alderman of London, and sit every Monday to hear causes in the Husting. As a man of law, I am bound by judgements of court as fast as my lord abbot himself. But no court has made this judgement, not even Tourneur's own manor court, and in my reading it binds no one. It is one man's judgement, and he the complainant, and I doubt not he meant it as a kind of hard mercy, and no malice, yet I call it bad law. There has no charge been laid against you. No one but he that's father to one of you and lord to the other has any right to pursue you, and I am not obliged by law to abet him. Be thankful you are not fallen in with nobility, boys. If I were one of your knights I should pack you back to your fate – the whole estate stands together. But I'm a merchant, born to trade and proud of it, and I know the worth of a hand that can make and do instead of hacking and piercing like a butcher's journeyman. Keep both yours, with all my goodwill, and make good use of them. The world will be the better off.'

He had risen from his chair, and was pacing the floor with long vigorous strides. He halted now before Harry, and looked him over steadily from head to foot.

'And you, my young sprig, I like you well for standing by your friend so stoutly. And even better for finding the wit and the courage to take to a trade and stand on your own feet, if you mean in good earnest to do it. Will you stand to it? And can you make it good?'

'Yes, sir, that I can. All that Adam told you earlier is truth, except that I am only his foster-brother. His mother nursed us together, and his father taught us together, and I have had mallet and punch and chisel in my hands since I was eight or nine years old. It's true we had but little training in carving at Sleapford, but we have stood at the banker and cut stone, and helped with the building of walls, gate-posts, all that was needed about the demesne. And at Shrewsbury we made friends with Master Robert, who is at work on the church, and when we had showed him what we could do he let us work under him. We helped in the carving of the rood-screen, and I also carved two capitals for the chapel of the infirmary.' He came to his feet in his eagerness, trembling a little in doubt of his own wisdom in committing himself so deeply to this man's discretion; but he could not keep it in. 'I brought away with me a work of mine to show what I can do. There was nothing of Adam's we could bring with us, but I pledge you my word he knows his trade as well as I, for we've done everything together. May I show you?'

'Ay, let me see what you can do.'

Harry ran out to the stable-yard and tenderly uncovered the wooden angel from its hiding-place. He brought it in and set it upon the table. Two days and a night in the cart had done nothing to dim the angel's wild brightness. With gold hair streaming upwards in the wind of his flight, and radiant wings arched and shimmering with tension, he plunged and lit upon the table-top like a shaft of sourceless light. The air of the chamber cried out about him in one golden chime. It mattered nothing to him that he bent his head and spread his delicate hands now before a merchant of London.

Otley uttered an exclamation of astonishment and pleasure, and put out his hands to the bright being. 'This is yours? Verily your own work? No copy of a known masterpiece? Give me leave!' He took it up and turned it in his hands, looking with delight into the narrow, fiery face. 'Here's a touch I had not looked to see! There's many a church and abbey would be well pleased to buy this of you, I swear. Are you being honest with me, boy? Your master had no hand in the making?'

'Myself I made it, every bit. I liked it the best of all that ever I did. Will it stand my friend, do you think, with a master? It is only wood, but there was no way of carrying stone, and I had no drawings by me. In stone I have much to learn, but I can learn, and I will. I want to learn.'

'That's the best of all teachers, the desire to learn. Hold fast to it. Stand your friend with a master? Ay, will it, with any worth his salt. Why, I have been in Canterbury and seen work set up to praise that was no match for this of yours. Young Talvace, you should get you to one of the great cathedrals and learn your business from the best in their line, for you have the matter in you.'

They had both drawn close to him, one at either elbow, tense with eagerness.

'Would they take us? Oh, I would cross Europe to get to a master like that, and to such work! Master Robert showed us some drawings of the new work at Canterbury. And I have heard that at Wells they are doing beautiful things. Father Hugh spoke sometimes of these matters with us.'

'And France, sir – do you know anything of what is doing in France? Master Robert talked of the rebuilding at Chartres, after the fire they had there. And in Paris – '

'Ah, France!' Master Otley set down the angel. 'You must talk to the master of my ship about France.'

'Do you trade to France, too?' asked Adam, large-eyed.

'Ay, do I, and to Cologne on the Rhine, too, and sometimes into the Flemish cities, though they want not for cloth, for indeed they furnish all Europe with fine stuffs. But though your Flemish tapestries and velvets and embroideries be the most sumptuous to be had this side of the East, yet there's nothing like good English and Welsh woollen cloths for gowns to keep out the cold. The lordly lads of the Staple think there's no great trade but in raw wool, but trust me, boys, we shall make our name yet for good English cloth.'

'But surely when we are in such hot dispute with the French king,' ventured Harry, 'there are heavy fines laid on ships that ply there for trade?'

'Why, so there are, when it can be called trading with the enemy. And from day to day, God knows, no master can tell whether he may not be landing a cargo on an enemy shore that was friendly but yesterday. But to levy a fine and to get it is two separate acts, and no king can be everywhere, nor his officers, neither. As for France, we are in no trouble there just now. Since Ascension Day King John and King Philip and the young Duke of Brittany are all come to an agreement together. If it hold! Who can tell with kings? I can compound with a French merchant, and we hold to our bargain like honourable men, but from a prince I should want heavy security. And from a baron, cash!'

'And have you been in France yourself?' they asked him, glowing.

'I have, a dozen times, though now I have a grown nephew who handles the French trade for me.'

'And have you seen Paris? Have you seen Notre Dame?'

'And St Denis?'

'And Chartres?'

'Three years ago I was in Paris. Chartres I have seen, too, but not since the fire. And at Bourges they are building such a great church as I had never dreamed of. High – ah, you should stand under the vaults there and see how lofty. Thus – even the aisles as high as our choirs – ' He sketched the elevation out with his finger upon the table, while they gazed passionately. 'And Normandy is full of building. Churches grow overnight, like spring grass, like mushrooms.'

They had forgotten all that had gone before; the young brothers for whom Adam had shed a few tears secretly in the night, the mother whose kind, pretty, foolish image had haunted Harry's uneasy dreams, pain, anger and fear, the strange journey they had made with the child out of the last frontiers of their own childhood, all were clean swept away out of mind. They sat down with him round the table, under the angel's burning eyes, and poured out questions in an ardent flood. By the time Otley marked the fading light, and remembered the morrow's early start, Harry was already fallen into an inspired silence, bright and distant of face, his eyes shining.

'You've kept me talking past sundown! To bed with you, we make a longer day of it tomorrow, and must rise with the dawn. There, lads, go join the rest of my rogues in the hall, we'll see you safe into London. Go ask for my foreman Peter Crowe, and tell him you are taken on for the journey.' And he called after them good-naturedly, as they stammered their thanks from the doorway: 'And if any among my hopefuls get playful with you – for they're a corn-fed lot, and the boys have a way of playing rough with newcomers – stand to it and give as good as you get. There's no malice in it.'

They assured him they would impute none. He had meant the advice for Harry, of course, taking it for granted that the villein's son would drop neatly on his feet in any testing company, by virtue of the toughness, good-humour and resilience bred into him in a hard school. With a knight's son all manner of considerations of privilege, dignity and high temper might be expected to complicate the process of initiation.

They smiled at each other, secure in their mutual knowledge. Harry had stood on his own feet with all the boys of the village from infancy, never even thinking to exact respect or look for quarter. By the time Ebrard had become conscious of his running wild, and tried to hammer into him a right sense of his own estate, it was already far too late.

'Goodnight, my honest masons!'

'Goodnight, sir!'

As they crossed the court to the hall where the commonalty lodged, Harry gripped Adam by the arm. The light, wild shining of his eyes looked yellow in the dusk.

'Adam, I am resolved! I am resolved on France!'

Every summer Nicholas made this journey to buy up the cloths woven during the long winter. From Shrewsbury his men travelled into the hill country to bring back the bales by pack-horse into the town clearing-house; but on this Roman highroad it was simpler, if slower, to concentrate all their goods into carts. The cortège was thereby more compact, the precious cloths safer from the weather and more readily defensible if attacked. Watling Street lay under the king's peace, and crimes committed upon it were the business of the king's officers, but their control was tenuous, and masterless men were everywhere. Nicholas Otley provided his own sturdy army, preferring prevention to reliance upon law.

It was a contented and high-spirited army, from Peter Crowe, the foreman, who was fifty-five, to the youngest of the archers, who was a bumptious sixteen; and it assimilated two new companions without heartburning. The Lestrange brothers, like any untried novices, had to be tested before they could be accepted; but the elder proved to have a temper as sunny as his face, and fists as ready as his laugh, and the younger, though no great man of his hands, took the worst of every rough and tumble with such pugnacious appetite and so little ill-will that both were taken into the confraternity on the night of their arrival, and fell asleep in the rushes of the hall already sworn members, and happy with the few bruises it had cost them.

They had what they wanted. Men among men, they fed and watered and groomed the horses, cleaned harness, ran Master Otley's errands, re-flighted arrows, lent a shoulder to the wheels where the road was bad, and in the evenings crowded in joyously among the grooms and teamsters in hall, listened to Peter's stories, wrestled with the boys, played at draughts and tables with any who needed opponents, and joined in the songs of the archers. A place had been willingly made for them, and they stretched themselves, body and wits and spirit, to fill it to the last corner. They had never been so happy in their lives.

By the fourth day, somewhat timorously, for fear they should be thought to be putting themselves forward too soon, they began to involve each other more deeply in the evening's entertainment. Encouraged by an approving remark of Peter's about the sweetness of Adam's voice in the choruses, Harry piped up that his brother sang well and knew a great number of songs in both Latin and English. Adam, stricken with an unusual shyness, protested his inadequacy and tried to avoid the laurel, and when they pressed him avenged himself by saying that he was used to singing only with his brother's accompaniment, and that Harry could play on both citole and lute, and very well, too. One of the young archers had a citole, though he was no great hand on it, and freely confessed as much. He flung it to Harry across the circle, so directly that he could do no other than catch it, and they were fairly in it.

They conferred in anxious undertones as Harry tuned the citole, reproached each other hotly but very quietly, and were deeply happy. Adam had blushed like a girl, Harry had turned grim and pale. They embarked on one of the decidedly secular songs they had so surprisingly learned, out of class, from Brother Anselm, the young precentor at Shrewsbury; in whom, it is to be feared, the devil of human delight had not yet resigned his claim. Adam sang, at first tremulously, then captivated by his own gift and confident as spring:

'*Suscipe flos florem,*
  quia flos designat amorem.
Illo de flore
  nimio sum captus amore.
Hunc florem, Flora
  dulcissima, semper odora –'

Bent over the citole earnestly, his hair shaken forward upon his forehead, Harry turned his head away from the company, the better to concentrate, and so chanced to stare fixedly and sightlessly at one of the long windows unshuttered on the soft summer dusk. When he had plucked the last chord, and had leisure to blink away the haze of absorption, the stone lancet suddenly came into existence for him as the space of pale green after-light it was, and no empty space, either. Two rounded arms were folded on the stone sill outside, and a dimpled chin rested upon the arms. She had the hood of her cloak drawn over her head, and her braids were unloosed for bed; and in bed she should have been, at least two hours earlier.

He turned, startled, to shake his head at the praise of his playing, and back out of the circle hastily, thrusting the citole back upon its owner. 'A moment – I'll come again. I have an errand I forgot to do.' And he slipped away quietly to the door and, tiptoeing along the wall, pounced upon her before she was aware of him. She was barefoot in the dewy grass, and as he made his spring she gave a soft little cry of alarm and slipped through his fingers like an eel and ran; but he caught her within a few yards, and held her struggling between his hands.

'Gilleis, what are you doing here? And without shoes! What would your father say if he saw you here running about barefoot so late? Back to bed, now, quickly!'

She looked up at him from under the shadow of her hood with great eyes glimmering in the twilight, and her small breast heaved. 'Leave go of me! I need not do what *you* tell me! *You* are not my father!'

'You may be glad of it,' said Harry, putting on the grimmest face he could manage. 'If I were, miss, you should go back to bed with a flea in your ear. And if you caught cold from going without shoes, you should have the nastiest medicine I could brew for you. Come now, before someone else sees you.'

'I *will* take cold!' she threatened, suddenly in tears. 'I *will*! You don't care! You don't play with me now! You never want me to help you. You don't sing to *me* –'

Too taken aback to say anything intelligent, he protested feebly that he had not been singing, but playing, but she rightly brushed that aside as a quibble not worthy of notice, and wept the harder, pushing him away ineffectively and pulling her cloak over her face. He stooped and, slipping an arm under her knees, hoisted her in his arms and sat down in the angle of one of the buttresses with her, on the projecting course of stone.

'Gilleis, how can you say such things? Not care, indeed! You know I care! I don't have time to play, or I would. You know I have to work now, and earn my keep. I gave you my angel to mind for me, didn't I? Would I do that if I didn't love and trust you? But I'm your father's hired hand now, I must do my share. I can't play children's games any longer.'

'You don't want to!' she wept inarticulately into his shoulder. 'And I'm not a child! You weren't working just now. You always say, presently, when I've finished my work, but when you have finished it you don't come – '

Children! he thought, sighing with exasperated tenderness. A man never knows how to take them. All these last days she's been under my feet. She has no companions of her own age here, and I suppose Adam and I are the nearest she sees. He hugged her closer, rocking her gently and coaxingly on his lap, and whispering comforting noises into her hood.

'Be my good little girl now, and I'll find a fine piece of wood and make a portrait of you before we get to London. And I'll play for you, and Adam shall sing. Don't cry, sweetheart! Hush! You'll have me in trouble for keeping you here in the night.'

But the more he crooned over her and soothed her like a baby, the more inconsolably she cried. Her black hair, smoky and soft, tickled his nose and made him sneeze. He was growing weary of his paternal role, and dear though she was and fond though he was of her, if she had really been his child he would have smacked her. Yet he remembered uneasily the halt within the gate at Shrewsbury and her full skirt spread out to cover his hiding-place, and every impulse of impatience in him was drawn in on a golden rein of something more than gratitude.

'Gilleis, my honey-bird, I'm going to carry you back to your own door, and you must run straight to bed, you understand? What shall we do if you make yourself ill? Everyone will be unhappy, I most of all, because I shall feel I am to blame.' He rose, steadying his burden carefully. She was small for her age and a light weight, but he was no nobly-grown Adam, and she was as much as he could manage.

'You'll drop me,' she said, for the first time unimpeded by tears. Was she not, even, laughing at him a little, or were those only subsiding sobs that shook them both? He could not be sure.

'I shan't. You're not such a big girl yet.' With determination he crossed the court and carried her securely to the door of the gentles' staircase. Her body was soft and cool in his arms, naked under the folds of her cloak. Probably he had offended her by catching her at such a disadvantage. That aspect of her complexity did not puzzle him, and he dealt with it with tactful respect, handling her as reverently as if she had been a princess in cloth of gold.

As he set her down gently within the doorway she stirred in his embrace and wound her arms round his neck, laying her soft cheek against his. She smelled of childhood and the after-warmth of the departed sun and the dewy grass.

'Will you make a portrait of me? Truly?'

'Truly, if you'll go to bed this minute.'

'Will you begin tomorrow?'

If he must! It would still leave him the last hours of the evening to spend in hall among his fellows. But why had he not ten more years on his back, and a beard on his chin? Then she would pester someone else to play with her in his stead.

'*Only* if you go to bed this minute! Without one more word!' He kissed her on the forehead. 'There, goodnight!' He pushed her firmly towards the staircase, and as she gathered her cloak closely about her and climbed the first step he slapped her cheerfully on her neat, round rump to speed her on the upward journey.

It was a sad miscalculation on his part, as she showed him by turning on him like a fury and hitting out at him with all her force. Her hard little fist stung his cheek-bone and sent him a step backwards in sheer amazement.

'Don't dare! Don't *dare*!' Her eyes blazed at him, dry of tears, full of a desperate sadness; he saw a woman staring helplessly out from behind the child's outraged grief, but did not recognise what he saw.

'Gilleis, what have I done? On my soul, I did not intend – '

She whirled away from him and ran up the stairs, and was gone. Rubbing his cheek ruefully, he went slowly back to his friends. He supposed he had trespassed on the field of liberties which belonged only to her father. And of course, like all girls, she wanted to have her cake and eat it, to permit herself whatever familiarities she pleased with him, but resent any he took with her. And yet he would not for the world have offended her so, if only he had known how to avoid the pitfalls; but where girls were concerned there was no rule and no law. A man had to accept the risks, and be prepared to be invited to an act one moment and belaboured for it the next.

Well, he'd make his peace with her in the morning, and seal it by carving the figure he had promised her. And in another week they would be in London. By the time he entered the hall again he was ready to laugh at himself and her, and when the citole was passed to him again with a request for a drinking song he had already forgotten her.

They broached their French project to Master Otley on the last evening of the journey, in the abbey guest-house at St Albans, over the painting of Gilleis's image. It should, by rights, have waited until they were in London, but the merchant, delighted with the little nine-inch figure of his daughter, could not wait to see it take the bloom of her face and the black of her hair, and had borrowed colours from one of the brothers so that the work could be done on the spot. They had even offered him a table in the corner of the cloister where the light lay longest and clearest, so that he could work in peace, if peace indeed this could be called, with Adam leaning over one shoulder and Master Otley over the other in absorbed admiration. If they crowded him too closely he said nothing, only halted his hand and looked up with the fierce frown and ominous forbearance of a Talvace crossed, and they drew off respectfully and gave him room.

Gilleis had conducted herself, during those sittings, as though she had never in her life shed a tear before him, or aimed a blow at him, or been in his presence upon any but these formal terms. And in that stiff ceremonial dignity he had carved her, a small, erect figure with hands demurely folded and head loftily raised. He found her amusing so, but had the sense not to show it.

'Master Otley, we've been thinking, Adam and I. You remember we were asking you about the church-building in France?' He drew in a delicate, arched black brow, taut as a bow, and frowned thoughtfully as the very look of her face sprang to life in the copy. This haughtiness and distance he had been so intent on reproducing that he had never before stopped to wonder about it. If he looked long enough at the statuette he might begin to understand the original. 'We have been thinking that the best thing we could do is to go on into France.'

He heard Gilleis stir, and looked up impatiently. She had turned her head and parted her lips, and the trick of the light in her great eyes was lost. 'Sit still!' he flashed in annoyance, and got up to take her by the chin and jerk her head into position again, not roughly but quite without gentleness. 'Stay like that, and don't fidget.'

Without complaint she held her pose. When he managed to remember, with surprise and compunction, that she was not a copy set by a master, but a living child, and one of whom he was very fond, he marvelled that she did not burst into tears a dozen times in an evening. But usually he remembered only when she had already gone to bed and it was too late to appease his conscience by complimenting and making much of her.

'That's a big step to take,' said Master Otley. 'Do you speak the language?'

'Both of us well enough, Adam better than I. There would be no difficulty there. And you see, sir, there are reasons. London is far from Salop, and a good city to hide in, I know it, but wherever we go in England Adam will always be in some danger. Even in a charter borough, even in London, he would not be free until a year and a day had passed. Runaways have been dragged back when their year was almost run, many a time, some have even been unlawfully seized afterwards, when they were free men, and have been hard put to it to get loose from their masters to have their cases heard in court. In a village there would be no hope of his escaping notice at the next viewing of frankpledge. You know these things better than we. Is it not better to go on into France? We can surely get service there with one of the great master-masons, and learn our trade as well there as in England.'

The merchant, watching the features of his child's face spring out like stars under the charged brush and the darting hand, smiled in his beard. 'Good reasoning enough, but desire came before reason, I fancy. No need to dress up your longing for me, lad. In your place and at your age I'd be across the sea like an arrow. My ship sails as soon as we have her loaded and provisioned. Are you for taking passage in her? She puts in at le Havre by the longer crossing, a good spot for trafficking into both Paris and Brittany – now the young duke's reconciled with his uncle there's good trade to be had there.'

'Do you think we could earn our passage on board ship?' asked Harry, smoothing the curve of a firm, soft mouth, and surprised to find in it so strong a suggestion of sadness.

'You've earned it on dry land. I've no complaints of my bargains. Why not aboard ship, too? Though it's likely you won't feel so spry when you get that ocean swell under you. You're welcome to try, the pair of you.'

Harry looked up from his work, and Adam held his tongue and his breath, brilliant-eyed with excitement.

'May we really cross in her? If we are not able to be of use, we could pay something for our passage – '

'You'll do no such thing. Keep your money, lads, to set you on your way over there, and see you keep it well out of sight, and have the other hand on your dagger. And when you have a fair price from me for this little beauty here – '

'No!' said Harry quickly. 'This is promised already as my gift to Mistress Gilleis. A most rare woman! For the past hour she has not opened her mouth.' And he lifted his head and looked at her teasingly, expecting to see the dimpling quiver of a smile pass over her cheeks and lips and be sternly repressed. But she neither spoke nor moved, not by so much as the tremor of an eyelash. Nor did she lower the great dark eyes that dwelt so faithfully upon him.

'A princely gift,' said Nicholas Otley. 'When you let her speak she'll thank you for it prettily. Show your master five such days of work as you have shown us, and he'll know how to value you. It's settled then. You shall come home with us, and stay in my employ until the *Rose of Northfleet* sails, and then you shall cross in her, with my very good will and my blessing, and try your fortune abroad.'

'Sir, we shall be most happy to take advantage of this, as of all your former kindness. We shall not forget it to you. And if we are to have an opportunity, then,' said Harry, straightening his back, 'I will finish the painting later. The light is beginning to fail, and I cannot handle the figure so well now until the face is dried. And I think Gilleis is very tired.'

It was not the word he had in mind, but the right one would not come. The large eyes, all of her that was eloquent tonight, spoke in an unknown language, disquieting him even in his joy and excitement.

'Rest, Gilleis, we'll go on another day.'

'Come and look at your sweet self, my dove,' said her father, 'see how beautiful you are.'

She got up from her place and came to stare at her image with the same unfathomable thoughtfulness she had bestowed upon the artist while she sat silent. And it was beautiful. The newly painted face had changed under the brush and withdrawn all its soft, confiding innocence behind a touching new aloofness. There was something melancholy in it, and something assured, too. She was as he had seen her tonight, and as long as he continued to work on the statuette he would be for ever puzzled and enraged by his inability to understand what he had faithfully recreated.

'What, nothing to say?'

'I see what it is,' said Harry. 'I'm to blame. I've threatened her into silence so long she's forgotten how to speak.'

'Let well alone, then. Tomorrow she'll chatter us all to deafness as usual.'

'I could speak,' said Gilleis, 'if I had anything to say.'

'Come, that's better, she still has a tongue. Say a word of thanks for so beautiful a gift, and prettily, mind.'

'Only if you like it,' said Harry, collecting up brushes and colours. He was sure by her stubborn silence that she did not like it, that to her it meant only a reminder of hours of motionless boredom, of being frowned at and scolded. Even his gift he had managed to spoil for her.

'You should, miss, for he's made you a beauty, funny little squirrel as you are. Give Harry a kiss for it and say goodnight.'

Obediently she raised her face, and offered the silent mouth, and when he opened his arms to her and hugged her with goodwill, she slid her hands delicately about his neck and gently laid hold of the thick locks of his hair, where it grew crosswise in curls in his nape. Her mouth was cool and smooth and firm. Kissed, she did not kiss him again, but only permitted the salute in an act of royal condescension; but her fingers, tugging softly in his hair, had no such lofty detachment about them. Looking at her serene face as she disengaged herself, he could hardly believe the hands had belonged to the same person. What she would have liked to do, of course, he reflected, was to pull his hair as hard as she could, in payment for his lack of consideration these many evenings, but before her father this was the worst she could do without being detected.

He watched her regretfully as she went confidingly into Adam's arms and gave him a smacking kiss, kissed her father, and went with unusual docility, and without a backward glance, to seek her bed.

He was sorry now, so far as he could spare a thought for anything but the future and France, that he had dealt so clumsily with her and made her dislike him so much.

In darkness, rolled up in swathes of felt in Harry's bundle, the angel took wing for le Havre. The wrapping was to protect his colours from the salt air, and his slight outstretched hands from the buffeting of the passage. Like the brilliant invisible creature within the chrysalis, he slept and dreamed; and the half-smile on his ardent mouth still made the unseen face beautiful and terrible. There was wonder in it, and wildness, and secret knowledge of everything that had been, everything that was, everything that was to come.

He saw in his dream all that passed about him and thought to escape the piercing intelligence of his hooded eyes: Gilleis clinging with one hand to the side of the little boat that heaved softly under the ship's stern, and with the other to her father's firm hip, the teeming wine-quays of London's foreshore, the needle-sharp gables gnawing the pearly September sky like uneven teeth, the two boys already half-drunk with excitement, half-sick with impatience, turning their backs even on the Tower to strain their eyes downriver, towards the future, towards the sea, towards a fantasy of living, growing rock, a tree, a grove, a forest of stone. He saw the cool, hasty kiss on the child's proffered mouth, the quick embrace, the good-humoured way the boy bent his head low for her while she hung her medal of the Virgin round his neck; and he saw the child waving constantly from the receding boat as she was rowed ashore with her father, waving long after the boys had forgotten her in their curiosity about the ship and its crew and its rigging and all the strange-smelling, salt-coated, strident life within it.

Afterwards, when the tide and the following wind had brought the *Rose of Northfleet* down to open water, and the great estuary had widened and widened into the still greater sea, and the waves had grown bursting rims of snow and plunged like horses, the angel saw his creator brought down to ignominious misery, hanging over the lee rail heaving out his heart in helpless convulsions, while a bewildered Adam, gay as a grasshopper and unable to feel anything but delight in this absurd motion, tenderly held and sensibly exhorted him, torn between laughter and concern.

The angel, tossed ceaselessly in his swathed darkness, still smiled, immune even from pity. The hands feebly wringing away tears of weakness and shakily wiping cold sweat from a clammy forehead and beads of sour vomit from grey lips, were the hands which had made him as he was. They were more and less than he, more vulnerable and immeasurably more wonderful.

Somewhere beyond the water, beyond the misery of sea-sickness and the disillusionment of experience, the golden fantasy grew and flourished immaculately still, a tree of stone tall as the sky, budding miraculously all the year round with new, exuberant leaves of worship and aspiration and knowledge.

PART TWO

PARIS

1209

CHAPTER SIX

The house in the Rue des Psautiers was double-gabled and somewhat broader than its neighbours, and beside it a great studded door in the wall led through into a stable-yard. Steep-pitched roofs thrust deep eaves forward over the street like jutting eyebrows, casting the house door into shadow. In an upper window a light burned, though a curtain screened it from direct view.

When the house had belonged to Claudien Guiscard, a middle-aged and wealthy widower who dealt in perfumes, silver, jewels, and carpets, and other commodities brought in from the Levant by way of Venice, no one who passed along the quiet street had paused to give it a second glance; but now that he had died and left it to his mistress it was a very different story. Traffic along the Rue des Psautiers was brisk these days. Young men came in their dozens to try their luck at catching her eye and ear and gaining entry to that lighted room. Old men who had no such expectation nevertheless went out of their way to use the quiet thoroughfare, merely in the hope of catching a glimpse of her at the window, or as she entered or left with her waiting-maid. Claudien's nearest relative, a second cousin, was said to be contemplating an appeal to the judiciary to dispossess the courtesan of her legacy. She, for her part, was rumoured to be quite unmoved by the threat, and had certainly done nothing to abate the scandal which centred upon her person. After her lover's death many people had thought she would sell the property quickly, while it was hers, and go back to Venice, from which city Claudien had brought her. Instead, she had settled herself comfortably in the house and entertained there like a duchess, admitting to her more intimate favours whoever pleased her, even though he were penniless, and declining whoever did not, though he came of the blood royal and brought purses of gold to sponsor his suit. She was the rage. She could sing and play, duel in verses with the poets, and argue philosophy with the schoolmen. Besides her native Italian she spoke Latin and French and even a little English, or so it was said. She kept herself in the modest, dignified state of a noblewoman widowed, but with the freedom and intelligence of an Athenian hetaera. And this curious disregard she had for the charms of money – presumably because she already had enough of it – gave an enchanted hope even to those young creatures who would not otherwise have ventured to fix their eyes upon one so sought after; so that almost nightly the several estates of Paris clashed upon her doorstep.

On this particular evening of late April two parties converged upon the house at the same moment from the two ends of the Rue des Psautiers. From the north, on horseback, followed by a manservant and a little group of attendant musicians carrying their instruments, came a young gentleman of the de Breauté family, dressed in his best and aware of his worth. From the south, strung four abreast across the street, and singing a scandalous parody of Sigebert's hymn to the virgin martyrs, with its catalogue of resounding female names, Adam Lestrange, the English mason, with his three attendant demons from the garret in the Ruelle des Guenilles; in his right arm his brother, in the left the lad Élie from Provence, with his choirboy's face and his street-arab's impudence, and arm-in-arm with him the saturnine baccalaureat Apollon, with his lute slung over his shoulder. They came formidably armed to the lists, with Adam's looks and voice, Harry's new verses, and a tune of Pierre Abelard's dredged up out of Apollon's capacious Breton memory to fit the song. Between the four of them, these last two years, they had produced some notable additions to the street songs of Paris.

Strolling behind them, drawn by the parody, the magnet in the Rue des Psautiers, and the prospect of mischief, came a dozen other students fresh from Nestor's inn and full of wine, come to see fair play.

Apollon first perceived the horseman, his servant and his players, and dropped out of the quartet in the last verse to exclaim: 'The enemy are in sight!' His jaw fell at sight of the array of instruments. 'God's wounds, they've brought the whole consort! Are they *all* candidates for paradise?'

'A rival!' said Adam, crowing with joy. 'The one stimulus I needed! Come on!' And he unlaced his arms nimbly from Harry's neck on the right and Élie's on the left, and led the dash for the doorway, his long legs flashing. They followed willingly, whooped on by the gay rabble behind. The horseman, awaking less readily to the situation, clapped spurs to his horse somewhat belatedly, and reined in in a flurry of sparks at Madonna Benedetta's door-step just as Adam set foot on it and spread his arms to bar the way.

'Give way, fellow,' said de Breauté, secure in his nobility but good-humoured still. 'Do you not know your betters?'

Adam planted himself firmly on the second step, and wagged a chiding finger at his rival. 'Come, come, sir, do you not know there's no better nor worse here, but only pleasing or displeasing to the lady? It was as close a thing as ever I saw, but I am here before you. Do you give way, like a fair-minded fellow, and take your turn another evening. I stand on my rights.'

'I'll see you to the devil first!' said de Breauté heartily, and pressed his horse close, in the hope of intimidating this bold young man into drawing aside; but Élie snapped his fingers loudly under the beast's well-bred nose, and sent it backwards in a startled plunge a yard or two across the cobbles, hooves slithering and clanging hard against the stones. If there was a woman in the lighted room, she could hardly be long unaware of the commotion beneath her window; even if she had been sleeping, she must be wakeful enough now.

The horseman, for a moment thrown off-balance, recovered himself with a rising temper, and swung his whip at Élie's head, but the boy ducked and sprang aside, and Apollon lifted a soothing hand and cried: 'Wait, now, not so hot! Do you want to ingratiate yourself with Madonna Benedetta by starting a brawl under her windows? Do you suppose she isn't capable of making her own choice? And is any one of us going to dispute it if she does? Are you afraid to enter the lists fairly, song for song?'

The rabble of students had closed in happily about the two groups, and linked arms to form a semicircle round the doorway. They raised a cheer at this suggestion, foreseeing delicious entertainment, whether the bargain held or broke.

'Song for song! Toss for first place, and give each other fair hearing.'

'And if she give either one a sign of her approval, t'other must pack and go, and no hard feelings. Right, boys?'

'Right!' roared the circle delightedly, and swayed inwards to see and hear the better. Such harmless townsfolk as happened to be passing through the Rue des Psautiers first slowed at sight and sound of this noisy assembly, and then halted to await developments, until the circle was three deep and others were craning to look over the shoulders of those in front. Of late it had become the habit with some to stroll by Madonna Benedetta's on uneventful evenings in the hope of diversion.

The musicians grinned with the superiority of professionals at the idea of competing with this shabby handful of students and craftsmen. Their master had nothing to fear. Plainly he thought the same, for he had lowered his whip and was laughing. Like Adam, he had been taking aboard courage and inspiration from a flagon, and as yet it had left him amiable.

'Done! If she signify her favour to you, I'll withdraw and leave you to your happiness. But you must do as much for me.'

'Willingly,' said Adam. 'What's more, I'll give you the precedence. Go first, and you shall be heard fairly.'

'Good lad!' whispered Harry in his ear. 'There's not a woman breathing could bear to say yes to the first till she's heard the second – and last heard's best remembered.'

'Silence, lads, give silence! Play fair by us both!' And in an undertone Adam besought anxiously: 'Shall I spring the new song on her direct, or open with some small thing?'

'The new one! Stake everything!' advised Apollon in an answering whisper.

The ring of students, more than commonly disorderly in pursuit of order, exhorted the world to silence, and had much ado to silence one another; but in a moment or two the last ripple of their hubbub sighed away into the shadows, and the consort, assembling in a little group at the foot of the steps, tuned their instruments and broke into a known melody.

> 'If I had lilies to bring,
> or were this the season of roses –'

'We're back with Fortunatus,' breathed Élie disgustedly, 'picking violets for Radegunde. For God's sake, where are the moderns?'

'Hush, give the man his chance.'

He subsided with a sigh of protest, and like his fellows heard the performance out with critical attention, and even some pleasure, for all its antiquity. Having paid for music, de Breauté contributed none himself; no doubt he knew his own capabilities best, and not every man can have a true voice. And if he must purchase his talents, he had got good value enough. The singer had a sure delivery and a sweet tone, and the players knew their business. He sat his horse in mid-street, his eyes fixed on that upper window, where the candle-light flickered a little in the freshening breeze of the night, and the arras stirred languidly, so that at times he stiffened in eagerness, expecting the apparition of a smiling, gracious face. But the violets of Fortunatus reached Radegunde, and still Madonna Bendetta did not show herself.

'Hard luck, friend!' commiserated the students cheerfully. 'She-hawks never come to the first lure.'

'Let's hear what the other can do.'

'She's there,' said one, his eyes on the window. 'I saw a shadow pass. She marks you, lads, you're not wasting your breath.'

'An omen!' piped up a youngster from the third rank, craning his neck and recognising the lutanist. 'He has Apollo himself to play for him!'

'Unfair!' cried another. 'What chance has the other poor devil against the gods?'

'Without his name be Marsyas,' shouted a voice from the back, and there was a howl of laughter.

'Will you hold your din, and let Apollo make himself heard, before he has the knives sharpened for the lot of you?'

They settled good-humouredly into silence, still grinning, and Apollon led softly into Abelard's forgotten air. One listener, catching an echo of something once half-known, drew back his head, and ceased to laugh. Here and there a swaying head picked up the time. They knew a tune when they heard one. They were quiet enough now. De Breauté looked on perforce, frowning to see the visible audience captivated, and fearing for the invisible.

Adam sang, his voice soaring fresh and gay and plaintive between the overhanging walls:

'Now is the time of maying.
Beneath thy flowering tree
I strip my bones with praying,
And yet thou wilt not see.

The sap of spring is leaping,
The love-dance takes the deer;
I cry thy name with weeping,
And yet thou wilt not hear.

Under thy sheltering blossom
The coney makes her cave.

The birds nest in thy bosom,
But me thou wilt not save.

Yet when the branch is shaken –'

The arras within the window trembled; he saw it, and his voice trembled with it for a moment, and then swept on joyously and steadily to the close:

'Yet when the branch is shaken
And summer's pride is past,
Me, naked and forsaken,
Receive and love at last,

And when the autumn dapples
Thy gilded heaven tree,
Let fall thy golden apples,
Bow down thy breasts to me.'

There was a moment of stillness and silence, and then a rising murmur and a triumphant cry:

'Look up, lads, the moon rises!'

A hand had appeared from behind the tapestry, and was stretched out over the street. They saw a round white arm from which the fur hem of a loose sleeve fell back to the elbow, as something was let fall from between her fingers and drifted down lightly towards Adam's ready hands. One of the musicians, encouraged by a cry of protest from his lord, leaped to intercept it, but Adam whisked it away and held it high. The circle of students stamped and roared.

'Violets! The ones your fellows tossed in at her window a minute ago! She gives them to me. Are you answered?'

'A judgement, a judgement!' they chorused. 'Go home, man, she's made her choice.'

The wine de Breauté had drunk was souring in him. He hesitated angrily for a moment, the horse shifting uneasily under him. The hand vanished within, the window was quiet and unrevealing as before.

'She said no word. How do we even know the posy was meant for you and not for me?'

They roared him down indignantly, but now his blood was up

and he would not give way. 'Song for song till she told us her mind was the bargain!' he cried, and signed furiously to the musicians to strike up again. Insistent above the hubbub rose another melody well-known to every minstrel in Paris.

'Stay by the door,' urged Harry, clutching Adam by the arm as he started angrily forward, 'for I think she means to open when she has her fill of this.'

'Let me alone!' growled Adam, struggling. 'I'll have him off his perch though he draw on me, the cheating hound!'

They held him back and thrust him behind them into the coign of the doorway while they shook some sense into him. 'What do you want with the man, you fool? The woman's yours, leave the man to us.'

For all their indignation, the audience had stilled to listen. The song was an old favourite, and this was not, after all, their quarrel; they were there to enjoy it, and perhaps to add a little fuel to the fire if it threatened to burn out too soon and too tamely.

'This is dull stuff,' said Harry, cocking an ear. 'Let's see if we can improve on it. Apollon, lend me the lute!' His eyes were gleaming yellowly, and he had a hungry, cat's smile as he bent over the strings and fingered his way into the air. It was already too late to do anything about the first verse, but he could surely liven up what was left.

'Now summer comes with splendour,
The zenith of the year,
And winter's frosts surrender
To Phoebus' burning spear,

But I, who dote upon you,
Your grieving suppliant stand – '

In came Harry with a vicious chord and a drumming of his finger-ends on the wood, and a voice far louder and more penetrating than Adam's, if less melodious:

' – While my hired gleemen dun you
For love at secondhand.'

A shout of joy went up from the audience. De Breauté's servant darted forward up the steps and lunged with his sheathed dagger at the lute, but Apollon and Élie closed in before Harry, received the attacker into willing arms, and held him a writhing prisoner. De Breauté, black with temper, set spurs to his horse again, but one of the students caught at his bridle and hung upon it with all his weight. The distracted consort, redoubling their efforts, blew and scraped and plucked frenziedly to drown the hubbub. The singer bellowed:

'O fount of pity springing,
Be your sweet mercy shed – '

There his voice cracked grotesquely with strain, and choked him to silence, leaving Harry's gleeful shout triumphant on the air, sharp as sour apples:

' – On one more skilled in singing
And better worth your bed.'

A howl of delight from those nearest greeted it, and clamouring complaints from those behind demanded to have it relayed to them, and so it was, flung back wave by wave to the most remote onlookers bobbing up and down at the back. The laughter followed it in widening ripples, echoing from the leaning gables in a riotous thunder. But high above it floated the loveliest, clearest, most candid peal of mirth launched in Paris that night. It fell from Madonna Benedetta's window like a flight of yellow rose-leaves drifting slowly down in a shaft of sunlight.

Everyone looked up, but the window was empty; and as they stared upwards, the door was softly unbarred below, and softly opened. Adam heard it and sprang round to see a girl's face glowing in the interstice and a girl's hand reaching for his to draw him in. Overwhelmed now that the heavens stood wide for him, he could only stare and wonder, until Harry, thrusting the lute back into Apollon's solicitous hands, took the dazed conquerer by the shoulders and pushed him into the house. The door closed smartly, and a bolt shot into place with a clang.

Too much occupied with keeping his seat to mark the opening of the door, de Breauté heard the bolt go home, and casting a frantic glance in that direction, saw that his rival had vanished. It was more than his pride could bear. With a yell of rage he lashed out at the student who clung to his bridle, and the horse, taking the worst of the blow as the boy ducked under its heaving neck, reared up with a scream and sent the front rank of spectators leaping back into the arms of their fellows. The youngster, flung off like a kitten, dropped as lightly as one, and rolled clear of the clashing hooves, to be hauled to his feet by his friends. De Breauté, freed of the hampering weight and no more than half in control of his mount, drove him straight at the steps.

The musicians embraced their instruments and scuttled aside, jostling one another wildly. Élie leaped from the steps in one direction, Apollon, jealously guarding his lute, in the other, and Harry, pinned in the doorway, took the lash of the whip about his upflung forearm to save his head, and clapping the other hand as far up the butt as he could reach, wrenched the horseman's lunging weight towards him. He meant only to disarm his attacker, but the whip had a loop which was fastened securely about de Breauté's gloved wrist, and man and weapon were dragged forward together over the horse's shoulder. Harry went down beneath the flying weight, and rolled upon the steps half-dazed, his enemy sprawling over him and the agitated hooves plunging and clattering on the cobbles not a yard from them, until Élie caught at the bridle and drew the beast away, trembling and snorting. He got it safely clear of the crowd, and then it tossed him off like a flake of foam from the bit, and took to its heels for home; and Élie, ever a practical man, wasted no time on a problem he could not solve, but picked himself up, rubbed his bruises briefly, and hurled himself bodily back into the laughing, bawling, cursing, grunting mass of bodies that filled the Rue des Psautiers from wall to wall.

The wiser citizens made all possible haste away from the battle; the students with whoops of joy poured themselves into it, took whichever side they fancied, and laid about them merrily. It was months since they had seen such a satisfactory affray, and one in which anyone might join. They settled down to enjoy it.

Even the musicians, inextricably tangled into the struggling mass, abandoned all thought of escape, and went to their master's support tooth and nail. There was no hope of withdrawing their instruments intact from such a turmoil, so they turned them into weapons, and trusted in de Breauté to replace them, since they served his pleasure and were being sacrificed in his cause. Élie took a crack over the head from a flute, and sat down hard again on the cobbles. Apollon, shielding his precious lute with his body, since he had no lord to buy him another, was felled by a blow from a viol, and heard its delicate, taut ribs crack and cave in with almost as much pain as if his own darling had suffered injury. Not until his cherishing hands had assured him that it was still intact did he find time to notice the thunderous music in his misused head. The rounded belly of a citole, swung purposefully at Harry's skull as he rolled clear of his antagonist, missed him by a foot and smashed like an egg against the edge of the stone step. He flung himself upon it and seized its slender neck, and planting a foot in the musician's chest from his vantage point on top of the steps, hurled him off to crash into a swaying wall of bodies. He had possessed himself of a weapon only just in time. De Breauté was on his feet and had his sword out.

Someone yelled: 'Steel!' and those who could fell back a little from him, for he was in so irresponsible a rage that to be within his range was a risk even these incautious spirits did not care to take. He lunged at Harry, and the shattered citole, cunningly advanced to meet the point instead of battering it aside, was impaled so deeply that the tip of the blade split the sounding-board and grazed Harry's fingers. He twisted the neck of the instrument through a full circle in his hands, and de Breauté screamed and let go his hilt rather than have his wrist broken. Harry uttered a shout of triumph, and swung citole and sword together about his head, intending to hurl both over the surging mass of combatants and out of reach; but at that moment a piercing whistle rang out from the northern end of the Rue des Psautiers, and every student head reared in one abrupt and incredibly brief instant of stillness.

'Scatter!' bellowed Apollon. 'The watch!' And the apparently inextricable mass disentangled itself miraculously, and made off like the wind in all directions but the north. The noise of running feet was like a sudden heavy shower of rain.

Élie leaped for the top of the wall which bounded Guiscard's stable-yard, and hauled himself up with a furious scraping of shoe-toes and knees, to straddle the wall and drop out of sight within. Apollon dived into a narrow gullet between the houses, and crept through, holding his nose as he paddled along the noisome gutter into the Rue du Lapin and safety. Harry, dropping the transfixed citole, took a flying leap down the steps to follow him, but the musicians, secure in their master's nobility and seeing a safe and easy way to ingratiate themselves with him now that the odds were so drastically changed, fell upon the fugitive as one man and bore him crashing to the cobbles.

By the time he had regained the breath they had knocked out of him, they had him propped on his feet before the provost and were volubly explaining how the whole riot was his work, how he and his cronies had molested their lord on his entirely innocent occasions, interrupted his serenade with ribald parodies, assaulted his servant, dragged him from his horse, and started a street fight in which all the other riff-raff of the student quarter had rushed to take part.

Harry's eyes grew large with admiration as he listened. 'On my soul,' he said, 'I begin to respect myself! It seems I'm a devil of a fellow.'

One of the sergeants clouted him lightly in the mouth with the back of his hand, to teach him to be silent until invited to speak. He shook the slight sting of the blow away without resentment, and looked round upon the empty street, suddenly so quiet. Every soul but himself had got clear away. But for the sad, splintered instruments, and the sword, still stabbing the citole to the heart, no sign of the recent bedlam remained.

The provost, frowning down from his lanky roan horse, was also surveying the battleground, and regretting that he had not delayed entering the street until he could post a second force at the southern end and net a whole shoal of the rowdy students who plagued him so constantly. But half of them, no doubt, would have laid claim to clerical privilege if he had, and been fished out of trouble by masters or canons. Well, at least there were no bodies to be accounted for this time, and no injuries.

'My lord de Breauté, do you bear out all this? You know this fellow for one of the ringleaders, do you?'

'The most impudent of them all,' said de Breauté, breathing hard and looking daggers as his servant brushed him down. 'It was he pulled me from my horse.' But he said nothing of Adam's part in the affair; perhaps out of generosity, but more likely, thought Harry, because the admission of defeat would have made him a laughing-stock.

'Well, rascal, what have you to say? Did you pull my lord from his horse?'

'I did,' said Harry, 'after he took his whip to me. But indeed it was more of a success than I'd bargained for: it was only the whip I wanted, I got the man as well. I was more surprised than he was. And I was underneath!'

'Wanted the whip, did you!' said the provost with a grim smile.

'We may be able to satisfy you there, my lad. What business had you here in the first place, ruffling it and howling gross songs on the public street to the annoyance of an honest gentleman? I mean to have the peace kept in my city, and you and your kind shall learn it.'

'Why, I don't deny the fight, but there are two sides to any fight, and I can hardly be supposed to have sustained both sides single-handed. This honest gentleman made a bargain, and refused to abide by it when he lost, and so we came to blows. Take him in, too, and do us both justice. Besides,' said Harry cheerfully, 'you're more like to get a good fat fine out of him than me, for devil a silver coin have I got to my name since I paid for the supper.'

'If you had half the year's minting, you should still cool your heels overnight, young man. It will do you no harm to lie hard for once. Unless you can produce witnesses to speak to your version of this evening's entertainment?'

There were indeed two witnesses almost within call, but to disturb them would have been a kind of blasphemy. The light was quenched in the upper room. Harry smiled, and shook his head. His hard night for Adam's soft one, it was a fair exchange.

'Now you've promised me a bed, how can I be so uncivil as to wish to excuse myself from occupying it? Yours is one guest-house that never turns away even a *vagus*.'

'You have a trick of speech that never was bred in Paris,' said the provost, frowning over him, and thoughtfully pulling a great nose pitted with pock-marks. 'What's your name, fellow? Are you enrolled as a student, or are you indeed *vagus*?'

'I am not enrolled as a student, but I have leave to hear lectures when my duties permit. My name – Master Provost, can you keep a secret? My name is Golias, master of the *Ordo Vagorum*, but I'm in Paris incognito, and you mustn't breathe a word of it.'

'Pay him for that,' said the provost, but so tolerantly that the sergeants dealt him no more than a couple of buffets on the ears with their heavy leather gloves.

'If you wish to make any claim to being a clerk, make it now,' said the provost shortly, 'and before witnesses.'

Harry shook his thick, disordered brown locks indignantly. 'Does this look like a tonsure?'

'I've known tonsures appear mysteriously, even in a cell underground. I'm taking no chances.'

'I'll strangle whoever tries to shave this,' Harry promised

heartily, 'even to get me out of jail.'

'Bring him along,' said the provost, 'and we'll see if he has a better will to answer questions in the morning.' And with that he shook his reins, gave de Breauté a brusque inclination of his head, and trotted away along the Rue des Psautiers. And Harry, held firmly by both arms and encouraged to speed by an occasional fist thudding into his back, stepped out philosophically after him. It was bad luck to be the scapegoat, but it might have happened to any one of them; and the evening had been worth it. He had no complaints.

The exhilaration of wine and action lasted him half through the night, though he did tell the sergeants, more in sorrow than in anger, what he thought of the narrow, damp, foul cell into which they thrust him. They answered, justly enough, that he had good reason to be thankful they had given him one above ground, with a window, small, high and barred, but undoubtedly a window, and giving on to the outer air. They might just as easily have put him underground in darkness. They rough-handled him a little before they left him, for his impudence, but without malice, almost playfully. Even sergeants have a certain sneaking fellow-feeling with those who are merry with drink, and they did not stop to wonder how much of his gaiety was due to wine and how much to satisfied excitement.

When he was alone he groped his way to the cold stone ledge, and sat down. Through the high window he could see a handful of stars, and the air, though laden with some highly unpleasant smells, was breathable. They were right, he had good reason to think himself lucky. If they had been in a bad humour they would have broken his head for him and pitched him into one of the fetid holes below, where a man could not even stand upright or lie at full length.

Now the worst problem he had was how to pass the time and work off the rest of his animal spirits, for he was too restless to think of sleeping. He eased himself into the most comfortable position he could find, discovering in the process some bruises he had not known he possessed, and began to go through his repertory of disreputable songs, tentatively at first, to see how soon they would feel it necessary to take steps to silence him, then, emboldened by having got through the first unthreatened, at the top of his voice. He was halfway through the ballad of a certain abbess of remarkably irregular private life, with his ears cocked for footsteps and his eye on the door, like an urchin essaying how far he dare go in provocation, when the key turned in the lock and a thread of light split the darkness. He fell silent, half regretting his recklessness and half exulting in it, and waited to see if he had tried his luck too hard; but the turnkey with his lantern brought in only one man, the provost's clerk, a sharp-faced fellow in a scholar's garde-corps and a skull-cap.

'I am come to advise you of the amount at which your fine is fixed,' said he, planting the lantern upon a wooden stool in the corner of the cell, and signalling to the jailer to withdraw and close the door until he wished to leave.

'Then you may spare your breath,' said Harry, swinging his feet to the floor and sitting up, 'for whatever it may be, I cannot pay it.'

He looked round his prison with interest, for he had had small opportunity to examine it when they bundled him into it, and this interlude of light and company was welcome to him. He had not, until that moment, realised that he had a stool, and a large, solid stool, too, with a top to it as thick as a refectory table. Nor that he had company of a kind in his solitude, apart from the vermin, for all the walls about him were written and scratched over with complaints, curses and ribaldries left by his predecessors, including some interesting reflections on the provost's parentage, scored deep into the stone above the bench with a knife or a nail.

'Then you may rot where you are, my friend, but it is my duty to acquaint you with the provost's judgement. Your freedom is set at twelve pounds, Paris. If you pay your fine, you may go free in the morning. If not, you may write a letter to someone who can raise the money for you. You must have friends who will bestir themselves for you.'

'My friends are all as wealthy as I. You have as much chance of getting twelve pounds out of the lot of us as you have of being taken up to heaven living.'

'That is your affair, not mine. But until the fine is paid you will continue to lie here. Have you no money at all?'

Harry turned out his pockets, and unearthed a few small coins, all that the merry party at Nestor's had left him. In the search he found also something which greatly pleased him, for he had forgotten he had it, and if the sergeants had been more thorough with him it would surely have been found and taken from him, along with his dagger. His favourite little pocket-knife in its worn sheath was strapped to the belt of his chausses, under his tunic, and had escaped notice. He took care to keep it out of sight now, for fear the oversight should be remedied. The very feel of it between his fingers, the way the haft settled and fitted into his palm, filled him with confidence and comfort.

'That won't free you,' admitted the clerk with a sour smile, 'but it would at least buy you a bite of bread and cheese if you're hungry, anda drop of cheap wine. I'm not obliged to offer you these services, nor good advice neither, but out of goodwill I'll get you food if you please to pay for it.'

Harry was on the point of closing with this offer, when the feel of the knife against his side, and the sight of the honest dark wood of the stool, filled him with a different hunger and a stronger anticipation. He shook the coins together in his hand, smiling delightedly.

'I'll tell you what I'd rather have, if you'll help me to it. Oh, nothing against your conscience, I swear. A light! A candle – a large one, mind, none of your ends – or the loan of a lantern for the night. What do you say? There's enough here to pay for it, and something over for your kindness.'

'It's a queer taste,' said the clerk, raising his eyebrows, 'to want to see this hole as well as feel and smell it. But if that's your wish, I see no harm in it. Keep this lantern, it's trimmed, and will burn all night. And if you please to send a message somewhere in the morning, I'll see it delivered. Don't thank me for that! How else should we ever see our money for you starved mice from the schools? There's not a one of you ever has the means to pay for his bed.'

'Your hostelry charges such high rates,' said Harry, grinning, 'that it's my belief you owe us that bread and cheese thrown in. And faith, I should only be doing right by my fellows in misfortune if I stood out for it. If they don't send me some food in, I'll go on singing until they do, and nobody shall get any sleep tonight.'

'That's one way of looking at the matter,' agreed the clerk drily. 'On the other hand, the provost lies well out of earshot even of your bellow, and the sergeants are dicing and not yet minded for sleep, otherwise they would have made shift to silence you before now. And my reading of the probabilities is somewhat at variance with yours. I should put it, rather, that if you do not hush your noise, they will soon be in with rods and an iron bridle, to hush it for you.'

'Say no more, I'm convinced! Only leave me the light, and I'll be quiet as the grave.'

He parted with his last coins upon these terms, without the slightest regret; and when he was left alone again, the jailer having re-locked the door upon him and withdrawn with the clerk, he went and set the lantern on the stone bench, and tipped up the stool to examine it more closely.

The top, seven or eight inches thick, projected at either end beyond the roughly carved legs, and made a fine jutting mass of wood. He thumbed it over, and it was shiny and smooth with long handling. To make the most of his light he sat down on the filthy floor with his back braced against the stone ledge, and the lantern shining over his left shoulder, almost on a level with the end of the stool, which he drew close between his knees. When he turned it sidewise to the light he could already see the thick, gross profile leaning out like a devil from a misericord. He drew out his knife, and the haft nestled into his palm like the muzzle of a favourite dog, ready and eager for exercise.

He did not sleep all night, but the provost had never had a quieter or a happier prisoner.

CHAPTER SEVEN

Adam walked through the early dawn to the Ruelle des Guenilles like one borne on a rosy cloud of delight, and climbed the stairs to the attic, singing softly to himself and unbuckling the belt of the good cotte as he went. At the sound of his step Élie flung open the door and rushed out to meet him.

'I've been waiting for you – Apollon had a six o'clock lecture he couldn't miss. Adam, they took up Harry!'

'They, who?' said Adam, lost in his own surpassing memories, and slow to recognise disaster. 'What are you babbling about, man?'

'The provost and his officers. Did you not even hear the alarm? Ah, well, I suppose not! They came soon after you entered the house. We all ran for it. Everyone got clear except Harry; they picked him up for disturbing the peace, and de Breauté and his men swore he was the ringleader. They took him off and tossed him in the provost's prison, and there he is now, and how are we to get him out? We haven't a thing of value to pledge, and if I ask my father for money before my next allowance is due he'll likely bid me come home and render account of myself, and I shall be hauled out of the schools and put to clerking. The last time he had to bail me out he swore he'd give me no more indulgences. What are we to do?'

Adam took him by the arm, and marched him into their room, and there began hurriedly to strip off the precious cotte and pull on his working tunic, shooting questions like arrows at the hollow-eyed and whey-faced Élie.

'How did you learn all this? Has he sent word?'

'I heard them take him away. I was hiding inside Madonna Benedetta's stable-yard.'

'What? You've known ever since it happened? You clown, why didn't you come and tell me at once?'

Élie clutched his aching head and rolled his eyes heavenwards. 'Talk sense, man. How could I? Can you not see me banging at the door? "My most humble apologies to Madonna Benedetta, but I must borrow my friend back from her, his brother's been taken up by the watch!" Besides, I didn't know then where they might take him, I had to follow them to find out.'

'Did they mishandle him? And did he manage to hold his fool tongue?'

'They were in good humour, no more than playful. But you know him – when the provost asked him his name he told him he was Golias, and that didn't please!'

'That's like him!' said Adam, savage with anxiety, tugging down his tunic. 'He never could let well or ill alone. Let me get him safe out of there, and I'll have something to say to him myself. Golias, indeed! And he knows the trouble they've been making about vagabonds lately! If he must make a joke at the wrong time, does it have to be the most provocative joke possible? Well, go on, what did you do?'

'Came back here to Apollon. He makes a better figure than I do when it comes to bearding officials. He went and argued the toss with them at the prison, and tried to threaten them with all the canons of Notre Dame. But they wouldn't turn him loose, and they wouldn't let Apollon see him. They want twelve pounds Paris before they'll let go of him. Apollon tried bargaining – you know he can *look* as if he has a few pounds about him even when he hasn't a penny. But he couldn't beat them down. It's twelve pounds or no Harry. Now what are we going to do? We can't put together two pounds between us until the beginning of the month. Apollon said if we could find some way of making up the rest we could pledge his lute.' He offered this extreme sacrifice round-eyed with awe as a child, for he knew its worth. So did Adam, and turned impulsively to fling an arm round his shoulders and hug him briefly.

'We won't cut Apollon's heart out, it's not as bad as all that. No, I'll go and cleanse my bosom to old Bertrand. He'll rave, but he'll pay up rather than leave his best sculptor in jail and have to make do without him, even for a day. I'll get my head in my hands, and so will Harry when he's loosed, but no matter for that. Go and sleep it off,' he advised, pushing Élie towards his bed, 'you look like a ghost. I suppose you've had no sleep all night.'

'Have you?' asked Élie with interest, and a reviving spark in his clouded eye.

Adam shot him a brief, preoccupied grin, and postponed whatever rejoinder he might have had in mind for that. There was no time and he was in no mind for fooling until Harry was free again.

He made all haste to the Ile de la Cité, and in the close of Notre Dame looked for Master Bertrand among the lodges clinging like barnacles to the foot of the new west front. It was early yet, but the old master-mason was often bustling about the site ahead of his men, ready to harry them even if they came before their time. Yet this morning Adam chafed in vain, waiting for him to put in an appearance, and at last had to entrust his vigil to the boy who swept and ran the errands about the masons' lodge. It was an hour before the child whistled up to him on the scaffolding, and fetched him glissading down the ropes from the putlogs embedded in the base of the south-west tower.

'He's just come, and Canon d'Espérance with him. And they have a third one with them. Somebody important. Not a churchman, neither, he looks like a lord. You'll never disturb them while he's there?'

'Needs must,' said Adam. 'If I'm torn to pieces, sweep up the shreds tenderly and give them to Harry for Christian burial.' And he brushed a hasty hand over the corn-coloured hair tousled by the breeze on the scaffolding, beat stone-dust from his sleeves, and approached the three figures gathered in the middle of the close, looking up at the west portals.

'Master Bertrand, by your leave – '

The master-mason was a venerable figure, bearded like a patriarch and aware of his massive dignity. He turned upon his man a frown of reproof, and waved him away irritably. 'At a more opportune time! Can you not see I am engaged?'

'I see it, indeed, and I ask your pardon, but this is urgent, and I think you would wish to hear it at once. It touches my brother. You have had no time to remark it, but he is not here this morning, nor like to be until we find twelve pounds to redeem him. To be plain with you, sir, he is in prison, and the provost will not let him go for less.'

'He is *where*?' thundered Master Bertrand. Canon d'Espérance and the stranger had withdrawn a few paces and were talking together in low tones, but they could hardly help hearing that bull's bellow.

'In prison,' said Adam uncomfortably. 'He was taken up after a street fight in the Rue des Psautiers last night, not having committed an act amiss more than the other thirty-odd of us, but being unlucky enough to be the only one caught. I am sorry, the thing was more my doing in the first place than his. But so the case stands. And if you would be generous enough to advance us the money, we could be about getting him out at once.'

He drew breath, and waited with interest to see if the explosion would come; but it did not. Master Bertrand swallowed his gall with difficulty, but he swallowed it.

'You and I, Master Lestrange,' he said, in a low voice half-choked by the effort at composure, 'will discourse further of this hereafter. And I shall have something to say also to that graceless brother of yours when next I see him. He does not deserve that I should advance him a sou, since he has not the wit nor the virtue to keep out of trouble. But he knows I am pressed, and he trades on it – he trades on it! He will do it once too often some day, and find he is left to rue it.'

'I cannot call to mind that he ever ended in prison before,' said Adam sulkily. 'The money shall be regarded as an advance on our pay, sir, and you may dock it from both of us till it be paid off. I am sorry I was the occasion of his ill luck, but I'll take good care not to let him be tripped so again on my account. I can say no more.'

'You could hardly for shame say less. How came you to be caught up in a street fight? Have you no discretion in you? Must you frequent the most notorious spots in the city?' And he could not refrain from appealing, with arduous self-control, to Canon d'Espérance. 'Your reverence, you hear this fellow? Do you wonder I have difficulty in keeping my times, when my rogues play me such tricks? Master Henry Lestrange, if you please, is taken up by the watch in a brawl, and in some weeks' time you will be asking me why the Calvary is not ready as I promised it. There are no reliable craftsmen to be had these days; the more gifted they are, it seems to me, the bigger rascals they turn out.'

Thus invited into conference, the canon bestowed on him a placating smile, and said mildly: 'Come, he has not been such an unprofitable servant, I think. He is not the first young man to fall from grace.'

The stranger, turning abruptly from his contemplation of the new portals, walked towards them at this moment, and said clearly, in a resonant voice that came rounded on the air like the complex note of a bell: 'Lestrange, did I hear? Is this he of whom we were speaking just now?'

Speaking of Harry, thought Adam, turning sharply towards the voice. To what end?

'The same,' said the canon. 'That is, he who is in prison is the same. This is his brother.'

'I have been hearing something of the pair of you,' said the ringing voice, 'from both your masters here. It seems you are English.'

'We are, sir.'

'Fellow-countrymen should stand together in a strange land,' said the unknown, with a crooked smile. 'I am English myself. I should like to hear the full story of your night's amusement, if Master Bertrand can spare you the time it takes to tell it. And if, of course,' he added, marking how the hot colour rose in Adam's cheeks at the idea of telling how the evening had ended for him, 'it is not too profane for the ears of Canon d'Espérance.' The smile drew upwards one corner of a long, embittered, expressive mouth, while the other half of his face remained almost still. 'You may omit the improper passages,' he said coolly.

It was put as a suggestion, but it was nonetheless an order. This man spoke in commands, and he would not often be disobeyed. Adam found himself telling the tale of Madonna Benedetta's serenade without embarrassment, even with gusto, while he took stock of the stranger.

He was worth looking at, tall and lean and graceful, a man perhaps forty-five years old, richly and sombrely dressed. His head, wonderfully set on a throat like an antique column, was carried very high, and the arrogance which was in every turn and every line of it had been born with him. He wore his hair in the older fashion, squarely cut, with a fringe over his forehead, but it was such a great forehead that it was not dwarfed; and his brows, of a brown darker than the hair, were long and level, and all but met over the long, straight nose. Sunk deep into his head, in great, shadowy sockets, his eyes stared forth restlessly questioning, measuring, assessing, dissecting, fastening with famished intelligence upon everything that came within their sight. Disquieting eyes they were, illusionless yet eager, calm yet full of a smoky secret rage, brilliant yet melancholy; and they were beautiful. His face was clean-shaven, and burned to a deep tan which he had certainly never acquired in France, nor in the England he claimed as his country. Observing it, Adam began to guess from what quarter he was newly come; the dark gold, so startling on the taut, drawn lines of his cheeks and jaw, would soon tarnish and fade in this climate, though the coming summer might preserve it for a while.

He wore a full surcoat of russet cloth, the wide sleeves and capuchon lined with tawny fur; and as he moved, two rings on his lean, bronzed right hand flashed gold and purple. The skirt of his surcoat, slashed to the waist, uncovered as he walked a long, elegant leg in a boot of soft leather, almost knee-high and of a most outlandish cut. Like his tan, he had got those somewhere much farther east than Paris.

Adam debated the wisdom of remembering Harry's improvisations word for word in this company, but when pressed he produced them, adroitly avoiding the canon's eyes. They had a second success. The canon kept his smile severe and academic, but his eye gleamed for a moment. The sunburned stranger threw back his head and laughed aloud.

'Oh, Master Bertrand, I see you did not tell me the half. You have a man of parts there, it seems. Well, and then?'

'Then the door opened and let me in. And it appears that a free fight broke out in the street, though exactly how it started I'm in no position to argue, for I knew nothing about it until this morning, when I went home and learned that the watch had taken my brother. No one was damaged, God be thanked,' said Adam, 'and no one was taken in charge except Harry. So I don't see that it would hurt them, or be bad for public order, to let him go. But without the fine they won't do it.'

'Irresponsible as children,' said Master Bertrand querulously, 'the pair of you. I've a mind to let him stew in his own juice for a day or two, and teach him a lesson, but that would hardly be fair unless we could commit you into the bargain. So I suppose we shall have to get him out.'

'To visit those in prison is a Christian act,' said the stranger with his crooked smile. 'I have a fancy to go myself and relieve this gifted young man of yours. Will you lend me his brother for an hour, to bring me to the place? I'll send him back to you as soon as may be.'

He used, then as always, the courteous speech of one asking favours, but he used it in the calm manner of one exacting dues so obvious that no man would dare gainsay them.

'You are too condescending, my lord, to two graceless young rogues, but take him, take him if you will.' He was relieved to be spared the expense, thought Adam, but otherwise he was none too well pleased about the stranger's interest. Masters may know the worth of their pupils, and to themselves even admit it, but they do not commonly enjoy being excelled by them; and Adam was not alone in holding that Harry had outgrown his instruction. Others, without his understandable partiality, had been known to express the same opinion.

'My lord, this is generous, towards two who are unknown to you. But I do not know how we are to discharge the debt.'

'There will be no debt.' There was a momentary flash of displeasure from the formidable eyes, like a single flicker of lightning out of an overcast sky. Then he emerged from behind the clouds and laughed again. 'What you mean is that *I* am unknown to *you*. You are nice in choosing your benefactors, are you? My credentials will pass muster, I trust. I hear you come from the marches of Wales. So do I. If you know Mormesnil, or Erington, or Fleace, or Parfois, you know me. My name is Ralf Isambard. Are you content?'

'My lord!' said Adam, overwhelmed by a name that rang in the marches as loud and as awfully as FitzAlan or FitzWarin.

'Come, then, we'll not leave your brother any longer in durance. Master Bertrand, they shall both come back to you within the hour.'

With the abruptness which marked all his movements, and the grace which clothed his naked arrogance and rid it of all offence, he swept away from them, swerving between men and piled building materials on the crowded site, the skirts of his surcoat flying, the barbaric boots spurning the dust of the close. Walking behind him, Adam could not take his eyes from the uncovered head, with its short, curled hair blowing back from close-set ears, and the beautiful subtleties of its modelling showing through the thick locks, as the slanting morning light touched every salient and the shadow clung in every hollow. Harry won't be able to set eyes on him, he was thinking, without wanting to copy that head in stone. He'd make a terrible fighting saint. Or a magnificent devil!

With the coming of daylight Harry, long accustomed to be sparing with candles, had put out the lantern in favour of the light from the small, barred window, lifted the stool on to the stone ledge, and continued his work kneeling before it on the hard, uneven floor of the cell. He was completely engrossed in what he was doing, and incapable of feeling either hunger or weariness.

Had he heard the key grate in the lock during the first hours, he would have clapped the stool hard against the wall and sat on it, and the knife would have been slipped out of sight in an instant.

Now he heard it, but as from a great distance, and he did not move or even look round, but went on paring to his exact delight the curl of a thick mouth within the bristling beard. He heard footsteps enter the cell behind him, but paid them no attention. His intent head, tilted a little on one side to let the light fall full on his work, had the look of a child's in passionate play, or of a devout man's in prayer. Not until a shadow crossed between him and the window did he acknowledge that he was not alone, and even then he only halted his hand for a second, without turning his head.

'Stand out of my light!' he said imperiously.

The shadow withdrew at once, but a second and a bulkier took its place.

'By God,' said the provost warmly, 'you have the devil's own impudence!' He came a single menacing step nearer, thus bringing into his view the carved head that leaned out from the overhang of the stool. He gasped, recognising the frowning brows, the great pock-marked nose, the jutting bearded chin. With a bellow of rage he lifted his staff and struck hard at the hand that was so busy with the knife.

The impact of the blow, and Harry's yell of pain and fury, and the clatter of the knife falling, all seemed to come together. Harry whirled round on his knees and flung himself along the floor, reaching for the haft with his left hand, since the right was paralysed. The provost raised his cane to strike again. The tall shadow within the doorway moved faster than either of them, and to better purpose.

Harry's groping fingers touched the haft just as a foot came down hard but silently upon the blade. Through the hot mist of his anger and pain he was aware, with grotesque clarity, of a boot such as he had never seen before except in some drawings at Caen once, made by a mason who had followed Richard to the Crusades, and left two fingers of his left hand in Acre, lopped by a Saracen sword. Leather worked as soft as cloth, and upturned toes drawn to a blunt point, and a small, fine pattern tooled in the upper surface, like Persian diapering. He looked up, by way of a long, muscular leg in dark brown chausses elegantly fitted, to lean hips circled with a gilded belt that supported two jewelled daggers, a spare, energetic body, a shadowed face dark as bronze. A hand as sunburned as the face had gripped the provost's wrist in mid-air, and now flung away wrist and arm and stave in one violent gesture of prohibition.

'If you have broken his hand – !' blazed Isambard, and bit off the threat with a snap of white teeth.

Harry came to his feet in a startled scramble, and stood staring at the lordly stranger in amazement, nursing his numbed right hand tightly in the left to help the pain to pass. Isambard had the advantage of the light. He saw a young fellow of twenty-four or twenty-five, in a shabby tunic of the common drab brown, soiled after his night in this foul cell, bruised and dusty from last night's fighting, a wiry brown lad with untidy hair and a frayed collar. What was there in that to keep him looking so long? The boy might have been any poor little goliard poet, *gyrovagus* from town to town and patron to patron, or a spoiled clerk on the run after his first essays in minor rascality. Just what the provost thought him, in fact. But for that dedicated face, fierce as a sword, single-minded as a hunting beast, insatiable for one thing he desired, into which, for him, the rest of the world crumbled and was swallowed up. Canon d'Espérance, holding up the wooden angel two nights ago, had said: 'You will see for yourself where he got the face.' At eleven years old, when his childish countenance could have had but the tender foreshadowing of this intensity, he had prophesied what he would become.

'You may pick up the knife now,' said Isambard, and withdrew his foot from it. 'Put it away. You need no weapon now, and your head, I think, is finished. If you worked over it farther I believe you might regret it.'

'I am afraid,' said Harry, sheathing the knife, 'that even as it stands I am like to regret it.' He took aside with a wry smile at the provost, who was glaring at his portrait and breathing hard.

'Count yourself fortunate, boy, that your fine is already paid, and you out of my hands,' he said grimly. 'If I had seen this before I accepted the money you should have paid for it with your skin, and handsomely. If ever you come in my charge again you shall lie in irons, and underground, and we shall see what mischief you can get up to then. My lord, I wish you joy of your bad bargain!'

'I am content with it,' said Isambard shortly. He stared for some minutes in silence, twice changing his position to have the light on the carved head move. The one-sided smile came suddenly, dazzlingly. 'I swear I think you ungrateful. The young man has made you immortal. Why, there is no malice in it, it is not even ill-natured. And touching the workmanship, find me another man who could have produced such a masterpiece by lantern-light, with a pocket-knife only, and I'll give him as warm a welcome as I do to this one. But if you regret parting with him so cheaply, there's more for you. I won't haggle about his price. And a word in your ear – the stool would fetch a price, too, if you show it in the right quarter. We'll not be niggardly over your bill for his night's lodging.'

He turned back to Harry, who was watching him in silent wonder and flexing his numbed fingers.

'Has he damaged you?'

'I think not. There's nothing broken. I shall be clumsy for a few days.' His eyes, sea-green in the fronting sunlight from the little window, and startlingly bright, questioned and found no answer. 'I expected Master Bertrand would send to buy me out. I do not understand, sir, how you can have involved yourself for me, and I am not happy to think I have cost you so much money. Why are you doing this?'

'Call it a whim. I was with Canon d'Espérance and Master Bertrand when your brother came to tell them of your misfortune, so I returned with him to set you free. He is waiting outside for you, and I have promised Master Bertrand he shall have you both back at work within the hour. Make your farewells!' he said, like one speaking to a child, and the crooked smile flashed.

Harry opened his mouth to question farther, and then shut it again helplessly. He looked at the provost, and then at his surly, vigorous effigy, and broke into the impish but sweet smile that belonged only to his moments of achievement and the lovely lassitude that followed them. 'Master provost, part friends! I own I did begin it in spite, but I ended honestly, I swear. If you did owe me somewhat for it, you've paid me.' He showed a hand already swollen and darkening, and looked a little reproachful through his smile. 'No hard feelings?'

'Be off with you!' said the provost gruffly. 'And keep out of my hold from this on, you rogue.' But Isambard's admiration of the carving, even more than his handful of coins, had disarmed him; it was with something very close to a smile that he let them out into the narrow courtyard and shut the door on them.

Harry looked up joyfully at the sun and drew deep breaths, suddenly aware of hunger and weariness as of luxuries.

'You have neither eaten nor slept,' said Isambard then, sharply practical. 'Are you fit to go to work? I would not trust you on a scaffolding myself.'

'Oh, I shall do very well. I must go and take my tongue-lashing. When he's done with me I daresay he'll tell me to go and get some sleep. Will you not give me another opportunity of thanking you? And tell me to whom I owe my freedom? I fear I was too much confused even to be civil, you came on me so unexpectedly.'

'You have not displeased me,' said his rescuer sombrely. 'My name is Ralf Isambard of Parfois – we are fellow-Salopians, so count me as a biblical neighbour, too, and I'll be content. Here I shall leave you. But if you are at liberty tonight, come to me at eight, for there is a matter I wish to break to you. I am lodged at the Maison d'Estivet.'

'I will come,' said Harry. 'And I thank you.'

In the street Adam was waiting with an overcast face; he saw Harry, and the sun came out.

'Crusades!' said Isambard, dangling the gold cup between his long hands and staring down into it with a sour smile. 'Never run from what disgusts you to look for a clean cause at the other end of the earth, boy. I took the Cross because I had my bellyful of squabbles and compoundings for earthly kingdoms – when King John made peace with Philip at the cost of Evreux and many another good town, and did homage to him for Brittany, that galled me close. And when he took hands with Llewellyn and secured to him all his conquests – to him who burned Fleace on his way to Mold, and left my garrison dead to the last man – that filled my cup. Now, it seemed, the Welshman was to be my king's liege man, and his son-in-law and bosom friend. So I left England and took the Cross, in the hope and certainty of one fight that might hold the ground firm under my feet. I must have been younger than my forty years, Harry! I'm wiser now. We set out for the Holy Sepulchre, but we got no father than the Rialto.'

Harry looked at him without understanding across the width of the table. 'But surely, sir, you did take Constantinople – '

'A figure of speech, boy. Where two Venetians are come together, there is the Rialto, and any stranger rash enough to venture there had better keep one hand on his purse and the other on his sword. Yes, we took Constantinople. A Christian city, head of a Christian empire! Strange quarry for Crusaders, if you consider it!

We took it from an able prince, who in his turn had taken it from his incompetent brother, and put the old fool in close ward before he could run his land quite to ruin.'

'Is it true,' asked Harry, 'that he blinded him?'

'True enough,' said Isambard indifferently, 'but so have others done, and worse, without having holy wars preached against them by other princes of the same faith, and, God knows, no better record. However! We put the doddering old man back on his flimsy throne, and within the year his ungrateful people had had their fill of him, him and that travelling packman son of his. He teamed well with the Venetians, that young man, but the Greeks wouldn't have him. He cost them a second siege of Constantinople, and a second capture, and there was nothing for us to do after that but set up some emperor of our own there, and hold it down by force. That was how near we came to the holy city! They celebrate the Latin rite again in Santa Sophia, but the Greeks still look to their own prelates in exile. Who has profited but Venice? It was markets, not miracles, they set out to achieve, and they at least succeeded. Their grasp is on every city in Romania.

'And do you know, Harry, what sent me home? Another treaty, just like those that drove me away. Our Latin Emperor, the champion of Christendom in the East, feeling himself insecure – as God knows he has good reason! – has allied himself with the Moslem Sultan of Rum against the Christian Greeks of Nicaea! A small thing to turn my stomach, after swallowing down so much. But it makes a neat end, don't you think so?'

'You make me feel,' said Harry slowly, 'that I have been fortunate in putting all my pains into wood and stone, and not into the affairs of men. And yet men are all the material we have, if the world is ever to be perfected. And I think you must have found, at home and in the East, something better than disgust. If not among doges and princes, among ordinary men.'

Isambard drained the cup with an abrupt toss of his head, and set it empty on the board. 'You think so? Lend me your eyes to look at the England to which I am returning. What am I going to find there? To what sort of household am I come home?'

Thus challenged, Harry cast his mind back in some astonishment, and was shamed to discover how little he had thought or questioned of England in the nine years since he had left it. 'A very troubled and much diminished one,' he owned ruefully. 'You'll have heard that it lies under papal interdict? The quarrel is over who shall be archbishop of Canterbury – the bishops and the monks were in dispute over it, and King John sided with the bishops and would have had Norwich appointed, but the Pope refused to confirm the election and would give us Cardinal Langton or none. And the King will not admit Langton to his see, and there they stick at odds. But you know the circumstances better than I do. And most of what was English here is gone – Maine, Touraine, Normandy – '

'Gone!' said Isambard with a short, hard laugh. 'You talk like what I remember of myself at your age – God knows why I should blame you for that! Nothing is gone, boy. Normandy stands where it stood, and Maine and Touraine. All that has happened is that a truth has been acknowledged for true. They are parts of this mainland of France, always were, and always will be, unless God send a miracle to translate them across the sea. Does that make you gape at me? Your willing exile has been better filled than mine, or it would have had you looking back and reconsidering, too. I have done much hard thinking, there in the East, and I have seen that I was wrong to blame the King for letting Evreux go. He would have been wise had he made what terms he could then, to part equably with all he has parted with perforce since that day. Do you know what has been the undoing of my family and many another like it for the past hundred and fifty years? The attempt to ride two horses. It is time and more than time to reconsider whether we want to be Norman or English, for we cannot go on being both. I do not know why I had to go to Constantinople to discover that I was English.'

He rose from his high-backed chair, and began to walk the room restlessly, from tapestried wall to tapestried wall, the tremor of his passing making the candles flicker. Harry's eyes followed him steadily, watching and wondering to what end all this tended. What could such a man want of him, that could not be asked outright, without preamble? Why should he be favoured with the confidences of Ralf Isambard, lord of Mormesnil, Erington, Fleace and Parfois in the marches of Wales, a dozen other properties in the north and the south-west of England, and God alone knew how many in Brittany, Gascony, Maine, Poitou and Anjou?

'I am newly come from Brittany,' said Isambard, halting abruptly face to face with him, as though he had been reading his thoughts, 'where I have been surrendering one of my two horses. I am English, Harry, but my elder son is French to the backbone.

Have I surprised you? You did not know that I have sons? Oh, yes, I have sons! The elder is of about your age. I was married at seventeen and widowed at twenty-five. I cannot call to mind that I ever seriously regretted either event. Now Gilles will be lord of every plot of ground I held in France, and do homage to King Philip for it, very willingly. And I shall go home to England and do homage to King John for what I hold there; and that I will hold with my life. One mount at a time is enough for any man. I have resolved my problem. And John would be well advised to cut the knot of his in the same way, sit him down squarely in England, and set his mind and will to work in making it strong and prosperous, and binding it to himself indissolubly against all comers. But he cannot do it. Even if he saw the need and wished to do it, he dare not. Do you know why? Because his people – not even we who are nearest to him, but those ordinary people of whom you were prating just now – would tear him limb from limb!'

He uttered a sharp croak of laughter, and turned away to the open window, drawing aside the arras to look out upon a dove-coloured sky and a rising moon, and floating against the soft, silvery light the lofty outline of Notre Dame above the roofs, quivering like a candle-flame with the reflected radiance from the Seine. 'The wine is with you, Harry.'

'I thank you,' said Harry, and did not touch it.

Isambard turned his head suddenly, and met the young, brilliant eyes full. They neither evaded him nor softened their intent staring.

'You are wondering,' he said, 'if I am always so talkative. The truth is that I have a desire to be honest with you, Master Lestrange. Before you commit yourself to answering either aye or no to what I have to put to you, I should like you to know something of me, of your own knowledge and not from other men.'

'I know you have been courteous and generous to me,' said Harry, 'and I think that is enough to know.'

'The more fool you, for I can be other things.'

'And what do you know of me,' went on Harry warmly, 'but that you took me out of the provost's jail, and that I have a little skill in carving, a very good conceit of my own work, and a nature incurably stubborn and unruly? I'm sure Master Bertrand can have left you in no doubt on that score.'

'Do you really believe that is how he speaks of you? You underrate him. Oh, he is jealous of your ability, that's easy to see, and he reports you as self-willed and stubborn, and a hard and arrogant judge of other men's work. He says also that you are the most gifted pupil he ever taught. It was he, not Canon d'Espérance, who told me that you have a daemon.'

He smiled, this time almost gaily, seeing Harry crimson to the ears with astonishment and pleasure.

'Did he truly say that of me?'

'That and much more, both bad and good. But as to your ability in every stage of your craft, good. How long have you been with him?'

'Nearly four years now. I did not think he held me so high,' said Harry, dazed. 'He never let me see it.'

'And before?'

'We were rather more than four years at Caen, serving under Master William at the abbey church of St Étienne. He is a fine master, difficult to please. He would not endure scamped work, he would have from us only the best we had in us.'

'And before that? But you can have been only a child before that.'

'For a few months after we came from England we were at Lisieux. I will not claim we learned much there, except quickness and obedience to orders. I was glad to get away to Caen within the year.'

'I see you must have brought a sound foundation with you from England. Who was your master there? He must have taken you young.'

'Adam's father,' said Harry without thinking, and could have bitten out his tongue. In nine years he had never made such a slip before, and now it was far too late to take it back. But Isambard, though he lifted one rapid flash of his shrewd eyes to his guest's face, made no sign of wishing to question the relationship. 'He was a village mason, with some practice about the lord's demesne,' went on Harry, making the best of it. 'I was not his own son, but he fostered me along with his own three.'

'So you began with practical labour, and not with the drawing-board. It is the right way round, and I am well content with your record.' He reached for the wine-jug, and filled both the cups, and taking up his own, began to pace the room again.

'This is the matter, Harry. I purpose to build a church beside my castle of Parfois. I began this work once before, and got nowhere with it. You know Parfois? It was named from the old Parfois which was my family's first seat in Normandy.'

'I know it,' said Harry, remembering the vast grey curtain wall that rose out of the rocky outcrop and undulated round the hill like a snake in motion, and the twin gate-towers jutting out over a ditch that was a natural fissure in the rock, forty feet deep. He had seen it only twice in his life, on rides to the north-west of the county with Ebrard to buy ponies, but it was not a sight ever to be forgotten.

'Then you know the hazards. In those days we were raided almost daily, either from Powis or Gwynedd, and though they knew better than to attempt Parfois, the site of the church was outside the walls, and they found it sport to steal materials and terrify my masons. I do not know why I happened upon so many timorous men. One after another my master-masons took fright and deserted me. I expended three, and then I razed what they had done to the ground and went off on my Crusade. But now I mean to return to the project, and see it completed. I have been visiting all the great building enterprises round Paris in search of a master to my mind. I think I have found him.'

Harry was on his feet, quivering.

'I offer the work to you. I offer you the virgin site, a free hand, and money enough for all you need. Whatever materials, whatever men, whatever engines you want, you shall have. But on one condition: that you will swear to me to stay until the work is completed, in the teeth of Llewellyn and all his men.'

In the hungry young face, suddenly grown pale as ash with desire beneath its weathered tan, the eyes glowed like topaz. It was in a husky whisper that he managed to say: 'I accept, and I swear!'

Isambard came down the room to him and stood close, searching his face with unsmiling eyes. 'You have no doubts at all. You know you can do it.' It was not a question; he was reading, and marvelling at what he read. 'How soon can you come to Parfois? I have some business here in France which I had better conclude now, while I have the safe-conduct of the Cross, but in three or four weeks I mean to sail from Calais. I should like to take you with me.'

'It will depend on Master Bertrand. I must finish the Calvary on which I am working.' He had command of his voice now, it came round and ringing with ardour. 'That means perhaps a month's work. Then, if he is pleased to release me, as for your lordship I make no doubt he will, I will gladly come. I would only ask you for one thing, that I may take my brother with me.'

'Surely you may! I have said that you shall choose whom you

will. If you wish to make other conditions, make them now, before you bind yourself.'

'Then I dare to ask that you will undertake not to displace me but on one ground – that the work I have done for you is not good enough.'

'And on that ground,' said Isambard, dazzled by the passion and certainty with which he said this, and the towering pride that blazed at him from the sea-green eyes, 'you have no fears.'

'No, none! In Chartres, in Caen, in Bourges, I have seen the splendour and energy of other men's creations, and ached for my own. Everything I have learned while I laboured to fulfil other men's designs has been food to what I have in me. I have carried it a long time, and thought of it much, and longed for it to come into the light. If I give it to you, you will not be disappointed.'

'With all my heart,' said Isambard, 'I believe you.'

'My lord, there is a certain quarry where I can get the very stone I want and have always wanted.' His voice gathered way, rushing joyfully after an entrancing memory. 'A warm grey stone in colour, with a pale amber grain in it that flushes to gold in the sunlight. The only difficulty is that the quarry is very close to the Welsh border.'

'No matter, you shall have an ample guard and a lease on the quarry for the duration of the work.'

'If you should be sending couriers to England before we leave, I should like to send a list of the materials we shall want immediately. It will save time on arrival. Stakes and cords for laying out foundations, leather thongs and wood for scaffolding, hurdles, timber for centring, lead, glass – and carriage for all these. It means the gain of a whole year if we make full use of this summer to assemble them, for we can spend the winter under cover, cutting stone, once we have it on the site. Can you guarantee me carts and teams enough?'

'All you may ask for you shall have. My steward will put forward all the orders you care to send in advance of your coming.'

'What manner of foundation shall I find?'

'Rock, and levelled already by those who went before you, though you may, of course, need to level more ground than they did, depending on your design.'

'Good, we'll lay the footings of the stonework well into the solid rock. There could be no better foundation, and it means we shall get little or no settling.'

'I see you are not afraid of Welsh raids,' said Isambard with a smile, 'for on that head you have said not a word.'

'Oh, I was born in that border country; Welsh raids were the common stuff of our lives there. I would not turn my back on such a commission as you have offered me, not for all King Philip's army, leave alone a handful of wild Welshmen. I pledge you the best work I have in me,' he said, suddenly raising his cup with a wild smile, 'and my word that I will not leave you until the church be completed. And to that I drink!'

'And I will never deprive you of that I have entrusted to you, until it be finished. That I swear.'

Harry had the cup at his lips and Isambard was raising his, when suddenly the ringed hand flashed in a violent gesture.

'Wait!' he said harshly. 'This is too easily and too lightly taken up for my taste.'

He put down his cup upon the table, and swept away in long, irritable strides to the window, where he stood gripping the arras hard in his long muscular fingers. Without turning his head he said more gently, but with a heavy solemnity: 'Harry Lestrange, you should go home and sleep on this. I have taken you in the sails of your longing and blown you away, and God knows that is not as I would have it. I want you, but I want you fairly. It was ill done to spring it on you today, with your foolish gratitude fresh in you and your eyes dropping with sleep. If you give your word to me, you are giving it to a hard master, one who will have no mercy if you break faith. I promise you the full support of my hand while you play me fair, and I promise you the full weight of my fist if you play me false, be it never so venial a default. Such as I am I am, I cannot be other, and if you enter my service you must abide by me as I am. Do not swear tonight! Go home and consider well, and come to me tomorrow.'

'No, my lord!' said Harry loudly and joyfully. 'I know my mind now. If you were the devil himself I would abide by you for such a prize as this. I pledge you now!'

Isambard had turned from the window, and was staring at him with the faint shadow of astonished displeasure in his drawn brows, for he was not accustomed to hearing the word 'no' flung at him so roundly. But the eyes in their deep caverns remained aloof and sombre, as Harry tipped back his head and emptied the cup and set it ringing down upon the board. 'I am your man. I swear, on this living heart, that I will remain with you and seek no other service until your church is finished. And if I play you false, you may have this same heart living out of my body.'

There was a long moment of silence, then Isambard walked slowly to the table and drained his own goblet and set it gently beside its fellow. 'So be it!' he said.

CHAPTER EIGHT

The splendours and audacities of Madonna Benedetta Foscari came to Isambard's ears in the common gossip of Paris, and quickened an amused curiosity even in one not greatly given to pursuing fashions.

'I hear she was brought back as booty from the Crusade,' he said to Adam one day, as they were rising all three from a long conference over the letters and requisitions to be sent in advance to England. 'It pleases me to think that Venice lost something, in the end – a loss to balance all she gained, if report does not lie about the lady. It seems old Guiscard had an eye for more than markets, in those business deals of his in the Adriatic. Is she as wonderful as rumour makes her?'

'Even more wonderful,' said Adam, smiling without even a shadow of regret at the memory of his one night in her favour. More than that he had not looked for, and yet he had gained something more, for she still tolerated him about her sometimes in the evenings, for the pleasure of singing with him.

'And you, Harry – are you, too, among her admirers?'

'My lord,' said Harry, frowning absently over his lists of materials, 'I never saw more of her than a hand and arm. They looked much like any other to me.'

'Never saw her, after all you paid for the privilege? This must be remedied! Adam, bring us to meet this nonpareil.'

The order was issued idly, perhaps even in jest; but as Adam said afterwards, at home in the garret in the Ruelle des Guenilles, even the jests of a man like Isambard had best be acted upon.

'You might be wise, at that,' agreed Apollon, 'to humour him. I know him by repute; he has a fief not far from my home. They say he's a man to be feared, very ill to cross, and merciless to his underlings.'

'Speak as you find,' said Adam, undisturbed. 'He's dealt fair enough by us so far, and very surely he knew how to pick a mason for himself.' Harry was not present, and so could be freely praised.

'Well, we are bound to him, whether it turns out well or no, and if he wants amusement during these weeks while he waits for us, I'll be a serviceable fellow and provide him at least the opportunity.'

'I take it very hard,' said Élie, looking up reproachfully from his books, 'that you'll do for him what you haven't yet offered to do for me, and we bosom friends so near parting.'

'My lad, you're never likely to have either the paying of my wages or the flaying of my skin, or I'd oblige you. The way will be clear for you when my lord and I are both out of Paris. And you'll be grown a little, too,' said Adam kindly, patting Élie unwisely on the auburn curls dragged every way by nervous fingers as he studied. Élie promptly slammed away his book and closed with his friend happily, swooping to take him about the knees in one arm as he passed, and drop him neatly to the floor. Apollon, without taking his eyes from the lute-string he was carefully fitting, stepped out of their way and let them roll together the length of the room.

Soon, he reflected sadly, he had better be looking round for two congenial spirits to fill the beds of Harry and Adam when they were gone; but they would not be easily replaced.

When next they presented themselves at the Maison d'Estivet Adam bore an invitation with him.

'My lord, Madonna Benedetta Foscari sends her compliments, and begs that you will come and drink wine with her at her house tomorrow evening at eight. She had the whole story out of me,' said Adam, grinning, 'and she asks that you will bring "your lively sculptor" to present himself. So she called him. Indeed, I think she missed very little of what passed that night.'

Isambard laughed, so carelessly that Harry was persuaded he had never seriously considered that his expressed desire might be taken literally. Nevertheless, his business in France was already completed, and his mind, restless for home, plagued by waiting and idleness. The woman who had diverted the whole of Paris might provide even for him an evening's diversion. 'The lady is gracious,' he said. 'We shall be happy to attend her.'

'Why the devil did you have to involve me?' demanded Harry ungratefully, when he was alone with Adam. 'I have a drawing for my east window half finished, and now nothing will do for him but I must go along with him and waste an evening.'

It was in this temper that they waited upon her, one idly curious, one openly displeased at being kept from his work, which for him was more enchanting than any woman who ever breathed. On

Adam's confident heels they stepped into her presence, in that upper room from which she had dropped the violets of her brief but gracious favour. The rich profits of Master Guiscard's Venetian tradings had draped the walls of the apartment with oriental carpets, and covered the floor with rugs of worked skins. The chairs were cushioned, the drapings of the table damask, the winecups of thin and glittering glass. And the woman who rose from her seat in the window and came sweeping across the room to receive them had the assurance of an abbess.

'My lord of Parfois, you are welcome to my poor house.'

'Madam, this is kindness in you, for my claim to your notice is small indeed, and my need of your grace is great. I am soon to rob you of this minstrel of yours.'

'So he has told me,' she said, and gave him her hand.

What had he expected, that his eyes searched her face with so urgent and single an interest? The noblest and most expensive of courtesans must always have been accessible to that bottomless purse of his, but he had chosen rather to buy beautifully-tempered swords, exotic animals, fine carvings, barbaric jewellery, holy relics and fragments of the saints, to judge by the great mass of baggage he had brought from the East with him. Moreover, he had come here at her invitation only out of curiosity, and no very profound curiosity at that. Yet his eyes hung heavy upon her now, and his face had the gravity and passion it wore when he looked upon works of art, judging hardly, fastidious in criticism, rejecting what was not unique. Her he did not reject.

'And you,' said Benedetta, 'are he who wished to improve upon "*Dum estas inchoatur*".' Her voice, which Harry had expected to be rich and sensuous and full of art, was clear and direct as a child's, and so unselfconscious that it seemed startlingly loud in the quiet room. It was pitched low, but its ring was of silver, not of gold. 'You ended vilely sharp,' she said.

'I know it,' he admitted, somewhat taken aback, and uncertain whether to be a little offended or to laugh at himself. 'I was straining against the odds. And no doubt you noticed that I am no Adam.'

'No,' she said, 'I see you are no Adam.'

'Howbeit, you laughed.'

What was the power she had to draw to herself even the unwilling mind that would gladly have kept its reserve in her presence and gone on considering in happy silence the exact line of an arch instead of the subtle shape of a face? It seemed that everything about her was as challenging in its unexpectedness as the candid, unflattering voice, that made no play with compliments. She should have been soft and sumptuous. Was it childish to expect a courtesan to be so? He saw her aloof and erect, impregnable within herself like a man, open to approach like a man. He had expected to have nothing to do here but to admire a body which could hardly fail to be beautiful; and here he found himself withdrawing his attention only with a kind of agony from the enigma of her mind and spirit, to look at the famous and resplendent flesh in which she walked.

She was just of a height with him, which was barely medium tall for a man, but more than common tall for a woman. Their eyes met on a level, close and searching, mutually intent. She was built like a tower, broad and noble, and moved with a vigorous grace that composed itself pliantly to the confined space within these walls, and yet suggested what breadth and largeness might be hers in freedom. For the dark red hair Adam had prepared him, and it fell nothing short of his description, with its crimson shadows and fiery highlights. But no one had told him how brilliantly white would be the broad brow beneath the coronal, and the throat on which the coiled hair cast reflected colour until it glowed like a clear glass goblet of wine. No one had warned him that her eyes would be set so wide apart, under such a bold line of brows; nor that their shape would be so full and clear, and their colour such a pure grey, with something of violet in it in the shadows. The chin was too generously rounded for beauty, perhaps, the mouth too full, though wonderfully set into that antique shape of rich, resolute curves. The body and face were all woman, yet Harry might have been standing eye to eye with a man, his opposite and his equal. He felt his heart and his mind rise to her; his blood and his body were at peace.

'And your song,' she said, turning with a decisive movement to lead the way towards the chairs grouped to receive them, 'for Adam tells me it was yours – it has opened other doors than mine, no doubt?'

'Not to my knowledge. When I gave it to Adam I renounced my rights in it.'

'And I've sung it but twice,' said Adam, 'and both times to you. I am not likely to offer it to anyone else.' He was at home in this house, as a cousin or a retainer might have been at home, and accepted his status with good humour. He made himself cupbearer for them when they were seated, curiously watching Isambard's face. It pleased him that beauty which had dazzled him should also blind others.

'I have not yet heard this song,' said Isambard, his eyes upon her face, and the faint, oblique smile plucking at the corner of his mouth. 'He makes none for me.'

'He made none for me,' she said calmly. 'This was made for his brother, and its passion is in the mind only. All the same, a good song. Adam will surely let us hear it again. Take my citole, or the lute if you prefer it.'

'He is no hand at it,' said Harry, reaching out a hand for the instrument. 'Here, let me!'

He bent lovingly to the tuning of the citole, pushing back his chair from the table; and finding its stall-like arms hampered his movements, he got up and crossed to a stool beside the window. The air came back to him tenderly and plaintively, whispering under his fingers. Isambard's imperious profile, sharp against the candle-light and glitter of glass on the table, had a stillness beyond natural, as though he held his breath, as though he had become stone, like the marble mask he had brought back from Greece, a fragment of some broken, beautiful god.

Adam sang as freshly as a lark, without a trace of that poignancy of love-longing the melody suggested. She is right, thought Harry. The passion is in the mind only. All the same, it was a lovely sound.

' – Yet when the branch is shaken
And summer's pride is past,
Me, naked and forsaken,
Receive and love at last.

And when the autumn dapples
Thy gilded heaven tree,
Let fall thy golden apples,
Bow down thy breasts to me.'

Suddenly he felt their summer warmth cupped in his palms, and the closing chords broke false under his hands. Heat swept upwards through his body and stained his face. Not her breasts; he could look at her unmoved, or if not unmoved, untroubled. He did not desire her. Her presence enlarged him, her beauty delighted him, he was at peace with her as with a man who was his match. But she brought with her glimpses of other women, some seen but once, some never yet seen, some known and forsaken and forgotten before he knew what he did. What she was, what she could be to so many men, some woman would be to him. She was the hope of that fulfilment, the promise, almost the certainty; and she was the foreshadowing of his monstrous loss if he should let the tide of the spring escape him.

He stretched his fingers tremulously along the shoulders of the citole, and the polished wood was cool and smooth to his hot palms. Why was he suddenly possessed by this agonising awareness of his senses, as though desire itself were something to be desired?

'You have a fine touch,' said Isambard, 'and a nice turn with verses. I see I have found myself a phoenix.'

'I'm out of practice,' said Harry. 'That was not well done. But it's a beautiful air. Since I spoiled "*Dum estas inchoatur*" for you, will you hear it now? Without the improvements?'

Adam sang it, untouched by the disquiet in the room. How pleasant and good a thing it must be to be Adam, and live on such close terms with the present that neither past nor future truly existed!

'The same metre,' said Benedetta. 'But the Sieur de Breauté was never a very original wooer. And he borrowed not only the song but the rendering, too, and made no acknowledgements to the singers.'

'Having paid for the performance,' said Isambard, 'he felt free to call it his.'

'Like Paulus with his poems,' she said, and then, seeing his hollow eyes burn up into astonished laughter: 'It surprises you that I should be able to follow you into Martial? Why? Because I am a woman? Or because I am the kind of woman I am? I'm right it was of that couplet you were thinking?

' "*Carmina Paulus emit, recitat sua carmina Paulus.*
Nam quod emas possis iure vocare tuum."

How should we translate it into this English of yours?

' "Paulus buys verse to read in his own name.
Why not? What's bought the purchaser may claim." '

'Martial is a dry study for a woman,' said Isambard, 'and we are not as generous in having our daughters tutored as we might be. It should not displease you that you show as the exception.'

'I was sister to two gifted brothers, and I read with them. It was not so much planned, it happened. I was curious, and I drew in on them before they were aware. Would you rather I sang you something from Catullus – our own Catullus, the stranger from the north? There's a poet for women! I was at his Sirmio once; the olives and the lake and the long arm of land are just as he left them.'

She had risen and taken the lute, and carried it with her to the cushioned seat which was built into the window. Her long fingers were rapid and impetuous on the strings, able but inattentive. Harry heard in their cascading notes here and there a chord that jarred, as though she had withdrawn her mind from what she did, and left her hands to fend for themselves.

' "*Ille mi par esse deo videtur,*
Ille, si fas est, superare divos,
Qui sedens adversus identidem te
Spectat et audit
Dulce ridentem – "

"– though to be sure he took that from Sappho, metre and all. Or do you know the "*Pervigilium Veneris*" written for the night festival of the goddess at Hybla, in Sicily? It's a beautiful thing, in its way.

' "*Cras amet qui nunquam amavit, quique*
amavit cras amet!
Illa cantat, nos tacemus. Quando ver
venit meum?
Quando fiam ceu chelidon ut tacere desinam? – "

' "She sings, we are mute. When comes my spring? When shall I become as a swallow, and no longer be silent?" A curious version, that makes Procne the swallow the sweet singer, and Philomela the voiceless one. Many critics have speculated on his meaning, but for my part I think he was human and made a mistake.

' "Who loves, love on! Who loves not,
learn to love!
Yesterday's drought tomorrow shall remove." '

She swept her fingers violently across the strings, and nstantly muted them with her palm.

'I am convinced,' said Isambard, smiling at her darkly over his wine; 'no need to dazzle me farther. You are as learned as you are beautiful. And indeed, if you go any deeper into the classics you must leave me behind. Tell me rather about yourself, and I'll forgo Venus. Gladly I'll be a celebrant,' he said softly, 'at the Pervigilium Benedettae.'

Harry sat mute, nursing the citole and longing to be away. What need had they of him or of Adam, to help them to duel with love and Latin across a room, like a couple of arid schoolmen trying to out-pun each other? And yet it could not be true that she was parading her accomplishments seriously; there was that in her voice and manner that mocked her own flourishes as she made them. She seemed to him more like a woman reading over the letters of an old, half-baked girl's love from her past, with satire and tenderness in her voice, before she tore them up and burned them without one look of regret. A little ceremonial pyre to end a phase, a folly, a wasted time. A burning of the weeds from a fallow field which is about to be sown and bear fruit.

They were talking now with quick intelligence of Venice and the East, of the Crusade and its consequences, of courts and markets and the vexed affairs of kings. She left the lute lying in the cushions and came back to the table to pour more wine, but Adam was before her with the crystal jug and the dishes of sweetmeats. Harry let his mind withdraw from them into his own world, where at this moment he should have been busy with his pens and his instruments, adding to the roll of drawings already made.

He knew exactly what he wanted, he had been working over it in his mind for some seven years now, and only in detail would the actual site at Parfois alter his conception. He had yet to see how much ground he had to use, but neither beauty nor splendour have need of great size. What he wanted was light, light and space, and the upward surge of stone like a growing tree from foundations to vault. No oppression, no darkness, no burden of thick, groaning columns and lowering roofs like the stony weight of guilt. He saw the shape clearly. No chevet of chapels, but a square east end, so that he could have a whole wall of invading light pouring in upon the high altar. Short, strong transepts, lofty aisles, and the clerestory tall and fully glazed above a shallow triforium. The west front with a great, deeply-cut doorway and a vast window above, set back in course on course of moulding, where the light could harp all day long on strings of stone, making even that greyer northern air shine lucid and sharp as the dazzling south. Over the west front two minor turrets, tapering to slender fingers of stone. Over the crossing the great tower, as in Normandy, binding all together, rooting all impregnably into the earth, drawing all erect with it towards heaven. In that tension was the significance of life, and next to light, this he wanted above all, the duality of flesh and spirit, manhood and godhead, the tension of man on his way to God. A noble tower, tall and tapered, its long surfaces so subtly fluted and moulded that light and shadow might stroke it into a hundred changing shapes of majesty and beauty as the hours of the daylight passed. Permanence and change, diversity and oneness, in that grey-gold stone that glowed in his memory like – what was Adam's phrase? – a mine of sunshine. There is no growth nor fruitfulness but rises from these paired opposites of darkness and light, earth and heaven. My feet as roots in the earth, my forehead straining into the sun. The tower at once anchoring my church fast to the rock, and translating it into a balanced arrow of light aimed at the sky.

And within, the three-aisled nave; not with austere, unbroken lines from floor to vault, and certainly not with these debased Corinthian capitals that leave me so unsatisfied. Trivial as ornament, and purposeless as halting-places for the eye on its way upwards – no, not those. Capitals that live as flowers live, animals, men, all that comes from the soil and springs towards the sun. They shall shoot strongly from the columns and leap upwards, thrusting the abacus as high as they can reach, straining to sustain the vault like trees growing. Not a single line, but a single unbroken impetus, one surge of energy and faith drawn taut as a bow-string, but as secure as the arch of the rainbow.

There is no beauty where there is doubt or insecurity. A sense of unbalance is the death of art.

That hair of hers, caught up by the wind, could well hold up an arch on its great tresses. Like the leaping flames it so much resembles. Or the breaking wave. Everything that reaches up, everything that stretches and exults, an arm and hand thrusting against the abacus, a squirrel's arched tail, a leaping child, an uncurling frond of fern, a climbing vine, all manner of leaves that lean upwards to the light. And my lord's towering pride, that all-but-visible presence that rears over him like the black shadow he casts above him now, as he leans over the candles.

All his household at the Maison d'Estivet are afraid of him, even his five squires, three of them from blood the equal of his own, go in dread of him. Why? I see nothing so terrifying in him.

Together with all these ascending creatures, angels descending, like my first angel, hair and garments torn upwards in the streaming air of their flight. He could serve for either a demon aspiring or an angel falling. Or for both, perhaps. His head is very beautiful.

The woman made a movement of hand and arm that drew his eyes back to her. What was it in her that dragged so deeply at the chords of his memory, plucking out echoes he had long forgotten? All her motions had a quality of reminiscent beauty about them, as though she comprehended within herself all the women he had ever seen or known. The richness and kindness of her flesh brought his mother back to him. And her voice he had heard before, somewhere long ago and far away from here, clear, candid, direct as her eyes. Across those eyes of hers, temple to temple, her face was as wide as its length from brow to chin. What are the true proportions of beauty? Where, in any case, does beauty reside – in what is seen, or in that which is called to mind by what is seen? And can both be put into stone together?

I must make a drawing of her before we leave, he thought, if she will let me. I wish I knew where I had heard her voice. I wish I knew what is so moving about it, what quality it is that makes it seem remembered rather than heard, as though when she speaks I am listening to someone else, saying to me words she has never said.

'Harry!' said Adam, jogging his elbow good-humouredly. 'Have you fallen asleep? Madonna Benedetta is speaking to you.'

He started out of his dream and looked up quickly, full into the grey eyes, so wide and limpid that it seemed to him he saw his own image there. It was in that moment, when she had spoken to him and he had not even heard, that he recognised the quality her voice had for him, and knew it for a daunting honesty like that of a child, a fearless and merciless innocence. So had a child spoken with him once. How long a time it was, how long a time, since he had thought of Gilleis!

He opened his mouth to make excuses for his absence of mind, and on the edge of speech was held silent by the apparition of Isambard's face. While the woman was not regarding him, his eyes glowed upon her from their hollows of shade; through the golden mask of his face the naked blaze of his desire shone molten for an instant, then the heavy eyelids closed upon the fire, and the bronze head was darkened.

The fever of departure had lain long over the Ruelle des Guenilles and the Maison d'Estivet, but into the busy, dusty, populous lodges at Notre Dame it penetrated late, and brought to light a curious accumulation of forgotten belongings. Last of all, neglected in a corner of a chest where it must have lain for over a year, Harry found the frayed cloth scrip in which he had brought his small baggage from England, nine years ago. He picked it out and shook the dust from it, suddenly moved to look back and remember with affection and curiosity the boy who had carried it. From its deepest corner his fingers unearthed what felt like a coin, but when he drew it out he knew it for a small, tarnished medallion, the Virgin and Child on its face worn almost smooth. It was still threaded upon the gold cord by which Gilleis had hung it round his neck in the boat, before he climbed up into the *Rose of Northfleet*. He had not paid sufficient attention to it then to realise what it was, but he knew it now for one of the gilt threads she used to plait into her short black braids of hair.

He stood holding it in his hand, suddenly shaken by such a convulsion of homesickness that tears came into his eyes. How old would she be now? Nineteen! A woman! Did she still travel to the midlands with her father to buy cloth? Hardly likely, he thought; she would be mistress of the household in London now, and have other cares on her hands. She might even be married and ruling another man's house. He tried to see her a woman grown, and could not, his memory brought back so persistently the small, charming child with her great eyes and her flower of a mouth and her stiff little black braids, thick as her wrists. She had cried because he was always too busy to play with her. He remembered holding her awkwardly on his lap, on the stone ledge against the guest-house wall, labouring to comfort her and half-tempted to shake her. He might have made a little time for her, he thought remorsefully, after all she had done for him and for Adam.

And he had not even recognised and appreciated the gold thread from her hair!

He was still clasping the medal in his hand when one of the apprentices came looking for him. 'Master Henry, there's one here asking after you.'

'After me? What does he want?'

'Not he, but she,' said the boy, studiously keeping from his lips the knowing grin that was bright in his eyes. 'I thought best not to ask her business – I trust I did right?'

'It's a sound principle,' said Harry, making a perfunctory feint at the youngster's ears for his impudence, which the boy as dutifully ducked. 'Is she handsome?'

Raised brows and rolling eyes informed him wordlessly that she was; nonetheless, he expected no one more disturbing than the canon's housekeeper, or Master Bertrand's maid-servant, and felt a shock of incredulity when he emerged from the lodge to see Madonna Benedetta moving alone between the stacked stones, splendidly incongruous and utterly composed, with the skirt of her long bliaut over her arm. She saw him and came towards him, and her walk was as direct as her voice.

'Madam, you wish to speak to me? I am at your service.'

'I should not be interrupting your work,' she said, in that clear voice that came to him now with so significant an echo, 'and I must not do so for long. But my opportunities for talking with you will soon be gone, for I hear from my lord Isambard that in two weeks more you will be leaving Paris with him. Is it so?'

'Yes, we are almost ready. Master Bertrand had been good enough to release Adam and me, and the sooner we are in England the better, for I cannot make final plans until I see the site. I am sorry that I cannot offer you here either refreshment or privacy –'

'I need neither,' she said simply. 'If you will show me your Calvary, I should like that. I have never yet seen anything of yours.'

'Willingly! You know it's finished?' He led her to the lodge, and brought her in under the lean-to roof to a solitude and a silence. 'My lord has kept you informed? He has – visited you several times, I think.'

'He has,' she said, something of amusement in her voice, and a certain dryness, too. There was a silence. She had not yet looked at the grouped stone figures. 'You,' she said, 'have not.'

He did not know what he ought to reply to that, and for a moment kept a lame silence, at a loss to guess what she wanted here with him, 'Was I – expected?' he asked hesitantly at last.

'Expected? No, not that. You owed me nothing. Hoped for, perhaps.' She turned from him and walked slowly about the stone group, examining with steady, intelligent eyes the dead Christ, a dragging weight upon the pierced hands, with the Vigin and Saint John on one side, the the holy women on the other, motionless figures of grief, terribly self-contained, each one of them a well-shaft of loneliness sealed up from all consolation. They touched each other, but remained irrevocably separate. 'So since you did not come to me,' she said, still thoughtfully gazing, 'I have come to you. Not expressly to see this, but I am glad that I have seen it, all the same. How did you come to understand so much about suffering? Is it something in your experience, or a motion of the will and the imagination? Most Christs have made but a symbolic gesture of dying. Yours has been dragged through the whole process of a cruel execution.'

'Have I over-stated?' he asked with real anxiety.

'No, that is how it must have been. I am sure He was spared nothing. And you have let Him keep the wholeness of His spirit. Everything is there to be read, but He does not assault us with it. We are left to choose whether we see or pass by. It was terrible, but He has sustained it. There is no room for pity.'

'You are comforting me,' he said. 'I do not know if you intended that. But it is not true that I understand suffering. Here I have been trying to explain it to myself, how a man could pass through that agony, and still come out of it a man. Dead, perhaps, but not violated.'

'That is what He has done,' she said.

'If that is true, then so far at least I have succeeded. But I suffered only in the imagination, and still I do not know whether I could undergo the ordeal in the flesh, and remain unbroken. Imagination is not enough. Perhaps those who have never tried to imagine it come best out of the testing of pain.'

'It is natural to be afraid of one's own human weakness,' said Benedetta, 'but not good to dwell too much upon the question until it arises. If you cannot imagine pain fully, neither can you fully imagine the resources you have in you to meet it and overcome it. Do you suppose you could have put into this figure anything you yourself lacked?'

Harry smiled. 'That is a very large artistic question, and I am not prepared to argue it.'

She stood considering the group still for several minutes. From the runways of hurdles above their heads the voices of the masons came to them distantly.

'They won't like it,' said Benedetta, shaking her head. 'They are not invited to take part in it, and that won't please them. To be challenged to think about it is the last thing they want.' She turned from it with decision, and stood facing him squarely. 'Harry!'

She used his name with a familiarity and authority that came, he supposed, of listening long to Isambard, who had made free with it from the first. 'Harry, you must know that I have lived a certain kind of life, spending myself and what was mine as I saw fit, taking a price when I chose, and giving when it pleased me to give. I am not ashamed of it, and I make no defence of what needs none. I see nothing dishonourable in disposing as one will of what is one's own. And hitherto I have owned myself wholly. But it becomes dishonourable to squander the same wealth when it ceases to be one's own. Harry, since that evening when you came to me with your lord my door has been closed at night, and my bed solitary. I will not give to any man but one what is no longer mine to give, but his.'

She had drawn a little nearer to him, and stood searching his troubled face candidly and proudly. He did not understand. He thought she must be speaking of Isambard, and wondered what need she could have of such a confidant as himself, if that were so.

'Madam, whatever you may ask of me – ' he began haltingly.

'I am asking you for nothing. I am offering you something – myself, myself entire, to be yours without reserve, yours once for all. If you are pleased to take me, I will be faithful to you as long as I live, and never know another man, as I shall never love another. If not, tell me so plainly, as I deserve of you, and I will never trouble you with my love again.'

Harry stood stunned and speechless, staring at her open-mouthed. He could think of nothing but that she must be mocking him, and it filled him with a sense of outrage that she should do it in that piercing, spontaneous, child's voice of hers, so wildly sweet in his ears. Closed fast in his left hand, the worn silver medal bit with sharp edges into his palm.

'I cannot believe in this,' he burst out, shaking his head in quick and helpless anger. 'You have seen me but once, you know nothing of me.'

'I know all that I need to know, and more than you think. My life turned from its course when you entered my house. Even before I saw you, your voice had fallen athwart my peace. Adam is Adam,' she said, laughter looking out of her eyes for a moment, 'and what woman could have the heart to wound him? But it was for you I opened the door.'

She could have reached out her hand and touched him, but she would not. It was for him to take her or refrain.

'I know my own mind,' she said. 'I know there is no returning for me. From the moment that you came into sight my heart fixed on you, and I have been mistress of my heart too long to question or distrust it now. Do you think I am a woman given to self-deceit? Or without experience? I did not choose to love you. Who but a fool ever chooses to love? But truth is truth, and I acknowledge it. This is something not even you can change. Even if you reject me, you cannot deny me the right to love you. Love you I shall, as long as I have breath, whether you will or no, whether I will or no. I know the absolute when I see it, and I am a practical woman, one who wastes no time in fighting God.'

She saw the play of doubt and unhappiness in his shadowed face, and even the flicker of a boy's wariness, and her mouth softened in a smile at once tender and ironic.

'Do not be afraid that I am come to plead. I came to give you what is yours, but if you do not want it I can take it away again. You owe me nothing. Unless, perhaps, I might lay claim to the grace of your trust, and ask truth of you as I have told you truth. Look at me, and say what you have to say, and see if I fail of what I have pledged you.'

Harry raised his head, and met her glance full. He had indeed considered the kind of evasions any man might have used to extricate himself from so strange a situation, half-protestations of respect and admiration designed to send her away appeased without making her any promises, until such time as he could remove himself thankfully into England. But he put them from him again, for she was worth something better than that. Encountering the proud and fearless eyes, he felt again, and strongly, that first delight of finding himself in her presence and recognising his match. No word or act of his should deface that balance. Truth he owed to himself and to her, and truth she should have.

He said: 'I do not love you. God knows I should be a happy man if it had happened so to me, but it did not. From my heart I thank you for the magnificence of the gift you have offered me, but I cannot take it. I will not pretend a passion I do not feel. I neither love nor desire you.'

She did not lower her eyes, her face did not change. She stood for a moment in silence, containing the wound, her hands quiet under her breast, and watched his eyes clear and soften from their cloudy frown. In the act of denying himself to her he had given her a fragment at least of his heart; he felt it pass from him, and was eased and glad that all the generosity should not be on her side.

'I was not mistaken in you,' she said, after a long moment, in a voice very soft and strangely content. 'At least, after so long of being free, I set my mark high. Now be generous in your honesty yet again, and tell me truly whether you are utterly indifferent to me. And if it is so, you are rid of me for ever.'

He lifted his head sharply, his eyes flashing as the light caught their startling greenness. A few words only, he thought, hard to say and harder to hear, but we should both be free. She would be rid of me for ever, as I of her, for she has a mind and a heart that cannot go cold through a long life, and in the nature of man there must come a day when she will forget me. I have only to strike her now, and we are both delivered. But when he opened his lips the words would not come. He could not do it. The one lie was as contemptible as the other. Between himself and Benedetta lies were unworthy and unthinkable.

'Only a clod could be indifferent to you,' he said deliberately. 'I delight in your beauty, your mind I honour, your gallantry I revere. Madonna Benedetta, I like you well and more than well. I'll neither feign what I do not feel, nor deny what I do. If God had pleased to have me love you, I would have accounted myself the happiest of men, and in having your faith and trust I still reckon myself blessed.'

Then she did put her hand upon him for an instant, only the touch of her fingers against his breast in an indescribably eloquent gesture of gratitude and acceptance. 'With that I am a rich woman,' she said. 'I shall never speak to you of love again, unless you so will it. Yet this which is yours I swear is yours for ever, and if the day should ever come when you want it, you have only to call to me and I shall come to you – you have only to reach out your hand and I will render you all that is yours. Now I am going. No, let me leave you here and go alone. And do not fear that you have hurt or harmed me or done me any wrong. You are as I would have you, and I delight in loving you.'

With that she caught up the skirt of her bliaut again, and flung it over her arm with one of those gloriously large gestures of hers, and would have passed by him with a raised head and a smiling mouth, but he put out his hand to her, and she swung back to lay her own in it for an instant.

'Sweet friend!' she said, and drew her fingers away again before he could kiss them, and so went forth and left him gazing after her.

Now he could never escape her, nor she him. Not even the dear talisman gripped so fiercely in his hand could set them free. Nor could he ever want for her, or take away that morsel of his heart from her.

'The summer can be beautiful at Parfois,' said Isambard, caressing the dog's head with his ringed hand and looking down with a faint, remembering smile into the crystal cup of wine. 'In spite of our border rains, it can be beautiful. That is good riding country, and full of game. I have taken wolf and boar there sometimes, but they're getting rare these days, even in the marches.'

'You are looking forward already to being home,' said Benedetta, 'I hear it in your voice. I believe you love your England.'

'After years of deluding myself that I had many homes, I have at least discovered where my home is. But late,' he said, with a melancholy smile, 'since it is now a home without a family. Gilles remains here in France, as he always preferred to do, and now he will have the sole care of those honours which used to be mine, and no leisure for visiting me – even if King Philip's policies were not making it hard to pass freely between France and England. And the younger boy, William, is in FitzPeter's service, the Earl of Essex, and comes home only on occasions to refill his pockets. Why not? What's mine in England will be his some day. William is his mother's son, he never liked Parfois, it was too remote for him. The king's court pleased him more than mine. It may be that I shall find nothing but disappointment even there.'

'You want too much,' she said. 'Men, and countries, and causes fail you because you expect too much of them.'

'It may be true,' he owned indifferently. 'I am what I am. Whether it is my fellows who have fallen off from me, or I who have cast them off, I begin to find myself appallingly alone. And sometimes I have a great longing in me for someone who will not fall away.'

She turned her head and looked at him across the room. In the great high-backed chair he sat leaning upon one arm, his chin cupped in his palm, the candle-light tremulous upon the tawny golden planes of his temples and cheek-bones and the fine, spare line of his jaw. A man of contrasts, all brilliance and blackness. Out of the caverns of shade the beautiful eyes, reddish brown like dark gilliflowers, burned steadily upon her face. He had a necklet of uncut, polished stones set in gold about his neck. Like his lord and friend King John, he had a liking for jewels and cared fastidiously for his person; and like so many of his fellow-Crusaders he had picked up some of the refinements of his Moslem enemies. But luxury could never soften so much restless energy; even his indulgences he used as whetstones for his mind, and his occasional dissipations were only a means of exercising and testing his body when no more violent occupations offered. She could well understand that he wore out his companions as he wore out shoes, and grew angry at finding them inadequate. And his women, too, perhaps, though she doubted if he had turned readily to women. His wife, a bride of policy nine years older than himself, had died early and left him free, young, wealthier than ever, and almost certainly ungrieving, too well-endowed to want for loves if he needed them, but too youthful, complex and energetic to devote to them overmuch of his time and vigour.

'Come with me to England,' said Isambard.

She was silent so long that he grew impatient, and sat up restlessly, pushing the hound's head from his knee and gripping the carved arms of the chair with both muscular hands. He had a way of turning any chair in which he sat into a throne.

'Why don't you answer? I cannot have surprised you. You must know that I want you, that I have wanted you from the first moment I saw you. It is not my way to make many words where I know I am understood in few. Come with me to Parfois, and you shall be nobly used and honourably attended. All that is mine I will share with you, and hold you in love and worship. Give me an answer!'

'I am wondering,' she said mildly, 'if you have really considered what you are proposing. Now, when you confess to a taste for permanence, am I the right person to invite to share your life? Does it seem to you that constancy is what I confer upon my lovers? I had thought I was more faithfully reported.'

'It is not like you to play with words,' he said, frowning. 'What you undertake, that you will perform, and well you know it. Where you have given only a fleeting pleasure you have never promised more. But I am asking for more. Come with me, and I will never have any but you, and you shall be my mistress and my peer.'

'You tempt me,' she said. 'I like you well and take pleasure in your company, my lord, and there is much to attract me in what you suggest. But there are things about me that you do not know. If you had come to me like the rest, looking only for a night's pleasure and ready to pay for it, it would never have become necessary for you to know them.'

'Do not attribute to me either coldness or continence,' he put in haughtily, 'for holding back until now. I want you body and mind and heart, or I will have none of you. To hold you in my arms for a night, and know myself one of a long line of fools who believe that they have possessed you, that I could not endure. I want a consort for my days and my nights alike, a partner worthy of my state.'

'You lay the more obligation on me,' she said, 'to make it clear what I can give you and what I cannot.'

She rose abruptly from the table and crossed the room to draw close the arras over the door, as though the May evening had turned cold suddenly. Her long skirt made a soft rustling like autumn leaves, and shed a faint perfume on the air as she passed by him. He followed her movements, and watched her standing motionless in the doorway, her raised hand still clenched in the tapestry. In the shadows her coronal of hair was darker than garnets.

'My lord, I have loved a man, and love him still. He has never been mine, and in this world I think he never will. I say it to my sorrow, he neither loves nor desires me. Nevertheless, I have given to him that love that cannot be given but once, and if that is what you look for from me, then go away now and think no more of me. The heart of love is gone, and cannot be given again. What remains is the woman you see. I am not of those who die of unrequited passion, though I live the poorer by what I have lost. I have respect for you, and liking, I have a mind that may serve you well, and a body I am free to pledge to you if I choose, and I have a strong appetite for life. If you still want me on those terms, we may be able to strike a bargain. But I will not come to you dishonestly, pretending to be what I am not.'

He had risen from his chair, thrusting the hound aside with a brusque movement of his foot. He came towards her slowly, anger and jealousy in the lines of his frowning face, but calculation in his eyes, and something of a hot, unquestioning tenderness, too, that reached for her through the bars of his pride. She loosed her hold on the arras, and went step for step to meet him, a rueful smile on her lips, but her eyes like clear steel mirrors in which he beheld his own insatiable face.

'I cannot believe this! I want you whole!'

'But I am not whole,' she said, 'the best is gone. And so goodbye, my lord!'

'No! Wait!' He took her by the shoulders, and held her hard between his hands, and she felt him trembling with the force of his pride and rage, that would not have less than all, and yet could not let her go.

She had no mind to influence him; her honour was involved. She stood calmly sustaining his famished stare, and out of her own experience she found a measure of true compassion for him.

'He still lives – this man of whom you speak?' he asked harshly.

'He still lives.'

'Here, in France? Or was this beforetime, in Venice?'

'I have told you all that you need to know of him,' she said. 'I'll tell you no more.'

His long fingers tightened tormentedly into her flesh, drawing her close against his breast. She had never been in England, the phantasm could not follow her there, into a new country. And he would be ever beside her, with the persuasions of his body and the graces of his worship for her, flesh and blood and present love for a fading dream. She could not live in memory for long, she was too intelligent, too honest, too keenly alive. With all things new around her, and all in his gift, she could not choose but love him at last.

'Yes, come!' he said hoarsely, suddenly laying his lean cheek against her hair. 'Come with me! Even so, come! If you knew my need – '

'Wait! Hear what I undertake, before you bind yourself.' She braced her hands against his breast and held him off from her. 'If you still desire it, I will come with you. I will bind myself in faith and loyalty to you, and only to you, until one of us two shall openly and fairly pronounce this contract at an end. And then it shall be void, and there shall be no redress. If it is you who cast me off, I will abide it and never complain. And if it is I who abandon you, you must do as much in your turn. But this I swear to you, I will never leave you, except it be to follow that creature I love more than my own life. And if that should befall,' she said with a bitter smile, 'as God He knows it is unlikely ever to do, you may well say of me, rather than "God curse her!" – "God help her!", for I shall surely pay in full any debt I owe to you.'

'I take you, then,' he said, the words strained out of him in a half-suffocated voice. 'I take you, on those terms, and will hold you against the world.' He caught her to him fiercely, his arms circling her body, his mouth kissing and murmuring against her cheek. The other, the enemy, the man from the past, would never come troubling them. He was a bloodless shadow, a poor thing without the wit to love her then, or the spirit to find her now if he came to his senses. The sea, and silence, and indifference would hold him distant from her. And even if he came – as he never would come – he was mortal and could die. So poor a spirit would need little quenching. 'Hold by me!' he whispered into her throat. 'Hold fast by me, for God's sake!'

'Until death or he call me from you,' she said, 'or you discard me.'

She marvelled at herself a little, that she, born of subtle, seafaring merchant stock without pretensions to nobility, should feel herself bound by the niceties of honour far more inescapably than by his arms or all the resources of his power.

He twisted one hand in the coils of her hair, and began to pluck out the bone pins that held it in place, until the heavy sheaves fell about her shoulders and drifted in a shining darkness between her uplifted face and his kissing mouth. She embraced him resolutely, straining to her heart the instrument of her power and means of her usefulness, and she felt neither fear nor regret for what she had done.

Harry picked his way across the courtyard of the Maison d'Estivet, between servants and pack-horses and corded loads, with the din of departure in his ears. The leaning face of the house, striped with fitful, watery sunlight and the tenuous shadows of clouds, sheltered with its overhang the piled furnishings of my lord's bedchamber and wardrobe, the most precious freight, just in process of being loaded. Three of the harassed squires were superintending the porters, and sweating blood for fear a few flecks of dust should be cast upon Isambard's silks and furs. The heavier and less precious baggage had already been dispatched to Calais in carts, some days previously, but these last and most closely guarded goods must travel by pack-horse to keep pace with my lord and his personal party. The sumpter column would leave this morning, the riders this afternoon, to make an easy first stage on the way to the port. Then there remained only the sea voyage, a brief but abysmal misery as Harry remembered it, between him and England.

Adam, somewhat below his best after a last boisterous night with

Apollon and Élie at Nestor's, had already ridden ahead with their instruments, the accumulated mass of Harry's drawings, and the attendant spirit of their travels together, the wooden angel. The angel's colours were a little dimmed and mellowed now by many lodgings; he had been the guest of three great churches and won the admiration of many sound critics, not least of them his last host, Canon d'Espérance. Now he, too, was on his way home. He was part of a debt of honour which had been long in the paying.

Half a dozen dogs ran between the stamping horses and bustling men, and were cursed and kicked and tripped over by turns. Most of them would be left here, but the three strange hunting dogs from the East were to be shipped to England after their master, and were intended, so Harry had heard from the youngest of the squires, as a present for King John. They had long bodies like greyhounds, and long, narrow faces, haughty as Saladin himself, and long, shaggy ears and flanks, and according to Walter Langholme they could outrun leopards on their own ground, and pull them down, too. They paced suspiciously through the teeming halls of the Maison d'Estivet, delicate and aloof, nervous but not timid, objects of terror and awe. Only the great wolfhound from Arabia, Isambard's special delight, was more feared. He was trained, so they said, to be one man's beast, and at his command would bring down and kill either man or leopard. He was never seen without Isambard himself holding the leash, or else his handler, a Christian Greek from Romania, bought with the dog. Nobody else could command him, for he knew his rights, and deferred only to his lord and his lord's deputy.

There were falcons in the menagerie, too, and a little green and gold singing bird in a filigree cage for the queen. And there were two caskets of gilt and inlay work containing fragments of the shattered bones of Saint Stephen and a lock of the red hair of Saint Mary Magdalene, which she tore out of her head in the hours of supernatural darkness on Calvary; and most precious of all, an amethyst flask of the water of Jordan, blessed by the last Christian prelate of Jerusalem, before the holy kingdom fell to Saladin, and a second time by the Pope in Rome. It was said to have worked several miracles already, and was intended as a princely gift to the cathedral of Gloucester. It travelled in a bag of worked leather, strapped to the thongs of one of the pack-saddles and watched with anxious care.

As Harry approached the doorway he heard Isambard's voice raised within in a brief but violent outburst of wrath. A servant came scuttling out, his eyes blank with fright, and the mark of a whip crimson across his cheek and chin. De Guichet, the oldest of the five squires, followed him with more dignity, but in equal haste to remove himself from his lord's vicinity. He was scarlet to the hair, and in a temper he would certainly vent on someone lower in the hierarchies before the hour was out. Encountering Harry outside the door, he raised his eyebrows and shook his head at him helplessly, but did not stop to exchange words. It was Langholme who tilted his head significantly towards the house, and said in an undertone:

'Keep out of his way. The signs mean thunder.'

'What ails him?' asked Harry, unable to take the storm too seriously, since it had never yet blown in his direction.

'Pinpricks. One of the Syrian hawks died, no one knows why. And now the horse the lady was to ride is gone lame. It wants but one more thrust and someone will bleed for it.'

'The lady? What lady is that?'

'Why, his Venetian beauty, of course, who else?'

'Madonna Benedetta?' cried Harry, staring at him unbelievingly.

'Did you not know? She has been here three days with him already. Where have you been hiding, not to have heard it? She's sold old Guiscard's house and is coming to queen it at Parfois.'

His first feeling was of alarm for his own peace, but he tossed that away contemptuously as a vanity on his part. If she had captured the lord of Parfois she was not likely to waste any thought on his master-mason, nor to thank him for remembering that she had once offered herself to him. No, he need not fear any vexation from her, she would surely play the chatelaine with a particularly forbidding hauteur towards him, to warn him not to presume on what had passed between them.

Thus far he pursued these sensible arguments, and then turned sick with his own shameful stupidity. She was no such person. He was lying to himself and defaming her. Whatever she did, she did with open eyes and with her might. What she had said to him stood; she would not take it back, and she had not repented of it.

It was for him she was coming to England! With what intent he could not guess, but he knew that it had to do with him.

'I've been out of Paris until last night, on my lord's business,' he said. 'I heard nothing of it. Is she within there now?'

'She is, and he's about choosing another mount for her, and God help the grooms if he fails to find what he wants. If I could, I'd put the width of Paris between myself and him. I've seen his lightnings kill before now.'

Harry curled an incredulous lip at what must be an exaggeration. 'What, in Paris, with men of law within a stone's throw?'

'Do you think the law cares what Parfois does with his own serfs? Or his free men, for that matter? Or that it dare touch him, if it did care? To those who fall within his honour he *is* law, the high justice, the middle and the low. There was a sheriff once in Flint who did try to move against him,' said Langholme simply, 'but it ended in the sheriff being thrown out of office and ruined. And law's lost a deal of its force in the marches since those days, let me tell you. Stand away. Here they come, the pair of them!'

The household had not yet grown accustomed to its new mistress; a hush and a tremor went before her as she stepped from the doorway, and covertly all eyes turned upon her. Then, as Isambard appeared at her shoulder, all faces were as quickly averted, and hasty hands, none too steady under that fixed and frowning eye, went on feverishly tightening girths and hoisting the corded loads into place.

He should have known that, however changed and disconcerting the circumstances, she would be their mistress. She moved across the crowded courtyard with that imperial calm of hers, untroubled by the secret assault of so many eyes, and when her glance fell on him she greeted him courteously and composedly, like any other of her lord's more exalted servitors. She wore a plain riding-dress, and her hair was hidden within a white wimple, so that for the first time he saw the pure, strong shape of her face without the distraction of that red splendour; and as the dress had a cloistral austerity, so the face had a power and a confident passion quite without fear of the world.

Isambard, all brown and dull gold from head to foot, had the Arabian hound on its short, thick leash at his hip. Its colour, like his, was tawny, and its hide, like his sun-gilded skin, had a golden lustre. They looked like a group in bronze when they halted for a moment, and in motion they were molten metal. The dog's head, jawed .ike a mastiff, came level with the man's waist. Its mask was ugly, but its gait was exquisite, the light ripple of controlled power moving that entire great body without a sound or an effort. The sight of every man in the courtyard shrinking furtively aside from his passage moved Isambard to a sour smile, but it was only the ominous flicker of lightning through the cloud that hung upon his face. The whip that had laid open the groom's cheek still dangled from a gloved wrist. By the look of him he would use it again freely on anyone who crossed him, from de Guichet down.

'Ah, you are back,' he said, espying Harry. 'Are you any judge of a horse?'

'No, my lord, or at best an indifferent one.'

'No matter, attend us! I am the worst-served and worst-provided master in Christendom, I think. I hope you have done your errands better than Despard did when he furnished me this stable of mine. Are the accounts all paid?'

'And the receipts are with your clerk, my lord.'

'Good, then at least we leave no debts behind us. Are you in mortal fear of this creature, like all the rest?'

'I suppose he was trained with that end in view,' said Harry. 'Why complain of a success?' But he fell in on the hound's other flank, watching the rippling of the great muscles under the silken hide with a delight which at least balanced his wariness.

The line of stables occupied one long wall of the courtyard. Benedetta sat down on the mounting-block, while Isambard had horse after horse paraded before him, and found fault with all. The two unfortunate squires who had been sent ahead into Paris to rent the house and fill the stables before his arrival sweated and endured humbly, as he pulled their work to pieces. Yet it seemed to Harry that the horses were well enough, if their master's heart had not been set on the Arab mare, now disastrously lame. She was a beautiful creature, but there were others no less fine, if the lady could manage them. He wondered curiously if she rode as well as she did most things. Benedetta on horseback would be a new revelation.

'The black is the best of a poor bunch,' said Isambard. 'Lead him out, and give him space to show his paces.'

'The black?' De Guichet hesitated. 'My lord, he'll be a handful for any rider, and if my lady – '

'Lead him out, I say!' snapped Isambard, with a sultry flash of his deep-set eyes. 'Am I to mount her on such poor jades as you would choose for her?' And he strode forward and took the halter himself, and brought the black horse out into the centre of the court, and wheeled him circling about him, with the first glow of pleasure he had shown. Benedetta looked on with a noncommittal face from her seat on the mounting-block, the shadow of a smile on her lips. The beast was too large for her, and far too nervous, Harry thought impatiently, and it was a vicious trick to loose him like this in the middle of the flustered servants and restive pack-ponies. A load was knocked over, and furs spilled across the dusty cobbles. One of the ponies shied. The hound, whose leash Isambard had passed to the Greek handler, lifted his tawny hackles and began to moan with contained excitement, deep in his throat.

'Here, take him, let me see him move.'

De Guichet took the halter from him gingerly, and in that moment the horse, sensing a less confident hand on him, suddenly took offence at the dog, partly in real uneasiness, partly in sheer high spirits, and plunged backwards, rearing and whinnying, and dragging the squire with him. He backed into the file of pack-ponies, and sent them scattering with squeals of alarm, and the liveliest of the line, with ears laid back and eyes rolling, went sideways in a series of stiff-legged leaps from the stamping black hooves, plucking his bridle out of the hand of the servant who held him. The load slid sidelong from his back, and cast a full pannier to the ground, spilling brocades and jewels across the cobbles, and the servant, struggling to avert the disaster, fell with it, his arms still outspread to try and save what could be saved. The pony's plunging feet, tangled in silks, kicked panic-stricken left and right, and stamped flat the leather bag that held the flask of the water of Jordan.

In spite of the clamour of the horses and the shouting of men, the small, terrible sound of the crystal shattering seemed to carry clear through all and reach every ear. De Guichet, cursing and cajoling, brought the black horse to earth again, and led him aside, trembling. The pack-pony, caught and held by one of the grooms, stood shuddering and sweating. Between the cobbles of the courtyard a little, dusty puddle gathered and seeped slowly away, leaving only a damp, dark stain.

There was a single instant of appalling silence. Then Isambard made a strange, soft sound, low in his throat, like a more terrible echo of the hound's moan of desire; and in the same moment the servant, sprawling among the ruins, uttered a hoarse croak of terror.

'My lord, mercy! I could not help it!'

The bronze face, fixed in a dreadful stillness, stared upon the trampled relic and the grovelling man for a moment in silence. Then, with a flashing movement, Isambard stooped and tore free the heavy brass clasp from the hound's collar, and setting his hand in the erected hackles, thrust forward savagely towards the poor wretch on the ground, and spat into the pricked ear a few barbaric words. Whether they were Arabic, Greek, or whatever other strange tongue, they needed no translating.

Harry uttered an almost voiceless cry of protest, and started forward, but Langholme took him by the arms from behind, and dragged him back, clinging to him obstinately as he struggled to free himself, and hissing in his ear: 'Let be, you fool! Do you want to be the next?'

Killing was the dog's business, he leaped like an eager craftsman to the word of command. The great paws bunched under him, and launched him forward in an easy, beautiful leap. A screaming and scrambling convulsed the courtyard, men and ponies ran confusedly for cover, and found none. The man on the ground had dragged himself up and cast one wild look all round him, and turned to run desperately but with frantic purpose straight for Madonna Benedetta, who had not moved from her seat on the mounting-block.

He hurled himself at her feet, crouched against her ankles, clutching her shoes against his streaming face; and with a swift movement she caught up the hem of gown and cloak together and cast them over him. The weighted corner of her cloak flicked the hound's gaping muzzle as it loped silently after its quarry, and sent it scrabbling and sliding back a yard or two on the polished stones. The woman sat quite still, her right arm spread over the servant's heaving shoulders, her face, composed but watchful, turned steadily towards the dog. Sensing that he trespassed here at his own peril, but reluctant to quit his victim, he circled her, head lowered, jaws slavering, and stared at her with baffled amber eyes, dubious of his duty.

In a second he might have made up his mind. But a second was enough for Isambard, ashen beneath his tan, to leap forward and slash the weaving jowl aside from her with a vicious swing of his whip. Benedetta looked up at him as he leaned above her, speechless with anger and fear, and said with the faintest of smiles and the mildest of voices: 'Yes, call off your dog, my lord, he's trampling my dress.'

He could not speak, his throat was constricted with the terror he had felt for her and the fury he had felt against her, an agony of hate and love. He stood towering over her in aching silence, as the Greek crept forward and leashed the dog, and retreating step by step, with held breath, drew it away with him to hide and tremble in the background. Silently Langholme relaxed his grip on Harry's arms, and silently Harry stood off from him, drawing long breaths of the charged air and getting no relief. Until the tension broke between those two facing each other there, no one dared move except softly and stealthily.

The lines of Isambard's mouth, drawn thin and grey, relaxed slowly, and blood flushed again beneath the stretched skin of his cheeks. Under the heavy eyelids the fires burned out to black. She held their hard stare until the anguish passed from it and the breath was even and quiet in his still dilated nostrils.

'My lord,' she said then, as naturally as if nothing out of the way had passed, 'if you do not want this man, give him to me. I shall have need of a man-servant sometimes.'

For a long moment he did not answer. Then with an abrupt movement of his whole body he straightened up from her. 'He is yours,' he said quietly, and turning from her, strode away into the house, men and dogs and ponies scattering hurriedly from his path.

She waited until he was gone, and then with a lift of her head and a marked glance about her sent the squires and grooms and porters about their business. Then at last she drew aside cloak and skirt from the prostrate man, and looked down at him with a face suddenly grave and thoughtful. His palms were folded about her feet, his face pressed against her insteps; he lay unmoving.

'Get up!' she said gently. 'He is gone. No one will touch you now, you are mine.'

The man lifted a soiled, drained face. He had bitten his lip so deep that blood had run down into his short brown beard, and with the exhaustion of relief from fear he was almost too weak to move. Harry, who had felt no dismissal in Benedetta's glance, went forward and lent him an arm to help him to rise.

'You were his serf? Are you French?'

'English, my lady.' His voice was flat and dazed. 'From Fleace, in Flintshire.'

'What is your name?'

'John the Fletcher, my lady.'

'Well, John the Fletcher, you are no serf now, but my liege man, and free. I do not expect to make any great demands on your skill in fletching arrows, but who knows, some day I may need you.'

'I am your man,' he said hoarsely, and caught up the corner of her cloak and pressed it to his lips. 'Body and soul, mistress, while I live.'

'Go now and bathe your face. And keep out of my lord's sight for a while. You are safe enough from him, but I would not have him reminded.'

When the man had limped away across the court, Benedetta rose. She encountered Harry's eyes, and smiled, rather ruefully. There was no constraint between them; the freedom he felt with her at once startled and reassured him. How could he have feared, even for a moment, that she would pursue him with the love he had refused? Love with her would be a field of action, not a need. She was complete whether she won or lost the world. She was her own fortress and her own sanctuary.

'We strike these attitudes,' she said, 'almost by accident. Now I feel more than a little foolish.'

'You risked your life,' he said, watching her face gravely.

'I think not. I was born with certain disabilities; among other things I am quite unable to feel any fear of dogs, even when I should. It is very disconcerting to the most dangerous of beasts not to be feared. And besides, you saw how fast my lord can move when he pleased. The hound would have had a sword through him before ever he got his teeth through my cloak. Not that I thought of it, either way,' she admitted, 'at the time. Unless sometimes the act is also the thought. In any case, I could not move aside, he held me by the feet.'

'That was not what held you,' said Harry; and after a moment, very soberly: 'Take good care with such a man!'

'That is good counsel for you, as well as for me,' she said, giving him a keen look. Then her eyes softened into a regretful smile: 'He has surprised you. I am sorry! As for me, I knew already that there is nothing so bad or so good as to be out of his compass. Except, of course, faith-breaking, the only mortal sin.' She brushed a few flecks of dust from her cloak, and turned towards the house. 'Ask Bertrand de Guichet to pick out a horse for me, Harry. He need not be a lady's nag. I can ride. I must go in and make my peace.'

She went, with that splendid, straight walk of hers, and she did not look behind. But she left with him one more, the last and most touching, of those unbearably lovely memories she seemed to quicken about her at every turn. He saw again the bold hand casting the hem of her skirt over the runaway, and before his eyes the hand dwindled into a child's plump little paw, gallantly spreading out her full skirts to hide two boys from their pursuers. Such a fondness came about his heart that he could not see for tears. This was Benedetta's gift to him, the recognition of the tie that bound him to Gilleis.

He opened his mind to love unresistingly, and it flooded his being, filling him with a sweet and poignant delight more overwhelming than pain. Body and mind, he ached for her. His need was as inordinate as his neglect of her had been innocent and long. Gilleis, I must find you, I will find you, he cried to her silently. Oh, love, Gilleis, wait for me, I'm coming!

It was time and more than time for him to turn homeward.

PART THREE

THE WELSH MARCHES

1209 – 1215

CHAPTER NINE

Adam awoke with the first sunlight on his face through the narrow east window of the upper chamber, and opened his eyes to see Harry sitting on the edge of the bed, pulling on his hose. He stretched and yawned luxuriously, looking up at him with a dreamy smile, and for a moment lay wondering vaguely and contentedly where he was. Then he remembered riding into Shrewsbury after dark, in the soft summer rain, the drowsy supper downstairs in the inn, and the pleasure of falling half-asleep and bone-tired into this capacious bed beside his brother. They had ridden out of their way to the lead-mines, because Harry would not let even the lead for his roofs wait its time, but must bespeak it from the source now, before he had even set eyes on the site where he was to build.

'Where are we going so early?' he asked sleepily, and groped along the bare floor with one hand for his shoes.

'Not we – I. You can go and look at the town, after all this long time away, and meet me here again in an hour or so.'

Then Adam remembered. The mist of sleep cleared from his eyes, they opened wide and blue as cornflowers in his sunburned face. 'I could very well come with you. Who's going to remember old scores now?'

'No,' said Harry with finality. 'You'll not set foot in their gates. I won't be long gone.'

'And what if they move against you? You're very tender for me, but foolhardy for yourself, it seems.'

'This debt is mine,' said Harry shortly, and rose from the bed with a bound that set the wooden frame creaking. Adam lay still and watched him dress, his hands comfortably linked under his fair head. It was characteristic of Harry that he had had to be bullied into buying new clothes in London, seeing no connection between the dignity and authority of a master-mason and the length and amplitude of his cotte. He scoffed at the full-length gown of the selfconscious master as the uniform of infirmity, and could not be induced to interest himself in what he wore, beyond demanding freedom to move as he pleased. It had cost Adam a deal of scheming and cajoling to get him into this trim light-brown cotte and the dark green surcoat with its full sleeves and capuchon elegantly draped. He surveyed his work with contented eyes as Harry combed his hair and buckled on his belt. The gravity, purpose and power of the face had never been in any doubt. He would have no difficulty in commanding respect and obedience, whatever rusty old tunic he put on him. Still, Adam liked to see him doing honour to his role. It was not every man who could set up to be a master-mason at twenty-four.

Harry caught the complacent blue eye, and grinned derisively at the reflection of his own magnificence there. 'They'll not know me.'

'They'll know you,' said Adam positively, with pride and contentment, and closed his eyes and slept again.

Harry went on foot through the town, downhill by the curving streets in the sharp, cool light of the morning. Nine years had not greatly changed Shrewsbury. The narrow shop-fronts between their dark, timbered portals, the leaning gables serrated against the pale, pearly sky were as he remembered them, and the people who rubbed shoulders with him were unfamiliar only in a degree of quietness and reserve, almost of suspicion, as though strangers were no longer so frequent or so welcome as once they had been. A sign of the times, like the silence of the bells. Here in the town which had been his home he felt the want of them again like a gnawing hunger. At this hour of the morning the roofs should have been rocking with sound; but for over a year now all the bells of England had been stilled, all the churches closed, the brides bedded with clandestine ceremonies or none, the dead buried without rites, in pits by the roadside. And the king, acting with as great audacity as the Pope, and as little regard for the effects of his strategy on the innocent and helpless, had appropriated to himself all the lands and rents and properties of the church, on the ground that it was no longer fulfilling those duties in consideration of which it enjoyed such privileges. Without income neither clerics nor monastics could feed themselves, much less provide for the sick and poor around them. It was always on the lowest and least that the weight came down in the end, just as debt found its way down from the king through his barons, through their tenants-in-chief and their subtenants, to the free cottagers and the bound villeins on their poor little yardlands of earth. Innocent struck at John, John struck at

Innocent, and both blows fell on the poor man in his field. Bishops and abbots could ship themselves abroad until the storm should blow over, but wretched little parish parsons, as poverty-stricken as their own flocks, could not, and now it was the poor who fed the priests and not the priests the poor. All over the appointment of an archbishop!

But no, it was less simple than that, that was the chosen occasion, not the cause. This Pope, able, brilliant and ambitious, was an emperor lost, and saw Christendom as a temporal as well as a spiritual empire; and John, the most stiff-necked of the princes of Christendom, and the one most likely to see his island kingdom as a secular force with an integrity of its own, stood squarely in his way. In their trial of strength the people of England were the pawns, expendable until the want of them threatened to decide the game.

Isambard talked often of John and of affairs in the world, thinking aloud in front of Harry with a freedom which he felt as a compliment, yet somewhat as a burden, too. Those trenchant monologues, so acidly clear and so unorthodox to come from a man so devout, had opened his eyes to new ideas, and compelled him to look a second time, and more critically, at everything he had been taking for granted. The habit of questioning everything can be dangerous, for sooner or later it will surely bring a man into head-on collision with the unquestionable, and he will not be able in conscience to draw aside.

At the foot of the sloping street the wall shut out the sunlight, and the tunnel of the gateway, between its two towers, was a shaft of golden light piercing the shadowy town like a spear. Harry passed through the gate, and crossed the stone bridge. Beneath him the Severn at its summer level ran quiet and green. He looked back at the buttressed face of the wall and the narrow terraces of the vineyard running down from its foot to the tow-path by the waterside. Had they left Father Hugh his vineyard, or did the king lay claim to that, too?

He looked ahead, and on the other side of the river rose the boundary wall of the abbey grounds, the mill, and the long line of the infirmary roof; and high above that, massive and rosy-grey in the morning light, the silent tower of the church.

They had ridden in from the lead-mines by the Welsh bridge on the far side of the town, so that this was his first sight of the abbey for nine years. He had expected a shock of rediscovery and a surge of memories, for the five years he had spent here seemed now to have been happy and fruitful, and a return after long absence should have moved him deeply; but now that the moment came it astonished him only by its naturalness. It was as if the interval had been no more than a few weeks, and he was returning after a holiday. When he approached the gate-house the shadow of a more piercing memory fell upon him, not of his childish years in this sanctuary, but of the manner of his leaving it.

The fair, dear face swam once again before the eyes of his spirit, half-remembered and soft and sweet in rounded childishness, half-dreamed and remote in daunting womanhood. It had wanted only a glimpse of a little girl by the wayside, or a woman's braided hair, or a child's tossed ball, all the way from London, and she had quickened in him like fire taking hold, and burned unbearably about his heart in a great, sweet pain. At every halting-place on the way he had asked after her, in case someone could call to mind the old journeys with her father, and remember when last she had passed along Watling Street; but no one had been able to give him news of her. He wanted to believe that here there would be a different answer for him, that where he had first found her, failing to recognise gold when he had it in his hands, he would find the way to her again; but now that he set foot in the shadow of the gate-house he was afraid.

He had been so sure that she would be waiting for him in London, that in a world of changes her environment would have stood fast. Even when her cousin's wife had opened the door to him, and husband and wife together had shaken their heads regretfully and answered his questions as best they could, he had scarcely been able to grasp that Nicholas Otley had been two years dead, and Gilleis almost as long withdrawn from London. She had been left well-provided, but had chosen to sell her share in the cloth business to her cousin and attach herself as tirewoman to some noble lady, a wise enough course for a young woman of means left without parents. But with what mistress she had established herself, or in what part of England, they did not know, for she had left London within a few weeks of her father's death, and they had had no word from her since. There had been certain pressing wooers, said the young wife, more pressing still after Nicholas died of his fever and left the girl well-to-do, and that, she thought, was the reason Gilleis had left behind her no word of where she might be found.

He had gone away stunned, telling over the poor facts like beads in his mind, and for a long time unable to grasp their significance. It was the only thing of importance in his life that he had never confided to Adam, and without understanding his own reticence he had been grateful for it. He could not have borne the sharing of this sorrow. So all the way north he had looked for traces of her and failed to find any, and all the way he had ridden in a tension of ardour and despair, delight and despondency, brilliance and blackness, unable to believe that he had lost her, yet day after day refused ground for hope. The world continued beautiful, friendship sweet, the future and the work that waited for him a passion and a wonder. Only she was wanting. The silent anguish she left in her place in his heart was a part of the fury that drove him, a dark source of energy side by side with the bright. But even Adam knew nothing of it.

Edmund came out of the gate-house as Harry entered the courtyard. His shoulders were a little stooped now, and there was more grey in his hair, but otherwise he was hardly changed since the day when he had lifted Adam out of the saddle at these gates, and carried him indoors in his arms. He turned and looked inquiringly at the entering stranger, and at first seemed not to know him, but as Harry drew nearer the peering eyes sharpened and stared hard, and the man's lips opened on a greeting, but hesitated still on the name.

'Say it, Edmund,' said Harry, feeling his heart lift with pleasure and hope at being known. 'You won't be mistaken.'

The porter's face broke into a broad smile of delight.

'Master Talvace! Is it you indeed? After all this time!'

'I would do better to toss my cap in first, maybe,' said Harry, 'and see what sort of a welcome it gets.' And yet he had no qualms now, the sight of an old friend had made all things simple. All things but one! 'And it used to be Harry,' he said, reaching out his hand.

'Ay, so it did, when you were a little, sharp thing no higher than my elbow.' Edmund gripped the offered hand with pleasure. 'But you're come home Master Henry at least, after all your gallivanting about the world. Lad, but it hasn't changed you!'

'Oh, a little, I hope! It was needful! Things are changed here with you, I fear, and not for the better.' He looked about the courtyard, and it was a sad and quiet place compared with its old bustle of life. A groom was bringing two riding horses out of the stable-yard to the guest-house, and a pack-mule belonging to some small merchant stood awaiting his load. The doors of the church were closed, and the lodges and scaffolding all gone, though the work was uncompleted. Building went on leisurely here, and now the interdict had cut off the funds and made progress impossible. Round the almonry a few beggars and cripples crouched, sunning themselves. 'I see you still manage to feed the hungry. But I fear these are hard times for you as for them.'

'Why, we have been lucky compared with most. Shrewsbury was always strong for the king, and has found him a mint of money in its time, for charters and the like, so we got off lightly. All the Abbey lands were turned to the king's profit except the main granges, but we've not been interfered with there, and the mills here keep us heads above water, and a little over to give. It's meant parting with all but a handful of the free men who got their livings here, and it's hard on them. But we shall weather it, we shall weather it. It can't go on for ever.'

'And travellers still come,' said Harry, his eyes on the packman loading his mule.

'We never closed our doors yet. Travellers? It's quiet just now, but sometimes you'd think the whole land was on the move, the roads seethe so with travellers – following the king's example, for, faith, he must know every inch of his own roads by now, he's never still. And the roads of France, too, belike, for indeed he's oftener there than at home, trying to get back his own. And every baron in the realm has half his household out riding courier for news and carrying letters, they're so hot to make alliances and so quick to grow feared of those they have and send out to make more. Harry, lad, there isn't a man here above the hinds who dare trust his neighbour.'

'Edmund!' Harry laid a hand upon his arm. 'You remember when I left here? It's a long time, but you wouldn't forget that. Do you remember a merchant who was here that day, leaving for London with three carts full of bales of cloth? His name was Nicholas Otley. He came every year in the summer, you may have had him here no more than three years ago. Do you mind the man?'

Edmund scrubbed thoughtfully at his chin, narrowing his eyes to stare back through time. 'I mind the day we lost you, well enough – the to-do there was about you, no one could forget it. We ended dragging the pool. Man, I'm right glad we got nothing but fish and weed in the nets! Sir Eudo very nearly had the place down stone from stone after you, and I wouldn't have given much for your skin if he'd found you, abbot or no abbot. But a cloth merchant – and carts – ah, so that was how you got past us, after all! Yes, I call him to mind now. A pretty little lass he had used to ride with him.'

Harry's heart turned in him at the mention of her. 'His daughter,' he said from a dry throat. 'She'll be a young woman grown now. Has she been here in the last year or so, Edmund?'

He held his breath and felt the pain of hope take him by the heart, while Edmund cast his mind back yet again, with maddening deliberation. 'The last time they came must be three summers ago now. I've seen nothing of man or maid since then.'

The fall was harder every time, and yet in his heart he had never expected success. 'You've not been away from your duties sometimes? If she'd been here, you'd surely know of it?'

'I'd know. I know every soul that comes through that gate, and those that come regularly I don't forget, you know that. If she'd been here, I should know it. Are you wishful to find her, then, Harry?'

'I have a debt to her father,' said Harry, turning his head away as he felt the blood mount in his cheeks. 'I looked for him in London and heard he was two years dead. I'd be glad to pay his girl what I owe, if I could light on her.'

'Likely she's wed,' said Edmund comfortably, innocent of the blow he was delivering, 'for I mind me there was a young fellow rode with them the last year or two they came, that seemed to be set on her. And indeed she was a fine lass. Are you for staying with us a day or two, Harry? You'll be more than welcome.'

'No, I must ride on to Parfois. But I must see the abbot, if he has time and will to see me. Will you sound him, and I'll be in having a word with Brother Denis while you go.'

'Brother Denis, is it?' Edmund took him by the arm gently as he would have turned towards the infirmary. 'You'll not find the good old man, Harry, sorry I am to say it. He's five years gone from us.'

'Dead?' He had learned to contain the repeated pain of Gilleis's loss, but this blow, which he had never for a moment foreseen, struck him to the heart. Old men die; there was nothing strange in it. Yet no omen had warned him that Brother Denis was no longer in the world; there should have been something changed in this familiar air, a shade of green lost from the river meadows, some kindly warmth gone out of the sun. Now he could never beg pardon for leaving him without a farewell and with a lie on his lips. He had waited nine years to cleanse his breast of that reproach, and now he was five years too late. 'I left him unkindly, Edmund – like a thief. Did he blame me? I'd rather it had been any man than him I cozened, but I was pressed hard.'

'God love you, lad, you knew him long enough – did he ever blame any child for defending himself as best he could? No more than you'd blame a hunted cat for putting out her claws.'

'Did he speak of us – after we ran?'

'Ay, did he, often enough, and always to wish you well. For weeks after, if it rained hard, he'd say: "I hope the children have a good roof over them tonight." And as late as the winter, every frost would have him worrying if you were clad warmly enough for the weather. It was your father he had trouble forgiving. Never fret about him, he's with the saints, and knows better what ails you than you can ever tell him. He's the most sorely missed man that ever left this house; the boys have a poor time of it without him to shelter them a little when Brother Martin blows north-easterly.'

The memories were coming back on him thick and fast now, crowding in upon him unbearably close. 'See if the abbot will admit me, Edmund,' he said, flinching from too much remembering. 'I'll need to be getting back into the town within the hour.'

'I was for telling you, Harry, if we had not got on to Brother Denis – the abbot's a sick man, and has been since Easter, though we think now he'll mend. Oh, likely enough they'll let you see him, most like he'll want it as soon as he knows you're here. He's clear enough now in the head, but it was a long fever, and he's weak and thin as a stray cat.'

'I'm sorry to hear it,' said Harry. 'If he's allowed visitors I should indeed be glad to see him, if only for a few minutes, but I'll not inflict myself on him unless he's fit for it.'

'Will you come across with me, or shall I look for you again?'

'I'll be in the church,' said Harry, and parted from him so.

He entered the church, as he had left it nine years ago, by the south-west door from the cloisters; all others were closed, and the parochial door locked and barred. The air inside was at once cold and close, and the heavy dimness came down upon his spirit like a threatening cloud. The old oppression of stone and darkness and the chill of the grave made his flesh shrink, even while he acknowledged majesty. He bowed his head before the high altar, and walked round by the ambulatory into the Lady Chapel. The founder's tomb rose like a barricade to block his way, cutting off still more of the precious light. Light, light! How could they bear to seal themselves in from it? How could they teach the soul to soar where there was neither space to unfold a wing nor air to sustain it? He smiled at the old Madonna, blunt-featured and massive, a heavy country-woman, out of fashion now, but dear to him for the many times when she had been his comfortress.

'Holy Virgin, I have brought you your own again. Take him back in your kindness and cherish him. He's no *vagus* at heart, he'll go wandering no more.' He unwrapped the cloth from the roll he carried under his arm, and set the little angel gently in his place on the altar, and the delicate wings stiffened and checked on the heavy air, the thin, frail feet stretched downwards ardently. He lit and hung motionless, quivering with joy, his hands outspread, his gleaming eyes averted from the ruby flame of the lamp. Wherever he went, his hour was eternally fixed in exultant arrival; he knew no separations and no departures.

'Take my thanks,' said Harry to the tired, patient, durable matron of stone, 'for all I have seen and known, and all that I have made and shall make hereafter. In my church you shall have an altar all jubilant with gold and amber light, where you shall see all the colours of the spring and summer, and never be cold.'

Her antique smile embraced him indulgently with the rest of creation, expecting nothing from the promises of children. He said a prayer for the certain and blessed repose of Brother Denis's soul, and then knelt thinking of Gilleis, but did not pray for her. And there Edmund found him when he came from the abbot's lodging.

In the curtained bedchamber a young novice sat reading to the sick man, but he rose when the stranger entered, and silently withdrew, closing the door behind him. Harry went forward and stood beside the great bed, looking down into gaunt eye-sockets in which the sunken eyes burned brilliantly. They searched his face in silence for a long moment, while the grey lips quivered into a faint smile.

'You'll have come for your horses,' said a voice that rustled drily, like the wind in dead leaves. 'The little cob died. You'll have to take one of my horses in his place, or keep back his price.'

Hugh de Lacy's face was a mask of fine, worn bone on the pillow, the parchment skin stretched over it tightly. The hand that lay slack on the covers had the look of alabaster, as though the light could shine through it. Harry had never noticed in the old days what beautiful bones he had; now there was hardly anything of him but bone.

'Sit down, Harry,' sighed the autumnal voice, and the emaciated fingers stirred in a gesture towards the stool the reader had vacated.

Harry remained standing, looking down at him with a still face. He drew out from the purse at his belt a little leather bag, and laid it upon the bed beside the lax hand.

'Eleven shillings and seven pence. And something over for the repair of your almsboxes. You will find the amount right, but if you would like someone to check it I can call your lector back again. Let us call the cob's price an alms to the abbey. I have no doubt he was well looked after.'

The smiling mouth tightened painfully, but he received the check without complaint. In a moment he said: 'Or we might devote it to candles for your father's soul. The Mass, of course, is out of our power.'

'My father's soul!' said Harry slowly, and drew off from the bed a little. Father Hugh had taken it for granted that he came from Sleapford; so had Edmund, or he would have told him of the old man's death directly. It must be ancient news, or they would in any case have been quick to offer him condolences as soon as he appeared. So Sir Eudo was gone to his fathers, was he? And Sir Ebrard Talvace was lord of Sleapford in his room.

No doubt it ought to move him, but he contemplated it and felt nothing, neither satisfaction nor sorrow. Old men die, Brother Denises and Sir Eudos alike, it's the common lot of man. He bore no grudges now against his family, and certainly had never wished his father ill. For nine years he had scarcely given him a thought, either vengeful or affectionate. This death seemed now so far distant from him as to be meaningless. When it came to absolute honesty, his father and he had never in their lives been within hailing distance of each other.

'As you will,' he said. 'It would be better spent on the living, to my mind, but your candles won't hurt the old man's soul, if they don't help it.' The words had a more churlish sound than he had intended, but he stiffened at the idea of feigning a grief he did not feel. 'I have put the angel back in his place, too,' he said.

'Ah, the angel! I've missed him, Harry.' Hugh de Lacy moved his hand upon the bed, as though he would have stretched it out to the young man, but his fingers touched the bag of money, and he drew them back with a momentary frown. 'Sit down with me,' he said again in a low voice. 'I ask it of your courtesy. They tell me it is only weakness, but I don't see as clearly as I used to. I cannot talk to you as to an oracle in a cloud.'

Harry drew the stool close and seated himself, flushing a little. Were the hollow eyes too weak to see the colour mount in his face?

'And how is your brother?' asked the abbot.

How often in the old days, thought Harry, I fell into this trap through not looking where I was going. It irritated him, I remember. Now I know where I am going, and I am going straight, not roundabout.

'I thank you, my brother still has both hands.' And after a moment he added mercilessly: 'I have not brought him inside your walls this time. I thought it best not to tempt your conscience a second time – he could still not prove free residence of a year and a day in any English borough, and I remember your devotion to the niceties of law, Father.'

The corners of the bluish lips drew inward sharply. The face could grow no paler. Motionless in its stony beauty, too drawn to reflect in any tremor or change the moving of the mind within, it stared upwards at the ceiling for a long time. At last he said, so low that Harry had to stoop his head to hear: 'Can you not forgive whatever wrong we did you, all those years ago?'

'I can forgive,' said Harry, 'for what it's worth, because I no longer need anything from you.'

'Nor from God?' asked the abbot.

'That is between God and me.'

He waited, watching the edge of sunlight creep towards the bed. The silence drew out into a fine-spun thread, like floating gossamer, drifting without tension. He looked again at the man in the bed, and now the transparent blue eyelids were closed, and remained closed, and the face was so still and remote that he thought the abbot had relapsed into a half-sleep. Silently he rose from his place and crossed slowly to the door. There was nothing more for him to do here. He had presented himself and paid his debt, and the debt to him had been acknowledged; what more did he want?

His hand was on the latch of the door when he heard the sick man draw breath in a rending sob, as quickly and fiercely suppressed. It pierced the shell of ice about his heart like a flame, and the molten heat of remorse and tenderness flooded him. He turned and flew to the bedside, falling on his knees and flinging an arm across the abbot's body. He laid his cheek against the bony hand, and then his lips.

'Father, forgive me, forgive me! I had nothing to ask pardon for until now! Arrogant and presumptuous as I am, why should you grieve over me? I never meant to hurt you so.' He caught himself up passionately: 'Yes! Yes, I did! I did mean to hurt you, I came to hurt you. God forgive me for it!'

The long body, all fallen away to bone, was so insubstantial in his arm that he was afraid to let the slightest weight lie upon it. The ashen mask, broken and contorted for a moment, relaxed into a smiling weariness, and was still. The abbot opened his eyes upon the young, bright face, wild with shame and self-reproach and tenderness. Now indeed he recognised Harry. He had not meant to call him back with pity, yet it was apt enough. Arrogant he was, a very tower of arrogance against every force that opposed itself to him, but one touch of the finger of weakness or suffering could bring him to his knees in a frenzied humility as passionate as the pride that engendered it.

'Even now I am doing you harm,' said Harry remorsefully. 'You should have quietness and peace, and I've left you none. I'll go, and trouble you no more. Only say that you forgive me my hardness of heart, for indeed I'm sorry and ashamed. I didn't even know I was nursing a grudge all this time. It was easy to forgive those from whom I hoped for nothing, but I put such reliance in you!'

'And I did not mean to fail you,' said Hugh de Lacy sadly, 'but it is done, and cannot be undone.' His thin hand, weightless as a withered leaf, rested on Harry's brown head. His voice, eased of its brittle dryness, said gently: 'I forgive, and do you forgive me, child. My blessing you had with you always. How happy I am to have my peace made with you, and part in kindness, since it may be for the last time.'

Harry smiled at him, bending low to the strengthless embrace. 'No, Father, you'll live and rule many years yet. You'll maybe see me into my grave before you.'

'God forbid, Harry! Sit with me a little while, I'll not hold you long, I soon tire. Tell me how you have fared since the day we lost you, for many a time I have thought of you, and found no comfort.'

'Yet, Father, perhaps all was well done, to take me out of a life in which I was unprofitable, and set me on a fruitful path. For I have made offerings of beauty and splendour to God with my own hands, and shall yet make more and better.'

He sat beside the bed, holding the wisp of a hand, and talking of Caen and of Paris, of St Étienne and of Notre Dame, until the dim blue eyelids closed again tranquilly over the assuaged eyes. The knife-sharp outlines of the face had softened, the parchment skin had regained a faint tinge of colour and freshness. And it seemed to him that there was some wound within himself which had healed miraculously when the abbot embraced him, and that the deep scar-tissue was growing lissome and smooth again with every easy breath the sick man drew. He kissed the dry forehead very softly, and went out from him on tiptoe.

Only when he was striding back through the town gate did it occur to him that he had forgotten to collect his horse, but he did not turn back; it was not for the horse he had come.

They came to the crest in the green track at sunset, and rounding the flank of the wood saw from the shoulder of the rolling ridge the river valley beneath them on the left, and before them, overhanging the slope, the sandstone outcrop, seamed with broken folds and shelves in which trees had rooted and grown; and on the summit of the rock, Parfois.

The level site that crowned the hill was not so great that the ambition of the Isambards could not encompass the whole of it. The curtain wall, overtopping the trees and rising sheer out of the stone on which it stood, wound round the hill-top like an enfolding serpent, six towers projecting their rounded sides so that there should be no foothold, even for a raven, that could not be brought under cross-fire. Within the walls the great hexagonal keep, with its three projecting turrets, caught the last rays of the sun and burned into a rose-red glow; the shadows from the valley, heather-purple, were climbing the shelves of rock hand over hand, and groping at the roots of the outer towers.

Three miles away beyond the river Wales slept in shade, only a distant hill-top here and there still golden. Half a dozen villages, down there in the valley, lived their lives perpetually in the darker shadow of that massy pile above them, their shelter and their burden. A dozen more in the folds of the hills on the English side of the castle hid in its lee from the encroachments of the Welsh, but feared their protector scarcely less than their enemies.

The shadow climbed, darkening as it mounted, engulfing one by one the arrow-slits in the rounded towers. The turrets burned like tall candle-flames. Behind the glowing machicolations of the keep the evening sky was a clear bluish-green, the colour of the eyes that stared so eagerly and so warily upon the castle of Parfois from the turn of the road.

The pyramid of the hill and its coronal of stone, shapely and secure, tapered into a burning apex of rosy light, no longer even a beacon lit on the earth, but a star suspended in the pure green heaven. Before they reached it all would be shadow. Already all was silence.

The track wound along the shoulder of the ridge, and then, curving to the right, began to climb the hill by the one easy approach. As they drew nearer to the walls, the keep vanished from their sight, and after it, on both sides, the towers withdrew sidelong out of range, and left them only the upper stages of the gate-house with its turrets. Halfway up the ramp trees closed in upon the track, and suddenly there was no castle, but only a dark woodland about them. Then they emerged again into open planes of grass, and the two outer guard towers came into sight, one on either side the way. The ramp broadened and levelled into a lofty field, a green island in air, for the broken formation of the outcrop severed it from the ground on which the castle itself stood by a fissure forty feet deep. On the far side rose the gate-house with its towers, the drawbridge down, the portcullis raised on the dark archway into the outer ward.

Harry halted on the edge of the green plateau. The track crossed it directly to the bridge, and on either side the rough grass stretched, a neutral grey now in the dusk. On the left lay the greater space, and here he saw dimly spread before him, visible by its own mysterious lambent light, the half-cleared rectangle of rock where three master-masons before him had begun to build. Beyond it confused and shapeless pallors marked where heaps of the old materials lay, and already Isambard's carpenters had thrown up lodges for the new masons soon to assemble here. The evidence of activity moved and excited him, but it was not at these he looked. The uncovered rock, a plan drawn deep through the grass and bushes and soil, held his eyes.

A noble space, and a marvellous setting. The faint luminosity of the rock, the harvest of the day's stored sunlight, seemed to float a foot or two in air over the place, as though the walls had already begun to rise. The north face would be presented to view from the castle, the south from the climbing track. He must consider the whole group, castle and church together, the counterpoise between them here, the unity they would present to those who looked up at them from the valleys on either side, the greater valley of the Severn to the west, the shallow, enclosed valley of the brook to the east. Building is sculpture on a grand scale. A building is as many-sided, as versatile, as complex as a man; it must be as whole and as well integrated as a man, and have regard to its neighbours.

He sat his horse, staring before him in the fading light, and the great reverence he had for form and proportion and the courtesy of shape to shape, his passion for stability and beauty and reticence and harmony, encompassed and transcended the castle and the rock, reached out to the hills of England on one side and the hills of Wales on the other, and found no enmity between them, passed beyond to the horizon, drawn in greenish golden after-light, and the vast profound of the sky, with its faint embroidery of stars. He saw the walls of his church take shape and stand erect towards those hesitant stars, and the tall central tower rear itself high and draw taut, like a worshipping man with his raised forehead tranquil in the radiance of grace. It seemed to him that in order to make it what he wanted it to be, he would have to stretch out the fingers of his senses and the cords of his compassion to the last reaches of the world, and relate every stone of his work to all that moved and breathed and hoped and loved, everything that had form or intelligence. Only so could it be perfect.

That was out of any man's reach. Yet it seemed to him then that he dared hope for it, and that as long as he had the hope he did not need the achievement.

'Let's get in,' said Adam, yawning as his horse stirred restively on the edge of the track, 'or they'll be raising the bridge on us. I don't know about you, but I'm more than ready to do right by my supper.'

Harry turned from his moment of prophecy with a laugh, and they rode forward across the drawbridge and into Parfois.

In this teeming household, where he kept the state of an early palatine, for ever hemmed about with squires and stewards and knights in attendance, and pages and musicians and a multitude of other hangers-on, Isambard yet contrived to live as solitary as a recluse. The great hall that clung to the curtain wall in the angle of the King's Tower was as populous and busy as any market-place, and he conducted the greater part of his day's business there and regularly dined there like any of his peers, presiding over an assembly which sometimes numbered as many as a thousand. But when he withdrew from them into the private part of his life there was not one of them who would have dared to intrude upon him, and not one who would have felt he could follow him there without intrusion. He had trusted servants, but no trusted friends; and that surely not out of fear, like his master the king, who collected family hostages about him as a miser collects money, but out of the long experience he had of disillusionment and disappointment, he who always asked too much.

He had made good use of the situation of Parfois by setting up his private apartments in the Lady's Tower, which overhung the sheerest face of rock and could never come under fire from any point or eminence outside the castle. The narrow shot-windows gave place here to generous lancets, and the heavy gloom within to plentiful air and light. Tapestries draped the stony walls, and the rugs and furs he had brought back from the East with him covered the cold, uneven floors. There he had installed Madonna Benedetta in semi-royal state. But it was a rare occurrence for any other to ask for audience there; and that he should be admitted was an earnest of extraordinary favour. Plainly this master-mason was a man to watch, if he did not over-play his hand.

'I ask your pardon, my lord,' said Harry, striding into the candle-lit tower room with a high colour and brilliant eyes, 'for interrupting you like this at so late an hour, but this is a matter of some importance. Since supper I have been going through the rolls with your man Richard Knollys, the first opportunity we've had. He is an admirable clerk and a good organiser, and I'm grateful for the work he has done for me here in preparation for my coming. But we are at odds on certain points, and I am obliged to confirm with you at once that there is only one master of the works here, and that is myself. If Knollys will work with me as clerk and executive, well and good, but we shall get nowhere if he is to consider himself joint-master with me.'

Isambard turned his chair aside from the chessboard at which he sat with Benedetta. Her hair was loosed from its coils, and hung to her waist in a thick, silken curtain of dusky red. She had a massive repose about her, as though she were so perfectly and so indisputably mistress of Parfois that her position held neither novelty nor gratification for her. She looked, thought Harry, like a wife, and a noble wife at that; and like a noble wife she made no move to withdraw from her husband's councils, but listened alertly and gravely to what passed, and held herself ready to give an opinion if it should be asked, and until then to remain intelligently silent.

And any man who had such a wife would be quick to make use of her wit, too, if he were not himself a fool.

'I had no intention of infringing your authority,' said Isambard somewhat drily, 'and I thought I had made his position clear. He is the most efficient assistant I could give you, but the responsibility for the works is yours. Why, what's amiss between you?'

'My lord, I find that several of the carpenters and masons he has assembled for me are pressed men, some of them brought from as far away as Somerset. Three of them are now imprisoned here for trying to run home. My lord, aside from my own views, surely no one but the king's own purveyor has the right to press men for his works?'

'You're over-hasty with your surelies,' said Isambard, 'for I enjoy the same right, granted me by the king himself. Within my honour I can hale a craftsman from one end of England to the other if I will, so he be not already engaged upon the king's works. It used to be "or the works of the Church",' he added with his crooked smile, 'but there's a new dispensation since king and Church fell out. And I can imprison fugitives, too, Harry, and turn them out to work in irons if I please, to keep them from running again. This I knew. Knollys has my sanction.'

'He has not mine, my lord.' The tone, though he had not intended it, had an arrogance which brought Isambard's head up with a jerk, and caused him to draw his brows together in an ominous frown. 'My lord, the right in law I don't dispute, though indeed I did not know of it until now. But for my part, I'll have no pressed men working under me. I think it beneath God's dignity to get his house built by aggrieved souls who hate what they do. A man should be able to sell his labour where he will.'

'You intend to teach God his duty, as well as me?' asked Isambard in a steely voice, and spread and closed his hands on the arms of his chair as on the hilts of daggers.

'I intend to make sure I can do my own duty, nothing more. I am here to build you a church, the best I have in me. I must protect my work from influences which would deface it. I'll have no forced men. It is not worthy of you nor of me, nor of the work we are about, to compel unwilling service.'

'You are employed to build,' said Isambard, suddenly on his feet. 'Stick to your banker, and do not meddle with what does not concern you.'

'This does concern me. Neither you nor I can get good work out of pressed men. You promised me a free hand in this enterprise, my lord, and I hold you to your bargain!'

They had both raised their voices, the high words clashed in their mouths with the very same sound, and the light eyes and the dark flashed with equal anger.

'Moreover,' said Harry, plunging precipitately on, 'there is something I like even less than this. I find we are carrying daily a separate roll of some hundred labourers on the site who do not appear among our expenses at all, apart from the cost of their food. Knolly says he had your authority to exact from your villeins two days of extra labour every week for the clearing of the site, and from time to time for fetching and carrying and unskilled work afterwards. I could not believe you ever gave him any such leave, and I am come to you to confirm or deny it.'

'I did give it. I maintain it. What offends your tender conscience in that? Is it beneath your dignity to have unfree hands carry away the soil from your site?'

'So far from it, my lord, that all I want from you is your leave to make no distinctions between free and unfree here. I'll welcome every man of them, so he come of his own will. But to take from them two full days of labour now, when the harvest will be coming on, is to take their livelihood from them. You must know, my lord, that the times come down hard enough on them already. Four days on your harvests and two on your church, and when are they to reap their own fields? At night? Even if there are two or three grown sons in a household, there's work for every one of them, and a small enough return. If they give their time to you, they deserve to be paid for it.'

'Paid? My villeins paid for their services?' He threw back his head and laughed, full and honestly, but still with rage in the laughter. 'Harry Lestrange, you are here to build a new church, not a new world. Be wise, and stick to your chisels and punches, and let my dispositions for my people alone. If you turn hedge-priest you'll come by a hedge-priest's end, and that would be a pity, for you're an able young man in your own line. I like you, Harry, but I'm the master of my own estates, and you had better not tell me too often what I may and what I may not do with my own. I am not always in so patient a mood as tonight.' He turned away suddenly to the table by the wall and poured wine, shrugging off the annoyance with a toss of his shoulders. 'Now abate your fine ardours for an hour or two, and put down a few quick cups of this, and you'll take yourself less seriously. You were not so tedious when I found you in the provost's prison.'

He turned, laughing, to offer the cup, and was amazed and affronted to see how Harry's face had flamed to the forehead, and how the flesh round mouth and nostrils had whitened in the red.

'It was not necessary, my lord, to remind me of your favours. I am conscious of them. It is my intention to repay the debt.'

'God's life, boy,' flashed Isambard, raging again, 'I meant no such reminder. On my soul, only princes can afford a pride like yours.'

There was a moment of thunderous silence, while they stared upon each other bitterly, like enemies feeling for a killing hold. Then, with a large, languid movement of hand and arm Benedetta smothered a yawn, and swept her fingers through the tension as through a cobweb.

'I'm sorry,' said Harry, low-voiced, 'it was ill done to attribute to you any want of generosity. I know you have never sought any recognition of your kindness to me. Yet I feel my indebtedness, and for my own peace I long to discharge it honestly.' His face was pale now, and his lips no longer pinched with anger. 'As you found it possible to trust in my ability to do your work, now I ask you to trust in my judgement as to the methods I use.'

'We are not talking of building methods, but of administration. Build as you please, but don't meddle with other matters.'

'I hold that it is a part of my responsibility, and I have already meddled. I had better tell you what I have done, and then you may tell me if our contract still holds good. It will never be broken by me. I have freed the three men who were imprisoned, and told all the pressed men that they are at liberty to enrol with me or go home, as they choose, and that if they decide to go – as certainly some who are married will do, but I think not a great number – they shall have journey money for the road back. And I have countermanded the order to your villeins, and let them know instead that any among them who willingly enrol with me for day-labour will be paid the same rates as the free man who are unskilled. True,' he said deliberately, staring full into the deep eyes that blazed at him across the forgotten wine-cup, 'I have not the money to make either promise good, unless you grant it to me. But that is for you to decide. If I am the master of your works, as you swore to me I should be, then you will endorse the measures I have taken and give me means to honour my promises. And if you override my decisions, then I am manifestly without authority, and no longer the master of your works. You promised me a free hand and all the resources I need. I am asking you to honour your promises, as I intend to honour mine.'

He was within an ace of getting the wine in his face, and most likely the cup after it. He saw the lean brown fingers tighten with deliberation on the stem of the goblet, and the hot red-brown eyes narrow calculatingly on him, debating the manner and measure of the blow and taking pleasure in it before it fell. Benedetta, watching them attentively across the room from the sheltering shadow of her hair, put a hand to the corner of the chess-board; but she found something in Isambard's face that caused her to sit back again and let the moment pass.

The hand that held the cup had relaxed. Harry stood motionless, never taking his eyes from his lord's face, until the flash of Isambard's rings in the light drew his eyes down.

'You had better drink it, after all,' said Isambard with the grimmest of smiles, 'it will do you more good inside than out. Here, let me pledge you! At least you have more heart in you than most of the fellows I maintain about me. Either that, or you are a plain fool, which I cannot believe. Take it, I say! I seldom play the page to any man, make the most of it. You might well be easier to live with, drunk,' he said, turning sharply away. His winged shadow swept across the floor. His hand, as he passed by, touched with a flying caress the smooth curve of Benedetta's shoulder. 'Harry,' he said peremptorily, turning again in mid-stride, 'I do not like having my hand forced. I advise you not to try this strategy again. You have left me no choice but between two extremes. There's nothing to be done with you but toss you into one of the cells under the Warden's Tower and undo everything you have done, or else lend my countenance to all and confirm you in your office. And, by God, I'm sorely tempted to take the first course, but that I should not savour even a masterpiece from the hands of a broken man.'

'You would not get one,' said Harry. He was glad of the wine, it had warmed the ominous chill out of him. 'I do truly believe, my lord, that only free men and willing can create masterpieces. And indeed, in this at least you do me wrong. I did not act first and ask afterwards to present you with an enforced choice. I acted because I believed I had your full authority to act. I am come to you now only because Knollys, in duty to you, I grant him, questioned that authority.'

'He will not question it again. I will not shame you before your workmen. Very well, let it be as you have ordained. But mark me, do not try me too far. Keep to your province, and trespass no further on mine.'

'My lord, I thank you.' He would not say more. What had he to be grateful for? This was no more than keeping to a bargain.

'In the morning I will speak to Knollys. Leave us now.'

'Goodnight, my lord! Madonna Benedetta, goodnight!'

He caught one flash of her eyes as he went out, and saw a salute and a smile there, the rueful, amused smile she had turned on him over John the Fletcher's bowed shoulders, that day of their departure from Paris. 'We strike these attitudes,' he heard her sigh, 'almost by chance.' Almost, but never quite. She, who knew all about the compulsions of her own nature, could not be astonished by any freak to which his might drive him.

He went out comforted beyond reason. Adam would have backed him cheerfully and wholeheartedly in any undertaking, however outrageous, but without bothering to understand why he acted as he did. She had done no more than slide the chess-board a few inches nearer the edge of the table, ready to overturn it if a diversion became necessary; but it had been enough to show that she understood everything. He was glad that she had been there. He was glad, wonderfully glad, that she had come with them to Parfois.

They made good use of the summer weather, and there was villein labour in plenty, once word had gone round that it was to be paid like the labour of free men and not exacted as manor dues. The site was completely cleared and levelled in a few weeks, since only a scattered, thin grass and a few starveling weeds had been able to find a foothold in the stripped rock, and the setting out of the plan showed that very little extra levelling required to be done. By the time Isambard rode to court at Woodstock in September the footing of the walls and the piers was laid, and the mason-hewers were hard at work at the bankers, and the setters already about the first courses of stonework for the walls. The carpenters were assembling poles and putlogs and hurdles and leather thongs for the scaffolding which would not be needed until the following spring. The master-carpenter, who had once been an assistant at Shrewsbury under Master Robert, was beginning the construction of centring for the great west window and the portal. And there were still six or seven weeks to run, with luck, before the onset of frosts would cause the setters to be laid off for the winter, and the rising walls would be bedded down warmly in heath and bracken.

Harry would have preferred to retain his team through the winter, but for this year that was impossible, since there was no indoor work for the setters. By next winter, if all went well, he would have a part of the fabric under cover, and keep his men on. Security and contentment made for sound work and rapid progress, in his experience. It had given him pleasure that more than half of the pressed men, once released to a free choice, had elected to stay with him.

Word of his straight dealings went round almost too successfully at first. Some of the brightest opportunists in the villages about the Long Mountain took this young master to be a simpleton, and came to hire their labour to him in the expectation of a soft living. Two kindred spirits with an empty hand-barrow between them could put up a very plausible appearance of zealous activity without any great expenditure in actual effort. Unfortunately for them the youngster turned out to have had experience with hard cases. They were marked down within a couple of days; those who were judged to be profitless were flung out without ceremony, and the few who seemed to be merely chancing their arm were picked out and set to work directly under Adam's eye, and kept hard at it until they had sweated out what they owed, with interest. Those who took exception to this treatment took themselves off in haste and were considered well lost; but there were a few who stuck it out in sheer obstinacy. determined to show they could do all and more than was demanded of them if they chose, and these Harry held to be worth the effort. When the driving stopped, they went on working; and they bore him no grudge for being their match, rather they liked him the better for it.

A few came who caused him more trouble. There were two big, bearded, weatherbeaten fellows whose looks he did not like, but he took them on as labourers none the less, and only at the end of the day had them stopped as they would have left the site, and found them swathed in cords and leather thongs from his stores. It seemed an insignificant haul for which to risk their lives, if they were what he deemed them to be, masterless men living wild in the forest. After some thought he made a search under the sheer edges of the plateau in the most secluded places, and found they had dropped a quantity of timber into the grass of a dingle on the English side, whence it could well be fetched away by night.

He turned them over to Sir Peter FitzJohn, Isambard's castellan, and before many hours wished he had not; for one of the two, recognised as a footpad who had preyed on travellers along the Roman road for two years and more, was hanged next day, and the other, almost certainly of his company, fared no better, for when he tried to break out of hold they loosed Isambard's Arabian hound on him, and with speed and efficiency it ran him down and tore out his throat.

Harry saw the beast come padding back docilely when the Greek called him off, leaving the carcase without reluctance, having done only what he had been trained to do. The tawny breast was streaked with blood, the beautiful, rippling body moved proudly and gaily, glossy with virtue. Harry felt the heat and filth of the blood sticking to his hands, and he had not the dog's appalling innocence to cleanse him.

'What are you fretting about?' said Adam impatiently. 'They were thieves, manifestly, and highway robbers by all accounts. What the devil else could you do with them but turn them over to the law?'

In spite of these endless echoes of law which left him so uneasy, Harry could not but agree with that. 'But what else could they do but steal for a living?' he said wretchedly. 'The big fellow was a smith in some village near Caus, they say, until he was laid up with a broken leg, and Corbett distrained on him. And the other was a runaway villein, and most likely with good enough reason to run, too.'

'I should be the last man in the world to question that,' said Adam wryly, 'but do me this justice, at least I never took to robbery and murder for a living, and he was not forced to do so, neither.'

Harry owned he was right, but could not feel happy about his part in the affair. And when, somewhat later, he caught the boy who clerked for him in his tracing-house abstracting cleaned parchments and chalks and other trifles for his own use, the first thing he did was to bar the door against any intruder, so that no one else should get wind of it. He could not let it pass, but he took care the law should have no part in it this time, and all the boy got for his pilfering was a half-hearted beating that fetched no tears, and a talking-to that provoked a cloudburst. It ended with his bringing some of his own tentative drawings to Harry, who commented on them with hard criticism and sparing praise, but showed him how to better them, and gave him all the materials he needed to continue his attempts, so that he no longer had any occasion to steal what he could have for the asking. The devoted shadow for ever under Harry's feet became a joke with Adam, but even Adam was never let into the cream of the joke.

That autumn the stone convoys from the quarry in the hills of Bryn came under their first attack from Wales. There was a mile or more to haul the stone down to the River Tanat, and then it was brought in boats down Tanat and Vrnwy and up the Severn, to a temporary quay in the meadows under the ridge of the Long Mountain. The haul of nearly two miles thence up to Parfois was a steep and hard one, but well protected. The trip by water was safe enough and cheap, though in spring, during the floods, they might have trouble. But the vulnerable part of the journey was the first mile to the Tanat, up there in the hills within a stone-throw of Wales, with nothing but the brook Cynllaith to fend off the tribesmen.

For a year now the prince of Powis had been kicking his heels as John's prisoner and living on John's sufferance, but for one incalculable neighbour they had gained another even more to be feared, for Llewellyn had swooped down like one of his own falcons from the peaks of Eryri as soon as Gwenwynwyn was under lock and key, and possessed himself of Powis to add to his northern stronghold of Gwynedd. It would be a marvel if he did not begin to style himself Prince of Wales soon. The unity of his country was clearly his ambition. And given the generous effort of the imagination to feel oneself Welsh instead of English, who could blame him?

He was, however, which was more to the point, at sworn odds with Isambard, and any baiting of his enemy which might be undertaken for sport by the hillmen of Cynllaith would certainly not be displeasing to their prince.

A messenger rode in from the quarry on a blown and foundering horse, with the news that raiders had come down on the wagons half a mile from the Tanat, killed two of the teamsters and scattered the rest, and dumped the loaded stone along the wayside, retiring with the oxen and the wagons. The teams were hired, and there would be compensation to pay, as well as an allowance to the widows of the men who had died. They could not afford constant repetitions of this expenditure in money; and men Harry never held to be expendable, on any terms. He flew to take counsel with

FitzJohn, and laid down his demands as briskly as any general planning a campaign.

A company of archers and one of men-at-arms must be stationed permanently at the quarry; it was less open to attack than the wagons in transit, but it was the next idea that would occur to the playful Welshmen. An armed escort must convoy every wagon that passed down to the river, and a small guard must be posted at the place of loading. When the hard frosts began they could draw off all, and still have enough stone in store to work through the winter.

Harry rode for the quarry that same night with a small group of archers and men-at-arms, leaving the main body to follow next day. He was uneasy until he had satisfied himself that no full attack on the quarry itself was planned. However, he found the place quiet as a churchyard, and the quarrymen roused and mounting guard. With the first light he rode over the approaches with William of Beistan, who had charge of the camp, and marked out the best spots to post sentries on the Welsh side, so that the quarry should never be taken by surprise. When the armed companies rode in, about noon, he turned them over to William, and having slept for a couple of hours with the aplomb of a tired puppy, woke no less refreshed, and with three companions convoyed the two dead teamsters sombrely back to Parfois.

One of the dead was a man of forty-two and the father of a family; the other was a young fellow of twenty. Harry went to see the widow and the parents, and slashed out of the building funds a sum of money in gift to them which would almost certainly be questioned by Knollys when they went through the rolls together. There was nothing more he could do, except give them the bodies for burial, and that must be burial without rites. These two had even died unshriven. He rode back up the ridge from the widow's poor hovel with a heavy heart. But at least he'd lose no more men to Welsh arrows if he could help it.

A week later word came that a second tentative attack had been beaten off without loss to the English, and though the raiders had carried away their three wounded successfully, one at least of them was thought to be mortally hurt.

'Well done!' said Isambard. 'But I would it were Gwynedd himself!'

Harry wanted neither Welsh nor English dead, but if they came baiting Isambard out of wantonness with little to gain, they could hardly complain of their reception. No doubt in time they would learn to let well alone.

'What fashion of man is this Prince of Gwynedd?' asked Harry, his charcoal sweeping down the long, beautiful line that outlined her cheek and neck and shoulder. 'Did you see him in Woodstock?'

'I saw him. Not at court, even Ralf would hesitate to present his mistress to his king,' said Benedetta, with the candour which no longer disconcerted him. 'I saw them meet in the street once and ride by each other, neither giving way. There was no more than a few inches clearance between their knees as they passed, but they would not rein aside. He has a quick, warm way with him, fierce but gay. He looked at us, and looked curiously, and I think would have spoken, but my lord looked through him as though he had not been there. And once I saw him walking in the garden with his princess on his arm.'

'And is he indeed the devil?'

'Only to an Englishman,' said Benedetta. 'To my alien eyes he is a goodly man. Uncommon tall for a Welshman, as tall as my lord and very dark. He shaves his cheeks and chin, but wears long, soft moustaches. He is all shadow and light, the lines of him are cut so deep. I found it a strong and clever face. But for all its boldness, too good-humoured to belong to a devil. Did you never see him, then? They say he has often met the king in Shrewsbury.'

'I've lived all my boyhood on earth that trembled when he stamped his foot, but never set eyes on him. My lord has had manors burned and garrisons killed by more than one honest enemy in his time; why is he so set against this one rather than the rest?'

She considered that thoughtfully for a while, sitting perfectly still as he had posed her, her head thrown back against the high back of the chair. The grey wintry light filtering in through the tracing-house windows, a dead, still, January light that would not last two hours past noon, burned into living warmth in the sheaves of her red hair, that grew from her temples with an upward curve like the curl of a wave.

'I think it is chiefly that he recognises a man who in more than stature is as large as himself. They are not so common, Harry. When he encounters one he cannot be indifferent. He might love, he might hate, but he could not be indifferent. And a little thing then is enough to decide between hate and love. Once in,' she said, turning her head suddenly to look directly into Harry's eyes, 'you know he knows no half measures. He both loves and hates to the death – his death or the other's. He has told the king to his face that he'll come no more to court while the Prince of Gwynedd is made welcome there.'

'Is Llewellyn such another, do you think?'

'Ah, Llewellyn is a man with a cause. He is safe from hates, I judge, for he has an overmastering love. I think he is no more aware of my lord than of any other peer of his who stands between him and the unity of Wales, or advances a foot across the border of her liberty. I think he is the most single-minded man I ever saw. Ralf would sacrifice his life, perhaps, for a cause, but nothing that touched him more nearly.' She smiled at the paradox, but let it stand. 'Not his faith and truth, not his pride. If John's life hung on Ralf's breaking his word, John would surely die. If Ralf could make England safe for ever by kissing King Philip's shoe, England would have to go in peril still. But – '

'But at Woodstock,' Harry took up gravely, 'Llewellyn knelt with the other Welsh princes and did homage to King John for his princedom.'

'That is something I am glad I did not have to see,' she said. 'And yet I dare swear that when he knelt to John and put his hands between John's hands, he never lost a whit of his dignity, nor the devotion of one clansman who looks to him as his prince. It seems to me, Harry, that sometimes honour may depend on abasing oneself rather than on guarding one's self-esteem, and faith on breaking one's word rather than on keeping it.'

'Not to me,' said Harry, curling his lip.

'No, I never supposed it would to you,' she conceded, smiling. 'You are utterly of Ralf's breed, I know it.'

'And you would not lie, nor break faith, nor humble yourself, either,' he said forcefully, his eyes flashing between his drawing-board and her face in fiery, absorbed glances. 'Not for any cause.'

'Would I not?' said Benedetta mildly.

'No more than I would. And as for the Prince of Gwynedd, he is in good odour with the king, and for my part I think he swore fealty in all good faith, and it will not be broken unless this goodwill between them is clean broken, too. It is not the first time the Welsh princes have done homage to the king of England. And he fought for him honestly against the Scots in the summer. After all, he is married to the king's daughter.'

'He is. Of all the women in this land, I think she has the most difficult part. If she were not his match I should pity her, but being the woman she is I think she needs no pity. Balancing such a father and such a husband, loving both, preserving either from the enmity of the other, that's no life for any but the greatest of women. Do you suppose she has not abased herself a hundred times, to John for Llewellyn, to Llewellyn for John? Do you suppose she has not lied and deceived to keep them from each other's throats? The pride of women must be a different kind of pride,' she said, and shivered a little, for in the tracing-house in the outer ward it was very cold, and she had been sitting still for him until she was chilled even in her furs.

'And their honesty another kind of honesty?' Harry laid down his charcoal, and stood back from his work. 'Come and see! Ah, you're cold to the bone! I'm sorry, I did not think. When I'm drawing I forget everything.' He had taken her hand with perfect simplicity, and stood chafing it between his palms. She drew it away only to take up the parchment and look at it more closely.

It was the design for a capital, not a portrait. Out of the neck-moulding the long line of her stretched throat grew like a lily-stem whitening into the flower, and her face, simplified and yet most vividly her face still, looked up into the sun from between the up-lifted wings of her hair. The blown locks, coiling and twining, held up the abacus as the strong jet of a fountain holds up a rose-leaf.

'It's beautiful,' she said, 'and I am proud. You must have a hundred such drawn out ready for the stone by now, I've seen you at it day after day since you put the walls into their winter sleep. But you'll have to trust many of them to other hands to carve. Are you not afraid they'll spoil your work?'

'I shall do the marking-out for them all, and see that they're properly executed. And all the piers of the nave I shall keep for myself.' He could not have borne to part with any one of them. He saw an aisle in a stone forest, with every slender tree bursting into matched bud.

'Will you show me your designs?' said Benedetta, turning on him shining eyes, in which the reflection of his own inward excitement burned generously.

He opened the chest gladly, and spread them on his tracing-tables for her to see, drawing after drawing; the bay designs of nave and choir and transepts, the plan of the nave vault, where all the sixfold buds of the holy forest burst at last into slender sevenfold branches, sealed together by a roof-rib, and knotted with clusters of starry flowers; drawings of the many separate mouldings for the west doorway and the great window above, with its multiple lancets and tracery of roses, of the elevation of the tower, tapered very subtly stage by stage and elegantly elongated by delicate free shafts, so that at any hour of day it would stand outlined in fine vertical lights and shadows.

'I have heard,' said Benedetta, 'that towers must be built by easy stages, not more than perhaps fifteen feet in a year, to allow for some degree of settling. Is it true?'

'It is, and you are always astonishing me by the things you know,' he said, smiling; 'but here we are on solid rock and could not be better founded, and I shall be able to build faster. And these, look, these are what I am hoarding up for myself. No one else shall touch them, except perhaps Adam. No, not even Adam! I can't give them up.'

His hands moved with love even on the drawings, he flushed like an eager child showing his treasures; and without words she was suddenly aware that she was honoured with a gift beyond price to her, though he laid it in her breast unawares.

The capitals of the nave, six to a pier, he set out before her one by one, tenderly and reverently. She saw everything that had breath praising God, her own wrists and hands reaching up to sustain the roof of his abode, the waves of the sea curling strongly upward, Isambard's face with parted lips and pulsing throat like a prophesying angel, his greyhound leaping, his falcon soaring on spread wings, branches blown in the wind, strong, vital flowers, all charmed into those pure, impetuous fountain-shapes, schooled to receive the upward surge of the columns and transmit it in a renewed thrust of exultant energy into the crest of the vault. She saw an entire world met in one impulse of worship, and giving to God the supreme service of its wonderful diversity.

There were many faces, many portraits. She recognised the thin, sharp, dark features of children from the villages in the folds of the uplands, where she often rode, and the misshapen body and derisory legs of a dwarf who begged food sometimes at the gates, weighed down by the great, patient head whose nobility she saw now for the first time. And this one was new, an old woman cradling a dead youth in her lap. At first she took it to be a pietá put into this local shape to bring it nearer home, then she knew it for the mother of the young teamster, nursing her dead. How much he had seen since this vision came upon him, and how much of what he had seen disquieted him! The hapless, wary, intelligent faces of the poor looked out at her from the work of his hands with a direct challenge forbidden to them in the flesh. Did he even know what he was doing, in setting before his lord and his lord's world the revelation that had visited him? Had he himself recognised it for what it was? Not, she thought, consciously yet, not with his mind; but the heart was aware of what moved it, and the hands knew what they did.

'I begin to know these leaves,' she said. They were everywhere, the arching, coiling, thrusting leaves, jets of life growing irrepressibly towards the light. Men and beasts and birds looked out from their shelter. 'They are like nothing I have ever seen anywhere else. Not in Italy, not in France. Those precise Roman capitals I know, but these are of another world.'

'And which do you like better?'

'These,' she said at once, and warmly. 'They belong to the stem. They grow. Those others are stuck on.'

Always, now, she knew when she had pleased him, though he never expressed his pleasure. When he was most glad and satisfied, then he was most silent.

'They live and grow, but they are like no leaves that ever grew in our world. The more's the pity!' She traced the vigorous, curling lines of them with a cold fingertip, and stood looking down with a faint and rather ironical smile. 'What are they? You made them, you should know.'

'You are right,' he said sombrely, gathering the drawings together. 'They don't grow in this world. They're the leaves of the heaven tree, this stone tree we're about growing outside the gates.'

'And what is the fruit of this tree?' She looked up at him just in time to see the gravity and doubt and wonder in his face, before he turned and smiled at her.

'Kingdoms. Little kingdoms of hope for the villein and the outcast and the landless man. Freedom for the unfree, ease for the overborne, plenty for the hungry, safety for the runaway. All the desire of the heart, for the heart that never yet had its desire.'

He fell silent there because of the look in her eyes, suddenly pierced to the very soul by all that she had not said, all that she had sworn never to say to him again. He felt Gilleis knot her small fingers in the roots of his heart, and knew in his own body the anguish Benedetta carried like a monstrous child in hers. He had never been so near to any living creature, not even to Adam, as he was then to her.

'But they never ripen,' she said, with the rueful smile that had grown to be one of the flowers of his world. 'We're promised that they will in the world to come, if we study to deserve. But they never ripen here. I see you know it, for you have drawn only the leaves, never the fruit.'

She shook her shoulders, shrugging off the suddenly-falling sadness that came so strangely out of the joy and certainty of the images he had made. 'I must go, he will be back from riding soon. But if you will let me I should like to be here sometimes when you are working.'

'Come when you will,' he said, 'you'll be welcome.'

She was at the door when he said her name, the first time he had ever called her by it. 'Benedetta!' And when she turned, startled and moved, he came to her quickly and took her hand, and kissed it. Wanting words of his own, he found her words in his mouth and they did well enough. 'Sweet friend!' he said.

CHAPTER TEN

Harry awoke suddenly in the young summer night, and turned over in his broad bed, and missed something beside him, a warmth, a soft sound of breathing, something without which his peace was gone. He stretched out a hand, feeling for Adam, and the other half of the bed was empty and cold.

It awoke him fully, but did not disturb him. Through the shot-window he could see the brilliance of the moonlight, and the night air was mild and sweet as noon. After the long winter and the slow spring it was delicious to be able to lie naked in the highest room of the Warden's Tower. Vaguely he wondered which of the many possible young women about the outer bailey could be the magnet which had drawn Adam out of his bed. It was past time for the boy to fall in love again. The marvel was that he had continued immune so long. Élie would never have credited that Adam could go a whole year with his eyes fixed only on his work.

He dozed for a while, but woke up again to a nagging uneasiness. Had there not been signs to be read in Adam lately? And not signs of his old spring fever, either. When Adam was in love he did not fall silent, he talked, and every well-disposed person about him soon knew all there was to be known of his condition.

Harry slid out of bed, wrapped himself in his surcoat, and went out to the tower stair, its narrow treads already hollowed slightly by many feet. The mere fretting of a man's feet passing once a day, he thought, can wear out stone in the end. The weather, and the wind, and the rooting of infinitesimal seeds in the crannies wind and weather have made, will fret away my work at last, but I shall be long dead, and my children and grandchildren after me. None the less, he thought of the ages smoothing away the clear lines of his carving, blunting the incisive edges of the leaves of heaven, rounding the sharp, wary features of the villein faces to a worn resignation before it returned them to stones; and a fiery pang of rage and jealousy pricked his heart, to think that even these into whom he had breathed a longer life than his own should die at last.

A good stone, a lasting stone; but even the mountains wear away slowly and crumble into dust.

He came out on to the leaded roof of the Warden's Tower, and the upper stages of the keep rose beside him, vast and pale in the moonlight. No sentry was posted here, for the turret on the King's Tower covered the same field of vision, and something beyond in either direction. Between the merlons of the battlements on the Welsh side Adam leaned on his elbows, staring down into the Severn valley, which lay open before him in silver and green, from Pool, up-river, where Wales looked near enough to touch, to the solid grey shape of Strata Marcella, down-river among its level meadows.

He walked across the open space to Adam's side, his bare feet making no sound, and laid an arm about the hunched shoulders. Adam started and turned great eyes on him.

'Oh, it's you!' he said with a faint smile. 'What are you doing awake at this hour? I left you snoring.' He frowned at the naked feet. 'Have you the wit you were born with, to get out of a warm bed and wander about barefoot on the leads?'

'I woke and missed you,' said Harry. 'What ails you, to get up like this in the night?'

'I couldn't sleep. The moonlight, most likely, it was full on my side of the bed.'

'There's more than moonlight making you uneasy,' said Harry, settling his arm about his brother's shoulders, and spreading an elbow on the stone beside him. 'My mind misgives me that there's been a deal wrong with you for a long time, and I've been too much occupied to take note of it. If it's been my fault for not listening, I'm sorry for it, and I'm listening now. What's amiss?'

Adam hoisted a shoulder against him ill-humouredly, and stared at the coiling ribbon of the river, far below. For a moment he was silent, then he rounded on him abruptly, and burst out: 'Harry, I must go home!'

'So that's it!' said Harry. 'Well, it's better out than in. What's come over you to turn homesick now, when you've been away from it for ten years, and never given it a thought?' He had not meant to sound that note, but already he felt himself stiffening involuntarily against the idea, and the asperity that spoiled the tone of his voice was the fruit of his own uneasiness.

'I have thought of it,' said Adam hotly, 'many a time, but it was a long way off, and what was the use of fretting about it when I'd no chance of getting back?'

'You were happy enough!'

'I know I was. Have I said I wasn't? We've seen and done fine things together, and I've enjoyed every day of it. But that doesn't mean I forgot I had a family. I didn't grieve about it when they were out of reach, but they're not out of reach now, they're here in the same shire with me. I want to see them, Harry. I've got to see them! My mother hasn't clapped eyes on me for ten years, and the boys will be men. And my father's getting no younger. I don't even know if he's still alive! I can't stand it any longer, I must go home.'

'If you felt so strongly,' said Harry, breaking into unreasonable anger, 'I take it unfriendly that you've never told me of it. If you want to leave me – '

'Don't be a fool!' cried Adam, outraged. 'You know I don't! I only want to see my mother and brothers again and let them know I'm in the land of the living still. And as for telling you of it, I've tried times enough. The minute I speak to you of anything that isn't stone you stop hearing me. I asked you for the time to ride down and visit them once, but I got my nose bitten off for it.'

'I didn't know it was for that you wanted your freedom. We were just cutting the voussoirs for the portal arch, you were needed here.'

'You didn't know because you shut your ears, then, for I said it plainly enough. But no, you gave me to understand where my duty lay and I let you have the last word. But now I'll not be put off any more, I'm going.'

'You'll go nowhere,' said Harry flatly. 'You're still Talvace's runaway villein, for all the ten years you've been clear of Sleapford. You'd be hard put to it to prove a year's free residence at law, for it's not yet a year we've been here at Parfois together, and all the rest of the time there's no English witness can answer for us. Even at best, we're in no charter borough here. It would go hard if you had to make your case in a court. Stay here and you're safe enough, no sane man would come and try to take you from Isambard. But once show your face in Sleapford, and Ebrard can clap you in hold whenever he pleases – '

'Ebrard?' said Adam sharply, jerking up his head to stare. He thrust himself off quickly from the parapet, and took Harry by the arms. 'What's this of Ebrard? Are we not reckoning with your father any more?'

'He's dead, three years and more ago. Father Hugh let fall the news when I visited him, thinking I was from home then, and knew it already. And afterwards Edmund told me the how and when of it. He had a falling seizure, and lay a month in his bed, and then the second fit carried him off. Likely my mother's married again by now, for she's in Gloucester's gift, and she has some land of her own. And Ebrard would be wanting her out of the house if he's married or thinking of marriage. Think of it he will, for land's land, and there are some heiresses growing up among the neighbours, or there were when we left home, if they're not all taken by now. But there's still Ebrard himself to deal with, and he'll not let go a possession easily, you may lay to that.'

'And you never said a word!' said Adam wonderingly. 'I tried to get news in the town that day, but I was chary of naming names, and I found folk too uneasy to give even the time of day to a stranger. Oh, I can be cautious, too, when it's a matter of my freedom.'

He shook Harry back and forth lightly between his hands, and grinned at him with restored good-humour. 'But now I'm resolved, and you won't turn me. I can be in and out of Sleapford unnoticed, before Ebrard even gets wind of it. I mean to see my mother if the devil himself stand in the way.'

'You shan't go! I won't let you take such a risk!'

'*You* won't let me?' mocked Adam. 'Do you want me to lay you on your back, lad, and trim your ears for you? I can still do it, one-handed, if you want to be shown.' He had made up his mind, nothing could put him out of temper now. Only irresolution could cast those shadows of silence and withdrawal upon him.

'Do you know why you don't want me to go?' he said, locking his arms about Harry and holding him fast. 'Because if I go, and find all well and the way open, and not a soul holding a grudge against us, you'll have no excuse for not going home yourself any longer. And you don't want to go! Or rather, you want it and you don't want it. You're afraid of what you'll find, afraid of being rebuffed, afraid of losing what kindness you have left for them, and gaining nothing. You're afraid of opening old wounds and starting old hates, when you feel the want of a fixed and quiet mind so that you can do what you have to do, and do it well. Don't you see that the only way to be free of them all is to go back and face them? You could be at rest after that, whether it turned out well or ill. It's the not venturing that undoes you, Harry.'

Harry twisted furiously in the prisoning arms, but could not break free. 'It isn't true!' he said hotly, turning his head aside to avoid Adam's challenging eyes. 'I haven't given them a thought, one way or the other, and I don't suppose they've ever a thought between them to spare for me. Why should they? All that's ten years past and over.'

Nonetheless, what Adam had thrown at him was no more than the truth. He had not, indeed, consciously been thinking of his family, but since he had returned to England they had lain secretly in his heart like a heavy burden, a duty on which he had turned his back, or an ordeal he shrank from facing. Adam was right, he would never be free of them until he had encountered them again. At the thought of meeting with his mother his bowels melted into a scalding liquefaction of tenderness and fear and grief. How if she were neglected in her widowhood and lonely, and he did not go to her? How if he heard of her death, and had to live out his own life in the certainty that he had shortened hers by his defection?

'It's easy for me,' said Adam gently, 'everything I left behind at home was love and kindness, and I want it back, and no buts about it. I'll bring you word, lad, and ride back with you if all promises well.'

'No!' said Harry fiercely, gulping down his lesson. 'I'll go first. There's still the matter of your freedom. I must talk to Ebrard and get his word for it he'll not claim you. I'll ride home today,' he said with decision, shutting his hands upon Adam's shoulders, 'and in two days more you shall have your will.'

From the head of the long, wandering track through the village he saw the church tower and the shingled roof that had grown dilapidated in the two years of the interdict. He saw the striped fields rising on the left, outlined in red because the headlands that divided the selions were full of poppies, and on the other side the fallow strips from which a few greedy souls, here and there, were trying to filch an extra crop. He had often felt it shame, when he was serving his brief apprenticeship as steward here and taking his new duties very seriously, that a whole moiety of the village fields should lie idle every year. Three fields would be better than two; if they put their minds and resources to work they could cut a third field out of the waste and bring it under plough.

He had ridden in by the mill through Tourneur land, and the memories crowded in upon him oppressively. Over there in the forest Adam had killed the doe. Here in the paddock at the mill they had left the horses, and from here he had brought them at dead of night down to the copse by the river. There was a young man stooping by the overshot wheel of the mill, just raising the sluice that blocked the head-race; he saw that it must be Wilfred, by the red hair, but this young giant looked so improbably a development of the Wilfred he remembered, and gave him such a hard, unrecognising look with his greeting, that he was too shy to make himself known. On his way down through the village no one hailed him by name, and his tongue stuck to the roof of his dry mouth when he would have claimed old friends. No, there would be time for that later, when he had faced whatever welcome awaited him at the manor.

He saw the long wall rise into sight, and the squat grey tower looking over it, and his heart turned in him. He did not know what he had expected, but now, as he drew near to the gate-house, he felt at once lost and comforted. The place was unchanged to outward view, and his recollections of it were sharp and clear and curiously ambivalent, charged with burning indignation and wincing guilt. But the porter who came out to ask his business was a stranger to him, and looked at him with the guarded interest he would have given to any unknown traveller. In that impersonal regard he felt all his expectations of pain and high feeling beginning to founder.

'Sir Ebrard's in the armoury,' said the porter. 'If you'll please to wait, sir, till I tell him who's inquiring?'

'I'll go to him,' said Harry, dismounting. 'I know my way. Time was when I was at home here. Never fear, Sir Ebrard knows me.'

The armoury had a new roof, and so had the dovecote. He was glad to see that Ebrard was keeping the place up properly. In the smithy someone was shaping a hilt for a dagger. It was not the old smith, but a lusty young fellow not above twenty-five. Likely the old man was gone to his rest like his master. One decade can swallow a whole generation of old men.

Ebrard was bending above the anvil, watching the work, his back turned towards the doorway, but he saw the fall of the newcomer's shadow athwart the light, and looked round casually, expecting one of the men-at-arms. He had filled out a great deal between nineteen and twenty-nine. It would take a stouter horse to carry him now. By the time he's fifty, thought Harry with astonishment, for he had somewhat envied his brother his elegance of person, he'll be fatter than father was. But with his height and his finer bones at least he'll carry it better.

The blue eyes narrowed, staring against the light. The tall body straightened, aware of a stranger.

'I trust I see you well, Sir Ebrard,' said Harry.

'You!' said Ebrard, and drew a long breath. 'Well, well!' he said. 'This is something we never looked to see.'

'I have been out of England until last summer, this was my first opportunity to visit you. And it is but a visit,' he said, to forestall any apprehensions Ebrard might entertain concerning his intentions. 'Make no special provision for me, I beg you. I have work going forward at Parfois and cannot leave it for long. I came only to assure myself that all went well with you here, and with my mother.'

Ebrard laid down the dagger and walked forth into the court. He took the hand Harry offered, and leaned to kiss his cheek, with so punctilious a civility that it was clear he felt himself to be entertaining a stranger, though with a stranger he would have been less at a loss.

'You'll have heard of father's death?'

The note of bewilderment in his voice was for their brotherhood, which he acknowledged but could no longer feel. The thought that they shared a father set them at an even greater distance from each other.

'I heard it only when I returned to England. It was late then to feel sorrow. I fear I gave him no great satisfaction while he was alive. I hope mother is in good health?'

'In excellent health. I might do well,' said Ebrard, checking in his march across the court and casting a frowning side-glance at his visitor, 'to send and prepare her before you go in to her. You'll understand, she's not looked for you these many years. First we thought you dead, and then – '

'Gone past returning,' said Harry.

'There was little in your going to make us think you would ever come back.' The blue eyes searched him again, rapidly and shrewdly. 'At least while father was alive,' added Ebrard deliberately.

'It wasn't fear of him that kept me away,' said Harry, taking this to be his brother's meaning, 'nor anger against him, either. Once Adam was safe from him I got over that quickly enough. But we had to keep running until we were clear of pursuit, and we ran ourselves into France before we ventured to stop, and with the novelty of it, and being very busy earning a living, we never had time to cast a thought back to Sleapford. I don't suppose father lost his sleep for long, either.'

'He was very bitter against you,' said Ebrard. 'It's so long ago now I don't remember the exact way of it, but I know he wouldn't have your name mentioned, once he'd fairly accepted you were gone. He came round in his later years, but I wouldn't say he ever really forgave you.'

'Then I have the better of him, for I forgive him.'

'It's because you had the better of him that you can afford to,' said Ebrard drily. 'What have you been doing since then? How have you lived? And is that foster-brother of yours still with you?'

This last question Harry chose to ignore, but answered the others readily enough as they climbed the steps to the hall door side by side.

'I marvel you could find any inducement to come back here,' said Ebrard at the end of the brief story, 'when you've done so well for yourself.' The name of Isambard had impressed him; the master-mason who had such a patron was clearly a made man.

'Inducement? After all, I am a son of this house, too, and my name is Talvace, like yours.'

Again he caught the narrow, sidelong flash of the blue eyes, and felt the momentary silence sharp as a knife slashing between them; and suddenly he heard his own words as Ebrard was hearing them, and could have laughed aloud.

So that was what worked so uneasily behind the fair forehead and probing glances! Ebrard feared that he was come to claim a share in what Sir Eudo had left, and was at pains to show him that he had forfeited the old man's favour and his own filial rights; and he, with his, "I am a son of this house" and his "my name is Talvace, like yours", had unwittingly caused the ground to tremble under his brother's knightly heels. He opened his lips impatiently to reassure him, and then thought better of it. No, let him sweat! Let him dangle on the hook for an hour or two. He had been on the point of exclaiming scornfully that he wanted nothing from him; but on reflection there was indeed one thing at least he wanted, and Ebrard might be only too pleased to compound with him on those terms. Why stick at demanding only Adam's legal freedom? He could very well bargain for the parents and the young brothers, too.

He had a good legal claim to some part of the estate, though it had always been accepted that the land must not be divided. By the time he had taken note of all the evidences of prosperity here, and shown a marked interest in every improvement to the demesne and every handsome beast in stock, Ebrard would think himself lucky to get off at the cost of only one villein family. In the long run he would not even lose by it. He would gain a rent for the toft, and William Boteler and his sons would be able to give all their time to their trade, and make more profit out of it, whereby the whole village would benefit.

Perhaps one of the boys might choose to come and work with Adam at Parfois. But first he had to play Ebrard safely to land, and if he took an impish pleasure in it, at least it was without malice; he had no ill designs on even one square foot of the poor soul's inheritance.

There was a newly-laid stone hearth in the middle of the hall, under the smoke-blacked beams of the lofty roof, and a new carved balustrade to the solar staircase. Harry admired both, and complimented Ebrard on his good management with a bright, appraising face.

'Mother's within,' said Ebrard, putting this aside quickly. 'I'd better go up first and let her know of your coming.'

'No, not for anything! I'll not be broken gently, like bad news. Let me go up to her alone, I promise you the shock won't harm her, I want to be recognised and taken to her heart, not ushered in like a packman trying to sell her pins.'

'She may not be alone,' said Ebrard with a wary glance. 'My young clerk reads to her sometimes of an afternoon. She finds needlework tries her eyes of late.'

Harry halted on the stairs to look back for an instant in doubt. 'You said she was well!'

'She is well, and blooming, too, you'll see for yourself. My lord of Gloucester wants her to marry again. There's a knight of his he wants to give her to, and I believe the match will be made very soon.'

'If the bridegroom doesn't please her – ' Harry began with a frowning face.

A brief, cynical and almost lewd smile twitched at Ebrard's handsome mouth for a moment. 'He does please her! He's ten years younger than she is, and a nice-looking fellow into the bargain. He's the one will need to have the draught sweetened.'

It was the nearest they had ever come to exchanging views on their mother, and Harry did not find it pleasant. Such disillusioning discoveries as he had made about her he had always kept to himself, and always forgiven, though sometimes after a painful struggle. He drew away hastily, and ran up the stairs, and with a sudden tremor of nervousness knocked on the door of the solar before he went in. There was a moment of silence, and then her voice, pitched rather high with surprise, called to him to enter.

She was sitting in the window embrasure, and he saw her first as a clear outline against the light, and thought her miraculously unchanged. She had on a gown of green cloth, and a bliaut of yellow brocade over it; in these, and in the coif of gilt net and the necklet of rough amber, there was more of the bride than of the widow. The young clerk, a boy of about twenty, frocked and tonsured, sat on a stool at her feet, bent attentively over his book, though if he had indeed been reading it must have been in a very subdued voice.

Lady Talvace was peering towards the door with a look of surprise and inquiry on her fair, soft face. Harry closed the door behind him, and came forward a few steps into the room, where the light could shine on him. She blinked at him, and looked again and caught her breath.

'Sir, I had not expected – my eyes are playing me tricks, for a moment I thought – You're very like Harry!'

'I am Harry,' he said, very gently.

She clasped and wrung her hands in a gesture of such spontaneous joy that his heart leaped in answer. Then she was on her feet, and had sprung past the tonsured boy, almost thrusting him from his stool in her haste, and in a moment she was in Harry's arms, weeping, laughing, babbling like an excited child, and covering his face with kisses. She wound her arms about his neck, and drew him down cheek to cheek with her, holding him with all her strength.

'Harry, Harry, my dear, dear Hal – !'

The clerk rose, drawing aside to the wall to creep about them as unobtrusively as possible on his way to the door. But over his mother's shoulder Harry saw the extraordinary look the boy gave him, the furtive, grimacing smile, half jealousy and offence, half sniggering collusion, and knew that she had found one more adoring youth to help her pass the time pleasantly, and one who had not been kept at arm's length, either. She could not help it, it was useless to blame her. It was not a vice in her, but only an instinctive appetite, like the earth's need of rain. A son, a baby-faced clerk, a new'young husband, they all came alike to her. Deprived of one, she would find another.

He held her in his arms, and was eased of all his fears. He had come here steeled in advance for tragedy and tension, but he should have known the reality would be small and ordinary and confused, the usual sorry condition of man. They were too slight to contain the passion his imagination had bestowed on them; he had better recognise his own inadequacy along with theirs, and resign himself to it.

'Harry, you wicked, cruel boy, how could you stay away so long? How could you forsake me? When you ran away like that you broke my heart.'

He held her tenderly and smiled over her shoulder. Surely she had wept bitterly over his flight, but there had been no breakages. His return made her happy, but she had no real need of him, she could get her happiness in a thousand other ways.

When she had cried enough, she held him off and examined him critically, emerging from tears resiliently, without disfigurement. She exclaimed with delight over him, said how well-grown he was and how handsome, which he knew to be false except as her eyes conferred beauty on him; and when he had told her everything that had happened to him since his flight, but for that part of the story which contained Gilleis and was for ever secret and holy because of her, his mother exclaimed over his prowess and his adventures no less generously, and kissed him again, and began to chatter of herself. Did he think she was looking well? She looked like a girl, and so he told her. She was a little plumper, perhaps, a little softer, her fair, pale flesh had slackened very slightly, a few lines marked the corners of her eyes, but her hair was as bright as ever, and her smiling face as charming. Gloucester's young knight would not need much persuasion to the match.

They sat together in the window, and she blushed as she told him of the projected marriage. She was already getting together her wardrobe for the occasion, and jumped up to turn slowly before him and ask if he admired her dress, for it was new.

'I have such a wonderful tirewoman now, Harry, she understands stuffs better than any maid I ever had. Do you remember Hawis, who used to weave cloths for me, the girl who wanted to marry a free man from Hunyate? She ran away with him, the ungrateful hussy, and left me with a gown half-finished.'

'Did you ever hear what became of them?' asked Harry innocently.

'Not a word from that day to this. I suppose they must have left the shire. I could never get a girl who knew her business for years after that, but now I have a real treasure. She can cut so beautifully – see the shaping of this sleeve. Her father was in the woollen trade, so she knows how to buy to advantage. She's making me a green pelisse.' She brought cuttings of cloth to show him, and drew him to her over them, her arm about his neck. 'Harry, must you gc away again?'

'I must, Mother, I must go back to my work. But I shall not be far from you now; if you need me you can send word to me.'

'At least you must sleep the night here; it's too long a ride to Parfois, and it would be folly to ride these roads at night.'

'Gladly and gratefully, Mother. Shall I have my room in the tower again? – do you remember how you came to me there? When I was locked in, that night? You came to comfort me and I knew I was going to leave you. I asked you not to think ill of me.'

'I never did, dear Hal!' she said and kissed him. And indeed she had never thought ill of anyone, or never for more than half an hour together. 'Wait for me a little while, Harry. I must go and see about making your bed, and set the supper forward. I'll come back very quickly.'

When she had left the room he picked up the shreds of cloth idly, and carried them to the window to examine the colours in a good light. All the tension had gone out of him, there were no more ordeals to face, no more pain or joy to be anticipated, he was tired out with relief. He stood looking out across the courtyard, without a thought or an idea in him, too content and too full of lassitude as yet to look even one step ahead. He must and he would talk Adam's full and indisputable freedom out of Ebrard, and deliver all his family with him, but that could wait until after supper, and until then Ebrard could fret jealously over his inheritance in anticipation of the attack which would never be launched. Now he felt nothing but a kind of helpless languor, at once pleasant and disappointing.

He heard the door open, but did not turn until some new lightness and length in the entering step, some different quality in the rustle of the flowing skirt made him aware that this was not his mother. When he turned his head the girl had her back to him, and was just closing the door. He saw the folds of the green pelisse draped carefully over her shoulder and arm, the hood swinging lightly against a waist he could have spanned in his two hands. This must be the wonderful tirewoman. Out of his lassitude he admired the long, smooth movement of her arm and hand in the close-fitting red sleeve, and the black coils of her hair braided high on her head within a narrow gold ribbon. But how truly wonderful was his mother's treasure he did not know until she turned to cross the room and lay out her work upon the table, and for the first time realised that she was not alone.

She made no sound, but she halted, and drew back her head with a start as mettlesome and wild as that of a forest creature recoiling from the touch of a hand. Great black eyes, gay and gallant, opened wide at him above pale cheeks that suddenly flushed radiantly red. A mouth like a budding rose opened and cried: 'Harry!' loudly and gladly, and curved into a laugh of joy.

He sprang down out of the window embrasure, trembling. 'Gilleis!' he said in a shout of delight, and snatched her into his arms.

'How did you get here?' he asked, when he had breath for anything but kissing, and without slackening his greedy hold of her for a moment. The pale prints of his lips on her cheek and chin and throat flushed slowly to rose. She kept her eyes tightly closed, and smiled and smiled on his shoulder with a triumphant delight. When she had her breath again she laughed aloud. 'I looked for you in London. They told me about your father. I'm sorry from my heart, love, that I never showed him my gratitude. And they told me you were gone to join the household of some noble lady, out of the city, but could not tell me where. Everywhere along the road I've been asking after you, and nowhere any word. And now I find you here!'

'They didn't tell you,' she said breathlessly, 'that my uncle wanted me to marry to his liking. The poor creature he threatened me with wasn't the only bidder, either. That's why I took good care not even my cousin, who's a harmless soul enough, should know where to find me. If I'd left a message for you, some other would have taken the advantage of it. And I knew you'd find me in the end.'

'But how did you come to know my mother in the first place?'

'It was very easy. You had talked of her a great deal, I knew she liked dresses, and I knew she had lost her special sewing-girl. The next year I persuaded my father to go a little out of his way with some of the Flemish stuffs he took north with him, and visit Sleapford, and she bought some brocades and velvet from us. We used to come here every year after that, and when I was older I began to show her how the stuffs could best be cut and made up, and then to stay with her and sew for her the week or two while my father completed his business in Shrewsbury, until she could hardly get on without me and begged me to stay and be her tire woman. But I never would, because I could not leave father.'

'But all this – I don't understand. To what end?'

'To get news of you, simpleton,' she said, and drew his head down to her and kissed the corner of his mouth. 'And you have no need to labour so to get such avowals out of me, for I'm ready to shout them from the battlements.'

'And I never sent word! If I'd known, if I'd known – !'

'It did not surprise me. I knew you for an unfeeling wretch, with no eyes and no wits for anything but your precious stone. But I knew you'd come in the end. So when father died, and I wanted to escape being pestered – and let me tell you, there were some better bargains than you among my suitors, Master Harry Talvace, if I were not such a fool as to love you! – I came here to your mother, and she received me kindly, and here I've been ever since. And a fine time it's taken you to remember you had a mother!'

'Until last summer I was in France still. And since I came back I've held off because – oh, because I wanted the courage to face it. If I'd known what I stood to gain I'd have been on the doorstep months ago. But how could I guess? How could I dream you'd be here, of all places?'

'Of all places!' she mocked. 'Where else should I be? Only here could I be sure that one day I should meet with you again. I knew you'd return to England some day, and then you'd surely come back here to see your mother. Not to stay, I knew that. Not to live in this house again. But you'd come! I could not come to you. I could only take my stand where you must some day come to me.'

'And if you had been mistaken?' he asked, tightening his arms about her fearfully. 'If I had never come?'

'If I had been mistaken in you,' said Gilleis, 'no one could have helped me. As well live out my life here as anywhere else. But I was not mistaken.'

'You love me!' he said in a hushed voice, not exulting, marvelling.

'Always, ever since I touched your cheek among the bales of cloth, when I reached for my ball.' She touched it again, very lightly, and felt him tremble. 'Do you remember? You couldn't speak, they were too near us. You caught my hand and kissed it. And I began to love you. You were full of tricks of the kind,' she said resentfully. 'When I was angry with you for laughing at me, you did it again. Oh, you were a great one for getting your own way with me, but you never gave me anything in return. Even when you made my image, you were so ill-tempered about it I was frightened to blink.'

'Is there nothing you've forgotten?' said Harry, aghast.

'Nothing bad. Your good points I forget. Perhaps there weren't any.'

'And yet you love me,' he said triumphantly.

'Oh, I claim only to be bold and resolute. I never said I was sensible.'

'If you scold,' he threatened, 'I shall beat you, when we're married.'

'Who said we should be married? Have you not heard that England's under interdict? There's neither marrying nor giving in marriage – we're one step nearer the kingdom of heaven.'

'Isambard's chaplain at Parfois will marry us. He holds that his lord is absolved because he was away following the Cross when the ban was laid. But if there'd been no Crusade he would have thought of another reason why Parfois should be exempt. The Pope is in Rome, and can threaten his soul, but Isambard is close at hand and deals rather with the flesh.'

'There'd be nothing surprising in your beating me, in any event,' said Gilleis, twisting her fingers into the short, curling hair in the nape of his neck. 'I think I was very near it once before, when you caught me peering into the hall where you were showing your paces on the citole, and you ordered me to bed, and I – '

'This I won't bear!' said Harry, roused, and caught her up in his arms and carried her to the window embrasure. She had not grown as tall as his chin, and she was slim as a reed; he had less trouble with her now than on that earlier occasion. All the same, she did not fail to remind him.

'You almost dropped me that time, too.'

He sat down in the panelled seat, and settled her on his knee. 'Now *I* shall begin remembering things. Thus I held you in my arms, and you cried and miscalled me.' He hugged her to his heart, laughing. It seemed that love had no language but laughter. 'You had nothing on under your cloak. And your hair was loosed from its braids.' He plucked at the ties of the gilt ribbon, and brought the black coils tumbling about them both, over her shoulders, over his cradling arm, heavy and silken and sweet. 'So, that's better! And as I remember it, love, it was you beat me, not I you. You hit out at me with your fist like a fury. And not the first time, either!'

'And yet you love me,' she exulted.

'I've not said so yet!'

'Too late to draw back. I saw your face when you recognised me. It was touch and go with you whether you shouted with joy or burst into tears on my breast.'

'That I may do yet,' he said, and set his lips to the opening of her gown, between her firm, small breasts. 'I do most truly love you, Gilleis. When I was grown a man I had the wit to know it. Oh, Gilleis, marry me! My lord's away in Ireland now with the king, and will be for a month or more yet, but as soon as he comes home I'll speak to him of our marriage. He'll give us a lodging in the castle, I know, and we can be wed in the chapel there. Oh, my love, how can I bear to ride back without you, tomorrow, now that I've found you? But I must make preparation to receive you at Parfois, and I must get on with my work, and you'll be better here with my mother until all's ready for you there.'

'I can wait,' she said. 'If I've waited until now, and never complained, I can wait a few weeks longer.'

'You won't vanish again as soon as I turn my back?'

'And you – you won't forget to come back for me?'

He buried his face in her hair and kissed her through the drifting silken curtain, eyes and cheeks and chin, and the soft round neck, and the eager mouth. With his lips against the delicate cup of shadow at the base of her throat he began to quake with laughter again, and laughed and laughed until it seemed he could not stop. She took his face between her hands and shook him into coherence. 'Oh, Gilleis, I'm in for such a scolding! What will my mother say to me when she hears I'm carrying off the treasure who makes her dresses?'

He rode back to Parfois singing, his mother's facile tears still moist on his shoulder, and Gilleis's kiss still warm on his lips. Ebrard had ridden with him to the edge of the demesne, so expansive with relief at receiving Harry's hearty consent in his proprietorship that he embraced and kissed him at parting with more warmth than he had shown since childhood. At this second departure the prodigal son carried everybody's blessing with him, not even excepting the baby-faced clerk, whose nose was clean out of joint as long as the interloper remained at Sleapford.

In Harry's saddle-bag reposed a parchment, drawn up by that same clerk and signed by Ebrard, testifying that William Boteler and Alison his wife, together with all their issue, were hereafter freed and loosed from villeinage, and that all the services by virtue of which the said William Boteler had heretofore held his yardland and his toft were hereby commuted to an annual rent of five shillings.

Adam was up on the scaffolding, watching the master-carpenter direct the striking of the centring from the deeply recessed arch of the west portal. Harry swung himself up behind him, and stealing up unnoticed to his back, stretched an arm over his shoulder and dangled the parchment before his eyes. Adam turned a startled smile on him, at once welcoming and questioning, and read the thing through twice before he could grasp it. He swallowed and stared mutely, his lips quivering. Harry seized him in his arms and hugged him boisterously.

'I wanted to go to them and tell them, but I didn't. You are to do that, and this very day, too. I wish I could come back with you, but we can't both be gone at this moment, and you can tell them I'll come soon, and that I send my duty and love before me. I hope they may be comforted for all the years they've lacked you, now that you come home with this in your hands.'

Adam, whose whole being was gaiety, Adam who had hardly ever cried even as a baby, stood trying to speak, and could not. His hands shook on the precious leaf of sheepskin. He put his head down on Harry's shoulder, and wept briefly and hotly, with all his heart.

'Ah, now, I hadn't meant to shake you so!' said Harry, too much excited and moved to be put out of his stride at being tossed into so unusual a role. 'It all turned out better than I'd dreamed, and getting this was easy, and on my soul I'm as wild with joy about it as you are. And think what it will be to walk into the yard and give this to your father! Come away with you now, and dress, and be off to get the best of the day. Everything's well at home, I promise you that. I saw the two boys, and heard your mother's voice in the house, and I asked at home about your father, and he's alive and well. So there's nothing to trouble you at all. Ranald's taller than you, I believe, and Dickon not so far short of you. And truth to tell, Adam, I've not been much missed at home, I did them no great wrong, and if they did me any it's long gone by. I'm mortal glad you made me go. Ebrard's concerned only that I shan't lay claim to any part of his manor, and my mother's meditating a second marriage, and happy as a lark, with or without me. Indeed, she has what she holds to be better cause to hate me now than ever in the past, for I'm robbing her of her tirewoman.'

Adam raised his head and scrubbed hastily at his eyes with his sleeve, uncovering a face absurdly contorted with laughter, tears and bewilderment. 'For God's sake, Harry, either you're out of your wits or I'm so bemused I can't take in a word. Her tirewoman? What can you want with her tirewoman?'

'Ah, but you haven't seen her, Adam!' Harry held him by the shoulders and shook him gaily, his eyes dancing with blue and green lights in the sun. 'She's no ordinary tirewoman. Her name is Gilleis Otley. I'm going to marry her.'

Isambard came home at the end of August, blazing with vigour and high spirits from the king's triumphal progress through Ireland and South Wales, where he had left his enemies disrupted and scattered. Better still, small seeds of suspicion concerning Llewellyn's loyalty had struck roots in John's mind, and three months of assiduous cherishing had brought the plant to the point of flowering. The charge was never likely to be proved, but then the charge was never likely even to be made; it was within his own walled-in mind that John indicted and judged in silence and without appeal. The execution of sentence was all that the world ever saw of his processes of justice. He moved deviously, even among those who had been most intimate with him, confiding in one only in order to counter the crumb of confidence he had been obliged to place in another; but if he still trusted one man above the rest of the world, the man was Isambard, and throughout that progress from Fishguard across Wales to Bristol, a demonstration of power designed to awe the natives into complete submission, Isambard had been busy pouring into his mind the idea of a final settlement with the Prince of Gwynedd.

The foray into his territories by the Earl of Chester, countenanced though not openly ordered by the king during his Irish expedition, had been useful in encouraging Llewellyn's many minor foes among the Welsh princes themselves. The greatest single blow John could deal at his enemy was to release Gwenwynwyn and set him up again in the southern part of his princedom of Powis, for his hot blood would never rest until he had won back the northern half from Llewellyn. Turn Gwenwynwyn loose this autumn to harry Gwynedd from the south, and by next spring the stage should be well set for a royal expedition to drive westward to the Conway and flush the falcon out of his crags under Snowdon.

Isambard rode home, therefore, well content with his summer's work. He brought his three score knights and his company of archers back to Parfois intact and with despatch, shed his mail for silk, and sat down in his great hall to hear suits and deal justice. At the clamour of his return the countryside, which had sweated to provide him the funds for the expedition, crouched lower between its hills like a hare in a furrow, expecting the next exactions all too soon.

'Marry?' said Isambard, when Harry came to him with his news. 'Faith, I thought you were married to your drawing-board!

He looked from the finished arch of the west portal to the great beams the carpenters were already shaping for the covering in of the aisles, and back to Harry's face, with brilliant eyes that danced with rare pleasure. 'It's plain being in love has not sapped your powers, even if you have been racing off to this girl of yours every ten days or so. I never saw a building of its size grow so fast. Ay, bring her to Parfois whenever you will. If you have her here you'll need no time out for the ride. Benedetta will take care of her until the wedding day, and you shall have a chamber in the King's Tower to yourselves, and welcome.' He clapped an arm about Harry's shoulders. 'And which of your names do you intend to marry in, Master Henry? Lestrange – or Talvace?'

Harry gaped so childishly that Isambard threw back his head and startled the birds with laughter.

'Never stare so, I'm no magician! I've known best part of a year. Do you not remember I told you last autumn that Hugh de Lacy sent you his greetings, when he wrote acknowledging the gift of wine I sent him after his recovery? With what name do you think he named you?

'True!' said Harry. 'I never thought of it. He knew but one name for me, for it never entered my head to mention the other. But why did you never question it?'

'Why should I question it? If you had had anything to tell me, you would have told me. A man's name is his own business – though for my part I'd rather he had but one, and that his true one.'

'And so would I,' said Harry, 'though it never troubled me when I changed it. Talvace I am, and Talvace I'll be from this on.'

So Gilleis came to Parfois in the second week of September, and two days later they were married in the chapel in the Lady's Tower, by the good-natured, subtle, pliant old man who was Isambard's chaplain and had served his father before him.

In the great hall that night they sat at the high table between Isambard and Benedetta, too full of their own happiness to eat or drink or speak. On Isambard's left Lady Talvace shone in the most resplendent of the gowns Gilleis had made for her, and basked in the attentions of her exalted neighbour. On Benedetta's right Ebrard wore his finest blue velvet, and drank for two. Below, in the hall, the entire household of Parfois chattered and supped. But in the middle of so many witnesses, those four were alone.

Benedetta looked along the table and saw the three profiles superimposed one upon another, like three heads on one coin. Isambard, the most distant of the three, flushed with wine beneath his tan, and with some deeper exaltation wine could never have given him, controlled the comings and goings of his underlings with flashing glances and eloquent movements of head and hand. When he laughed and turned his warmth and intelligence outwards on the world, as now, he burned into such lively beauty as could charm the birds from the trees. She understood, with her blood rather than her mind, one reason for his good spirits. It was pleasing to him to see one man about him helplessly in love, and not with her. There was also the pleasure he had from his summer of relentless intriguing against the Welsh prince. But there was something more, an air of having come to a happy decision, a shining elation for which she could find no sufficient reason.

Against his dark brightness the girl's rose-and-white profile was clear and pale as a pearl. A little creature, slender and beautiful, with great black eyes that observed fearlessly, and a mind behind them that judged with shrewdness and without mercy, after the fashion of children. When I received and kissed her at her coming here, thought Benedetta, those eyes pierced me to the heart, and that mind understood something, at least, of what moves me. I knew she would be young. I thought she would be soft, sweet and timorous; but she is gay and bold and gallant. I thought she would be no match for him, and he might some day look for another; but she is his match and mine, and she will not fail him. She is the death of hope, if that was hope I had and have no longer.

And now, Harry, what remains for me?

On this third face, the most beloved, so close that she could have brushed the flushed cheek with her lips as she turned her head, she dwelt longest, and with the most passionate and wondering attention. His eyes had a light, changeable brilliance, startling as topaz and aquamarine, and all the impetuous bones of his face stood outlined with the sharp pallor excitement. He had gone to some pains to make himself fine for his bride, he who cared not a fig whether he pleased anyone else, or what old clothes he wore, so he was neat and covered. The thick brown hair was newly trimmed, the fine-drawn cheeks and arrogant chin shaven smooth as ivory, and a necklet of polished brown stones circled his throat within the high collar of his golden surcoat. Talvace was Talvace again. Ebrard was a clod to him, for all his graces.

Touch him where you will, she thought, exulting in the fondness and pride that gathered about her heart like fire, and burned out of her even the agonising envy she felt towards Gilleis, lean on him as you will, and he stands firm under your hand. Sound him where you will, and he rings true. Who but Harry would have stood his ground with me, never hiding behind coldness, never compounding with his difficulties by a kind or a cruel lie, never shunning my company, never shaming me by an evasive compliment or an insincere caress, never in anything that rested between us two taking the false or the easy way? Who but Harry would have come to me straight and told me with his own lips of his love and his intent to marry? Not one of these knights and warriors but would have run from me as from the plague in the same case, though they think themselves heroes, and him a mere artisan who has chosen the poorer part. He came to me not even as an act of courtesy or mercy. He came as to one having rights in him by virtue of my love, one who should be encountered fairly, eye to eye, and trusted with the truth. He has done me more honour in the manner of his rejection than any other man with the offering of his heart's worship. And I do not repent me of my love, I exult in it. I gave it where it was due, and by God, I will never take it back!

I have lost nothing, she reasoned with herself, while some shell of her mind attended to Ebrard's gallantries. Not Harry, for he never was mine. Not the hope of some day winning him, for there never was such a hope. Only, perhaps, the illusion of hope. If she had been a slighter thing than she is I might have kept that illusion even now. But she is his true match, and I am glad of it, though it strips me of the last of my possessions. So noble a creature should mate nobly. If he had taken an unworthy consort he would have abased me as well as himself. So the delusion is over, and my sense of loss is the greater in measure as I worship and revere him more for his honourable and loving dealings with me.

Now there is nothing to gain. Now, therefore, she thought smiling over her wineglass, we shall see, Benedetta, whether you came after him to England to get, or to give.

In the quiet of the bedchamber Benedetta sat before the polished mirror, combing her long hair. Her eyes looked back at her from the shining surface with a sombre metallic lustre. Her hands, moving in the heavy coils of red, were slow and languid. She had never been so weary.

In the chamber newly prepared for them in the King's Tower bride and bridegroom lay closely folded in each other's arms, between waking and dreaming. They were sealed about with the impregnable armour of their happiness, exalted so far above the world that the world could not reach them. Yet some measure of their joy distilled into the air, and filled the night with a sweet, disturbing awareness, sharpening every desire to anguish.

Isambard, naked beneath the furred robe he kept for wear in his own chamber, came to her back, and buried his hands to the wrists in the masses of her hair. She heard his quickened breath, and the long, fulfilled sigh as he laid his cheek against her neck. Over there in the coign of the inner ward, did Harry twist his fingers so in the black hair, and even so smooth his palm down over the bud of the young, round breast and along the ivory of her side? An unpractised hand, but this skill came by nature; art could only elaborate and perfect it. I wish them well, she said silently within her heart. I wish them this good joy with all the rest. How could I grudge him his pleasure with her, I who would give him the world if I could? Their happiness is my joy, as well as my sorrow. Let him have everything this life has to offer a man, she prayed indomitably, smiling into the mirror at the darkly smiling face that looked over her shoulder.

'Benedetta!' he said in a low voice, and turned his lips into her cheek, kissing and smiling. She raised her hand and held him so, her fingers threading his hair 'My lord?'

'This marriage is a strange matter! How often I have seen my friends wedded and bedded, and never been stirred to feel anything but pity for them, that they should have to submit themselves to such tedious embraces with such unpleasing partners, to add a few fields or one more manor to their honours. Only a landless man can afford to plunge into marriage like this boy, without a single furlong to gain. What's to become of our morality if young men are to marry for nothing more substantial than love?'

'And what's to become of women like me?' she said. 'One should be properly practical about marriage. Sir Ebrard, they say, is conducting a long, cautious negotiation for his neighbour's daughter. Since Tourneur's son died she stands to bring three manors to her husband. She's thirteen years old, and pockmarked, or she might have been pledged already, even with her smaller dower. Ebrard was contracted once himself, it seems, but the girl died before she was old enough to wed. You'll not catch that Talvace with the bait of a black eye and a rosy mouth. No family can afford more than one fool like your Master Harry.'

'No family dare hope for more than one,' said Isambard, smiling. 'I'm glad I've seen his happiness. Something, it seems, I had to learn from him, how to value this vexed business of love.'

His hands gripped her shoulders and held her drawn back against his body. In the mirror their eyes clung.

'Benedetta, I see that I wrong myself and you in denying the name of marriage to this union of ours, that lacks nothing of peace and certainty and permanence. I want none but you, now or ever. I desire with all my heart that you will be my wife.'

Her face neither moved nor changed; only it seemed to him that a veil was drawn over the brightness of the eyes. Quiet under his hands, she sat and watched him through the veil, and was silent so long that a coldness came on him.

'What is it? Why don't you speak? Are you angry because I am come only now to this simplicity I might have seen long since? But I am not a simple person. It wanted the directness of children to charm me into simplicity. What was marriage to me while it marched in my mind with haggling and grasping for a few barren manors? This is a new vision of the paradise of the innocent, where the kiss comes from the heart. I should have done you no honour and myself no credit if I had asked you to be my wife in the old dispensation. But enter here with me, and we may be as the children.'

He saw tears well in her eyes, the first he had ever seen there, and did not understand that they were for him. They brought him to his knees at her side, his long arms clasping her close. 'Ah, have I hurt you? What is it? Best and dearest, what have I done?'

'Nothing!' she said. 'Honoured me! Laid me deeper than ever in your debt! Charmed me to the very soul! Nothing but good. But I am not and cannot be as the children, until time goes backwards. And I cannot and will not marry you. Not you nor any!'

The ready fires burned up in his eyes, darkly red with offence. 'Why not? What is this? You accepted me; why do you refuse my name and estate? Is it that other? Do you still cling to him? Has he ever shown you such a love as mine?'

Benedetta laid her hands about his neck and held his face before her, eye to eye. 'This I promise you, and be content. There never yet was a moment when I drew so close to you in the spirit as now, or was so moved towards you. The vow I made you I repeat and will keep, upon that honour the world would say I have not, but which you will not deny me. If ever I married man, it should be you, but I have that in me that will not let me marry any. Have you not been content with me as I am? Have I not faithfully given you my body, my counsel, whatever wit I have for your service? Let things alone! Let me alone!'

'There is a place in you I cannot come at,' he said violently, and plucked his head from between her hands and leaped to his feet, dragging her up with him. 'You touch me gently with your hands, you open your breast to me, you give me your body, but I cannot get to your heart.'

'You have no need,' she said. 'A morsel of my heart I gave you long ago. There is nothing left me to give that I have not given you. Be satisfied! If you had means to measure and tell over what I have in my heart, you would surely find yourself there.'

'Then give me what I ask! Marry me!' Bending his head in sudden desperate desire, he kissed her from brow to breast, closed her eyes with kisses, and fastened his lips so long upon hers that she struggled to wrench aside from him for breath.

When he withdrew his mouth from hers, the blanched lips flushed slowly back into red, bright as blood. They opened only to repeat, with a vehemence and resolution as inflexible as his: 'I will not.'

CHAPTER ELEVEN

'Madam, and most honoured lady,' wrote Walter Langholme by a courier from Aber, in the middle of the harvest, 'this campaign having now been brought to a successful conclusion, I am commanded by my lord to write to you that full account for which his duties about the person of the King's Grace leave him no leisure, and to convey to you therewith my lord's most faithful greeting and service. My lord is well, and has taken no hurt in the fighting, in which, indeed, our losses have been light, though some companies less well captained than our own have suffered much from the skill of the Welsh archery.

'As you know, we assembled at Chester in early May, our lord the King having summoned there all the leaders of the Welshmen saving the Prince of Gwynedd only, against whom our campaign was directed. These came in obedience to the summons almost to a man, even some among them who had hitherto held fast to Prince Llewellyn, but whether out of duty to our lord the King or envy to Llewellyn I know not, for in truth there are many who envy him and would gladly see his downfall. But at this first muster the King's Grace unwisely paid no heed to my lord's counsel, but would advance into Tegaingl without delay, though warned that our supplies were not sufficiently assured for so early a campaign. Howbeit, advance we did, and the Welshmen after their invariable custom withdrew before us, making no pitched stand but harrying us from the flanks, and so retreated before us with all their possessions, cattle and horses, into the mountains. We came to the Conway at Degannwy, having consumed the greater part of our supplies by reason of the season, for that countryside provided no food whereby we might spare our own, and of beasts it was stripped bare. It was thus clear that we could not survive a campaign of any length, for already such trifles of food as could be found commanded their weight in gold rather than silver, and to go forward was to reckon with famine. Our lord the King therefore commanded that the army should withdraw to England, and on the march we ate such of our horses as could be spared, and for the rest went hungry.

'Howbeit the King's Grace was not turned from his intent against the Prince of Gwynedd, but made new provision to better purpose, and we were appointed to assemble a second time in the opening week of July, at Oswestry. And thence, assured of our supply columns, we advanced into Gwynedd and drove fast for the mouth of the Conway, sweeping Prince Llewellyn before us across that river and into the mountains of Arllechwedd. The Welshmen fought as Welshmen ever fight, in flying skirmishes and by means of light-armed bowmen, the main army dissolving before us so that we could not come to grips, by which means they avoid heavy losses. But they could not halt us by such means, and so we came in triumph to Prince Llewellyn's court of Aber, and there took possession of the town, the prince having withdrawn into the mountains.

'Now Prince Llewellyn is returned, with his lady, and there is much haggling over the peace. Our lord the King has an affection for his daughter, and I make no doubt she will get for her husband the best terms that are to be had. My lord would have had him stripped of all he has, but that can never be while the Princess Joan lives, since his ruin would be hers also. The prince bears himself in no wise like a defeated man, but very proudly, though I have heard tell that he is bitter at this invasion of his realm, and myself I have seen at whose door he lays it. In the presence of the King he turned to my lord Isambard, and: "Well I know, my lord," said he, "that I have you to thank for traducing me to the King's Grace. You are he who put it into his mind to believe that I was conspiring with de Breos against him. Here at this time I am but a suitor in my own court, and cannot call you to account for it. But at another time I shall seek a settlement. Until then, keep this for me." And with that he drew off his glove and let it fall at my lord's feet. Whereupon my lord would have snatched it up, and there would have been swords out, for my lord is, as you know, of no temper to withhold his hand even in the presence of kings. But certain of the barons laid hold on them both, and the King forbade that the gage should be received, and charged them to forgo this quarrel now and hereafter. Nevertheless, neither one of them has promised obedience, though they parted without more words. So the matter stands, and it has been the King's chief charge that they shall not meet again so long as the army remains here. For my part, though in this I speak only for myself, I believe the prince when he swears that he made no compact with de Breos who is broken and fled, though he may well have been approached, and perhaps even tempted.

'It is not yet known what the terms of peace will be, nor when we shall be leaving here, but it is certain that the King's Grace is well satisfied with what he has accomplished, and holds that all Wales may now be held subdued, thus the better freeing his powers for the project which he still has dearly at heart, namely, the recovery of Normandy.

'Believe, most honoured lady, that to my lord's expressed duty and homage I add my own, and at all times pray for your safety and good, and am your most devoted and humble servant

Walter Langholme.

'Given this eighth day of August, the thirteenth year of the King's Grace and the year of Our Lord 1211, at Aber, in Arllechwedd.'

'Writ in haste at the courier's departure. Madam, it is now known to what terms the King has consented, and I must acquaint you they are not pleasing to my lord, for he holds that they leave to the Prince of Gwynedd too much scope for mischief hereafter. All four cantrefs of the Middle Country are surrendered to the King, leaving to Prince Llewellyn those parts which lie beyond the Conway. Gwynedd must pay to the King a ruinous tribute also in cattle, horses, hounds and falcons, and surrender hostages from the children of the nobility. I have heard that Prince Llewellyn's natural son is to be among the number, a handsome boy some eleven or twelve years old, who is well liked among the Welsh because his mother was a Welsh lady of note, daughter of a lord of Rhos. But whether it is true that this boy Griffith is expressly named hostage for his father's fealty is not yet certain. Some thirty more noble children will accompany him.

'My lord is greatly angered, none the less, at what he holds to be a victory thrown away, and has said openly that this whole enterprise will be to do again within a year. But I hope he may be proved too cautious a judge. Herewith I salute you reverently, and trust to see you in good health on our return.'

'One thing at least goes well,' said Isambard, 'and one man knows his business. It's rare enough these days. Do you mean to have the nave wholly roofed in before the winter?'

'Yes, my lord, and with your permission I should like to keep on all my hewers and setters this year. The vaulting will more than keep them occupied, we lose nothing by paying them through the frosts, and gain months of time. And we gain in goodwill by the security we give them, believe me. It's much, these days, for a mason to have his work safe and assured before him twelve months in the year, he'll give you value for it.'

'See to it, Harry. For it's in my mind that you spoil your workmen.' The long mouth snapped at the words, biting them off grimly.

'No, faith, my lord, that's not true. Many of my men must keep a family fed and housed on their few pence a day. The usage they have from you relieves them of anxiety. Never think that matters only to them. It sets their minds free to provide you the whole-hearted service you ask of them. And they respect you for it. Is that nothing?'

'Oh, you are on your old hobby-horse again. Turning artisan in your boyhood has given you an artisan's eyes. But at least I grant you,' said Isambard, his eyes fixed on the double lofty arch of portal below and window above, drawn back from light to shadow through eight courses of delicate moulding, 'what you have produced is much to my mind. The variation of the colour from dawn to dusk is beyond belief. When the light is slanting on these curves of stone they vibrate like the strings of a harp, such a tension they have. I see them sometimes when I ride out early, and they sing like notes of music.' He saw the vivid colour rise in Harry's face, and the pleasure that flamed up in his eyes, and smiled. 'Praising you is a luxury, you reflect back so warming a delight. You are like a child who has done his task better than he knew, and gets commendation where he looked for scolding.'

'It is not that,' said Harry, laughing. 'It's the terms of the praise. If you are content with your mason, I am content with my patron. Come and look within.'

He led the way between the slender mouldings of the doorway. On a level with Isambard's eyes, as he followed, the delicate columns burst into jubilant leaf. He halted, face to face with himself, startled yet again by the beauty and savagery of that simplified image, with its uplifted hair and passionate bones, and the stony calm of the eyes, staring forth from between the leaves of the holy tree. Angel or man or demon, this creature could have been any or all of the three.

On the other side of the portal the face of Benedetta looked out, bearing up the abacus and the lofty spring of the voussoirs on the erected masses of her hair. It seemed that Isambard would have passed her by without a look, but he could not. His feet lagged in the doorway; he turned about with a sudden helpless motion, and his hand flew to touch the lovely, taut line of the stone throat. The strong fingers lingered with so involuntary and so intense a suggestion of pain and longing that Harry drew off from him and waited with held breath, shaken out of his absorption into wonder and disquiet. Isambard's eyes burned upon the beloved face, searching hungrily and finding no reassurance. He plucked himself away at last with a violent movement, as though it cost him a struggle to release himself, and went on without a word into the lofty, airy shell of the church.

The aisles, not yet vaulted, stood beneath their timber roofs; the nave was still open to the sky, but the transepts were covered, and the base of the tower hung square against the clouds. The aisle windows and the windows of the clerestory printed their empty tracery on the light, laced with the wrought iron window-bars to which the painted panels of glass would some day be affixed.

'You see only the form and proportion,' said Harry. 'Give me this coming winter, and you shall see all the vaulting in place, at least the ribs. Next spring we'll need to get the heavy hoist installed in the tower, it's bespoke from Shrewsbury, we'll be bringing it up by water. Why build a new one when theirs is sitting idle? For this year I can make do with the two lighter hoists I've got. Richard Smith has a warm winter's work cut out for him, making rods and cramps and dowels for the vaults. Sweating over his tallow-vat proofing iron will be a pleasure through the frosts. He's a good fellow, and knows his trade, none better. I have but to show him the manner of device I want, though the like never was used before, and he'll shape it to the exact pattern. Do you like the line of it? That's what counts. Line, form, proportion, these are the body of beauty, the rest is but the dress.'

Isambard stood beneath the western window, gazing before him at the beautiful enclosed shape of air and light. He heard the clangour of hammers on the timbers above, the voices of the mason-setters working on the base of the tower, and shouts of the men bringing up ashlar with the hand-hoist. The whole site hummed with sound and movement like a hive of bees; but it seemed to him that the voice of the builder, leaping with ardour, rang louder than all.

'You are a happy man,' he said, in a voice of wonder and envy. 'You love what you do. You create, and that which you have made stands. No folly of others unmakes it, it has not to be done again and again, and still to no purpose.'

'I am fortunate,' said Harry, 'I know it.'

'The happiest of men in your labours.' Isambard turned his face into shadow, leaning his hand upon the pier between them. 'And in your love also, Harry?'

'In that also,' said Harry in a low voice.

'To have all!' The voice laboured with astonishment and despair. 'To have everything there is in life, even that last and greatest of all! What right has one man to so much? Where is God's justice?'

They were suddenly upon ground that trembled beneath their feet, and Harry would gladly have drawn back to the rock, but he could not.

'My lord, I think I have been visited with mercy rather than justice,' he said slowly. 'I make no claim that I am used according to my deserts.'

'Ah, Harry, I should ask your pardon! There's none I would more gladly see happy than you. Yet I cannot choose but envy you, and sooner or later envy will grudge to another the good fortune it cannot share. I think you have your deserts. Indeed, I think so!' He turned about suddenly, and the air between them quaked with the compulsive passion of his vehemence, an inexplicable anguish. 'And yet, Harry, how do you know, how can you be sure – '

A quick, light step and a sudden shadow in the doorway cut off the words on his lips, and Gilleis stood silhouetted against the light. In the vigour and rapidity of her movements she was like a bird, and the brilliance and audacity of her glance had something of a bird's knowing wildness about it. She looked quickly from one to the other of them, and stepped forward into the open, sunlit space of the nave.

'My lord, Madonna Benedetta is here with Langholme and the falconer, if you are pleased to be ready.'

She spoke to Isambard, but she looked at Harry. Something out of reason flashed between them when they beheld each other. Her lively face seemed to blaze into the proud, piercing image of Harry's countenance, even her great eyes, opened wide at him, reflected the shifting brilliance of the sea. And such a softness and radiance came upon him that it seemed he took her womanliness into his being, and gave her in exchange some part of his steel. Isambard saw the budding rose of her mouth quiver and part, softening without speech, as though she kissed her husband across the space of charged air. 'How can you be sure,' he had been about to ask, 'that you are loved?' Beholding her, he was answered.

'I will come,' he said, and turned to the doorway.

'You were about to ask me something,' said Harry, following; though if his mind and his eyes had not been upon Gilleis he would have been alert enough to let the question lapse.

'Was I so? No matter! I have forgotten now what I was going to say.'

At the edge of the site, where the track crossed the grassy plateau, Benedetta sat waiting on a tall roan mare. Langholme held his own horse and his lord's, and well back from them, in silent attendance, John the Fletcher watched from the saddle of a raw-boned grey. The falconer with his birds had ridden ahead, but Benedetta carried her own little merlin hooded on her wrist. She looked down from her high-pommelled side-saddle, and her smile was warm but weary. Her face had grown a little thinner of late, and a little graver. The spark of laughter that still lit in the limpid grey depths of her eyes had always something of irony in it, though something of tenderness, too.

'I did not mean to interrupt you, Ralf. If you have matters to discuss with Harry I will wait.'

'No need, I'm ready,' said Isambard, his eyes intent upon her face, where no revelation showed him his own image. He took the bridle from Langholme, and without waiting to be squired made a leap and drew himself up easily and gracefully into the saddle, sending the horse forward with a thrust of his knees before he bothered to feel for the stirrups. Benedetta wheeled and followed him, her close white coif shining in the sun; and after them Langholme cantered at a discreet distance, with John the Fletcher at his back. The deep thudding of hoofbeats descending the grassy track pulsed through the rock and subsided.

Gilleis looked after them thoughtfully. 'I marvel,' she said, 'that she chooses such a surly-looking fellow to attend her. He's always at her heels like a shadow.'

'She has good reason to trust in his loyalty, and he has good reason to guard and cherish her. It's thanks to her he's man alive.'

Gilleis slanted a quick glance at her husband and bit at her underlip with white teeth. 'She rides well,' she said judicially.

'She does,' he said with unthinking warmth.

'But then, she does so many things well.'

Harry caught the significant note in her voice, and looked round with a jerk, searching her face warily.

'She has an admirable intelligence, too,' said Gilleis earnestly. 'See what an interest she takes in your designs, and how constantly she visits your tracing-house.' Sidelong, she watched the shadows of doubt and consternation pursue one another over his face.

'Madonna Benedetta has taken an interest in the church from the beginning,' he said. 'Why should she not? She has as good a mind as any man, and I value her judgements. Moreover, she is the lady of this castle, whether by right or by custom, and goes where she pleases. She has been always generous and kind to me.'

'And how gladly would she be kinder and more generous still,' said Gilleis roundly, 'if you would but let her!'

The fiery colour mounted in his brown cheeks, and flamed to his hair. 'Gilleis, you surely cannot think – Dear, when have I given you cause – ?' He reached out his hand to catch at hers, but she snatched them away and turned her back on him, and all he could do was to take her by the shoulders and draw her back against his breast, his cheek against her cheek. She felt the burning heat of that touch, and suddenly repented of her ungentle game.

'Simpleton!' she said, and turning quickly, kissed him at random near the angle of his jaw, and plucking herself clear picked up her skirts and ran like a hare for the rim of the trees, laughing at him over her shoulder as she ran. Between wild relief and real anger, he turned his back on his duties and launched himself in vengeful pursuit. She was surefooted and fleet, but among the trees she stumbled, perhaps of design, and he caught her about the waist and pulled her down into the grass already growing dry and colourless with autumn.

'Tease me, would you? Make a fool of me, would you, miss?'

'Mistress!' spat Gilleis sharply, reaching for her favourite hold in his hair. He freed himself, not without difficulty and pain, and held her down in the rustling grass by the wrists, his weight lying over her; their hurrying breath mingled, in slightly savage laughter.

'What shall I do to you, hussy, for plaguing a good husband like me?'

She fought him for a while with all her strength, then with all her strength wound her arms about him and caught him to her breast. They lay intertwined, kissing and laughing and murmuring until they were spent, and for a moment sank together into the borders of a sweet drowsiness.

'All the same,' said Gilleis, 'you defended yourself before you were accused.' She turned her head, and closed her teeth gently on the lobe of his ear. 'I never said you cared for her, I said that *she* –'

Harry silenced her in the most effective way he knew, and emerged with just enough breath to gasp guiltily: 'I must go back to work! What will they think if they've seen us?'

She lay still for a moment when he had withdrawn his weight, her hand in his, her face smiling. 'Harry!' She drew him down again, lifting her mouth to his.

'I love you dearly, Gilleis, and only you, and always you. You know that!'

'I know it! And I love you, too.' But he saw by her smile that she had confirmed to her own satisfaction that this Venetian woman, who meant nothing to her, loved him no less surely, and that he was well aware of it. How had he come to betray them both so easily? It was more than he could do to keep any secret from Gilleis, she was so much a part of his very flesh and blood. Yet if she was too perfectly a woman to be compassionate, and perhaps too young to have room in her as yet for pity, she was also too secure in her happiness to be jealous. Had she not reason to be secure?

He drew her gently to her feet. The small nest their two clinging bodies had pressed out in the long grass seemed still to keep the very print of passion, and a warmth of its own. Surely no snow could ever lie there, and no frost whiten the grasses. He thought of Benedetta keeping her promised silence, abstaining from touching so much as his sleeve. He remembered Isambard's voice in its muted howl of desire and despair: 'To have all! What right has one man to so much?'

'What is it?' said Gilleis, folding her arms about him in sudden anxious tenderness. 'You're trembling, Harry! Dear love, what's the matter?'

'Nothing!' he said, shaking off the shadow hastily. 'Nothing in the world! A goose flying over my grave!'

Before the end of the year Isambard's prophecies with regard to Wales began to show signs of coming true, but it was not at Llewellyn's hands that the peace was broken. The chieftains who had willingly joined King John against him had soon awakened to certain disquieting discoveries. It was understandable that the king should feel it necessary to build castles in the Middle Country, the better to hold what he had taken from the Prince of Gwynedd. But hasty new mottes and timber keeps began to rise also in Powis and in other parts of Wales, until chief began to whisper to chief that this encroaching power which they had helped to supremacy was aiming its lance not at the throat of the Prince of Gwynedd, but at the heart of Wales itself. Let the English king once establish his castles throughout the countryside, and there would be no safe foothold left for any Welsh prince in his native land. Before the leaves had fallen Rhys Gryg and Maelgwyn, brothers of the line of Deheubarth, had captured and burned the unfinished castle at Aberystwyth, and Cadwallon of Senghenydd was in revolt in Glamorgan. The Prince of Gwynedd had not raised a hand to break the peace enforced upon him in the summer; but many of those who had been the king's allies had become, openly or secretly, his enemies.

'He is throwing away Wales and risking England for the sake of Normandy,' said Isambard, thinking aloud before Harry in the tracing-house. 'There's still but one man in Wales who can unite the whole country against him, and yet in his haste to make one frontier safe he is playing into that man's hands by offending all the lesser fry. He should have wooed them a little longer. It was too soon to frighten them with a rash of castles.'

'Yet you'll not deny,' said Harry, 'that the Prince of Gwynedd himself has kept the peace loyally. It is not he who has burned Aberystwyth.'

'Why should he, when they are willing to do his work for him? But be sure he misses nothing that passes. When he judges the time ripe he will take up the weapon of a Welsh national grievance, and we are the fools who will have forged it for him.'

'What, when the king has I know not how many hostages in his hands, and young Griffith among them?'

'Hostages! I'll tell you this, Harry, there are so many hostages in the king's hands, Welsh and English, too, that there's hardly a house in the two countries but stands to lose a son at the least step astray. Years of that, and not so much as knowing how to step to be above reproach, and seeing others, like de Breos, brought to ruin and death for no treasonous act that ever showed – why, those who have sons in hold must begin to despair of knowing how to keep the breath in their children. There comes a time when it seems a lesser risk to act, with some hope of success, than to hold back from action, and still be charged with treachery and pay the same penalty. One more thing I'll tell you! Of all the boys the king holds in ward, the only one he dare not touch is Llewellyn's son. It is not fear. It is a kind of respect for the man, even while he hates him, that holds him back from abusing what belongs to him. I take it, Harry, that what I say here to you goes no further?'

'You may so take it, my lord,' said Harry haughtily.

'Ah, now I see all the Talvaces stirring in you! There were clues enough to your line, when I think back, before ever Abbot Hugh wrote me his charge to you. When we rode to Calais, and in my ill-humour I told you you rode like a ploughboy, and you laughed, and said: "So my father used to tell me" – do you remember? – I should have known then, by your impudence, as well as by the words, where to look for your father. Well, be content, for I speak with no other as I speak with you, Harry.'

He moved restlessly away across the room, but in a moment took up again, without turning his head: 'I was much with John when we were younger, I had some love for him. I tell you, he could have been a good king and a happy man, who now is neither the one nor the other. Richard with his recklessness and his empty gallantry, who saw in England only an asset to be squeezed dry for his holy wars, him they praised and worshipped. John, if he squeezed them in his turn, at least began with some knowledge of them and some thought for them, and might have made them a nation and a power had he had even moderate fortune. But him they hate. It is too late now to undo that. As for his own peace, it is gone past recall. He trusts no one. And he cannot reconcile himself to the loss of any part of what was his. Normandy will be his death. He still dreams of recovering it, and for the sake of that delusion he is risking all that he has. For what purpose do you think he is now levying these new aids that are causing my stewards so much travail? To equip his fleet and army for the invasion of Normandy! For what purpose did he accept the risk of this reckless pressure on the Welsh? So that his rear might be safe from attack while he sails for Normandy!'

'It seems like to have the opposite effect,' said Harry, busy over his tracing-tables, but listening intently none the less.

'It does, for it has raised the very devil he hoped to bind, and before the chains were ready for him. But I tell you, Harry, if these

Welsh rebels can make the border so hot as to turn the king from his enterprise of Normandy – if they can do that, and do it in time – they will have done England a good service.'

'In time! And how soon is "in time"?'

'By this coming summer,' said Isambard, 'for that is when the king purposes to sail. And if he does spend so much energy clutching hopelessly at what's already lost, not only Wales will slip out of his hands, but England, too.'

Into the groves of Harry's stone forest, now magically coming into full leaf before the passing of the frosts, these echoes of the turmoil of the world came strangely and distantly, dulled of most of their import before they reached the ear. And like the undertow of a loud and dangerous tide, the long, submerged groan of the ultimate victims tore at his senses with a far more desperate vehemence. The king's tenants-in-chief complained of the burden they bore, and indeed if any among them lay under his displeasure he could readily turn their debts into their death. But the small farmers and the villeins in their fields could never escape the load. Not the king's caprice, but the precise operation of social law let fall upon them, in the end, the full weight of the royal debts. Through baron and tenant and sub-tenant the burden of extortion came down on the poorest, and through them upon their labouring soil.

How many more such fittings-out, how many more such expeditions, could they bear? And when would they find the common sense to condemn the futile fantasy of honour for which they were wrung, and not the mere act of extortion? They lamented and complained of the tallages that bled them, but they fulminated like outraged princes in the next breath against King Philip who had curtailed their majesty, and boasted how his conquest should yet be wrested from him. If there were other voices, they kept their views within their own doors. Only the women, struggling to feed their growing families, sometimes gave vent to their exasperation. Normandy? What was Normandy to them? They had only the haziest of notions where it lay. They could neither spend Normandy to buy cloth, nor give honour to their children to eat.

Before Easter the king's courier rode in from Cambridge, with a letter summoning Isambard to join the court there for the festival. He entertained his guest lavishly, but made no attempt to prepare for the journey until he had asked who was to be present, and cut short the imposing list of names and titles with a dry query touching the Prince of Gwynedd. Yes, Prince Llewellyn and his princess would be there in the king's entourage.

'Then he wastes his time sending for me,' said Isambard. 'He knows well that I have sworn not to attend on him on any occasion when the Prince of Gwynedd is received at court. Tell him that in all other matters he is assured of my duty and service, but in this I beg he will hold me excused.'

'I cannot give him such a message,' said the courier, aghast.

'I will have you deliver it under seal. You cannot be answerable for what I write.' And he called in a clerk, and dictated a letter of such elaborate courtesy and such inflexible insolence that even the clerk ventured to attempt reasoning with him.

'My lord, would it not be better – may I not write that you are indisposed and cannot come?'

'Do so,' said Isambard with a wolfish grin, 'and you shall hang for petty treason. After you have been flogged forinsubordination, of course. Write what I bid you write, and be sure I shall read it before I seal it, so let it be accurate. You will make it clear to the King's Grace that I *will not* come. Say also that when he sends for me to attend him in arms on a further visit to the Prince of Gwynedd, as I foretell he will do very soon, he will find me as forward as any.'

The terrified clerk wrote accordingly, as well as he could for the trembling of his hand, and the reluctant courier took the letter away with him, though Isambard doubted whether he would deliver it.

He did not have to wait long for the echoes of his prophecy. Whatever Llewellyn saw and heard in his Easter visit to his father-in-law, it did not dispose him to fear any very effective counter-action against whatever action the indignant Welsh chiefs might be contemplating, and it did incline him to give serious consideration to joining them. The new castles on which the whole wild, proud population of Wales turned suspicious eyes had not been in the bargain struck at Aber. Who was first breaking the terms of the peace?

But it was another voice, a voice at once infinitely distant and as close and urgent as the well-being of the soul, that sounded the decisive note of revolt. Pope Innocent, that spoiled emperor, took fire with opportunist alacrity from the first mild spark of Welsh insurrection, and hurled his last and most irresistible bolt against his obstinate enemy.

'Did I not tell you?' Isambard erupted in the lodge like a storm-wind, between rage and contempt and pure enjoyment of the complexity and ruthlessness of the pontifical mind. 'Did I not tell you, Harry, in Paris, that we had started a dangerous precedent with our Crusade against a Christian monarch? Did I not tell you the weapon would be too alluring to lie neglected for long? The Pope has profited by the example, and been seduced by the temptation. There is not a more subtle or a more able villain in Europe than our Innocent!'

He laughed at the startled face Harry turned from the capital on which he was working, though the astonishment was due rather to the sense of shock he always felt at the world's invasion of his rapturous peace than to any surprise at hearing Isambard so outspoken.

'God's deputy on earth has preached a holy war against the enemy of God, John. He has not only urged the King of France to invade him, but also absolved the Welsh princes from their allegiance and Wales from the interdict. There'll be bells ringing across the border, Harry, and Mass will be sung again. Maids can marry, and old men can be buried in holy ground. If they hesitated before, what is there to hold them now? They're up in arms from Gwynedd to Glamorgan, on God's business. Llewellyn is storming through the Middle Country, sweeping all before him. Everything we were at such pains to take from him has fallen back like a ripe plum into his hand. Rhys has burned Swansea, and the prince of Powis is battering at the gates of Mathrafal. Farewell, Normandy! Now if John can but keep his head we'll have it out with Llewellyn once for all.'

'Have you had word yet from the king about his muster?' asked Harry, caught up into this whirlwind of excitement almost against his will.

'Not yet. I've sent a messenger to ask what force he wants of me, and where, and when. Oh, God!' he said, gripping Harry's shoulder with fingers that bit like steel, 'bring me face to face with him this time, and no king by! Give me Llewellyn, and whatever the price may be here or in purgatory, I'll pay it laughing!'

The king's summons this time made no reference to the last insolent refusal. The matter was too urgent for remembering such minor scores. He appointed a muster at Chester on the 19th of August, and named the force he required from Isambard; who promptly raised more than the number of knights and archers, and double the men-at-arms, and lashed the husbandmen in all parts of his widely-scattered honour with aids and tallages to pay for the expedition. He was possessed. A trail of distraints, imprisonments, floggings and hangings marked the course by which he advanced upon his enemy. When he marched his levy out of Parfois at the end of July, the villages lay stripped of almost everything that could be commandeered as funds or supplies, their ablest men, their best horses. Even such iron as they possessed had been seized for arms. With the harvest hard upon them they had lost half their means of reaping it.

Harry, who was deaf to the greater voices of the outside world, caught the suppressed whisperings of the helpless little people with an infallible ear. Even if he had not, Adam would have seen to it that they were relayed to him. No one was likely to go to FitzJohn for help. He was my lord's voice in my lord's absence, and dared not stray from his orders, even if he would.

'The want of labour is the worst,' said Adam. 'That, at least, we have in plenty. And he never touched Richard Smith's supplies of iron. I'm not one for filching from a job, but this is a matter of their living through the winter, and the material and the making for a few new flails and sickles he can better afford than they can, God knows.'

They looked at each other speculatively, and began to smile. 'We'll have all the masters talk to their men,' said Harry, 'and spare all they can, all who're willing to go to the fields. Please God he's safely out of Parfois for two months, at least. We'll have everything in by the time he comes home.'

But on the 20th of August, long before they were done with the grain, Langholme rode into Parfois with word that the muster was dispersed, the Welsh venture cancelled, and the returning levy only a day away on its march home. He waited only for a change of horses and rode on to the manor of Erington with his news, leaving them to prepare in haste for a homecoming they did not understand, and which could hardly mean anything but disaster.

Harry and Adam were at work in one of the villages on the English side of the Long Mountain, when Gilleis herself rode down to warn them that they had best call home their volunteer harvesters, and be manifestly about their own work before the lord of Parfois arrived. Harry, stripped to the waist and brown and bitten as any villager, stared up at her blankly from the stubble and with a run and a leap scrambled up to join her on the headland. He kissed her almost absently, and: 'What, called off?' said he. 'Not even delayed? But why? What's gone amiss?'

'I know nothing but that they're coming home. Langholme was not within the ward more than a quarter of an hour, and if FitzJohn knows what's happened he must be the only one, and he's said no word. But it's certain they'll be here by tomorrow.'

'Ah, there's time enough, we'll have every man back on the site before morning. It goes hard to leave it unfinished, though,' he said reluctantly, looking round with delight on the baked, blonde harvest fields. 'It's long since I sweated the mischief out of me this way. They'll have their men back to see it completed, and their horses, too, but I'd have liked to finish what I began. Still, better not give him a holt to take out his spleen on them. I'll come back and put on my gown again, and he'll never be the wiser.'

'Never be the wiser, and he has only to cast an eye at the colour of you,' said Gilleis maternally, 'to see you've been playing truant.' She tidied his wild hair with her fingers, teasing out a few blanched husks of oats from the tangled locks. 'Show me which girl you've been tumbling in the back of the wagon, to fill this thatch of yours with chaff! I knew I should have come with you.'

'You do me great wrong,' he said, injured. 'Ask Adam if I have not worked like a Trojan. But faith, there's time yet to make up for that, now you've put the idea in my head. You'll be riding back at once, sweetheart, I take it?'

'And so will you,' said Gilleis firmly. 'Ask Adam, indeed! After all the covering-up you've done for him in your time! I won't stir from here until you put on your tunic and come with me.'

They rode back together happily in the decline of the afternoon, now racing like children, now dawdling like lovers. The sky was without a cloud, and their pleasure in each other without a shadow. Only as they climbed the steep track to Parfois did the sudden chill of the troubled world fall upon their hearts again, and wonder and speculation agitate the surface of their happiness; the inner security they had between them could never be touched.

Isambard rode in towards noon the next day, with only a handful of knights in attendance. In the outer ward he dismounted, walking away from his steaming horse before the grooms could run to take it from his hand, and shed cloak and gloves on the steps of the Lady's Tower for Langholme to pick up as he hurried to help him disarm. The squire was back from Erington only an hour before his master, and came breathless and nervous into the private apartments, to unbuckle sword-belt and unlace hauberk and carry away out of sight all the accoutrements of war. Isambard turned about beneath the trembling hands with a stony quietness, surrendering to these symbolic rites a body from which the mind seemed to have withdrawn.

When he was stripped of all the useless trappings he stretched back his long arms for his gown, and wrapped it about him, and made a single curt motion of dismissal that sent Langholme scurrying thankfully out of the room. Not one word had yet been said. Benedetta brought wine and offered it, standing squarely before him so that he could no longer maintain either the assumption or the pretence that he was alone.

'So there's to be no reckoning with Llewellyn,' she said.

The eyes which had been staring through her shortened their range slowly, were aware of the room, of the wine-cup, and at last of her face. He took the cup from her and walked away to stand at the window, looking down into the river valley.

'The plans were well-made, for once,' he said in a dry, quiet voice. 'This time we need not have halted at Aber, we could have wrested from him the last corner of Anglesey. The king was to join us on the 19th, but I left Chester with only de Guichet, and went to meet him at Nottingham. The Welsh boys were all brought there. On the day he rode in, before he would break his fast, he had them dragged out and hanged.'

He reached this close with no change of tone, but something in the look of his back, the rigidity of the broad shoulders, the strained stillness of his head, made her aware of his detestation. Not the savagery of the act, but its meanness and irrelevance, revolted him; there should have been no energy or hate to spare for such petty revenges while Llewellyn lived, and with Llewellyn dead there would have been room enough for magnanimity. He saw the death of the children as a meaningless and contemptible dissipation of the hatred which belonged all to a more satisfying adversary.

'All?' she asked in a low voice.

A short, hard laugh broke out of him like a cry. 'No, not all! Not Griffith! If he had to kill, I might at least have kept a spark of respect for him if he had killed Griffith. Did I not say he would never dare? The father's hand was over him like a canopy, he could not be touched. And John had just enough wit to realise that if he spared only one, and *that* one, the meanest must despise him. No, he left a handful of them to bear Griffith company. I don't know how many survived – I did not count the wretched little bodies.'

'We were not unprepared,' said Benedetta sombrely, 'for we have had news from Shrewsbury in your absence that marches with this. It seems Robert of Vieuxpont held one Welsh prince in the castle there. He received the king's order to hang him, and it was done.'

'He is the king's lieutenant, he must do the king's bidding or quit his office. But the end of it all – the cream of the jest! Three days after this miserable prentice butchery the king countermands all the preparations for the campaign, dismisses the levies and shuts himself up from us all. It was two days before he would receive me, and me he comes as near trusting as any. He had had letters, from the Princess of Gwynedd among others, and all to the same purport. He undertook this Welsh campaign, they said, at his own peril, for there was a conspiracy afoot among his own vassals to take this opportunity of betraying him to his enemy, or else making him their prisoner. He believed it, and called off the muster.'

'But if his daughter was the source of this,' said Benedetta with a faint and rueful smile, 'it is not hard to see her purpose. She has a husband and a father to save by such an invention.'

'So I told him, and begged him to go forward and pay no heed. There were others to confirm it, he says, but would not tell me who. And if it were true, what does he gain by this? There will be other opportunities. The poison is that they should desire to bring him down. If that be truth, they will not want occasions. What falls not out of itself they will make. And if he has enemies all round him, yet he might at least gain by going forward boldly and wiping out one, the rankest of all. But no, he would not be turned. He could have saved himself. He could have taken the field and dared them to act, met them and outfaced them on their chosen ground. It was the only way to salve anything out of this ruin, with all to gain and nothing to lose. And he would not do it! I prayed him for his own sake, for England's sake, even in mere justice to those poor hanged puppies who were being hurried into the ground, and their sires who had a right to confront him with the sword. I knelt to him!' groaned Isambard, and suddenly laid his arm over his eyes to ward off the remembered image. 'I went on my knees and implored him to go forward. And he would not! There'll be no reckoning with Llewellyn, now or ever. It is over.'

The autumn and winter passed, and the ribs of the vaulting soared under the timber roof of the church, graceful, impetuous, lofty, until the nave stood like the beautiful, strange skeleton of a fabulous ship sailing keel-uppermost through air, in vindication of its name. Before the frosts ended they had completed the filling in of the cells, and the lovely bones put on spare and shapely flesh.

In his safe, sufficing world Harry scarcely heard the confused rumours from outside the walls. The king's splenetic shufflings to find a champion to fight his Welsh war in his stead, his gift to various cousins of the house of Gwynedd of cantrefs he did not possess, and promises of yet other cantrefs if they could win them, while the Welsh laughed at his promises and threats alike, all these spiteful and ludicrous expedients by which he sought to buy off destiny passed by the builders like withered leaves blown in the wind. They had more important things to think about.

Only when Isambard came out to the church and stood watching them at work, as he did daily, some emanation of unassuageable grief reached out to them from his silence to discomfort and dismay.

Another Easter came and went, and in France King Philip, according to reliable reports, was building up a fleet and an army for his holy war against England, in derisive echo of John's ruined plans for the invasion of Normandy. If John did not move soon England would slip through his fingers like Normandy, like Wales; but there was no move left for him to make.

There was, however, one, it seemed, the last and most irretrievable; and on the 15th of May he made it. And in its immediate effects it was a master-stroke, though it proved in the long run a death-stroke, too. He had received, some two weeks previously, certain Knights of the Temple fresh from France, though not even his household officers knew what had passed between them. After their audience with him they sailed for France again, and in due course returned to Dover escorting the papal legate Pandulf; to whom, as vicar of the vicar of God on earth, the rebellious son of the Church surrendered, in return for the Church's protection, his kingdom of England and Ireland, and at whose hands he received them again as the Church's vassal, and accepted with them the archbishop he had so long refused to recognise.

A stroke of magic passed with the crown from hand to hand. It transformed the crusading Welsh princes into common rebels against the Lord's anointed. It snatched from Philip all claim to the prize he had been promised. It interposed the Church's protecting authority between John and his own discontented vassals. It gave him security, established him firmly in his curtailed rights, confounded all his enemies.

It also dishonoured him and broke his heart.

'But to kneel to him! Harry, to kneel to him and offer him the crown! It was England kneeling. How could he do it? How could he abase himself and us? If he had defied him, we could but have died, and we should have died unshamed. What is there in dying? Every man comes to it, it's nothing to fear. But to unman us all is worse than a death.'

After seven days of absence from the church and the world Isambard stood again in the nave, between the stony trees of heaven, in the silence of the twilight. The beautiful serried windows of the clerestory, open upon a soft green sky, looked in upon him like rows of luminous pale eyes in shadowy faces, watching and wondering. They said he had not eaten for four days, nor drunk, nor spoken a word since the one muted cry he uttered when the news was brought to him, before he fell senseless and was carried to his bed. He looked as if it might well be true. All his golden Grecian tan was long since faded; English summers had left him only the dull brown weathering of all men who lead outdoor lives. Now that, too, was blanched to a grey pallor, and the flesh worn away beneath it. His face was a mask of bone, but because his bones were ample and splendidly shaped his beauty was enhanced rather than impaired. The fine eyes, enormous in their cavernous sockets, were windows into a frenzy of pain, and the worst of the pain stemmed from that desolate intelligence of his, that would not let him leave one implication of catastrophe unexplored. His body was fallen away so that the most passionate ascetic of Clairvaux could hardly have matched his emaciation. Seven days of fasting could not account for this dissolution; it came from the spirit.

'Harry, Harry, in the night I see it, I cannot stop seeing it. The crown lay on the ground at his feet, and he spurned it with his shoe. He delayed giving it back, to assert his possession. England! We did not consent to it! Our name was taken in vain. But, oh, Harry, we cannot get clean of it now.'

He had reached the midmost point of the nave when he began to speak. It was the quietness and the loneliness that invited speech, here where the coming of night turned all that cheerful, busy, happy turmoil to stillness and peace. The first words came out of him like the first tears of one who has not wept for a lifetime, with spasmodic anguish, rending the tight cords of his throat; and then more freely, and then in flood. He lifted his contorted face to what light remained, and strained for breath as if he could not get enough air to keep life in him; but for the rest he stood very still, his clenched hands pressed together before his breast.

'My lord, it is not for me to accuse or defend him,' said Harry, shaken with the intensity of this agony. 'And yet I know this, that he also suffers. Out of the many dangers he saw for England, he chose to take this way, and the choice is his, as the burden was his. He sought to deliver England. My heart and my mind cry out in me, like yours, that he was wrong, yet I feel that his intent was not base. It was deliverance he sought, and by an act for my very life I could not match. Remember it to him, and forgive.'

'Forgiveness is not mine to give, and England will never give it. I would have spat in Pandulf's face rather than kneel to him.'

'And so would I,' said Harry, 'but who's to say if we should have been right?'

'Everything falls away, Harry! England I loved, and he has so befouled England that I cannot look on it without revulsion. Christendom I revered and trusted, and this is the voice of Christendom, the regen of God, this tortuous schemer who blows now east, now west, as his advantage lies. And thus shamelessly! Last year it was bell, book and candle out, and eternal salvation to all who take arms against God's enemy, John. This year, let all princes restrain their hands on pain of excommunication from the person of our beloved son. Oh, Harry, Harry, is it for the God of such a contemptible brazen weathercock as this that we've built a house fit for archangels?'

He clutched at Harry's arm; the convulsive grip of the bony fingers, so long and able, and now so helpless, the veins standing like blue cords between shrunken skin and starting bone, went to Harry's heart. He felt the shuddering tension of Isambard's body pass into him, and was flooded with so unexpected and uncontrollable an affection that it loosed his tongue from all the restraints of ceremony. He cast an arm about his lord's erect and fleshless shoulders, and clasped him warmly.

'What has Innocent to do with this? Often and often I have caught myself wondering about these same things. But always, when I felt my work growing beneath my hands, I wondered no longer. I build, and I feel no intervention of pope or priest between myself and God, and no doubt in my mind that this act of praise and faith is justified. King John may have failed you, but England has not. Innocent may shuffle his little blessings and bans without scruple, like loaded dice, but I swear God does not. I have not been building for pope or bishop or priest. The house *is* for the archangels.'

'Ah, it's well for you, who have to do with honest stone. But I am for ever bound, not to England, but to John. I am bound to him by oath of fealty, by the lands I hold, by the many times I have laid my hands between his hands. I am his man, whether I will or no. He has degraded and shamed me, but I am his man still. Let him be what manner of worm he will, I am not absolved from my oath, I can never be absolved. My allegiance corrupts and sickens me, but I cannot get free. I am his man till death, and I cannot get free!'

The hoarse, labouring voice, half-suffocated with raging grief, brought forth the words with convulsive effort, like gouts of blood breaking from a wound. He drew back his head, turning tormentedly to right and left, as though he struggled to evade the compulsion that drew him forward along the inescapable path of faithfulness. The arm that held him tightened. He closed his eyes for a moment, and opened the heavy lids again to behold the young, grave, troubled face, heavy with tenderness, regarding him as a loving child regards a parent overwhelmed with incomprehensible sorrow.

'Oh, Harry!' he said in a great sigh, and let his forehead rest for a moment in the hollow of the homespun shoulder. 'Oh, Harry, but I'm weary!'

CHAPTER TWELVE

Benedetta came down alone to the lodge, where Harry and Adam were inspecting the newly-cut voussoirs for the last of the tower windows. It had been raining, in the fitful April manner, with flashing sunlight between the showers, and the skirt of her green gown was dark from the wet grass. She ran her fingers along the joggled faces of the moulded stones, cut in deep, smooth waves, and asked curiously: 'Why do you cut them like that?'

'They key together more securely so. Look, they're matched to bind so close, you'll never see the join when they're raised.'

She fingered the mouldings and listened to the grinding hum of the wheel in the tower, hoisting stone, and the snatches of voices that the breeze brought from the scaffolding.

'How much longer now? A year?'

'Maybe a little longer. Call it a year, you won't be far out.'

'It seems impossible it can be so nearly finished.' The sadness came into her voice against her will. From beneath lowered lids she watched Adam take up mallet and chisel, and return whistling to the corbel on which he was working. 'When will the fabric be completed? Before the winter?'

'God willing! We're in the last stage of the tower. But there'll be work enough left for the winter inside. There's the floor tiles to lay, and the screens and stalls to fit, and the altar-stones and sedilia to put up. I doubt the glazier won't get all his windows in until the spring, so the scaffolding will stay up until next year. You should ask him to let you see the panels he has in their cames already, they're a wonder.'

'So by next year's summer,' said Benedetta, 'it will all be over.' She looked along the stored stones, fantasies of springing, burgeoning growth, crockets and mask-mouldings and bosses, and lengths of the prepared brattishing for the cornice of the tower. 'What will you do then?'

'I haven't thought of it yet. My lord has hinted at keeping me in his service. So great a landlord must be for ever building somewhere or other, there'd be plenty of work for me.'

'Yes,' she said, leaving the word solitary and lame on the air, though it seemed she must have intended something more; and she listened to Adam's whistling, and waited, he could not guess for what. 'You know the king is for France again?'

'So we heard. There's no curing him of this hankering after Normandy. Since his fleet made such short work of the French ships last year off Flanders, he's taken heart again, and no wonder. The churchmen may claim it was a divine judgement on Philip for striking at England sideways, after the Pope had forbidden him to go about it the direct way – but I doubt providence would have had its work cut out but for the king's energy and ability. But he'll find it a harder thing to get the better of Philip on his own soil. And the Emperor Otto isn't the ally I'd have chosen myself. What does my lord say?'

'I should ask you that,' she said drily. 'It's long since he confided such matters to me. But you know he holds the French possessions well lost, and wills that lost they shall remain, however it may displease his peers to part with half their revenue. He sees the only hope of England in accepting the loss of Normandy. A victory in France could set the king up in popular esteem, I suppose, at least for a time. But I'm sure Ralf prays for a defeat.'

'He has not sent for my lord to join him, at any rate,' said Harry.

'God be thanked! No, he is too distrustful of the Welsh; he wants Ralf here to hold the march for him. He puts little faith in this truce the archbishop has patched up between Welsh and English.'

She looked round quickly, hearing the light feet of the boy clerk from the tracing-house, running as usual. He bounced eagerly between the stacked stones, saw that Harry was occupied, and applied instead to Adam, in a breathless whisper.

'The devil!' said Adam, cheerfully enough. 'He could have chosen a better time. No matter, I'll come.' And he laid down his tools and went off briskly, his hand on the boy's shoulder.

As soon as they were well out of earshot Benedetta turned vehemently from her examination of the worked stones. 'Harry, send Adam away from here!'

His head came up with a jerk; he stared at her in blank incomprehension. 'Send him away? But why?'

'Because he's in danger here, or at any moment he may be. I had thought it might last out the time safely, but I'm no longer sure of it, and he must not be risked. Surely you can make use of him somewhere else? Send him out on your errands to the glasshouses and the pottery where you buy your tiles. But don't let him remain here at Parfois, constantly in my lord's sight.'

'My lord?' Harry put down his mallet and chisel among the array of punches laid out on his bench, and stood staring at her in doubt and wonder. 'What's awry between him and my lord? I know of nothing. He's taken little note of him all this time, but that little friendly enough. Why should he be dangerous to him now?'

'Because,' she said bluntly, 'he has begun to brood upon the remembrance that once, for the sake of a song, I received him into my bed. The time will surely come when that recollection will become unbearable. Don't let Adam be within his reach when that happens.' It was difficult to say, and ill to hear, and to be harshly practical about it was the only way of keeping it endurable. But his astonishment and reserve drew a smile from her. She had dragged him so abruptly out of the happy glades of his stone forest that he was at a loss with the complexities of a less perfect world. 'Have you not seen that he is fallen into a desperate jealousy of me? He talks to you more than to any. Has he never spoken of me in – strange terms?'

'Never!' But he had no sooner said it than he realised how seldom, in these last years, Isambard had so much as mentioned her name. He remembered, too, occasions when strange things had indeed been said, not of her, and yet closely touching her, now that he considered them more sharply. He had been too much engrossed with his own happiness to have much attention to spare for the dissatisfactions of others. He blamed himself for his blindness. 'And in your love, Harry?' the distant echoes mocked him. 'To have all, even the last and greatest! What right has one man to so much?'

'I see,' said Benedetta, 'that you have second thoughts.'

He shook his head helplessly. 'I've been a fool, I should have seen that there was grave matter in his moods. But indeed there was very little ever said, and nothing of you. And we knew he had always his time of darkness. But I cannot believe in his jealousy. That way it never tended, I swear. He knows well that you are honest in your dealings, he cannot be in doubt of your faithfulness.'

'Ah, faithfulness!' she said with a sigh. 'You are making my mistake, Harry. He wanted more than faithfulness.' She put up her hands and threaded the long fingers into the hair springing so vigorously from her temples; he saw how thin they were, pale among the dark red, and marvelled that he had not seen how she had lost flesh, as though she were being fretted away like her lord by the friction of the dual hopeless passion that at once joined and severed them.

'You'd better know how this thing stands,' she said almost roughly. 'You will need to regulate your acts accordingly. When he asked me to come to England with him I told him plainly there was one I loved, and in a measure that never comes again. I said that if he was willing to accept what I still had to give, I would be his, and never leave him unless for that one who had my heart's love. And God knows I did not lie, saying that *he* was never likely to beckon me! On those terms he took me, and I have held to my bargain faithfully. The more fool I, to think he could long hold to his! Did ever you know him content with second place? I should have known it could not so continue.'

She shook her head wearily between her hands. Harry did not touch her. Often in the past he had laid a hand on her easily, without a thought; now he perceived how terrifying was the power she had conferred on him to give her both pleasure and pain, and held back for fear the pain might prove the greater. And even this constraint between them seemed to him a false quantity, but he did not know how to master it.

'I begin to see,' he said in a low voice, 'how he has been cozened. Oh, not by you. He compounded for what you agreed to give, but he trusted in time and his own worth to have all at last. He could not know that he was bringing to England with him the very man he hoped to put out of your mind. And this, I misdoubt, you did not tell him.'

'You men,' she said, suddenly herself again, and looking up at him with a smile half scornful and half tender, 'are all the same. You have no more faith than Ralf, I see, in a woman's constancy of purpose. There was no need to tell him. It made no difference to the case whether you were near or far, living or dead. What I gave to you I gave once for all. I told Ralf the truth entire; that to this last sanctuary of my heart he could never come. My sin was not a sin of deceit, only of want of understanding. I should have known that was enough to bind him to the siege for ever. I did not know him so well then as I know him now. But now it too late to set it right.'

'Yet you may yourself be deceived. Benedetta, I am at a loss what to do. Surely if I should go from here, then in time – '

'You cannot go,' she said, 'until your work is finished. You pledged yourself. But even if you could, it is already too late. He knows he is not – no, I will not say "is not loved"! How could I not have some love for him, after all that has passed? But he knows that he will never enter the place of his desire. He knows I have not changed towards that other of whom I told him, and that I shall never change. Resignation is impossible to him. The struggle will go on, until one of us is destroyed – one, or both. I am only afraid that it may involve others, and I would not have Adam one of them. Get him away out of sight!'

'Oh, that's the least of the difficulties. I can send him to take charge at the quarry, you'll have heard that we're being raided again from Cynllaith, and we still need stone these next few months. But what of your own safety? If he cannot lay hands on – that other – may he not turn on you in the end?'

'Does it matter?' she said indifferently, not seeking to sting him, but honestly putting aside what seemed to her irrelevant. The consequences of what she had undertaken it was for her to abide.

'You know well it matters,' said Harry angrily. 'It is in my mind that you must leave him – '

'Then you may put it out of your mind, for I will not.'

'No,' he agreed, clutching helplessly at his temples, 'I see I should be wasting my breath to urge it. You'll hold by your word though it kill you, I know that. But for God's sake, what is to be done for you? I cannot leave it so. I would you might have loved him, for he was worth it, and now what's to become of you both? Oh, Benedetta,' he said wretchedly, 'if you had been less than you are, life would have been easier for us all.'

'I could say as much to you,' she said, looking up with that sudden indomitable flash in her eyes, the worn ghost of the old gallant laughter. 'Do you think I would have followed a lesser man across Europe? Life is always easy for those who have little mind and less heart. But indeed you need not fear for me. He loves me. He trusts me. He will not harm me unless he come to utter despair, and that I think is a state as impossible to him as resignation. It is not even a matter of pride in keeping faith now,' she said gently. 'He is mine, even if I cannot love him as he understands love. As for me, I no longer know what love is, it has so many faces. Even if – that other – beckoned me now, I could not go. What I did to Ralf I did unwittingly, but it binds me to him so fast that I can never get loose until death, unless he cut the knot and cast me off. So you see there is no profit in caring what becomes of me. Though

I'm glad,' she said, with a long, smiling glance of her grey eyes, 'that you feel it has some importance. That sets me up again in my own esteem.'

'I wish someone would do as much for me,' said Harry ruefully, 'for indeed I've been but a poor, unprofitable friend to you. At least promise that if you ever have need of one to do you a service, you will send me word before any other.'

'Gladly, if you will do as much for me. And it is in my mind, Harry, that I must not approach you so often or so freely as I have done in the past. It would be well if we had some other means of keeping in touch. I have often wished that I might know your wife better. Will you be my advocate to her? Say that I am lonely that I earnestly entreat her of her grace to spend some part of her time with me daily.'

She laughed at the sudden boyish flush that coloured a face mature, resolute and grave. 'It is not all strategy, I give you my word. I could love her, if she will let me. But there is art in it, too, I grant you. Wives and mistresses do not keep company. I would have him in no doubt of your position, and I would have a reliable contact with you, in case of need. Tell her as much as you please of the reason. All, if you will. What you do not tell, I think she will guess.'

'I will talk to Gilleis,' he said very quietly. 'She will come to you. I think she will be glad.'

'Ask her to visit me tomorrow while he is about his business with the steward and the rolls. And take care of the matter of Adam. I must go back, I have been longer over my errand than I meant.'

'Benedetta,' he burst out abruptly, as she made to turn from him, 'what was it awakened him?'

She opened her eyes wider upon his face, in quick and wary surprise that he should penetrate so surely into the one corner of her mind she had kept from him. He went on hesitantly: 'When we first came here, I swear, he was happy – as happy as it is in his nature to be. I blame myself that I did not mark when he began to change, but I think this was no gradual corruption that came upon him. He knows his worth too well to be lightly persuaded you could hold out against him lifelong. He would be hoping and believing yet, if something had not happened to show him the truth. What was it?'

It was the only moment in which she had ever been tempted to lie to him. He saw the grey eyes veiled and withdrawn for an instant, then they cleared and shone upon him, and he knew she had put the shadow by.

'It was your marriage,' she said gently. 'It was a novel conception for him that marriage should be the crown of love, instead of a bargain struck as a means to land or wealth or blood alliances. I suppose he had never been so close to such a match before. It went to his heart. That same night he offered me a princely gift. He offered me marriage, a marriage after the new dispensation.'

He stood staring at her steadily, while the blood drained from his face. He could not speak, there was nothing to be said to her. He had been always the fool of God blundering about her life without ill intent, innocently smashing all that she valued, breaking down the walls of her peace, complicating all her straight courses into a labyrinth.

'I refused it,' said Benedetta simply. 'I could do no other. So he could hardly fail to understand.'

She turned her head, and saw Adam coming across the trampled, threadbare grass. The gay, light sound of his whistling went before him like a blackbird's rich notes. He had not a care in the world.

'I would I had never set foot in your life,' said Harry in a low voice. 'I have brought you nothing but sorrow. I pray you pardon me!'

'*Pardon!*' She turned on him suddenly a startled face, bright and fierce as a flame, the eyes enormous with astonishment. She opened unwary lips to pour out to him the spring of molten gold that gushed from her heart. But Adam's foot was already light on the beaten earth under the penthouse roof, and a snatch of laughter, and a voice complaining querulously of the inattention and levity of boys nowadays, followed him in. Benedetta turned and left the lodge without a word.

There were no lives lost in the little war of Cynllaith that spring, though there were a good many knocks exchanged and a few minor arrow wounds to tend and the constant annoyance of losing horses and oxen. It seemed that Llewellyn was doing no more than tease his enemy. Only occasionally did the tribesmen launch an open raid. They sank one cargo of stone in the Tanat, and held up operations for ten days, while the river was cleared again. They made one testing raid on the loaded wagons after Adam's arrival, to see what mettle of man they had to deal with, and drew off with honours even. But for the most part they preferred to thread the picket line by night and filch a horse or two, or drop a tree neatly across the wagon track, or steal the harness. Theft, the most despised and condemned of crimes at home, was an honourable amusement once it crossed the border.

The Prince of Gwynedd had not, apart from these playful activities, laid a finger on the truce which Archbishop Langton, once established, had made it his business to prolong between England and Wales. Such pinpricks could hardly be regarded as an infringement of the terms; and indeed, why should Llewellyn want to renew hostilities, when he had consolidated all his gains and retained them unchallenged? Innocent had not, after all, quite forgotten the services of the wild hillmen he had never seen.

But at the height of the summer Adam, who had taken to this skirmishing like a duck to water, dealt all too competently with a raiding party by the riverside, and took three prisoners. He sent them under escort to Parfois. Isambard, without hesitation and without even having set eyes on them, had them hanged. After that it was *galanas*, blood-feud, but without the possibility of an atonement price being paid. The clans of the three dead men, all local, began to pick off stragglers from the stone convoys, and any man who unwarily showed himself too near the border was bound to draw an arrow from the thickets beyond the brook. Before July was out it became clear that the Prince of Gwynedd also considered himself to be at feud on his men's account. He had a country at peace, a vigorous little household army of a hundred and fifty men spoiling for work, and many hundreds of his free clansmen willing and ready to provide reserves if they should be needed. Private hate could never have deflected him from the larger affairs of his country; but now he had leisure to indulge it without risk to Wales. The little war of Cynllaith had become more than a game.

Adam held his own through two probing attacks, and sent back information which indicated that Llewellyn's own household troops had come into Cynllaith, and that the prince's captain of the guard, if not the prince himself, was directing them.

'Good!' said Isambard grimly. 'There'll be neither king nor court to run between us this time. We'll lead him on so far there'll be no withdrawing.'

'Shall I send reinforcements to the quarry?' asked de Guichet. Parfois carried at this time only its normal household companies, but they made a sufficiently formidable array.

'Not a man! No, you take one company by the inland road to

Oswestry, and I'll take the second by Careghofa, and we'll lie off until he moves in, and circle him from north and south together.'

The quarry continued under increasing pressure, but was not directly attacked, as the two forces closed unobtrusively into position north and south of the outcrop of hills, waiting for the Prince of Gwynedd to ride into the trap. Their scouts filtered towards the border and beyond, and found no Welshmen under arms. Isambard, chafing at Careghofa, devoured his own starving heart and waited.

Two messengers rode into Parfois on the seventh day of August. The first brought the news that at Bouvines King Philip of France had won a resounding victory over the Emperor Otto, scattering the great coalition in fragments about the fields of France, and forcing John to enter into negotiations for a long truce. The second reeled in from the south on a lathered horse, and slid from his saddle in the outer ward to gasp out news that touched Parfois more nearly. While Isambard waited for Llewellyn in the north, Llewellyn had transferred his forces to the south, and struck at the manor of Erington, on the border of Herefordshire.

Every man in the castle who was fit to ride and had any skill in arms was drafted into the motley company FitzJohn flung together within the hour. It had taken him no more than five minutes to send off a courier, on the best horse he had left in the stables, to carry the news to Isambard, but Erington could not wait until the cheated companies rode south. The palisade had been breached before the messenger broke through to ride for help, and the garrison in their timber keep would be only too vulnerable. Harry dropped his tools and offered himself with the rest, a score of his men on his heels. He was no great swordsman, but he could handle a blade in an emergency, and arms they had in plenty.

They rode out from Parfois and galloped south on the ridge road under a cloudless sky faintly shimmering with heat haze.

'August!' said FitzJohn bitterly as they mounted. 'No rain for a month, and his reverence preening himself on the success of his prayers for good harvest weather. If he's in his wits he'll be on his knees now praying for a downpour.'

The bells were loud in England again; they heard them ringing for vespers from all the churches along the valley as they forded the Clun, hardly slackening speed to find a good footing through the shrunken summer waters.

'And all the brooks dry,' fretted FitzJohn, 'and the manor well will be low. It they're out of arrows they'll have no choice but to make a sally against odds, or stay and be roasted.'

From the crest of the hills, as they climbed out of the river-valley, they saw smoke rising sullenly black against the pale blue sky. Long, drifting plumes of smoke, disseminating very slowly in an almost motionless air, hung like a grey ceiling above the skyline. They fetched a new burst of speed at the sight, though the horses were in a foam of sweat and had been pressed hard all the way.

For all their wild ride they came late. Llewellyn had played his cards well, and he was always a quick worker. Galloping from between the low, rolling hills, they saw the whole broad enclosure of the motte gushing smoke, and heard the crackling of wood as the flames twisted it, and it seemed to them that the whole of the manor was afire. Then, as they rode shouting down the curve of the fields and plunged at the steep sides of the mound, they saw the Welsh tribesmen scatter from the ditch and fling themselves towards their tethered ponies, and marked how one at least dropped and lay kicking with a clothyard shaft through him. The archers within the keep still had arrows, though how they could see to aim them was past guessing.

Under the pall of smoke the Welshmen drew off into the trees, but before many of them could untether and mount the motley muster of English had ridden into them, and they turned to fight. Great tongues of woodland came down here between the hills from Radnor Forest. Such of the Welshmen as broke away and found their mounts could be as elusive as foxes in that covert.

Harry leaned sidelong from the saddle to evade a braced lance, and wheeling his horse, ran his assailant through the upper arm and caused him to drop his weapon. The Welshman promptly sprang within his guard, and clamped his one good arm round his enemy's waist to drag him from the saddle, but Harry reversed his sword and clubbed at the uplifted forehead with the pommel, and as the dazed man relaxed his grip a little, kicked a foot free from the stirrup and hoisted his knee under the bearded chin, to hurl him off like a stone from a sling. He crashed among the roots of an oak, and lay winded. Harry hesitated only a second, looking down doubtfully at the gasping body, and then swung away to look for an undamaged opponent.

In the confusion of that brief battle in the edge of the wood he did no further hurt to anyone. Twice he pursued fugitive shapes that lay upon the necks of their ponies and rode through the coverts as daringly and smoothly as running wolves; but the first outran him easily, and the second he left at the summons of FitzJohn's horn. The English drew together out of the forest and converged upon the blackened shell of Erington, bringing six prisoners with them. The rest of the Welsh were safely away, and without fresh horses they were unlikely to be overtaken now. Far more urgent was the plight of the garrison, or what remained of it.

The gates of the palisade hung charred and glowing on their great hinges, sagging open on the smoky pale within. They hacked their way through into the bailey, and set to work to hew down the timbers that were still burning, and beat out the flames where the fire had taken less firm hold. All the stables and storehouses along the curtain had been plundered and fired, and there was no saving anything there, all they could do was use the axes on them wherever approach was possible, and bring them down. But the keep was still intact, only blackened with smoke and smouldering dully on the windward side. The timbers of the undercroft were hot to the touch, and the archer who threw open the door above and leaned out to hail them was smoked like a herring; but the garrison within were alive. They let down the ladder, and climbed out with their wounded, hoarse and parched and reaching eagerly for the offered flasks of water.

'If we had not been well-found in arrows,' said the castellan, 'and had four crack shots among us, they could have burned us to the ground long before this. And you come just in time, for we were down to our last dozen shafts. They drove off the stock hours ago, as soon as they had us bottled in here.'

They told over their losses, bringing out the wounded and the dead to the open meadow out of the heat and suffocation of the motte. Seven English bodies and four Welsh lay together on the cool turf. There were three English badly wounded, and five with lesser hurts. Two tribesmen were brought out alive to join the six prisoners taken in the fight on the edge of the wood.

'We're here for the night,' said FitzJohn, looking round on the falling dusk. He made his dispositions briskly: three parties to make the round of the nearest villages, where no doubt the inhabitants were huddled within barred doors at the rumour of the Welsh raid, to commandeer fresh horses and supplies of food; a line of pickets to cover the Welsh approaches, in case the raiders should be contemplating another visit by night; a lightweight on a fresh horse to ride back along the road to Parfois and intercept Isambard with the news; and half a dozen volunteers to scout through the woods into Radnor and try to get word which way the drovers had passed with the cattle and oxen. Oxen, of all living creatures, will not be hurried. If they could be recovered, so much the better.

Harry undertook this forest patrol gladly. If he was to remain a second day absent from his work, as well get all the freedom and exercise he could out of it.

'Make what use you can of the light that's left,' said FitzJohn, 'but don't push on after dark. We'll look for you back in an hour or so.'

Isambard's land fingered the edge of Wales here, as at Parfois, but with no river between them. Harry rode through the woods alone, in a silence so profound that the blazing turmoil of Erington became a fantasy. Twice he came upon forest hamlets, but the villagers had neither seen nor heard anything of the raiders, or else they made a habit of closing both eyes and ears whenever there was a possibility of such visitors passing close to their solitude. There was a good deal of Welsh blood in some of the veins on this side the border, too, and even those who were indubitably English had to live at peace with both sides if they wished to make their homes here. And once he found a small, isolated clearing of plough-land with a mean little dwelling upon it, almost certainly an illegal assart, but law limped with both feet these days. How long was it since the king's justices had been on circuit in any of these border shires? A matter of years? And no prospect of much improvement in the future, now that there was open talk of an alliance of barons to put an end to the king's infringements of their rights. When Corbett and FitzAlan and their kind began to talk of defending their rights, there was not likely to be much attention paid to the rights of lesser mortals.

Harry rode silently in the spongy turf, and was deeply content with his loneliness. He did not really want to find any traces of the Welsh. Let them have their spoils, they had lost several men to gain them, and it was Isambard who had first aggravated the rivalry into a blood-feud. He was on the point of turning to make the best of his way back to the manor, when he caught a glimpse of something small and furtive that ran aside among the falling shadows, and vanished into a clump of bushes. The quivering of the branches subsided slowly as he walked his horse past the spot; whoever had dived into cover there was crouching within the thicket.

He drew a yard past the place, and then kicked his feet from the stirrups and vaulted down almost on top of the watcher in the bushes. A shrill cry of fright startled his ears, and a wiry little body, slippery as an eel, fought to elude his grasp and narrowly failed. He caught the sudden narrow gleam of steel darting at his breast, and his parrying hand closed on a wrist so slender that he almost let it go again. A breathless voice bubbled Welsh curses at him, spitting like an angry cat. He had much ado to keep his hold on the furious, frightened little creature, it fought and struggled so; but in a few moments the struggles began to flag and breathless sobs to disrupt the curses. Harry plucked the dagger from a tiring hand and tossed it away into the bushes, and folding his right arm firmly round the boy, hauled him out into the open ride and stood him on his feet.

'Hush, now, hush your noise! I won't hurt you. Do you understand English?'

He got no answer at first. The child stood trembling under his hands, tensed to run like a hare at the first opportunity; a small, dark boy in brown hose and tunic, with a little homespun cloak buckled with gold on his shoulder. The face that stared sidelong up at him looked all eyes in the gathering darkness, a bright, moon-like shining of eyes, wild and wary as a fox's gleaming glance. He could not have been more than nine or ten years old, and small even for his age. Harry saw that the cloak was torn and the left cheek bruised and grazed. He dropped on one knee to bring his face on a level with the child's, and asked again gently: 'You understand what I'm saying, don't you? Don't be afraid of me, I don't want to hurt you. But what are you doing here by yourself in the forest? Did you fall from your horse?'

The dark head nodded slowly. 'I tried to catch him,' said the boy suddenly in English, 'but he ran away.' He trembled more violently, but he was less frightened now.

'Are you hurt?' But the question was more by way of establishing sympathy than to extract information; to judge by the way he had fought, he had got nothing worse than a shaking. 'Well, now, tell me how you came here alone? They surely didn't bring you raiding with them?'

Surprisingly the boy burst into tears at this; plainly there was something here that weighed on his mind even more distressingly than his fears at finding himself alone and benighted on the wrong side of the border. Harry was startled into offering a comfortable shoulder, and held and gentled him while he poured out his trouble in mingled English and Welsh. There was nothing new or surprising in it, after all; disobedient brats grow everywhere.

'Ah, so your father left you safe at Llanbister, did he? And gave you orders to stay there, and never stir a step. And there he'll expect to find you safe and sound when he comes back from his foray, no doubt. And this is how you've obeyed him!'

'I wanted to see,' said the child, with a spark of the spirit that had got him into trouble.

'Curiosity killed the cat, did you never hear that? You should have done as you were told, and you'd have missed a fall and a fright. Never mind, we must see about finding you a place to sleep the night, and some food to put inside you.'

'My father'll beat me,' said the boy, and wept again heartily.

'Very possibly, and well you deserve he should. But not tonight. And who knows? By the time he gets you back he may be so glad to see you, he'll forget about your sins. Come on, now, I'm going to take you back with me. Don't be afraid of anything, I promise you shall be safe with me.'

The dark head came up nervously from his shoulder, like a young horse shying. 'You're English!'

'So I am, but I'm no monster, all the same. Child, if I left you here what would happen to you? Come along, and trust me to take care of you. I'm better than the wolves, at any rate.'

He lifted the child to the saddle-bow, and mounted behind him, and so brought him back to Erington. It was dark by the time they emerged to the acrid smell of smoke and the dull glow of flattened timbers just burning out. Heat still quivered on the air. The boy, whose head had been nodding upon Harry's shoulder during the ride, started awake and looked round fearfully with great eyes and clung tightly to his captor's sleeve as he was lifted down among the strangers.

'God's wounds, Harry!' said FitzJohn, staring. 'What have you got there?'

'A venturesome young man who went where he was told not to go, and got himself lost and thrown in the woods. He's shaken and bruised, but nothing worse. I'll share my cloak with him tonight, and see about getting him back where he belongs tomorrow. If you'll feed him you'll have his love for life, I see it in his eyes.'

'Welsh?' asked FitzJohn, his eyes sharpening.

'I thank God!' snapped the child, before Harry could answer for him; and he stiffened and drew back his head like a hound raising its hackles.

'And a very proper spirit, too,' said Harry, laughing. 'Come, we'll find you some food to keep that temper of yours in good heart. Is there news from my lord?'

'He has sent de Guichet from Clun cross-country with most of his force to try and intercept Llewellyn, but it's certain even he expects nothing from it, or he'd have gone himself. They have too great a start of us. The rest he has despatched home, but for his immediate attendants, and they lie at Clun tonight. In the morning he'll be here.'

'At least he knows by now that most of his garrison still live,' said Harry, and took the boy by the arm to guide him through the camp. He gave him oatcakes, and some of the foraged beef that was already cooking, and watched him eat his fill. Then he cut swathes of the long dry grass from the headlands, and piled it for a bed on the springy turf at the edge of the trees. The child sat hunched, hugging his knees and staring all round him at the alien faces, suspicious and lonely. Harry said nothing to him, but wrapped himself in his cloak and lay down. In a few minutes the dark eyes turned wistfully upon him and the boy edged a little nearer. Harry rose on one elbow, smiling, and opened his cloak without a word. It was invitation enough. The child crept thankfully into the hollow of his arm and curled up against his side; the cloak wrapped them both.

'What's your name, imp? I forgot to ask it.'

'Owen ap Ivor ap Madoc,' murmured the drowsy mouth into his shoulder, and yawned hugely.

'Then, Owen ap Ivor ap Madoc, goodnight! Don't be afraid when you wake, I shall be here.'

Isambard rode in at dawn, before the sun was up or the camp fully astir. He had shed the weight of his arms at Clun, but for the light hauberk of banded mail, and his sword. Three of his squires rode behind him. He looked upon what was ruined and what was saved of his manor with an equal attentive calm, his motionless face lean and fierce as a haggard's mask. He looked upon the six living prisoners and the two who were half dead, and said: 'Hang them!'

'My lord! – all of them? There are two who cannot stand.'

'It will be but two yards farther to hoist them,' said Isambard in the same flat voice, and looked indifferently along the edge of the woodland. 'There are trees enough.' The cold glance ended in the piled dry grass, where two slept in one cloak. 'What's this? Where did you find the child?'

He went close and stood over them, looking down beneath drawn brows at the boy's flushed face and tousled head, pillowed on Harry's arm. FitzJohn came to his shoulder.

'Harry caught him in the forest, near the border. It seems he must have followed the raiding party out of curiosity, and in the alarm when they withdrew he was thrown, and lost his mount. I think he may be a most profitable capture.'

'He's Welsh?'

FitzJohn laughed. 'To very good purpose he's Welsh! I asked the same question, and he all but spat in my face. It wasn't till the cockerel crowed that I knew him. Do you not recall that face, my lord?'

Isambard pondered, frowning. 'It seems to me that I have seen him before, though I don't know where. Well, speak if you know! Who is he?'

'You must have seen him at Aber. Oh, there was no reason you should mark him there, you had to do with the men and not the children. But when I was there on your lordship's business, after you returned home, I saw this boy very often about the court, in company with the son of Princess Joan. He's heir to Ivor ap Madoc, who was the prince's *penteulu* – the captain of his guard – until he died, some years ago. The boy is Llewellyn's own fosterling.'

'Some say he's more,' said Langholme, half respectful and half knowing, looking sidelong at his lord.

'What do you mean by that? Ivor ap Madoc I remember well. It was natural enough for Llewellyn to take his child, it would be but a modest extension of their usual custom.'

'Yes, my lord, but there's more to it than that.'

'I may trust you,' said Isambard with a curl of his lip, 'to know all the kitchen gossip of Aber after one visit.' But he listened, none the less, with a gleam in his sunken eyes.

'Why, there's none bold enough to say it aloud, and I would not claim it's general, even in a whisper. But Ivor had been married nearly seven years to a lady of Lleyn, and was childless, to their great sorrow. He did not want to put her away, being very fond, but he needed an heir to keep his lands intact from three or four quarrelling cousins. I think they came very near parting, when suddenly the lady found herself with child, and all was well for them. The Prince of Gwynedd was dear friend to them both. And it was well for him that there should be a son, too, to keep the land together. Some say they compounded all three. But the usual whisper is that the prince and the lady conspired to make Ivor happy. He died when the boy was rising two years old, but he died content.'

'It may be true,' said FitzJohn, low-voiced, looking at the child. 'He's as black as Llewellyn, and as proud. And it seemed to me in Aber that the prince doted on his fosterling as on his own boy. But the tale of his getting I never heard.'

'It may well be true,' mused Isambard darkly. 'She would not be the first to make shift for an heir with another man's help. Yet Llewellyn acknowledges his known bastard proudly, it would go against the grain with him to hide this one.'

'My lord, he could do no other, for Ivor's name and the lady's, even after Ivor's death. The boy inherits handsomely from the father who acknowledged him, he has lands in Arfon and Ardudwy, he has no need of endowment from the prince. And as for any desire he had for the child himself,' said Langholme, 'you see he has him. On the mother's re-marriage – her clan married her again to a lord of Eifionydd, and she has two children by him now – Llewellyn took the boy into fosterage at his own suggestion, or so they say. It was shortly after young David's birth, they grew up together. Whether the tale's true or not, the prince loves them both alike, by all that I saw at Aber. My lord, I think he would compound an eternal peace with you and pay you indemnity for Erington into the bargain, to recover this boy.'

The rising sun laid long fingers of brightness across the sloping meadows to eastward, and threaded the branches of the trees above the sleepers, creeping upwards from Owen's soft, parted lips and round cheeks to stroke his long lashes and smooth eyelids. The touch penetrated his sleep. He stirred within Harry's sheltering arm and stretched and yawned pinkly, like a waking puppy, before he opened his eyes. Then the sharp flash of the sunlight from Isambard's rings made him screw up his eyes and jerk his head aside, starting into wakefulness.

He found strange faces and pale sky and the faintly-stirring branches of trees hanging over him, and felt a man's hard body beside him and the ground under him instead of his own rustling, sweet-smelling bed and his foster-brother's warm softness. He uttered a sharp whimper of fright, and started up, waking Harry, who had the gift of springing immediately into wakefulness and coherence. His reassuring arm tightened round the boy and held him close. His voice, already familiar again where all was unfamiliar, said easily: 'Now, now, Owen ap Ivor ap Madoc, where's the need of a noise like that on such a fine morning?'

He turned his head to smile at the boy, and saw the three men standing silent over them, with a strange and somewhat sinister significance in their hooded stares, or so it seemed to him. Recognising Isambard, he flung off the cloak, smiling, and scrambled to his feet.

'My lord! I did not know you were here. You had me at a disadvantage – I trust my sleep was seemly?'

'As the child's,' said Isambard without a smile. 'I have been hearing about your prisoner, Harry. It seems you have made a capture of some importance.'

Harry followed the look and the tone together, and came towards the truth by blind leaps. The smile left his face. He put out a hand and drew Owen close against his hip. 'I did not – I do not look upon him as a prisoner, my lord.'

'Then you had better begin, for that is what he is.'

'He was not involved in the attack made on your manor,' said Harry. 'I found him benighted in the forest, and it is my intent to set him safely on his way home.'

'Instead, you may take him back with you to Parfois, suitably escorted. I am not sure, Harry, that you might not lose your way with him if I let the pair of you go alone.' He would not be angry; he could even smile on them, though the gaunt face looked strangely cruel, smiling.

'It was never your way,' said Harry, matching stare for stare, 'to make war on children.'

'Not on them, Harry. But with them, perhaps. I think you do not know that what you hold there under your hand is the price of peace along this border. Tell him, boy,' he said, looking down at Owen not unkindly, and modulating his voice into a cold gentleness, 'what is your relationship with the Prince of Gwynedd?'

Owen, perhaps as a gesture for his people, perhaps in offence at being discussed thus openly, chose to answer in Welsh, and with a defiant sparkle in his eyes.

'Did he not say "Father"?' asked Isambard, who had but few words of the outlandish tongue.

'No,' said Harry, 'The word was "foster-father".'

'There's little difference to a Welshman. They fight to the death for their foster-brothers, and for their fosterlings, too, if need be.

You did not know of the connection?'

'I did not, but it alters nothing. The child is not to blame for this feud, whoever may be. He is not a prisoner of war.'

'It is arguable. He was taken on my land, and he was attached, however loosely, to the party that made this havoc here. He is the king's prisoner, since he was taken on land I hold from the king and in infringement of the king's truce. He goes back to Parfois.'

'I promised him shelter and safety,' said Harry. 'Will you do as much, my lord?'

'I need make no promises to my prisoners, and I'll make none to my underlings.' By the dryness of the voice and the tight pallor of the lips from which it spoke Isambard was surely drawing near the always abrupt breaking-point of his patience. From no other did he bear so much as from Harry Talvace, but the limit was dangerously close. 'If you wish to take him, take him. If not, Langholme shall, I care not so we have him safe. Llewellyn shall not have him back cheaply. I'll make him sweat for him.'

There was no help for it. The boy stood straight, glaring silent defiance, but the small hand gripped Harry's sleeve with a desperate anxiety. 'I'll take him back, then, if I must. And give me this, at least, that my wife and I may have the care of him while he remains at Parfois.'

'As you please,' said Isambard, with a faintly scornful smile. 'FitzJohn, find the boy a horse, and have six archers escort them back. Archers, Harry!' he repeated pointedly. 'I shall find the pair of you at Parfois when I return – dead or alive.'

'I've said I'll take him!'

'That's well! And you had best have him away from here quickly, before we deal with his countrymen.'

Harry understood, and felt his heart shrink for the bearded fellow he had wounded. So brief and inimical an encounter, and yet it made them men to each other, as none of his enemies was a man to Isambard. He made haste to feed the boy and get him mounted; they would not delay their grim work out of tenderness to him. Owen, anxious as he was, ate with an appetite that reminded Harry to fill his saddle-bag; small boys are always hungry. The child brightened, too, once they were on their way; his lost and frightened condition was not past comforting by a sunny day and a ride and the near presence of someone whom he felt to be friendly. Still silent and nervous as they threaded the low hills, he took heart from Harry's relief as the blackened shell of Erington vanished behind the ridge, and the woodland and its bitterly misused trees disappeared with it.

'Who is that terrible man? Is he the lord of Parfois?'

'Yes, but you'll see little of him, you'll be with me. My wife will make you welcome. Never worry about him.'

'Shall I have to stay there long?'

'Not long,' said Harry, with more conviction than he felt. 'They'll soon come to terms over you and send you home.'

'My foster-father won't know I'm gone until he reaches Llanbister. Even then he won't know where I am. No one knows!' He jutted an unsteady underlip, tears not far away. 'He'll worry about me.'

'Never fret so,' said Harry cheerfully, 'they'll send him word where you are.' But he wished he knew if they would. To leave Llewellyn to his anxiety, scouring Radnor Forest and the border country far and wide for his wayward fosterling, might appeal to Isambard as a sweet first move in the exploiting of his unexpected advantage. 'Think that you are come to visit an uncle at Parfois,' he said, 'and be sure you'll be home soon enough, and forgiven for all your sins. But you'll never disobey again, will you?'

Owen promised, but with markedly less fervour than he would have shown an hour ago. He was beginning to enjoy his ride and almost to look forward to Parfois, and he found Harry's reassurances convincing because he wanted to be convinced. By the time they splashed through the ford he had rebounded into gaiety and was preening himself on his prince's escort of archers, who rode behind at a respectful but watchful distance. Long before they rode up the green track to Parfois he was chattering and singing like a blackbird. The first pair of guard towers on the steep rise awed him into silence again, but when they emerged upon the plateau, to see the castle rising before them, and the church, warmed into gold by the sun, stretching its tall tower skywards in the rigid net of scaffolding, his eyes grew great and round with wonder and excitement. He was too deeply enchanted and too insatiably curious to be afraid. Even Llewellyn's great timber maenol at Aber was never like this. His head began to turn left and right wildly, staring at everything. The questions would come later, in an inexhaustible flood; for the moment he was speechless.

Gilleis was crossing the inner ward towards the King's Tower when they walked in together through the dark passage from the outer ward, Harry's hand on the boy's shoulder. She stood at gaze, astonished and moved as by a moment of prophetic vision.

How often since her marriage, and recently with what insistent and increasing longing, she had thought of the delight of having Harry's son in her arms. They had spoken of it together frequently, always as something that would surely come, but of late she had begun to wonder. After four years of marriage without issue people begin to call a woman barren. Love remains, love always, love without a shadow, but without its crown, too. And suddenly here came Harry, unexpected and without his companions of the muster, bringing her in his hand a straight, sturdy, staring child like a miraculous gift. A bold, black-haired, sweet, striding boy, as dark of eye and as red of mouth as his mother, and as brown and tough and proud as his father. They came straight to her, Harry smiling, the child grave and on his best behaviour.

Gilleis was smiling, too, though she did not know it, a wondering, dazzled smile, as though the sun had shone in her eyes.

'Gilleis,' said Harry, his free hand reaching for hers, 'I've brought you a guest. Here is Owen ap Ivor, who is going to live with us for a while. Make him welcome!'

The child, anxious to do honour to himself and his blood, made her a bow of such solemnity that only the deep obeisance to a king seemed appropriate in reply, and then redeemed himself by looking up at her as candidly as a flower and holding up his face to be kissed. She took his round cheeks in her palms, and kissed him.

'You are welcome to my heart, Owen. Indeed, indeed, I am happy to see you.'

She drew him into her arms, and the stiff little body melted into warmth and softness on her breast. He put his arms round her neck and his grubby cheek against her cheek. She felt the springs of her being rise in flood and spill over in a torrent of silent joy.

In the columns of the south porch, which Harry was carving *in situ*, appeared a small, hilarious angel on one side, and an unruly but engaging imp on the other, both with the face of Owen ap Ivor. A somewhat turbulent and spoiled angel he made, and a warm-hearted and affectionate imp, so that no one could ever be really sure which of the figures was which aspect of him.

By mid-September he was very much at home in Parfois, though his movements were restricted to the two wards of the castle, and he chafed at being turned back every time he followed Harry to the drawbridge. There was scarcely room within the gates for his energy and enterprise, and others, as well as the boy himself, found his confinement hard to bear. The falconers in particular, whom he especially elected to assist, added their heartfelt prayers to Harry's when he begged that the boy should be allowed at least as far as the church. They liked him well enough, and owned that for his years he was knowledgeable about birds, but he was so perilously innocent of fear that he treated even the great gerfalcons like pet merlins for ladies, and they lived in mortal dread that he would lose at least a thumb at any moment, if not an eye.

'He has no notion of running away,' said Harry. 'But even if he had, there's but one way down from here; you could as well turn him back at the lower guard as here at the gate-house. And he'd be the better for it if you'd let him ride sometimes. If two of the archers rode with him you'd be in no fear of losing him. You could see to it they're better mounted than he is.'

'You're mighty solicitous for him,' said Isambard, curling his lips in the angry smile that was never far from his countenance.

'I know how I should have felt if I'd been mewed as close at his age, and for as long. I'd have had the towers down round your ears by now.'

'I can believe it! Well, let him ride, if it will keep you content. I'll have FitzJohn give him two reliable men as escort, and he shall have his freedom as far as the lower guard.'

Harry thanked him, and was at the door, well pleased to be running with such good news, when Isambard called him back. 'Does he ask? About when he's to go home?'

'Yes. But not quite so often now. Not every day.'

'And what do you tell him?'

'What can I tell him? I say it will be soon.' He hesitated, looking down at the bony hand on which the rings hung so slackly. 'Does Llewellyn know that he's here?'

The smile flashed from the lips to the deep eyes, and kindled two red flames of bitter amusement that seemed to burn in a waste of hatred. 'He'll know by tomorrow. The messenger is on his way at this moment. Did you not know a courier came from him three days ago? Who would have thought it would take him so long to think of inquiring here? It's a long way from Llanbister to Erington, and it seems the pony made the best of its way home before they found it, so there was no way of knowing which way the boy had taken. They've been combing the wilds all this time. There are still wolves in Radnor.'

'Not only in Radnor,' said Harry bluntly.

Isambard's head went back in a brief shout of laughter, and the feral movement and the savage sound had indeed something of a wolf's howling about them. 'You still want to be my conscience, do you, Harry? Did I not tell you once, if you turn hedge-priest you'll come by a hedge-priest's end?'

'There are worse ends,' said Harry. 'But you will give him his nurseling back, won't you? Since you've let him know that he's here, I take it you've named your terms for handing him back? I tell you honestly, my lord, I'll be happier for you, as well as for Owen, when he's safe home again, though Gilleis will miss him sorely.'

'She will have him for a while yet,' said Isambard with bitter satisfaction. 'It isn't Llewellyn's purse that will buy him back, nor his black cattle, nor an indemnity for Erington, nor his pledge to keep the peace. I have not stated my terms yet, Harry, it's too soon, he has suffered nothing yet. A great many messengers will pass between Aber and Parfois before I talk of terms, and then they'll be terms of delay and doubt. The Prince of Gwynedd shall dance to my tune all the autumn, and then, when we're done with the quarry, I'll make him come here to me in person and beg for his brat on his knees.' He waited, watching Harry's face, and there was a silence. 'You disappoint me,' he said, mockingly, 'I had thought you would exclaim: "He will not do it!"'

'He will do it,' said Harry simply. 'He has done it for Wales and he'll do it for Owen. And it's not he who will have lost stature when it's done.'

He turned on his heel and went out, slowly because he expected to be called back yet again, but no soft, cold voice spoke his name, and no cry of rage halted him. He closed the door of the chamber behind him and went down the stone stairway still listening for the angry summons, even hoping for it; but it did not come.

However, he had the concessions for which he had asked. Owen rode out joyfully with his two guards, esteeming them a fitting tribute to a Welsh princeling; and when he was not scouring the countryside and flying the well-schooled little hawk they had entrusted to him, he was usually under Harry's feet about the church and the lodge, poking his nose happily into everything, misplacing tools, tinkering with the hand-hoists, borrowing drawings to try his own hand on the reverse, all in disarming innocence. The sole way to keep him still was to use him as a model. Harry had only to ask him to sit for one more figure, and he would endure for an hour with cheerfulness and devotion. On the frontal stones for the high altar he appeared as every one of the twelve little angels who played and sang in a seraphic consort. Rebec, harp, citole, shawm, gittern, bugle, cornemuse and organ, he played them all with a rapt solemnity, and four several images of him sang lustily out of one great psalter.

Inevitably he took mallet and chisel to a stone he should not have touched, but hit his own fingers before he did much damage to the stone. Gilleis scolded and comforted him, bathed his bruised hand, and lost him again to Harry as soon as the pain passed.

He was forbidden, under the threat of dire punishment in which he did not really believe, to set foot on the scaffolding except in Harry's company; but that, too, he had to try for himself. They thought nothing of it when they missed him from the lodge, since he came and went freely; but when all the masons had come down from the tower in the evening he was still missing, and the hunt for him ended only when a shrill yell, curiously compounded of bravado and fright, drew their eyes to the highest walk of hurdles that surrounded the half-completed parapet, more than a hundred feet from the ground. The cry came down to them thinly, falling through the clear, still air like a little bird's call; and there sat Owen ap Ivor, clinging to one of the poles very tightly with both arms, and dangling his feet over the void.

Suppressing an instinct to roar his rage and alarm in terms which might well have scared the imp over the edge, Harry called to him firmly and calmly to stay where he was and sit still, and himself went up and brought him down. When he had him safely on the ground, he flew into a temper all the more formidable for being deferred, and bundling the sinner headlong into the tracing-house, faithfully performed everything he had promised him.

Owen would not for the world have cried under punishment, though for less obvious reasons he would have liked to cry. When he was plumped unceremoniously back on his feet, and the hazel switch flung into a corner, he turned his back on Harry and stalked out with his head in the air, like the offended princeling he was, not even deigning to rub his hurts. But in ten minutes he was back again. He peeped in at the door gingerly, first one large, sullen black eye, then both. He put one foot into the room, then the second, and sidled along the wall with elaborate unconcern, as though he had not made up his mind whether he wanted to be noticed or not.

Harry was bending over his tables, assembling the drawings he had made for the altar of the Virgin. He observed the sidelong approach out of the tail of his eye, but made no sign. Owen leaned against the end of the trestle, and drew industriously in the grain of the wood with one finger-tip, and presently prolonged one of his imaginary lines so that it brought him gradually nearer to Harry's hip. Still the fish did not rise. A moment later the boy's shoulder pressed insinuatingly into Harry's side. For the first time he looked down, and beheld the curly head obstinately averted; but as he watched, it turned sidewise, just far enough to bring one reproachful eye to bear on his face. He smiled and dropped his dividers to open his arms, and instantly the child was in them, hugging him passionately. He said not a word, but buried his nose in Harry's cotte, and clung to him, making his peace in silence.

'Owen ap Ivor ap Madoc,' said Harry solemnly, hugging him back with goodwill, 'you're a terrible fellow! Will you mind me, the next time, and not frighten me out of my wits?'

The dark head nodded contentedly in the hollow of his shoulder.

'I was afraid you were going to hurt yourself – so I hurt you, instead. There's logic for you!'

Owen did not seem to find anything unreasonable in it; the same kind of thing must have happened to him before. Satisfied now, the security of their relationship re-established, he wriggled free and ran off to Gilleis, whistling tunelessly.

Only occasionally now did the anxious thoughtfulness fall upon him, and the familiar question come to his lips again:

'When shall I be going home?'

'Soon,' Harry would say quickly, looking round in haste to find a new lure to distract him, 'very soon now.'

Owen had a bad dream in the night, and started out of it in a panic to the palpitating darkness, out of which it seemed to him the denizens of his nightmare still hunted him. Desirous of company and comfort, but too proud to cry for them, he began to whimper and draw great sighs, as though in a troubled sleep, and presently had the satisfaction of hearing a light footstep in the doorway of his tiny room in the tower wall. The door that separated him from Harry's bed chamber stood always open at night, so that Gilleis could hear if he called to her, but he had never yet done so. At Aber he slept well out of earshot of his foster-parents, but at Aber everything was familiar, and he had David always in the bed beside him, so that he was never afraid of anything.

Gilleis had a small lamp in her hand, and her hair was loose upon her shoulders. She looked down at the restless sleeper, and smiled at the too tightly closed eyelids and the look of sharp, listening consciousness that betrayed him; and stooping, she kissed him on the cheek, so that he could awake and enjoy his success. He opened his eyes gratefully, and stretched up his arms to her, and the denizens of the dream were gone in a moment.

She knelt by the bed and held him half asleep on her breast while he babbled out his confused recollections of pursuit and terror. His trust and warmth and weight filled her with joy, and with that deeper content and fulfilment that made joy seem a slight and ephemeral thing. He lay on her heart, and it seemed to her that the newcomer, the wonderful creature under her heart, already drew breath with him.

'Silly boy, as if we'd let anything hurt you! No one can get in to you here, there's no one but the three of us, and God. So you know you must be safe, don't you? As safe in the darkness as in the day. I'm always close to you, you need only call me. Go to sleep again!'

When he was asleep, she laid him gently down in the bed, where he stirred and stretched, and subsided more deeply into slumber. She watched his sweet, easy breathing for a little while, and marked how all the foreshadowings of manhood, which showed so clearly in his waking face, withdrew from him in sleep and left him as innocent and defenceless as a baby.

She had had him for nine weeks now; one week for every year of his age. She could not hope to have him much longer. Llewellyn's couriers rode persistently between Aber and Parfois, carrying offers of ransom and pledges of peace along the march. When he had tormented the prince long enough, Isambard would surely send him his strayed chick home again. She no longer feared his going; the miraculous bud of promise her spirit had put forth at his coming had flowered triumphantly, and was already rounding into fruit, and the void he would leave in her heart the child of his heralding was waiting to fill.

She drew the coverlet closer round Owen's naked shoulders, for it was more than half way through October, and the nights were chilly. Feeling the touch, but undisturbed by it, he laughed in his sleep, a dazzling gift he had, and she felt herself filled to overflowing with his laughter as with a golden spring of sweet water gushing out of her heart. She was sorry for everyone in the world who had not her overwhelming reasons for happiness: for Benedetta who was childless and loved where she never could possess, for Isambard who broke every creature on whom he leaned, and then loathed them for breaking, even for the king, newly landed in the south from one humiliation to face the threat of another, the wretched king who was sick and angry and harried, and had lost his last gamble for Normandy. She was even a little sorry for Harry, because his part was only to beget and not to bear, and because he did not yet know how happy he was; and at the same time she envied him because he had yet to hear it, and that was a joy that could be tasted only once.

The child was deep asleep, the curves of the laughter still on his mouth. She went back into the chamber where Harry lay, and shading the tiny flame of the lamp with her hand so that the light should not fall directly on his face, stood beside the bed and looked at him earnestly.

Sleep took away years from him, too, but the lines of manhood, once graven, could not be erased. He had a touching duality, child and man together. The innocence and tranquillity that spring from knowledge and experience instead of from childhood and wonder belong only to the saints, and Harry was no saint; yet in sleep these were present in his face.

Gilleis set down the lamp, feeling the world shaken by one of those moments of unbalance and lightness that came on her sometimes now without warning. She was standing with both hands clasped to her body, her face bright and strange in the small light from below, when Harry opened his eyes, and sat up in bed with a soft, startled cry.

'Gilleis, love, what is it? What's the matter?' He reached for her hands, drawing her down to him. 'Little heart, are you ill?'

'Not ill,' said Gilleis, smiling. 'I've been to Owen, he had a bad dream, but he's asleep again now. Not ill, no. Indeed, it is very well with me.'

'You frightened me. You looked so strange.'

Smiling still, she blew out the lamp, and let fall the cloak she had wrapped about her to go to the boy. He turned back the covers of the bed, and she lay down beside him, shaking off the chill of the night in one tremor before she relaxed in his warmth. He laid his arm over her, and drew her close.

'I am strange,' said Gilleis, her lips against his cheek. 'I am a wonder. I am with child.'

'Gilleis!' It began as a shout of joy, but he suppressed it hastily to a whisper because of the boy. 'Is it true? Are you sure? Quite sure? Oh, Gilleis, when did you know? Why didn't you tell me?' He was incoherent and trembling with excitement. She laughed and embraced him, holding him to her heart as she had held Owen, and talking to him in the selfsame tone.

'Hush, you'll wake him! Yes, I'm quite sure, I waited to be sure. A month ago I thought it was so, but now I know it. It must have been in August I conceived, soon after Owen came. Harry, do you remember how you brought him to me, that day, and I not knowing who he was or how you came by him? It seemed to me like an omen. And ever since then it is as if the last secret place in me has opened and let you in. It always belonged to you, it always wanted you. But Owen opened the door.'

'Oh, Gilleis!' he said in a great sigh of delight. 'Oh, my lamb, my love, my rose!' He laid his hand softly upon her body below the heart, and lay quiet with it resting there. 'I'll be good to him. I'll make him a cradle fit for a prince. He'll be as beautiful as you.'

'And as foolish as you,' she said fondly, laying her hand over his. 'And as dear to me.' She turned her head upon the pillow and kissed him tenderly, as she would have kissed the child. 'Are you happy now?'

'Happy? More than happy! I have everything!'

He lay still beside her, their linked hands reverent upon the marvel, in a touch between adoration and caress. It seemed to him that all the darkness and cold of the autumn night grew warm and lambent with the happiness that ran over from his cup. 'How grateful I am!' he said. 'How grateful!'

CHAPTER THIRTEEN

Isambard came into the lodge in the bright early afternoon, when the light was at its best, and stood unnoticed for a while, watching the balanced, easy strokes of Harry's mallet as he used the finest of his punches on the wings of the angel of the Annunciation. The slender, kneeling figure lifted to the Madonna a face there was no mistaking, though no man had ever yet borne it; the face that would be Owen ap Ivor's when he came to manhood.

'A pity,' said Isambard, 'that you'll not be able to finish it from the living model.'

Harry cast a surprised glance over his shoulder. 'Not be able to finish it – ' He found for the words the meaning he would have wished them to bear, and his eyes shone, kindling from sea-green to gold with joy. 'You mean you're sending him home? Ah, but I'm glad! I knew you'd give over plaguing them in the end. Why, I know every line of the child's face by now better than his mother does, I don't need his living presence. I shall miss the imp, but for his sake I'll be glad to see him go.'

'I do not think you will,' said Isambard, 'not by the way he is to take. But you may see it if you wish, Harry.'

The words effectively stopped Harry's mallet, but it was the tone that brought his head jerking round again, and this time without a smile. 'What do you mean? Speak plainly, my lord. What's in your mind for him?' He put down mallet and punch, and came striding out from behind the stone group, wiping his hands on his tunic in the bad boyish habit he had never lost, and for which Gilleis was always scolding him.

'It did not come from my mind,' said Isambard, in the same flat, deliberate tone. 'I give you my word for that. I have had my orders from the king.'

'The king? How does the king know anything of Owen? He has his hands full in the south with Langton, and the rest of the pack who're massing for the kill now he's down. What's this child to him?'

'I hold this march for the king, and whatever happens in it touching the Welsh and him I must submit to him. My messenger went to him as soon as he landed from France, with my full report of all that has befallen in his absence. The boy was merely mentioned along with the rest, and there's but a line in the king's despatch about him, but it's very much to the point.' He had the parchment in his hand. Harry had not remarked it until that moment, for the hand that held it was down in the shadow, in the folds of the blue surcoat. 'It came but a quarter of an hour ago.' He held it so that Harry could see for himself the royal seal.

'Shall I read it to you? "For the boy ap Ivor, follow your own inclination and my desire and interest. Hang him, and send Llewellyn his body." '

'Christ aid!' said Harry, and clutched at the wall.

Isambard looked up over the roll, but there was nothing to be read in the look, neither regret nor pleasure, neither disgust nor approval. The cavernous eyes burned, but fire was their natural element; within the great smooth, translucent lids they must burn even when he slept. Harry could neither speak nor move for a moment. The thing came so unexpectedly, he could not grasp it.

'You'll never do it!' he said, dragging a voice out of himself as arduously as though he dragged his heart out by the roots. 'The king himself will wish it undone. He'll not thank you if you act on an angry word he surely never meant. God's life, my lord, the child is his grandson's bed-fellow! And think, now that so many of the barons are turned against him, he must look for allies where he can find them. How if he's wooing his son-in-law before the year's out, and you've been too hasty and set the child's murder between them? Do you think he'll be grateful?'

'Since when have I looked for gratitude?' said Isambard, rolling up the parchment. 'He is what he is, but he is my sovereign. What he orders I perform. But he will not repent of it. His hate to that man is second only to mine.'

'So he'll wreak it on a child of nine years, who has never stood in his way, who is not even Llewellyn's seed, but only his fosterling, and dear to him – '

'Ah, so they never told you the full tale,' said Isambard with a hollow smile. 'For they say, Harry, that he is Llewellyn's seed, if all was known, got for his friend who needed an heir but could not furnish one for himself. And for my part I think it must be true. Not even for Griffith has Llewellyn so persistently dunned us as for this boy.'

'You do but confirm me! This is not policy, it is only spite. He dare not touch Griffith, though he still holds him, because Griffith is acknowledged, and the charm of the father's name is over him. But this poor little creature is vulnerable, the charm does not cover him. The king can slaughter him, and stab Llewellyn to the heart, and yet pretend ignorance of what he does. Owen is to pay for Griffith's immunity. You'll surely not lend yourself to so mean an act?'

'Call it what you please. I have my orders,' said Isambard shortly, two hot discs of colour darkening on his cheek-bones.

'You cannot do it, I'll not believe it of you! You are nobody's hired murderer, not even the king has the right to ask it of you.' He caught at Isambard's lean wrist, and it felt hard and rigid and cold in his hand, like the hilt of a sword. 'My lord, this is a *child*, one who has been in my care, one you've seen yourself often enough, running about the wards. His death serves no purpose – '

'It satisfies a hate,' said Isambard, and shook him off, but without anger or impatience. 'Where is the boy?'

'Out riding.' He passed a hand over his eyes, and said dully: 'I wish he might never come back.'

'If he does not, the two who guard him shall hang for him. But he'll come. When he does, he shall have a brief while with Father Hubert, and then we'll make an end. I am the king's man, I shall do the king's bidding. To the last letter!'

The voice had not quickened from its sombre quietness, nor the face stirred out of its iron calm, and yet the air between them was suddenly bitter with so intense and incurable an emanation of grief and rage that Harry jerked up his head to stare at the source of it in horror, as though he found himself face to face with a demon. It was Isambard who turned away his eyes, but too late to contain the brief, blinding glare of a hunger that might well devour children.

'Lord God!' said Harry in an appalled whisper. 'You are *glad*! This is what you wanted! This is what you planned! It is not the king making use of you, but you making use of the king. You are to have the terrible joy of it, and he the everlasting shame! How many more, how many more have made him the scapegoat?' Isambard would have turned and flung away from him, but he thrust out his arm, and, setting his palm against the wall, barred the way. 'Show me his words, or I'll not believe in them. *You* have done this, not he. You are sick to the soul – '

'Sick to the soul!' repeated Isambard in a low voice, halting with his breast against the wiry brown arm. 'Sick I am, God knows! There, read! See if you can find some loophole I have failed to find.'

The words were there. He had not even read all. 'My grandson is too young,' the king had written, 'to cry for him long.' How could a man have the understanding to think of that, and still demand the death? He let his arm fall. There was nothing more to be said, no plea that would be heard, no goad that could sting Isambard into failing in his ghastly duty. His fealty would not stop short of one child's death; and the joy was surely there, whether he knew it or not. Killing the boy would placate for a moment the devil that fed on his heart, the hatred he bore to life, which had disappointed him, to love, which had eluded him, to beauty and innocence, which had abandoned him.

'As God sees me, Harry,' said Isambard with weary gentleness, 'I'm sorry! I'll have Benedetta keep Gilleis within doors when the time comes. You may tell her he's sent home, if you will.'

Harry made no answer. He stood staring unseeingly at the lively head of the unfinished angel; and in a moment he heard the rustle of Isambard's brocade against the timber posts of the lodge, and the rapid, incisive sound of his footsteps receding across the trampled waste towards the gate-house.

Words had lost their potency, and there was no time now for thought, unless, as Benedetta had once said, the act is also the thought. Everything took shape as it must. There was no other way.

He left his work as it stood, the tools lying, and went to his tracing-house in the outer ward, where his clerk was busy cleaning parchments.

'Find John the Fletcher for me, Simon, and ask him to come to me in the lodge, will you?'

The boy ran off willingly. Gilleis was with Benedetta at this hour, they were working together on the altar cloths for the church. To approach them himself would have been simple, but the occasion of surprise and therefore possibly of suspicion. And quite certainly unbearable. John the Fletcher was Benedetta's own man, and had access to her at all times; his comings and goings would excite no comment.

'Get her away out of his reach,' wrote Harry at his desk in the lodge, 'for I am about to do that for which there is no forgiveness.'

He did not sign it; she knew the hand. He added nothing; there was neither time nor need for anything more. By the time he had sealed it John the Fletcher was already picking his way between the stacked stones.

'You wanted me, master?'

'Will you take this to Madonna Benedetta, at once?' said Harry. 'You need say nothing to her, she will understand. If my lord is there, get it to her nonetheless, but see that it is done so that he knows nothing of it. I'm trusting you with what's more to me than my head.'

'She shall have it,' said John the Fletcher. 'He'll not be there, he's within, in hall, hearing some plea between two of his tenants, and there's another case to be heard after it. He'll be a good hour by the sound of it.'

'So much the better! Then, John – if they're alone – say to my wife that I send her my love and service. Will you do that?'

'I'll do it.' Out of the brown, bearded face sharp eyes studied him with narrowing attention. 'Nothing more?'

'Nothing more.'

'If you should be in want of a hand to second yours, master, she'd spare me to you.'

'I thank you,' said Harry, startled and moved, 'but I can make shift alone.'

'God be with you, then,' said John, unquestioning, and hid the message within his tunic, and so was gone.

Harry made his way to the storehouse which stood nearest to the English edge of the plateau. There was a coil of knotted rope there, formerly one of several used by the young masons as a quick means of descent from the scaffolding, but banished when it showed signs of fraying. He took it on his arm, and slipped unobserved into the fringe of the trees. Below this sheer, rocky face lay the dingle where the two masterless men had dropped their haul of wood, long ago in his first summer here. That was the one occasion when he had paid any attention to this cliff edge, but he remembered it well. There was a drop of perhaps fifty feet, and then some broken shelves where a starved tree or two clung, edging the soft, deep grass of the dingle. Thence the descent to the hamlet was easy. He made fast the rope to the bole of a larch tree close to the rim, and paid the length of it over, leaning out to shake it clear of the stunted trees below. It lay against the rock and vanished, being of much the same straw-pale colour. He debated for a moment whether he should risk leaving by this route and picking up a horse in the village, but speed was more vital than complete concealment. How could he be sure he would get a good mount? He needed a horse on which he could rely. Moreover, he had many valid reasons for leaving and entering Parfois freely, and they would not yet be questioned.

No one but Isambard was likely to find anything suspicious in the fact that Master Talvace was saddling up and riding out at this hour, and he would not see. Harry took the best and fleetest of the horses at his disposal, and rode across the drawbridge and down from the plateau, unchallenged but for the master-carpenter's hail as he passed the lodges.

'Harry, would you cast an eye at the screen with me, now it's in? I've a notion yet the line of it could be bettered.'

'When I come back,' said Harry. 'I'm going down to the quay, with luck they should be landing my last sliptiles before evening.'

At the lower guard they passed him through without a glance. Now how far dared he ride, and still be sure of intercepting Owen and his escort? The boy had fallen pliantly into the habit of telling him exactly where he meant to go; today he had said he would ride eastward between the hills on to the Roman road, and then south to the great open place where the old earth fort reared its ringed mound. The little hawk would be showing his paces in that bright, still, sunless air above the spongy, blanched turf of autumn. It was long odds they would not turn down into the river valley from there, to give the horses the steep climb at the end of the ride. However they varied their way back, they would stay on this level, and that meant they must use this path between the crests to reach Parfois. He took his station at the edge of the wood, on a grassy mound that commanded a view of the windblown levels over which they must come.

He had not long to wait. They appeared below him, riding in single file along a thin green track, for the tussocky grass was treacherous and full of warrens. He went down to meet them, and Owen saw him, and spurred towards him with a jubilant shout. For the first time he wondered what he was to do if the guards distrusted him, and he without so much as a dagger on him.

'I am sent by my lord to meet you,' he said, hushing Owen's chatter peremptorily with a raised hand and keeping his eyes upon the archers. 'Something has fallen out which makes it seem to him better you should not go back to the castle with your charge. He bade me say that like Robert of Vieuxpont he has received an order he would liefer not obey.' He cast one significant glance down at the child, and they understood him. Why, after all, should they doubt him? He had grown closer to Isambard of late than any other man at Parfois; if their lord wished to evade an unpleasant issue, Talvace was the very person he would choose to be his agent and lift the burden from him.

'It's that way, is it?' said the elder of the two archers, and whistled soundlessly, eyeing the boy. 'What's his will now?'

'That I should take the child as far as the quarry in Bryn and start him on his way home.'

Owen pricked up his ears at that, and shouted and clapped his gloved hands, startling the little hawk on his wrist so that it ruffled its wings and hissed indignantly.

'Silence, pest!' said Harry, shaking him gently by a handful of curls. 'Your elders are talking.' And to the guards: 'It was always his will that it should end so, and you know he has ways of getting his will.'

'Ay, has he, and can go roundabout as well as straight when need be, well I know it. But our orders were plain. He bade us never let the lad out of reach except within the gates.'

'Have I asked you to leave him? You are to come with us to Bryn. Understand me, none but my lord and I, and now you, know of this matter. He sent me because the child has been in my care, and will readily trust himself to me. There was no time for writing and sealing of credentials. His name in my mouth should be enough for you.' He wheeled his horse. 'We'd best be moving. Come, Owen ap Ivor ap Madoc, you've a long ride ahead of you.'

In their shoes, he thought, I would believe it; it has the sound of truth so strongly that I wonder if there is not a grain of the real thing at the heart of it. Why did he come straight to me and tell me? Out of rueful courtesy to me as the boy's keeper? Or to torment me because I am too fortunate, and have too much? Or did he tell me in order that I might do exactly what I am doing, and spare him this horrible duty? For all these reasons, it may well be, and which of them was strongest he of all men is not likely to know. God may know. As for me, I do what I must, and that is enough.

They were following. He did not look round, but he felt that the moment of hesitation was over, that they were satisfied of his good faith. He thought of Benedetta talking in paradoxes about honour and faith, of how honour might sometimes depend on abasing oneself and faith on breaking one's word. I am on my way to illustrating her argument for her, he thought wryly, but how it will come out none of us knows yet. Yes, they were following, and they were satisfied. They had fallen into their usual station, six or seven lengths behind their charge. How emphatically he had drummed it into Owen that he must never try to outride or elude them! Thank God the child had never understood why!

'Am I really going home?' asked Owen eagerly, bouncing with excitement on his brown pony.

'You are indeed.'

'But I have not said goodbye to anyone. They'll think no one has taught me good manners at Aber.' He was seriously worried; the reputation of the Welsh was in his hands. 'At least I ought to make my farewells to Mistress Gilleis, when she has been so kind to me.'

'Why, it was all arranged in haste, we may waive the niceties for once. I have said goodbye to Mistress Gilleis for you.'

And for myself, he thought, feeling the realisation close in on his heart like an iron frost. When I turned back to kiss her once more, there on the stairway on my way to work, and I did not know why it came on me so – that was goodbye.

'His love and service!' said Gilleis, stiff and pale in the window embrasure with the brightly coloured folds of the tapestry fallen round her feet. 'And gone! Why? Why? Why could he not send his message to me?'

'Because it's to me that John has ready access. And perhaps because he knew you would need persuading. He did send you,' said Benedetta with a wry smile, 'the message I would gladly have had. It remains only to do his bidding, and quickly.'

'I will not go!' said Gilleis, clenching her hands. 'If he is putting himself in danger, so much the more must I be close to him. What's my life to me without him?'

'You will go. You will go because he asks it, and because only he knows what he has done and what he means to do, and therefore none of us can hope to better his plans. You will go because it would be the cruellest blow of all to him if you should stay here to become the instrument of his undoing. You will go not because you are afraid, or do not love him enough, but because you are without fear, and love him more than yourself. Even enough to live without him – except,' said Benedetta, folding the parchment and hiding it in her breast, 'that you can never be without him now, together or apart.'

Gilleis turned her back on the room and looked out from the window into the sheer plunge of air. She kicked the embroidery out of her way with a swirl of her green skirt. 'You love him, too,' she said.

'God's death!' said Benedetta. 'Is that any secret? From the first moment I saw him, and shall do till I die. I would have told you so long ago, if I had thought it needed saying.'

'Ah, you mistake me! I meant that – that is a reason for trusting you. If I go – if I must indeed go – you will stand his friend here – '

'His, and yours, too.' She saw Gilleis start forward and catch at the stonework of the window, and the marriage ring gleamed on the small hand that pressed hard against the green girdle. Benedetta ran and caught her in her arms, and held her until the faintness passed. Tears were welling slowly from the great eyes and falling heavily upon the trampled needlework.

'That's no secret, neither,' said Benedetta, gently, 'at least not from me. And that's why you'll go. You have two hostages to save, and one of them a morsel of Harry's very life. Fetch your cloak, quickly, and I'll have John saddle the horses.'

At a farm between the rivers they asked for food, and the goodwife found them some oatcakes and apples and eggs, and brought a bowl of warm milk for Owen. Harry gave her three silver pence for the meal, and Owen offered her a kiss of his milky mouth, and she was content. They crossed Vrnwy with Owen still chattering and singing, more often in Welsh than in English, but soon he began to tire, and to nod in the saddle. 'Take the poor bird,' said Harry, smiling, 'and give me up the child, and he can sleep as we go.'

'I am not asleep,' said Owen indignantly, stiffening as he felt himself lifted from his saddle.

Harry settled him before him in his arm, well wrapped from the chilling wind in his cloak. The boy sighed, and stirred a little until he found the right place to rest easily, his head nestling in the crook of arm and shoulder, his cheek turned comfortably into Harry's breast. 'And I am not a child,' he said, taking firm hold of the folds of the green cotte that pillowed him. 'I am a boy, nearly a man.'

'You are an imp, and a sinner, but you have the makings of a man. Don't be in too big a hurry to leave being a child,' said Harry. 'It's no great blessing to be grown.'

Owen slept, flushed of face and moist of lip in the warmth of the cloak, as they rode into the quarry in the October twilight. A voice challenged them out of the dimness where the woods closed in upon the walk.

'It's Talvace,' said Harry, tightening his arm reassuringly about the child as he started awake at the cry. 'Hush, they're all friends here. Where is Adam?'

'Master Talvace, is it you?' William of Beistan's great beard bristled out of the dusk. 'What brings you here at this time? What's the news from Parfois?'

'There is none yet,' said Harry. 'That's to come. Where's Adam?'

'Within, at the huts. You'll see by the light of the fire as you round the trees.'

The rock walls of the quarry stood pale in the flickering light of a fire that burned in an open hearth fenced with stones. Owen awoke fully, and peered out of his nest at the strange faces that gathered from all sides to surround them. Adam came running from the huts to catch at Harry's stirrup.

'Take the boy,' said Harry, fending off welcomes, 'and let me get down. I must trouble you for fresh horses, Adam, and I could find a good home for a drink and a bite.' He dismounted, and a small, anxious hand reached to clutch at his sleeve; he detached it calmly from its hold, and shut it warmly in his own palm. 'I'm here, imp, never fear. These are all friends to me and to you.'

'Come into the hut,' said Adam, 'and we'll gladly feed you. Horses we have, too, but why should you want them tonight?'

'I'll tell you while we eat, for there's no time to lose. Owen ap Ivor, now's your chance to be a man. Will you wait here by the fire, and not worry if I stay out of sight for ten minutes? Here, Robin, take care of him while I have a word aside with Adam.'

Over the ale and meat and bread that Adam provided he said what he had to say, and briefly.

'This boy is foster-son to the Prince of Gwynedd. I want you to take horse at once – you yourself, Adam, mark me – and carry him to Aber and hand him over to Llewellyn in person. That done, on no account come back here.' He looked across the candle-flame at the archers. 'I have to ask your pardon for the trick I played on you to get you to come here with me. It was no lie I told you when I said that the king had sent orders to my lord to put the child to death. The lie was that he desired to be spared the duty of obeying. He was and is set to hang the boy. It was I who willed to carry him off and send him home. I could get him from you by no other means than I used, and I could not allow you to go back to Parfois and tell your tale, to set the hounds after us too soon. Now you may choose what you will do. But forget that you carry bows! All in this place will do my will, not Isambard's, and you had best not brave them. If you want my rede, I should throw in your lot with Adam here, and go to Aber with the boy. Llewellyn's gratitude will be assured, he'll receive you like princes.' He yawned, and rubbed his hands over his stiff cheeks. 'I am sorry I had to lie,' he said. 'There was no other way.'

The three faces stared in upon him in silence. 'What is it? What ails you?'

'What ails *us*!' said Adam. 'What of *you*, Harry?' By the tone in which he asked and by the look of his face, from which the smile was gone beyond even remembrance, he already knew the answer.

'I am going back.'

'No, by God, you're not!' swore Adam, scrambling to his feet. 'Not if I have to bind you over a horse to get you into Wales with us. Are you mad? He'll hang you out of hand.'

'He will not. He swore to me that he would not deprive me of the work he had entrusted to me – never, he said, until it be finished. And you know he keeps his word. And I swore to him,' said Harry, 'that I would not leave his service until the work was done. I keep my word, too. I am going back to keep it.'

'Your word, man! This is your life! Do you think he'll let you live, when in some sort you've made him traitor? And do you think there's any law left in this country now strong enough to take you out of his hands? Harry!' he begged, groaning helplessly. 'Don't throw your life away for a scruple! Come with us!'

'I shall live until the church is finished, some months yet. Indeed, there's only I can fix the term. Who knows, my lord Isambard and King John himself may both be gone before me. I don't think any more,' said Harry, emptying his horn and getting to his feet. 'Thought's unprofitable. Get me a horse, Adam, and leave plaguing me. Go I will, and there's no time to lose.' He caught Adam by the shoulder, and held him hard. 'No tricks in my defence, mind! I charge you on your soul, get the boy safely home, or you will have wasted my labour and my head, and for that I'll never forgive you.'

'On my soul be it,' said Adam, eye to eye with him. 'He shall be the first charge on me. After he reaches Llewellyn's arms my actions are my own.'

'Very well so. And you two, are you resolved to go on? I hope,' he said remorsefully, 'you have neither of you wives and children in his hold, but I pledge you my word I'll do my best to hold you clear of this treason and protect them from his anger.'

'My family are all grown and out in the world,' said the older man, 'and my wife's dead these seven years. And Harald here has girls enough about the shire, but no wife. We'll take your counsel, master, and go the rest of the way with the boy. I don't know but Llewellyn's service may be more to my mind than Isambard's, and we'll surely start with a foot in the door of his favour.'

'Then I shall have done you no wrong, and for that I thank God. I thought fast enough for my own,' he said, and turned his face into the shadow and went out from the hut, Adam at his back.

Owen was sitting by the fire still wrapped in Harry's cloak, eating hungrily, half a dozen of the hewers and men-at-arms gathered curiously about him. He was already friends with them, and his strange journey had ceased to be frightening and resumed its character of a high adventure. His large eyes shone splendidly in the firelight.

'It's a wild bird, but a true one,' said Harry. 'Be good to him.'

He thrust through the circle about the boy and dropped to the grass beside him. 'Owen, here I leave you. But here is Adam, who is foster-brother to me as David is to you. He will take you home to Aber in my place. Mind, now, his will is my will, and you're to mark him as you would me. And now give me a kiss, and God be with you, child. Wipe the grease from your mouth first, I like my kisses clean. That's better!' He kissed the soft, uplifted mouth and laughed. 'This time tomorrow night you'll be in your own bed. Carry my greetings to the Prince of Gwynedd and tell him if he gets as good sons as he fosters there'll be a Prince of Wales from his blood yet.' He embraced him briefly and rose. 'Where's that horse you have for me?'

His hand was on the bridle when Adam said despairingly in his ear: 'Harry, will you not change your mind? Think of Gilleis – '

'For Christ's sake!' said Harry, in a whisper that was like a howl of pain. 'Who else do I think of, every moment I sleep or wake?' He kept his face turned close into the horse's chestnut shoulder for a moment, but it passed and the calm came again. 'I do what I must, Adam. That makes all easy. I shall trust to see you again, in this world or another.' He turned a face now perfectly at his service, and leaned and kissed his brother. 'It was a mistake to sit! Squire me, Adam, I'm main stiff.'

Adam held his stirrup and helped him into the saddle.

'Get to horse yourself as soon as I'm gone. Goodbye, Adam!' He wheeled the horse and trotted towards the dark space where the rock walls parted.

'Goodbye!' said Adam after him, barely audibly.

Owen, grown anxious because of the disquiet he felt in the air about him, had crept away from the fire and stood looking uncertainly from one to the other of them as they parted. He caught the falling note of Adam's voice and saw the helpless grief in his face, and broke into frightened crying; and in a flash he was off after Harry, calling through his tears: 'Master Talvace! Master Talvace!'

Harry swung round at the cry, and the small hands caught at his ankle and clung desperately. He leaned resignedly from the saddle, took the child under the armpits, and hoisted him up to perch before him. Owen clasped him fiercely round the neck and hid his face against him, sobbing desolately. He felt the child's heart pounding as though it would burst out of his body.

'I don't want you to go! Don't go! They'll hurt you, I'm frightened for you!'

'Now, now, Owen ap Ivor ap Madoc, is that a noise for a prince to make? Is this the fellow who told me he was almost a man? No harm will come to me,' said Harry firmly, patting the quaking shoulders. 'Put it out of your mind. You're overborne with the journey and the strangeness, and you're imagining evil where none is. Look at me! Do I look frightened? Or sad?' He forced a finger under the quivering chin that pressed so desperately into his breast, and hoisted the tear-stained face out of hiding. 'Here's a countenance to scare the crows with! Let's see if we can better it.' He wiped the round cheeks dry with a corner of his cloak, and smoothed back the rumpled hair.

'He'll be all right once we're started,' said Adam, waiting to lift him down.

'He's tired. You'll need to carry him through the night hours, but I'd liefer you got him well into Wales before you take time for rest.'

'I'll do that.'

'No more tears? That's my true goshawk! Be a good boy, now, and mind what Adam tells you.'

He kissed the child once more, and handed him down. The small body lay on Adam's shoulder as horse and horseman dwindled in the shadows and the hoofbeats receded until the wall of rock cut them off sharply. Owen slid an arm resignedly about Adam's neck, and transferred to him faithfully the allegiance that belonged to his brother.

They turned back into the quarry together, and would not look after the vanished rider. For a few shared moments, before the child, childlike, let fall the premature burden of love and loss, and the man, manlike, refused it recognition, each of them knew that he would never see Harry again.

The hunt was up for him, and did not slacken with the night, but he was prepared for that. Most of the searchers would be out along the river valley, expecting him to make directly for Wales with his charge. Not until he was beneath the shadow of the Breiddens did he hear the clatter of riders on the road ahead, and them he eluded by slipping sidelong into the woods. When he returned to the track he took care to use only the grassy verge, where he could ride almost silently; and wherever the shelter of trees offered he took advantage of it gratefully. He was not going to be dragged back like a captured runaway; he was on his way home of his own free will, and of his own free will he would re-enter Parfois and take up the tools he had laid down yesterday.

He had had time to think on that ride, and even time to rebel in his heart against the wanton chance that had cast this inescapable need in his way, and not into another man's arms. Why should God confront him with this cruel choice a second time, and thus freakishly, when his happiness was at its fullest flower? But in a while he perceived that there was nothing wanton in it, and nothing that befell by chance; and that so far from being the second time he had had to choose, it was the hundredth time at least; or, to look at it from another and perhaps a truer viewpoint, it was but the latest reaffirmation of a choice which had been made long ago, and once for all.

From Adam's hand to Owen's head, there was no inconsistency and no chance stroke. The deliberate assumption of responsibility, the affirmation and the challenge, had to be repeated over and over, because the world was still as it had been, and he was still as he had been, and as he would be to his death. Once he had set his own judgement against the world's judgement, the end was implicit in the beginning. Somewhere at the bottom of his heart he had always known that the last choice he made in the teeth of power and privilege and law must be mortal, and that nonetheless he neither could nor would turn aside from making it.

So he had no just complaint against God or man, and he would prefer none. He had what he had chosen, he had never been one to haggle about the price.

Twice on the cautious climb up the flank of the hill he had to draw aside and take to the trees while horsemen passed by; but after that it was quiet enough. They must be seeking him farther afield by now, probably well into Wales. He came without mishap or hindrance to the foot of the grassy ride that led to Parfois, and there dismounted, knotted the reins on the horse's neck, and started him uphill with a slap. The gentle climb round into the dingle under the cliff he made afoot, and found the rope still dangling. The pre-dawn light was just singling out shades of colour, and severing pale from dark, as he hauled himself up hand over hand, and crept over the edge into the long grass, drawing up the rope after him.

Silence hung over Parfois. The drawbridge was raised, and in the quietness he heard the tramp of the guard on the walk between the gate-house towers.

When he had disposed of the rope he went into the lodge, and sat for a while with his forehead against the cold, smooth breast of the Madonna of the Annunciation; he almost slept, but shook himself awake again as often as he found himself drowsing. As soon as there was light enough he took up his tools, but the face of Gilleis smiling on him from the stone was more than he could bear. What was it he had promised to do when he rode out of Parfois? The rood-screen, that was it. The master-carpenter had never been happy about its proportions, its modest height and spare and delicate tracery disappointed his desire to display virtuosity, and he could not reconcile himself to the banishment of the cross. Harry was sure of his judgement; he would not tolerate anything that broke up that great, soaring, shapely space of air and light which was his best achievement, but this fragile and yet strong erection he loved, because it played with the light without opposing it, and its upright, filigree shapes made so many more small, springing fountains reaching towards the vault. Still, he had promised to look critically at it yet again, and at least the looking would be joy. He rose stiffly, and went into the church, mallet and punch still in his hands.

The pre-dawn light was dim but clear in the lofty vault of the nave. The enclosed space filled him with fulfilment and peace; it was like being compassed about by two praying hands. He stood within the west door, filling his eyes and his heart with it, for a long time, while the dove-grey light grew and brightened. He heard, but did not notice, the first horsemen returning empty-handed; they passed by his sanctuary, and the watch let down the drawbridge for them, but he stood untouched, charmed into quietness, no longer even weary. The eastward sky had cleared, and the first long rays of the rising sun, launched clear across the shallow valley of the brook, lit like golden birds upon the rock plateau of Parfois. They threaded the great lancets of the empty east windows, and flying level and radiant from end to end of the church, rang like gold along the western wall. Who would build a barrier in the skyway of the doves of God? Who would shut them behind a lattice of wood and stone, as in an elaborate cage? Suddenly the very vault was full of reflected light that trembled over the slender, braced ribs like fingers among harp-strings, and all the round-cheeked cherubim in the bosses glowed golden and shouted for joy.

The low rood-screen was perfect, delicate, austere. Master Matthew should not touch it again; he should not add one flourish to its spare simplicity. Its springing stems fretted the light into golden ladders across the patterned slip-tiles of the nave. No cross and no figures of mourning should ever cast long, asymmetrical shadows over that field of brilliance, and shatter its unity. He felt for his master-carpenter, but he would not have such beauty marred. He stood and gazed, and he was immeasurably happy, he who had thrown away all the remainder of his life and should have been immeasurably sorrowful.

Presently he climbed up into the triforium and walked along the narrow passage-way to the eastern end. Here he had left a whole range of corbels to be carved on the spot, and had not yet touched them, because this was easy, accessible work which could be tackled at leisure in the winter. He stood in the last of the trefoil openings, just tall enough to hold him upright, close to the east windows and above the high altar, and looked along the flying path of the light. Some of the clerestory windows at this end were already glazed, the rays of the sun slanting through them bordered the vault with burning jewels, emerald and ruby, sapphire and topaz, chryso-beryl and amethyst. He stood in the shadow, but all this light was his.

He was still standing there when the west doorway at which he had entered darkened suddenly with the outline of a man. He came in slowly, his arms hanging wearily, and advancing to where the soft reflected light plucked him out of the anonymity of shadow, lifted to the quivering radiance the ravaged face of Isambard.

He was quite certain that he was alone. How was it that no sensitivity of flesh or spirit warned him? The bitter countenance stared up into the vault filled with the morning, and like a flower in the sun warmed and flushed and opened, clean open to the heart, but upon such a naked anguish of pain and despair that all the air within the church shuddered and ached with it. Love was in it, too, and worship, but love without compassion, and worship without peace. Dark and gaunt with wonder, his eyes adored the beauty and splendour he had caused to be made, and could find no flaw in it and no joy. He bared his teeth and wrenched his head aside, and clenching the fleshless hands that still had such violent strength in them, struck with them hard against his breast.

'Even he!' he cried in the voice of a tormented demon. 'Even he! Traitor to me, and forsworn to you!'

The vault was built true, it brought up the suffocating cry magnified but undistorted to where Harry stood, and prolonged it in sad, diminishing echoes from end to end of the roof-rib. He leaned out between the cusps of the trefoil opening, his tools in his hands.

'Who says I am forsworn?'

He had said it quietly enough, but the nearness of the vault took it and turned it into a loud and challenging cry. Isambard's head jerked back, the deep eyes flew to find him, and having found him, there in the trefoil like a stone saint in his niche, hung upon him for a long moment in absolute silence, absolute stillness. Then he flung up his arm and laid it over his eyes, against the light or against what he desired not to see, Harry could not tell which.

'Why did you come back?' he cried.

How was he to understand such a question? Why did you come back to confront me with the necessity of killing you? Why did you come back to force upon me the terrible pleasure and the more terrible pain of revenge? Why could you not lift even this burden from me?

'To finish what I have begun,' said Harry, 'as I am bound in honour to do, and as I would do even if I were not bound. I well remember my oath. Have I to put you in mind of yours?'

Isambard uncovered his face. Behind the sheltering arm he had composed again the stony mask, beautiful and fierce, that was his public countenance. He looked up fixedly, and smiled.

'You shall finish it,' he said. 'My memory is also good. All shall be done in accordance with your oath and mine. All! Do you remember the very words, Harry? I hope you do. "On this living heart", you said. "If I play you false", you said. You have played me false indeed, for you have caused me to play false.'

Never once had he asked about the child, never mentioned his name or Llewellyn's. Perhaps even at this moment that disrupted heart was split between gratitude that the boy was got clean away, and rage against the instrument of his escape. The enforced dishonouring of the king's word there was no forgiving, but neither would he ever have forgiven himself for the slaughter of the child. Of all the hatreds that racked him, the sharpest was the hatred he bore to himself.

'Come down!' he said harshly. 'I weary of talking to you as to a god.'

Harry came down the winding stairway and across the pale, sunlit space of the nave, and stood before him. Now it was he who had to look up. He smiled, acquitting Isambard in his mind of valuing that small advantage. 'The boy is safe,' he said mildly. 'I think you may like to know that. And I remember my oath very well.'

'So be it. You shall have all the time you need to finish your work. But when it is completed,' said Isambard very softly, 'you shall die a traitor's death, you who made me a traitor. I will exact the full forfeit you pledged to me. I'll have that heart of yours living out of your body, and burn it before your eyes.'

CHAPTER FOURTEEN

The guards who came to fetch him dragged him headlong away over the drawbridge and into the gate-house while the site was still deserted, mortally afraid that some of his workmen might try to rescue him. They need not have worried, and so he told them; labourers and artisans have their own skins to take care of. But they were taking no chances with a charge so precious as Harry Talvace, for their necks would certainly have paid for any miscarriage. They bestowed him in a cell of the guard-house under lock and key, and hobbled with leg-irons into the bargain, and there left him immured most of the day; but they gave him a plank bed and food, and he ate with reasonable appetite and slept as soon as he lay down. Now that it was over, now that he had not to act any longer, but only to sustain what was enacted upon him, he could afford to sleep.

He slept all through the morning and into the late afternoon, while horsemen rode to Fleace and Mormesnil to bring back from among Isambard's other households certain men who would be better qualified for their duties by being strangers to their charge. Too many at Parfois, officials, armourers, archers, grooms, liked him far too well to be trusted with him.

The first to come was a smith from Mormesnil, who stood over the bed and looked at the sleeper in blank astonishment.

'Is that him?' said he. 'Why, he's nothing but a bit of a lad. You could have shut one of your iron neck-collars round his middle and spared bothering me. I thought we were chaining a wild bull by the to-do there is about him.'

None the less, he settled himself in the armoury, and made them the harness they demanded. Master Talvace must be free to use his hands for his work, and free to climb about his scaffolding as he pleased, and yet be always closely secured. A length of chain joining two hinged belts of steel, fastening with concealed locks that could never be picked, was to link him to his perpetual companion, the thick-set Poitevin man-at-arms, master of sword and dagger, brought from Fleace in Flintshire.

'Mind you make no mistake in the two girdles,' said the smith when he saw the squat bulk of Guillaume, 'or the lad will step out of his noose and give you the slip.'

'And if he does,' grunted the Poitevin through his bushy black beard, 'my fellow here can bring him down at anything up to five hundred paces. I should like to see him get past the pair of us, without some saint wafts him away in a cloud.'

'Saints,' said the smith with a grin, 'come very seldom to Parfois.'

Harry remained in the guard-house all that day, while rumour upon rumour went the rounds among his men, and hardly a tile was laid or a stone touched in the church. Parfois shuddered with the vibration of his treason, and engendered a hundred different versions of his fate. He was taken. He was dead. He was safely away into Wales with the boy. The boy was dead, but Harry had escaped. He had been seized on the very border and taken to Fleace.

John the Fletcher reported back to Benedetta a dozen times that afternoon, but always to the same purpose. 'They say many things, but they know nothing. He has not been seen since he fled with the child, or not by anyone who is willing to speak.'

'The horse!' said Benedetta, when he came again in the early evening. 'Ask in the stables, someone may know which horse he took.'

He brought back an answer which he could not get to her until supper in hall, because Isambard was with her in the private apartments. Then he made shift to whisper in her ear as she withdrew from the table: 'A horse from the quarry came in without a rider.'

'He is here,' she said with certainty and clenched a hand under her heart. But she maintained a calm face and a quiet manner, and said not a word of Harry to Isambard. The truth would come out without that, and she would neither betray herself nor beg for him until she must.

In the night they took Harry from his bed, and lodged him unshackled in a cell beneath the Warden's Tower. It was approached through an antechamber, in which for the first time he saw his two guards, the swarthy, squat Poitevin and the long, sad, red-haired crossbowman Fulke. They looked at him with impartial professional eyes, as he would have looked at the plan of a building not his own, which gave him no particular pleasure, but did provide him with problems he would get satisfaction out of solving. He saw that Isambard had been careful to put him in the hands of strangers, and he felt that he had been paid a compliment.

His own cell, the inner one, was small but dry, and, being cut down into the rock, warmer than the draughty precincts of the great hall. It had no window, but a narrow shaft slanting downwards through the thickness of the wall brought in air, and by day at least a feeble shaft of light would find its way down to him. He had a bed and adequate bedding; evidently my lord's master-mason was not to be allowed to die of a chill or grow crippled with rheumatism before he could be half-hanged and ripped open at the brazier by my lord's executioner. For the same reasons there would be food enough, and whatever he needed to keep him active and presentable. He was still master of the works of Parfois, and must continue to command the respect of those who worked under him. He had expected to lie awake, thinking too feverishly, feeling too bitterly, telling over within his mind the steps by which he had destroyed himself. Instead, he slept peacefully and awoke refreshed. There was something dreamlike in the apparition of Fulke at his bedside, with a candle in one hand and a trencher of food in the other. And the coming of Guillaume was even stranger. He brought water and a napkin, and when Harry had washed offered to shave him. Harry stared for a moment and then laughed.

'So I'm not to be trusted with a razor in my own hands! Well, it's an unnecessary precaution, but it's a luxury I never tasted before, to have such a service done for me. What of letting me handle mallet and chisel? Have they thought of that? Am I to be allowed to work today?'

It seemed that he was, for they brought in the harness the smith had made, and locked the smaller of the two belts about his middle.

'Which of us,' he asked, plucking experimentally at the chain, 'is the hound and which the handler?'

'You have a fine, bell-mouthed bay on you,' grunted Guillaume, unimpressed; 'we shall see if you'll still be giving tongue so boldly at the end of the day.' He had seen a great many jauntily defiant prisoners in his time, but never known their good spirits to last long.

'Well, we'll try the issue,' said Harry, stretching and turning to test how freely he could move. 'This is well designed. I like to see a man take a pride in his work. My lord promised me a free hand and time to finish mine. That holds good?'

'We are to attend you wherever you go, but so far as the works of the church are concerned you are the master. But mark, no one is to speak to you on any other matter but the work. You'd best warn them of it, for it's they who would pay.'

He heard that with the first stab of true terror that had yet touched him. Eagerly he had turned to the doorway, straining towards the one certain and unshakable joy he had left, which was his work, and the one comforting hope, which was for news of Gilleis. Was she safely away? Was she well? Was she with him in what he had done? Did she understand and forgive the enforced abruptness of his farewell? No use asking these two, who were strangers, and in any case surely had orders to carry back to Isambard every word he spoke. But once he was active about the church again, he was certain Benedetta would somehow contrive to send him word. Even if he was to be so closely hedged about from the world, some day his guards must let some whispered word slip through. He would not believe, he refused to believe, that he could be asked to suffer and die without knowing that she was safe – she and the boy, his boy, whom he would never see.

'I see you have second thoughts already,' said Guillaume, grinning. 'Have you just determined which end of the leash you are?'

'I was debating what I shall need from the tracing-house, so that we need not come back into the wards,' he lied firmly, laying his hands for a moment on the cold band of iron about his waist.

The doors opened before him one by one, the layers of stone that walled him in from the world. He stepped out into the grey, sad and yet lovely daylight, chilly and wan after yesterday's splendid sunrise, and passed through the outer ward to the tracing-house with his usual impetuous stride. There was but one thing to be done with chains, and that was to put them out of his mind. He walked as though fetters did not exist, and let Guillaume scurry after him to gather up the slack weight of the chain as best he could. Fulke came behind, his arbalest on his shoulder; he kept the keys of the harness, so that even if Harry disabled or killed the Poitevin he would not be able to rid himself of the incubus of his body.

The reappearance of Master Talvace in the castle of Parfois, and the manner of it, brought the cooks and kitchen-boys from the buttery, the grooms from the stables, the armourers, the waiting-maids, the men-at-arms, the chamberlains, the clerks, the squires and pages, all running from their work to peer and pity. He was not fled to safety, then! He was here, a prisoner and yet stepping out to his own tracing-house with the old authority, in chains and yet neither ashamed nor subdued. He passed among them as if he felt nothing of the dread and awe that shuddered through them at sight of him, and was quite unaware of the two who followed him so close. Word of his return went round like a fire in dry grass, as though his cortège had been a comet casting sparks from its flying tail.

In the tracing-house young Simon was sitting over his accounts with his head in his hands, not attempting to write or reckon. By the look of his swollen eyes he had already cried himself half blind. He saw Harry framed in the doorway, and his face lit up with such an incredulous radiance of joy that the very air brightened round him. He opened his mouth to burst into eager speech, and in the same moment he saw the escort and the chain. The light went out in his eyes. The broad smile of joy froze into a horrified grimace. He groped his way from behind his stool and would have flung himself upon Harry like a stricken child running for comfort, if Guillaume had not thrust himself between and driven the boy back hard against the edge of the tracing tables.

'Hands off! You may say what you need to say to him for the sake of the work, but not a word more. And touch him, if you want a whipping.'

'Let him alone!' said Harry sharply. 'He is my clerk, I will tell him what he may and may not do.' He looked over the Poitevin's shoulder into the boy's tremulous face, and smiled at him. 'Never grieve about me, Simon, you see I am still hale, and still master-mason here. We shall go on with our work, and finish it as properly as we began it – both you and I. When that's done it may be time for fretting about other things, but not before. For the present do as he says, speak to me only of the work we have in hand. That you may do, freely. And after all,' he said gently, 'what need is there to tell me that you feel with me and will be, as you have always been, a good lad and a loyal friend to me? I know it, and am glad of it.'

'Watch your own tongue,' said Fulke warningly; 'it's straying beyond bounds.'

Harry laughed aloud. 'What bounds? Do you think you can silence me? How, with whippings? Who loses by that? I have only to die once, but if I die too soon my lord will not get his church finished, and if you cripple me with rods or racks he will not get it, either. You dare not lay a hand on me without his word, and you know it. There never was a tongue freer than mine. Don't talk to me of bounds.' He turned his back on them coolly, and went to the chest that held his drawings. 'Has Knollys been through the rolls yesterday, Simon?'

'Yes, Master Henry, and passed them. The tiles have cost us less than we allowed for.' The boy's voice was unsteady, but he controlled it; he had his pride, too. 'There was so much uncertainty yesterday, because you were not here, that I think you should make haste to determine what Master Matthew has in his mind. Without you, he conceived it his duty to take charge, but you know he has ideas somewhat different from your own.'

'He's a good fellow,' said Harry, smiling, 'but he would fill the church with fabulous woodwork if he were let. Never fear, I'll guard my rood-screen. He's had full scope in the stalls.' He gathered his drawings and turned to the door.

The tremor of excitement and terror and pity passed before him like a fanfare through the gate-house and over the drawbridge, and the labourers, the tilers, the plumbers, the glaziers, the joiners busy on the choir stalls, all stood at gaze, open-mouthed and great-eyed, as he came to the church and entered it, with the alert step and high look he always had. Master Matthew was at that very moment stroking his chin and pondering the rood-screen which was such a disappointment to him; and he had a sympathetic group round him, for it seemed that his star might be in the ascendant now that Master Talvace was fled, or dead, or disgraced, whichever was the true version of his fate. For those slight vertical lines and spare, springing leaves, said Matthew, rubbing his hands, he would have a burgeoning forest of ornament, rich and deep. There was nothing to be done with this but rip it out and replace it entire.

'Over my dead body!' said Harry roundly, appearing unheralded on the borders of this conference. 'And that may be possible one day, but not yet, I think.'

They swung round in amazement, disconcerted and yet glad, and the apparition of the chain and waist-belt brought the glaze of shock over their eyes and froze the words on their lips. The effect it had on them startled even Harry; he had to clap a hand to his middle to remind himself of the cause of their petrifaction.

'Oh, never let that deceive you, that's my lord's thorough way of ensuring that he shall not lose my services. You will find I am still the master of the works here, and anyone who questions my authority had best apply to my lord for a judgement. I'm sorry I lost a day's work yesterday – events were out of my control. I make no doubt you used the time faithfully.'

Confounded, relieved, dazed, horrified, they found themselves back at work as though nothing had happened, though the very shape of their world had changed. The pointed tone of his voice, the critical glances of his eyes, denied the change, even the hours of the day, passing methodically in the ordinary tasks, conspired to make them doubt it; but the clash of the chain was a continual warning. All day long they heard it at intervals from the triforium, where he had begun the last series of carvings. It made a jarring counterpoint to the measured strokes of his mallet, and the tiny, rustling sound of the falling fragments of stone.

John the Fletcher, who had seen the strange procession cross the outer ward, came out to the site at midday and made to enter the church boldly, as though he had the highest authority. Within the portal two men-at-arms started up. A lance was lowered across his path, and a great hand flattened against his breast.

'Not here, John! None come in here but those who work here.'

'That's new,' said John equably. 'I was here yesterday. Madonna Benedetta wants to have the measurements taken for the cloths for Our Lady's altar, but if you see fit to deny Madonna Benedetta what she wants, on your own head be it. I'll tell her.'

It was no small matter to cross the lady of Parfois, but they had their orders, it seemed, for they did not step aside or lower their lances. 'If you were here yesterday, why did you not take the measure then?'

'Because the altar's not yet erected and Master Talvace was not here, and only he knows the details she needs. The worked stones they have in store I'd liefer not meddle with. Suppose I should be blamed for a breakage? It's a matter of a minute with him, no more. She sent me down because we heard he was back.'

'It's because he's back that no one can go in. With respect to your lady, but we have strict orders. No one, John!'

He shrugged with seeming indifference and went back and told her. If there had to be a struggle for entry, she would be more likely to succeed than any other. Shortly she came herself, sweeping across the trampled waste and in at the west portal with a high, imperious face and a frowning eye. Lances and arms crossed before her, closing the way. In the pale, haggard, lovely face the grey eyes were hard as glass.

'What is this? Who gave you authority to prevent me from going where I will? My lord shall know of this.'

'My lady, our orders are from him. We are to admit only those who work within, and else only my lord himself. He made no other exception. Well I understand that he may have had no thought of banning you, my lady, but without his permission we dare not let you in.'

'I am coming in,' she said, her eyes flashing, 'and you will answer for it if you hinder me.' And she gathered her skirts in her hands and made two bold paces forward up the steps, her breast to the crossed lances. They quivered before her, almost they were snatched aside from touching her; but the guards were more afraid of disobeying their orders than of offending her. They held their place, though they quaked in their shoes. She leaned hard against the lances, but could go no farther.

Before her the doors stood open. She saw Harry between the choir stalls, the two attendant shadows at his heels. As if her eyes had power to draw his, he turned his head and saw her braced against the barrier. He swung away from the joiners and came striding towards her into the nave, with such forgetful urgency in his step that Guillaume knew, even before he observed the woman at the door, that this was no errand he need countenance. He said not a word, but braced his solid weight, grinning, and let Harry plunge unrestrained to the end of his tether. The chain tightened, jerking him to an abrupt halt. She saw him lay both hands to his waist as the breath was clutched out of him, and marked the gleam of the iron. She heard the Poitevin break into guttural laughter, and her heart was sick with helplessness. They were too far apart even for a look to convey anything of meaning, she could not so much as nod to him that she had done her part. The dimness of the autumn air within the portal clouded their faces, so that they strained their eyes and their hearts to no purpose. And to betray their alliance too clearly was to have no second chance.

She remained for a moment motionless, devouring the very outline of his shoulders, the desperate poise of his head, all that the grey light showed her of him. Then she turned, with one of those wonderful, sweeping movements of hers that caused humiliation to fall aside from her like the dust shaken from the hem of her bliaut, and walked away without a word and without a glance behind.

'It's a long leash,' said Guillaume, still guffawing, 'but it has its limits. Our lymer hasn't learned about choke collars yet. Give him time, he'll come nicely to heel.'

Harry said nothing, though he was white with anger and full to the brim with the scalding realisation of his helplessness. She would try again, a thousand times, she would never give up trying. She would complain magnificently to Isambard of her usage, and he would offer with elaborate courtesy to do all her errands to the church in person. If she pressed the indignity to herself he would have the guards whipped, so that she should feel the injustice to them laid at her own door and never try to pass them again. She would send other messengers, variously, ingeniously, but none of them would ever get to him. Provision had already been made to counter her every move. He was to be incommunicado, to know nothing but the work for which he was being kept alive. But for that, he was already a dead man. He had no wife, no friends, no rights among the living, he had not even nationality or estate, no king, no stake in the happenings in the world. Benedetta would never be allowed to exchange one word with him again, nor could he ask Simon or any other of his subordinates to take the cruel risk of showing pity on him.

So there was one resource left to him, and only one, and that was himself. Come nicely to heel, will he? Not for your training, he thought, nor for my lord of Parfois's whistle. Since I must get my satisfactions where I can, and make shift for myself, let's see how my trainers will take to my element.

The glaziers were at work on one of the tower windows. It was easy to make occasion for climbing to the highest tier of the scaffolding, and his guards had no choice but to go with him. The pace he set them would have terrified even some of his own masons, but they panted after him perforce, sweating horribly in fear of their lives. Once he had to go back and extricate a green-faced Fulke from an exposed corner where he had stuck fast, unable to move either forward or back. When he had got them to the topmost walk and stepped calmly to the edge of the hurdles, they clung desperately to the wall, trembling and sick, not daring to look down. The Poitevin cursed monotonously in a vicious undertone, his bushy beard shaking. Harry stood with his toes over the void, laughing. Parfois was a grey hulk in the fading light, for the evening came on early; the river valley, far below, was a velvet bodice laced with a silver ribbon. A coldness and a calm smoothed the air before the slow approach of night.

Suddenly he was possessed with such a frenzy of desolation that all his body ached with it. He picked up a tiny stone someone had carried up here on his shoe, and dropped it into the void.

'What's to hinder me from following?' he said, turning upon Guillaume a savage smile. 'Unleash your hound, Poitevin, unless you want to go down with him.'

Guillaume opened agonized eyes and made a clutch at his arm, but he eluded it and slipped along the hurdles, grinning, and laying both hands to the chain, began to haul his fetter-fellow after him. The black-bearded man locked his arms despairingly about one of the poles and clung there, shaking from head to foot.

'Had you not better unlock him, Fulke? Or are you coming with us? Better that than face my lord without us!'

They cursed him, and then as helplessly pleaded with him.

'Ah,' he said at last, sick of the game as of them, 'you need not fear, your fool necks are safe enough with me. If I wanted to kill you I could have done for Fulke a while ago, I had only to leave him there to shiver with fright till he shivered himself over the edge. Come down, then, if you still have nerve to stir. Do as I tell you and you're safe as in your beds.'

He brought them down safely enough, but Guillaume, as soon as his feet touched earth, went on his knees and was direly sick. Harry dangled the chain at him and laughed, though already he felt a world away from laughter.

When they took him back to his cell that night and brought him food before they left him, all three of them were subdued and silent. Freed of his chains, Harry lay on his back on the bed, his hands linked under his head. His anger was gone, only the desolation remained.

'That was an unfair advantage I took of you,' he said, with a sudden grudging smile, 'and I'm not proud of it. It's a skill a man gets from long use. No shame to you that you were not born with it, for neither was I. I've no choice but to take you up there again sometimes, in all honesty, but I'll take you at your own speed next time, I give you my word.'

Dumbfounded, they stared at him speechlessly. It was the first time any of their charges had asked their pardon for misusing them.

'Is there aught you want?' asked Guillaume gruffly, before they left him to his darkness.

'Only one thing,' said Harry, rising on his elbow. 'For myself I've no complaint, if I could hear news of my wife. If you could but get me word whether she's in Parfois or safe away from here – '

He saw the closed look that came over their faces, and the side glances they cast at each other, and he understood that it was useless. They were set to spy on each other, no less than to guard him, and neither of them dared offer him comfort, for terror of his own neck.

'No matter!' he said with a sigh, lying down again. 'It was too much to ask.'

When the door was locked, the great door that was like a stone sealing a tomb, he turned on his face and lay with his head in his folded arms. The lightness and emptiness, the irresponsibility that had clouded his judgement when all possibility of action passed out of his hands, was clean gone now, like the passing of the numbness that follows a wound. The longing and hunger for Gilleis came on him like the throes of poison, griping his body until he felt that the very heart's blood was being wrung out of him. He lay hugging the agony to him, and biting deep into the hard brown flesh of his forearm, until the paroxysm passed in a brief burst of scalding tears.

Hard on its passing the agony of the mind began, the long anguish of thinking and feeling and fearing, that would never end this side of death.

The last great work of Harry Talvace at Parfois, second only to the capitals of the nave, was the gallery of portrait heads on the corbels of the triforium, the fruit of his captivity.

Because he was still a warm and living man, even though they had banished him into a companionless world not unlike a grave, his energy and passion, dammed up from all channels but one, flowed into that last course as an irresistible flood. One remaining happiness and joy he had, the only one now permitted to him, the exquisite thing he had made. All his virtue flowed into the stone and burst into flower.

By day he moved among his fellows, intent, competent and demanding; and as the weeks and months of the slow, dark winter crept by, what had been strange and terrible became customary and accepted. Men can get used to anything. For days together they forgot about his chains, only to be hustled away from him with reminding blows if they fell into the trap of drawing too near to him or addressing to him some few casual words with no bearing on the work in hand. They pitied him, but even pity flagged with use. They outlived it, as he seemed at last to have outlived fear and regret, and perhaps even longing. The heart can bear only so much and continue to suffer for only so long.

But the stone did not fail him. The stone survived.

He forsook his drawings and made new. All the corbels of the internal wall arcade in the triforium, between the shallow lancet windows, became as chapters in the story of his life. Here, in this most obscure place, away from the public eye, he might justly record his testament. He began drily and with deliberation. As long as one corbel remained uncarved, he would remain alive, he had his judge's word for that. It did not matter that the floorings were laid, the altars raised, the stalls fitted, more than half the windows glazed and the others ready and waiting for the spring; he would not die until the last carving was complete, and complete to his satisfaction. Well, he could make the work last a long, long time, if his life depended on it.

But they sprang to life so readily, they pressed forward under his hands so insistently, that he could not withstand them. There had never been carved heads so sudden, so urgent, or so economical. Guillaume and Fulke rolled dice idly on the flags of the triforium, and took their eyes off him for an hour or two, and when they turned about there was another living face looking down upon them. They came, and he could not maim them by working over them still when he knew they were finished. His father was there, his mother, married now to Gloucester's young knight, thank God, and far away from a death she could not have prevented, his brother Ebrard, and Adam Boteler his foster-brother. Poor Adam, fretting helplessly in Wales, perhaps, and trying to get reliable news in a distracted land where there was precious little of the commodity to be had. Abbot Hugh de Lacy was there, austere and aristocratic, Norman to his finger-ends, and Brother Denis the infirmarer, no doubt busy finding excuses now for the most unruly of the cherubim and seraphim at every celestial chapter; and Nicholas Otley, merchant and alderman of London, who had in him the large nature proper to princes, and which princes so seldom show; and Gilleis the child; and Apollon and Élie, wrapped in the one gown they owned between them. Benedetta was there, and the provost of Paris, and Ralf Isambard, and John the Fletcher, and Owen ap Ivor ap Madoc in his own proper person for once; they crowded out of his memory and sprang into the waiting stone.

The self-portrait that began the sequence, the several faces they recognised, started an unexpected curiosity in Fulke and Guillaume. They followed him from corbel to corbel, waiting to see who would appear, and they asked him many questions concerning those they did not recognise. If he had outlived his anger, they had outlived their indifference. From a leash the chain had become a link. It was late to begin a new relationship, but it was on them before they were aware.

Gilleis the woman came out of the stone with the first flush of spring, like a waking flower.

'That's her that's below on the altar,' said Guillaume, watching over Harry's shoulder. He had lost the last of his pay to Fulke and had nothing left to dice for. The winner sat comfortably propped against the wall in a patch of sunlight, at a little distance from them, drowsing within closed eyelids, but how soundly there was no telling.

'It is,' said Harry, in a voice that caused Guillaume to turn and give him a keen glance.

'She's a beauty. And by this, then, she's a real woman?'

'She is my wife,' said Harry.

Guillaume drew breath sharply and cast a glance at his fellow. Fulke's right hand relaxed slowly, and slid down from his knee; his head nodded gently back against the stone and rested there, and he did not open his eyes.

'I can get no certain word of your lady,' said Guillaume in a rapid whisper in Harry's ear. 'Some say she's vanished. Some say she's here but kept close. No one's seen her.'

Harry turned his head in astonishment to stare at his gaoler, touched to the heart. Even to speak of her, even to hear her spoken of, was like food after long hunger; and to know that his keeper had remembered and tried to do him so much kindness, brought gratefully back to him the world and men and all his faith in them. The touch of humanity came even through the stone walls of his cell.

'Friend,' he began, 'this was kind – '

Guillaume clapped a hand softly over his mouth, and looked again at Fulke, and leaned closer still. 'A word more, while there's time. Every night when you're safe in your nest one of us must report to him on your day. Never a day but he questions if you have not asked to see him. I think he wants it. I think if you begged for your life he might give it back to you yet.'

'He would not,' said Harry with conviction. 'He gave too much of himself to me ever to forgive me my treason against him.'

'Then why does he ask? Send word to him, ask him to see you. At least try. If he wants you on your knees to him, isn't your life worth it?'

'He'll wait a long time,' said Harry grimly, 'before he brings me to my knees.'

'But for your life, man! For God's sake, you're as mad as any mad marcher lord of them all.'

'What's between him and me won't let either of us kneel. But he'd never forgo the pleasure of killing me, even if I kissed his feet. Trust me, I know.'

'Then at least go slowly with your stone-chipping, lad, and live longer. You're bringing the day on yourself.'

Harry opened his lips to protest that he had been trying all these weeks to hold his hand; but before he could say a word Guillaume mouthed at him soundlessly: 'He's ware!' and stepped back from him to the length of the chain. Fulke had nodded himself clear of the pillar at his back and shaken himself awake. There was no time for Harry to express his thanks even with his eyes. He turned to his work again, and chain and chisel rang together.

'But four more to do,' said Guillaume, gruff as ever. 'What are they to be?'

'That you will see in good time.'

He was smiling as he shaped the beloved rose of a mouth. Two of the four would show them their own faces. Perhaps if Guillaume had nodded, Fulke would have hissed advice in his ear just as benevolently. Kindness and compassion and liking go right to the edge of the grave, like the bright gold dandelions that thrust up to the light even between the sealed stones of tombs. And the third of the four heads belonged to a man he himself had not yet seen, though according to his gaolers he was already arrived.

He saw him next day, as he was escorted through the outer ward. A tall, thin, rather elegant fellow in bright red and black stood with Isambard a little apart from the tracing-house, leaning on his horse's shoulder with one long arm. He was there to observe Harry, but in some degree it disconcerted him when Harry halted to make an intent and leisurely inspection of him. Even Isambard probably mistook it for a gesture of bravado, though he should have known better.

'Is that the man?' asked Harry as they moved on.

'It is.'

'French, you say? It's a fine, sinister head. He's never a Norman?'

'From Gascony, I heard. They say he's very skilled.'

Harry threw back his head and laughed aloud, without a shadow of bitterness. There were no double meanings in Guillaume's head, he meant it in consolation.

'Man, man, if that means he's expert in this new trick of taking out a man's bowels and still keeping the life in him, I'd rather they got me an honest English butcher, used only to coarse work like quick killing.' He threw his arm round Guillaume's shoulders. 'Never fret, it's all one. Guillaume, get that fellow to come to the tracing-house this evening, I need a better look at him. I'd like to make a drawing.'

And the fourth head, the last, he thought of with such secret love that he was glad no one else would ever realise whom it represented. They would take it for one more self-portrait to close the story, and discount the elements in it which did not stem from him. It was never likely to occur to anyone to match Gilleis's face with his, and recognise their son.

The need to prolong his life he had forgotten in the more imperative need to perfect his work. He could neither delay nor deface the issue of his hands, any more than he could have maimed the issue of his body. Daily his life flowed away into the sacred stone, as the fruit must fall and rot that the seed may germinate and the tree grow, the heaven tree of his achievement. He was the human sacrifice sealed into the walls, he was the ceremonial blood mixed into the mortar. Nothing was left him but the dedicated skill of his hands, the possessed fury of his creative dream. But the day had come when it was enough.

CHAPTER FIFTEEN

She came to him in the May evening in his bedchamber, as he was dressing after his ride, and waited motionless by the great bed until his squire had left him. Then she came forward and knelt at his feet. Her hair was unbound and her feet were bare, she had no jewel or ornament upon her. Never until then had she asked him for anything. She laid her hands about his ankles and her face upon her wrists, and the flood of her hair gushed over the skin rugs like an effusion of blood. In the nape of her neck the short tendrils curled small and fine as finger rings.

'I waited long for this,' he said, looking down at her with a still face. 'It used to be I who knelt to you. That prayer was denied. Well, speak, if you want aught from me.'

'Why should I speak,' she said, 'when you already know what I want? You made me a part of yourself. Now listen to your own prayers, and I will be silent.'

'I am doing what I wish to do,' he said.

'That I believe. But it is also what you loathe yourself for wishing, and will detest yourself for ever for having done. I ask you to deliver yourself, for no one else can. Send the Gascon away, and set Harry Talvace free.'

'There is no price even you can offer me now,' said Isambard, smiling into the mirror, 'that could buy his life.'

She lifted her face to him and joined her hands, and said: 'I am not offering to buy. I ask you to give.'

'Go on!' said Isambard. 'You brought more words than those with you. Let me hear them all.'

She knew then that it was useless. Nevertheless, she embraced his knees and said all that could be said of the six years of his acquaintance with Harry Talvace, of the incomparable work Harry had done for him, of the extenuations of affection and pity that made his crime no crime, and of the unquestionable love there had been between them. She begged for Harry's life in measured words and a low and level voice, without tears or reproaches. Even in abasing herself she matched him in dignity. Perhaps she would have shrieked and wept and loaded him with hysterical entreaties, if she had known how to do it, but it was a skill she lacked. In the end it would surely have been all the same. He was irrevocably set on destruction. Not on Harry's destruction only, but on hers and on his own, on pulling down the whole structure of their life headlong upon them to crush them.

He drew himself out of her arms, not ungently, but with such deliberation that she was confirmed in her despair. She let him go and remained kneeling where he had left her, her hands joined.

'The last scaffolding is down. By the tenth the lodges will be down, too, and the site cleared.'

She neither spoke nor moved.

'On the morning of the eleventh, soon after dawn, we'll make an end.'

Out of the following silence she spoke at last, quite gently. 'You think you will be healed of your hell when you have made hell everywhere about you. But it is your own heart the Gascon will be ravishing. And you will have to live on after it. He will at least be able to die.'

'It will take longer than you might think,' said Isambard, clasping an amber necklet about his throat. 'De Perronet tells me on one occasion he kept a client alive and conscious for more than half an hour after disembowelling. The heart is more difficult, but he assures me Harry shall live to feel the want of it. Of course, he may be exaggerating his skill – he is a Gascon.' He turned his head and looked at her, and she had not moved. Her profile was clear and still. 'Of what are you thinking, Benedetta?'

'I am wondering,' she said, 'what terrible penance you will exact from yourself some day for what you are doing now.'

Only silence answered her. She did not look round until she heard the door close after him.

That was over. She had never believed in it, as she had never believed in the letters she had helped Gilleis to write and send to this lord and that along the march, imploring their aid for Harry. It was every man for himself in this distracted England. Who meddled with such as Isambard?

It remained to save what could be saved. She rose and dressed, and before she went down the stone stairway and across the inner ward to the great hall she sent for John the Fletcher. She was sitting before the mirror when he entered; their eyes met in the glass, and they understood each other.

'On the morning of the eleventh,' she said, 'at dawn. He does not intend Knollys to pay off the men until it is over. There will be a great many people. That should help. Have you considered the ground?'

'The roof of the tower is the only sure place,' said John the Fletcher. 'It commands the whole field from the gate to the gallows, and the range is easy.'

'But it makes withdrawal more difficult. I can have a rope secured for you down the cliff on the Welsh side, and a horse waiting in the woods below. We must look at the place together. But getting down from the tower and out of the church will take a dangerous time.'

'There'll be confusion enough,' he said, 'and the church between them and me, and the trees close. I'll take the risk. It's the one perfect place.'

'The light will be on your right hand. Are you sure of your skill? Can you do it clean?'

'Madam, I can.'

'Good! I'll see that you have money, and you must get out of the shire as quickly as possible.' She twisted the mass of her hair into a great, shining coil, and drew the silken net over it. In the mirror her eyes had a shadowy silver lustre, as though they were great with tears, but her mouth was smiling faintly. 'When they lead him out from the gate,' she said, 'the dawn light will be on his church. I hope there will be sunshine. He will look up to take his farewell of it, and stand still to adore the work of his hands. That is your moment. Promise me, John, that he shall never turn away his eyes from the church to look at the gallows.'

'As I hope for the mercy of God,' said John the Fletcher, 'he never shall.'

One more thing she had to do, but it could not be done until the last evening. Father Hubert was old and wily, but in some respects also gullible, a circumstance of which she could make good use, but which she did not intend should be of use to any other. If she prompted him before the event he would have time to betray her design by accident, or, no less disastrously, think it over quietly and think better of having anything to do with it. On the last evening, shortly before they supped in the great hall, that was her time.

The guard was gone from the church now. Harry had looked his last on that prayer-shaped space of air and light between the two folded hands of stone, and there was no longer any need of lances at the portal. She went alone, in the close of the afternoon, to pray at the altar of the Virgin with the face of Gilleis. On the other side of the grassy plateau the gallows stood waiting, the tree of death opposed to the tree of life. She did not avert her eyes from it, she even turned as she was crossing the bridge, and measured it with her glance again, like a soldier measuring his opponent's sword. Then she went in and dressed herself as carefully as a bride, in a cotte of dark blue velvet and a surcoat of gold tissue, and coiled her hair on her head within a golden circlet. The time for despair was over, and the time for mourning was not yet; tonight was a time for triumph, if she played her cards well.

She went down alone to the chapel to find Father Hubert. The old man had been most of his life in service at Parfois, and was treated as a privileged person, a position on which he prided himself not a little.

'Father,' she said mildly, turning the rings on her fingers, 'I am exercised in my mind about Master Talvace. You know it has been always my lord's custom, as I think it was also his father's, to offer to every condemned man on the eve of his death whatever comfort or entertainment he most desired for his last night. He has not mentioned it in Master Henry's case, and I fear that it has slipped his mind, and that he will be distressed afterwards if he omits it. But I would not myself remind him; it is too like a criticism of him, which I do not intend. But you, Father, can speak of it most fittingly, as a part of your office. You will be visiting the prisoner after supper, will you not?'

'That is my intent,' said the old man.

'Then could you not remind my lord at supper, and say that you will, if he so pleased, be the messenger of his gracious clemency? I fear he will feel it as a point of honour that Master Henry should not be excluded from grace, and if he fail in it through forgetfulness it will wound him deeply.'

'My lord is always punctilious,' agreed Father Hubert, preening himself. 'It is my duty to see that all is done as he wishes. Certainly I will speak to him before I go.'

'And, Father, for my part you may say to Master Henry that I commend to him my lord's merciful dispensation, and pray that he may use it to his best comfort, God guiding him. I should like him to know that he is prayed for.'

'It is right and meet to remember the prisoners and the unfortunate. I will tell him what you say.'

'You have greatly comforted me,' said Benedetta, and went smiling into the great hall. Now, if I have not over-prized the love we surely have between us, she thought, Harry will know what to ask. And you, Ralf, who perform all your promises, good and evil, you shall have your hand so forced that you cannot withdraw.

He came to table that night in a magnificence as striking as her own, with glittering eyes and high colour, and the oblique smile frozen on his lips. The presence of his entire household never touched his mood; he was so used to them, and so indifferent to them, that he created a solitude about him. Nevertheless, it was well that there should be so great a cloud of witnesses. He ate little, but drank well, he who was usually a sparing drinker. Her sleeve brushed his with stiff whisperings of brocade and velvet, the fine Flemish stuffs he loved, and she felt in every touch the contagion of his dangerous excitement and his appalling unhappiness. She would have pitied him, but she knew he would esteem it the last cruelty.

The chaplain rose from table early and came to his lord's shoulder. He had a good, sounding voice, a dozen or so of the knights and squires could not choose but overhear.

'My lord, I am going to visit the prisoner. All is to be done according to custom? I know the magnanimity of your mind, and I know you would wish me to observe all the forms honoured in Parfois.'

'It is a case like any other case,' said Isambard. 'He has the rights all condemned men have.'

'Then I shall ask him, as is customary, what privilege or comfort he most desires on his last night,' said Father Hubert.

'Do so, Father!' He smiled, not displeased with the reminder. To offer a crumb to a man starving for life might well be the last refinement of his revenge. 'Short of liberty, he shall have whatever he cares to ask.'

It was done, that ringing voice of his had committed him too deep to withdraw. Now let Harry do his part, and God give the old fool who brings his reply the courage to speak it aloud, thought Benedetta.

He would be a long time gone, he was invariably long-winded about his office. She could not sit still, nor did she wish to be within touch of Isambard when the answer came, but fronting him and at a distance, that she might see his face full. She rose from his side and came round the high table to the corner of the dais where the musicians sat, and held out her hand for the citole the youngest of them was idly clasping. The boy leaped up and brought a cushioned stool for her, and she sat down calmly and retuned the instrument at leisure. Isambard had turned his head and followed her movements with attentive eyes that revealed nothing of his mind. She let her fingers stray into Abelard's forgotten air deliberately, and watched to see if his mouth tightened or his eyes kindled, but there was no sign. Wait, she thought, there's no hurry, I'll prick you home yet.

It was three-quarters of an hour before Father Hubert reappeared at the end of the high table. What ails him, wondered Benedetta, playing a false note at sight of him. Nervous of his errand he might well be, but this was fear itself. His fingers were scrabbling agitatedly in his venerable tonsure, and his eyes looked sidelong at his lord. Whatever Harry might have said to him, it was more than she had foreseen, and more than the old man had bargained for. He might even lie; she had not thought it needful to take that into consideration, but she questioned if he was as much in awe of hell, in the last estimate, as of Isambard. True, he took his little customary liberties, but he knew where to stop. Yet a dying man's charge is a terrible thing to betray.

'Well?' said Isambard, frowning because the chaplain hung irresolutely silent.

'My lord, the young man is in no proper frame of mind – it is an obdurate soul – '

'He is paying for his obduracy,' said Isambard, and his crooked smile was more bitterly twisted than usual. 'He has a right to it. He flung my offer back in my teeth, did he?'

No, she thought, her hands rigid on the citole, it is not that, it is something more.

'No, my lord, not precisely so. Though in effect, what he asked being so insolent and malicious – '

'Come to the point! Did he make a request or no?'

'My lord, he did, but – ' Father Hubert was more afraid to remain silent than to speak, and too confused to lie fast enough for conviction.

'Then repeat it! In his very words, Father!'

'My lord, he asks – may God forgive him! – he asks for Madonna Benedetta to be his bedfellow.'

It carried halfway down the great hall, and in a flurry of frantic whispers that hissed like snakes it was repeated back and back to those who had not heard. The stem of the Venetian glass snapped in Isambard's fingers, the delicate bowl shivered among the silver dishes, and wine gushed across the table like blood. Below the salt the household of Parfois had become a forest of dilated eyes; and in a breath even the whispers died, and silence closed on the hall, and stillness, as though all in it had been turned to stone.

It was better than she had designed, it was a thrust to the heart. Her own heart was leaping in her with so large and jubilant a pulse that she could hardly contain it. She rose, drawing all eyes to herself, and slowly, slowly she began to cross the hall, the citole in her hand. For a moment none of them, not even Isambard, understood what she intended. But as she passed along the dais and drew abreast of him and still did not halt, he realised her purpose. He leaped to his feet with a scream such as she had never heard or thought to hear from that imperious throat. His great chair went over backwards with a crash upon the floor, and the silver trenchers rang as his fists thudded on the board.

'You shall not go!'

She turned and looked at him with full, mild eyes, sustaining his frenzied stare with the utmost resignation. 'I will go, my lord,' she said loudly and clearly. 'It touches your honour. What am I, beside the sacredness of your word?'

It drove the breath out of his body and froze the words in his mouth. He was taken in the snare of his own inflexible pride; what he had said he could not unsay, what he had given he could not take back. Before the eyes of all his household he was silenced and helpless. Short of killing her, there was no way of stopping her.

She looked him steadily in the face, and suddenly and blindingly she smiled. The dove-grey softness of her eyes darkened and brightened into purple, shining with triumph; the full mouth curled exultantly. She straightened her shoulders, drawing herself up before him in such a transport of defiant joy that the dullest among them could not but understand. She was going not to sacrifice, but to triumph. The unveiling was done deliberately, with a barbaric delight in the opulence of the gesture. If she had cast down her eyes and preserved the pretence of sacrificial devotion she might have gone on living, thought more than one who looked at her. She has just tossed her life away for the pleasure of striking him to the heart.

To Isambard that look of naked joy uncovered a greater

mystery. The moment of the dissolution of their compact was come upon him without a word spoken. She had pronounced the contract at an end, and there was no redress. She was abandoning him to follow the creature she loved more than her own life, and he must abide it without complaint. If she had seen the end in the beginning, she could not have found fitter words for it.

'Father,' said Benedetta, again veiling her face, 'I do not know where his cell is. Will you bring me to the place?'

She went out on the old man's arm, and in stillness and silence all the fixed and fearful eyes followed her withdrawal. Only Isambard stood where she had left him, his hands over his face, and no one dared even approach him to pick up the fallen chair.

In the antechamber of the cell Benedetta paused to look sharply at the two guards, who stood back from her respectfully, as much in awe of her cloth of gold as of her authoritative bearing.

'Wait!' she said. 'Before you open the door let me give you a word of warning. When you have turned the key upon us, for your own safety leave this room and lock the outer door also. Sleep across the threshold if you will, but be so far from us that you may be under no suspicion of seeing or hearing anything. Father, tell them what would happen to any man who dared to witness this coupling.'

'She is giving you good advice,' said the old man, trembling. 'He would tear you in pieces.'

Afterwards, she thought without astonishment or concern, he will tear me in pieces; but by then it will no longer matter.

'Father, remain with them, and bear them witness if they are called in question.'

'Madonna, I will.' The hand he held in his was warm and easy; he clung to it to steady his own trembling.

'And pray for us.'

Guillaume turned the key in the great sunken lock.

'Mistress, when shall we open to you again?'

'When they come for him,' she said, and gathered up her long skirt and went into the cell.

They had left him a great candle for his last night; it burned in an iron candle-stick on the rock ledge beside his pallet, and wavered softly and constantly in the air from the shaft. Harry was lying on his back on the bed, his head pillowed on folded arms, but at the sound of the door opening he turned on his side and rose on his elbow to stare at the glitter of gold in the doorway. He had not believed that they would ever let her come. The flame of the candle shone in his astonished eyes, turning their shadowy blue back to green, and the reflection of her splendour transmuted the green to burnished gold. Between the black lashes, beneath the dark, straight brows, that brilliant, dancing light startled and moved her like the apparition of stars in a night of storm. He swung his legs over the edge of the bed in trembling haste and scrambled to his feet, and the hurried sweep of his arm set the candle rocking. He clutched at it to steady it, and she saw how his hand was shaking.

The door closed behind her. The key turned. The candle-light shuddered up the stony walls in ripples of pallor, and slowly stilled.

He tried to say her name, and his mouth was too dry for speech. She saw him swallow and moisten his trembling lips with a tongue almost as dry. He had not believed she would come, and now that she was here, she who alone could tell him what he ached to know, he was afraid to ask her, for fear the answer should be harder to bear even than the wondering.

'She's safe,' said Benedetta, leaping to fill his need. 'She's well. She sends you her heart's love.'

'Oh, Benedetta!' he said in a long, soft sigh, and the trembling tension ebbed out of him. His cast shadow on the wall seemed to soften and dwindle. '*Nunc dimittis*!' he whispered and suddenly bowed his head forward into his hands and wept, wearily, gratefully, freely, like an exhausted child.

She took him in her arms and drew him down with her on to the bed, and the brief storm spent itself in the shoulder of her magnificent surcoat. She smoothed back the thick brown hair from his forehead and let her hand rest about the back of his head, holding him gently upon her breasts. She had the whole world in her hand. 'There, lie still, we have time. We can speak openly, and all night long. No one will disturb us, no one will spy on us. I've seen to that.'

'Where is she?' he asked, when he had his voice again.

'Safe with the anchoress sisters at the oratory of Saint Winifrede, in the hills by Stretton. They're kind and loyal, and so holy no one dare meddle with them. And good nurses, you can be easy about her when her time comes. Soon she'll have the child to live for, and neither of them shall ever want for a friend.'

'I'd have given my right hand if I could have come to her, that day, but there was no time, if the boy was to live. I was afraid! She's headstrong! I was afraid she would refuse to go.'

'She didn't want to leave you, it wasn't in her nature to take cover when you were manifestly putting yourself in peril. But we didn't even know what you intended, and for the child's sake she had no choice but to obey you.'

'It was hard for her,' he said, and shook in her arms at the memory. 'And not even to know for what end I was asking so much of her – '

'She knows now. She's with you heart and soul. What else could he do, she said, being Harry? The hardest for her to bear has been staying there in hiding all this time, knowing what was fallen upon you.'

'She knows about me? The whole of it?'

'Not the whole. She knows it's death, but not that it's on us already. God knows I have no right to keep anything from her, and yet I could not tell her, and the child so near. I told her – ah, I hoped it would be truth! – that you would spin out the work you had left and make it last months yet. I hoped there'd be time for his rage to pass, or that the king would call him hence and you be forgotten. For there's a great contention between John and his barons, and Langton has his arms in it to the elbows – some matter of a reaffirmation they want the king to make, securing them all their old rights. Even FitzAlan and FitzWarin are siding against the king, and now it's come to an issue of arms. A few months more, and there might have been no thought to spare for you. Oh, Harry, why didn't you hold your hand and give your friends a little time?'

'I meant to,' he owned. 'I as good as told Adam I should. But when it came to the point I could not. The work came so quick upon me, I could not turn my hand to abortion. Not even to save my life! Benedetta, does she know – the manner of it?'

'No!' she cried, her arms tightening jealously about him. 'Nor shall not! But that none of us knows, Harry. Only God knows it.'

'Never tell her! Where's the need? By the time she knows of it I shall be past troubling. I would not have her grieve over what's done. You've seen her since you took her away?'

'Three times. I dared not go oftener. And several times John has been my messenger.'

'Did *he* look for her?'

'I know he did, though he never spoke of it to me, beyond asking if I'd seen her that day you took the boy. I said she had been with me in the morning and I had not seen her since. He ransacked Parfois for her, and even after you came back he was still searching for her through the villages below. But it did not continue long.'

'Tell me of her!' he begged hungrily. 'Tell me everything! Does she speak of me?'

'Speak of you! Oh, my heart's dear,' said Benedetta, laying her cheek against his hair, 'you are her sun and her moon. You are the spring and the summer to her.' She smiled over his head into the candle-flame, and talked to him of Gilleis until she had exhausted every detail of the time they two had spent together loving him. 'Only the child has kept her still and silent. When she has put your son from her and placed him in safety, I know, I feel, she means to return and fight for you – '

'Yes,' he said, fondly and proudly, 'that I can believe.' He turned a little in her arms, and rested with his cheek upon her breast. 'Now that won't be needful. Benedetta – ' He hesitated upon her name, and she looked down to find his eyes searching her face. 'When you tell her, carry my undying love to her. And kiss my son for me.'

'My best and dearest, you know I will.'

'You've eased me of such a load!' he said, and drew a long, weary breath. 'Now that I have her blessing and yours, the rest is almost easy. I thank God!' And after a while: 'I have been most happy, and most blessed. It was ungrateful to forget.'

'How long is it since you slept?' she asked, passing cool fingertips over the blue-stained arches of his eyelids. 'Two nights? Three?' He shook his head, faintly smiling; he did not know. 'Sleep now, and I'll watch by you.'

'Oh, no!' he protested, tightening his arms about her. 'I shall be sleeping soon enough.' The shadow of the terrible portal of that sleep lay heavy upon his face. Through the breast of his crumpled shirt she felt the strong, indignant beat of his threatened heart. 'Let me enjoy you while I have you. I never thought he'd let you come. It was the only bolt I had to loose at him, and I hoped it would find its mark, but I never believed it would win me the prize.'

'He'd pledged himself before everyone, he could not evade it. "It touches your honour," I said. "What am I in comparison?" But I laughed in his face, I could not for my life refrain. If you won't sleep, at least lie down and rest.'

'If you'll lie beside me. It's but a narrow bed for two, but we're neither of us so great that we need a lot of room.'

'True,' she said, smiling, 'I'd forgotten. You asked for a bed-fellow.' She rose and kicked off her shoes, and stripping off her surcoat, let it fall in a corner of the cell. 'Take the inner place,

Harry, I would be between you and the world.'

He lay down close to the wall, and watched her as she lifted the circlet from her head and loosed the flood of her hair. 'God knows I should ask your pardon for that,' he said shamefacedly. 'I am not proud of myself now.'

'You did well! I meant you to ask for speech with me, but this was more than I'd hoped for. You pierced him to the heart.'

He opened his arms to her, and she lay down beside him in her velvet cotte and clasped him close. He filled his hand with her hair and drew it over them both like a silken coverlet, and she heard and felt a sudden honest crow of laughter go bursting up out of his throat to make the candle flicker again. 'It's well seen he lacks experience of my situation, or he'd know I'm in no case to afford you much pleasure or do myself much credit in that kind tonight. But it's a narrow life he's led, when all's said and done.'

'Never fear,' she said, settling herself warmly in the crook of his arm, 'I'll not hold you to your bond.'

'Ah, don't mock me! It was a poor joke, I know, but I'm out of practice. If you knew how long it seems since I laughed!'

'You have no debts to me,' she said, with the old, large candour. 'I want for nothing. I have everything.' And indeed she had outlived, how long ago she could not even guess, the anguish of not being able to be more to him than she was. It had passed unnoticed, some day when it had dawned upon her heart, though not upon her mind, that what Gilleis was to him was not more, but only different. They lay together now marvellously at peace, and not the humble peace of resignation, but the lofty peace of achievement. All that she needed of him she had. It did not matter how small it might seem to others, when it filled her life to overflowing and had been given with a generosity as absolute as love itself.

'Harry, are you afraid of death?'

'Who is not a little afraid of it, if he's in his right wits? We're all in awe of the dark, when it comes to it. But it's not death appals me, it's the dying!' He stiffened angrily against the shudder that convulsed him. 'I'm afraid of pain. I'm afraid of that devilish violation of my body. And of being a spectacle, long after I've ceased to be a man. Ah, why did you ask me? I wanted to spare you this.'

She laid her hand upon his cheek, and holding him so, said with passionate gravity: 'Harry, with all my heart I ask you to trust me. Leave reasoning, leave preparing yourself, leave fearing. You will not be shamed. He'll have no triumph over you. He'll never see you broken. I swear it! Death, we can't avoid, but its coming is in God's gift, not in Isambard's.'

'Ah, girl!' he said with a whisper of laughter, 'you lift up my spirit. If you could speak so to me at the last, before you leave me, I believe I might not break.'

'I shall not leave you. And you will not break. Trust me, and don't be afraid.'

'A miracle!' He lay smiling at her with a sudden unquestioning weariness sweet and heavy in his eyes. 'You draw out fear with your fingers. I can almost believe that if you have asked it of him God will make the way easy for me and take me to Himself unbroken. The other – ah, the fear of what comes after is a good fear, hardly more terrible than when I had to go before the masters in Paris and submit my master-work. I was sick with fright the night before that, too; Adam had a time with me. But they gave me their approval.'

'I am not afraid,' she said, stroking him softly, 'that you will fail of getting God's.' But whether the master-work he was to offer must be his church or his life, or whether indeed the twain were one, she did not trouble to question; they were of one quality both, and God would know how to value them.

'What will you do, Benedetta, afterwards? You have no thought of – of dying? You wouldn't do that!'

'Not while you have a child living for me to love and serve.'

He heaved a deep sigh of wonder and content. 'What have I done, what have I ever done, to deserve your love?'

'Loved me,' she said, smiling, 'after your fashion. And it's a good fashion, I wouldn't change it.'

He turned his head upon the pillow, and taking her chin in his hand, softly, tenderly kissed her. They lay together a long moment thus, a sweet, cool, tranquil joy possessing them, their mouths married in quietness. When he drew away, as softly as he had come, she lay still with her overwhelming happiness.

'That was no kiss for wife, or love, or mother, or sister, or child,' she said at last, marvelling.

'No, it was only for you. For my sweet friend – from the most grateful to the truest and dearest of all sweet friends who ever loved each other well.'

She would have spoken, she would have poured out her heart to him like a libation, but his peace was too precious and too fragile a thing to be so shaken. She lay still in his arms, holding him to her heart, and they were silent for a long time; he said at last, in a soft voice already blurred with sleep: 'Death is in God's gift! If it might come now!'

In a few moments she knew by the languid weight of the arm over her, and by his gentle, deep breathing against her cheek, that he had fallen asleep.

He slept in her arms through the hours of the night, while she cradled and guarded him as jealously as a mother; and when the first pallid light cast a faint ray through the shaft in the wall she took his face, all softened and flushed with sleep, in her hands and kissed him awake. He opened his eyes and smiled at her brilliantly. Then realisation closed on him, and the smile grew wan.

'Yes!' he said. 'How kind you are! Yes, I must be ready.'

He sat up and swung his feet to the floor, and shook out the crumpled sleeves of his shirt. 'They'll bring me fresh clothes. One must make a good impression. I've told you nothing about my life here, have I? A pity, but it's too late now. It's more interesting than you might think. Guillaume shaves me beautifully every day. I never had so smooth a chin before.'

'It's prickly enough now,' she said, laying the backs of her fingers against it.

'No matter, you shall kiss me goodbye after he's shaved me. I would his hand might slip,' he said candidly, 'but there's no hope of that. And look, your beautiful dress thrown down on the floor! For shame!' He picked it up and shook out the folds, brushing off dust with his hands. 'Put it on, I like to see you so fine. Let me be your tirewoman.' He held it for her to slip head and arms into it, and drew it down admiringly over the velvet of her cotte. Thus having her by the shoulders as he smoothed the shining tissue, he leaned and kissed her forehead. 'Sweet friend! And now, when they come to dress me, you must go.'

'As far as the next room,' she said, 'to wait for you.'

'No, you must go. Somewhere out of sight and out of hearing, so that you will remember me only as I am now. I will not have you see me cut down and ripped apart. I will not become a howling animal and a mess of butcher's offal in front of you.'

'Have you forgotten what I told you? Leave lashing your courage, it's a shame to treat so fine a horse so cruelly. Leave fearing, it won't be as you fear. I shall be with you while you live.'

Did he believe, now that the morning was come, and the ordeal had drawn so close to him? She could not tell. Perhaps even he did not know. He had a kind of grace and lightness about him, half of deliberate pride, and half of irresponsible serenity, as if he had drawn some degree of comfort and reassurance from her certainty. But she thought it was only the comfort of having eased his heart to someone who loved him, and talked his fill of someone he loved.

Guillaume and Fulke came in with the dawn and brought him his best clothes. They took the precaution of turning the key loudly and then waiting some minutes before they opened the door, and Benedetta came forth with her hair all about her in a shimmering crimson cloak. Fulke called her back timidly from the doorway.

'Mistress, you've forgotten this.'

It was the gold circlet she had worn round her coiled and braided hair; she could not conceive that she would ever need it again. She looked at it indifferently, and then at them. The two wary faces, hard enough perforce in a hard world, and constrained in front of her, looked upon Harry with a rough, regretful kindness. After their fashion they had been good to him, once prisoner and gaolers came to know one another. 'Keep it,' she said, 'and share the worth of it between you. Drink it to his memory.'

In the antechamber Father Hubert waited, uncombed and rosy with sleep. He began to babble commiserations and civilities, which caused her some surprise until she realised that he was hoping for her confidences. She listened to his assiduities with a faint smile she could not repress. He was not sure if she was still worth cultivating or if her star had set, and she was in no mind to help him to a decision.

'My lady, will you not go from this place? My duty is here, but yours is nobly done.'

He is still wagering on me, she thought, amused. I ought to warn him how the wind is likely to be blowing from this on.

'No,' she said, 'I shall wait for Harry. Where is my lord?'

'He has already taken his place.'

Close to the gallows and the brazier and the butcher's slab of stone, she thought. She saw the level field of young grass, green and fresh beneath the tree, the great cleared square and the path to it lined with men-at-arms, lances slanted across the curious breasts of the spectators. Outside that armed barrier all the household would be gathered, and all the workmen who had built the church, the plumbers, the glaziers, the masons, the joiners, the clerks and draughtsmen, the labourers. The old man who had coveted Harry's place, though never at this price, he would be there, and that poor boy from the tracing-house, who had smudged Knollys' accounts with so many bitter tears over his master's fall. On both sides of the cleared square and along the rim of the rocky fissure companies of archers would be spaced out for action in case of trouble. And placed alone within the charmed enclosure, Isambard's great chair, and the man himself enthroned in it. He would have it set where he could command a clear view not only of the executioner's proceedings, but also of the whole of the wide gangway cleared from the drawbridge to the gallows. He would want to see all, every step of the way to death, but whether to exult over his enemy or to crucify himself in his friend not even she would ever know.

'And the Gascon?'

'He is in attendance.'

So they would be men of Parfois who escorted him to his death. De Perronet in his black would be waiting by the foot of the ladder. With his pride in his appalling skills he seemed to her an abortion, not a man. Man begets; this thing's function was to destroy, and not only the flesh; to reduce God's best to a jerking, mangled, mewing horror as long as possible before he let the spirit out of it. I would I had half a company on the tower, she thought, instead of one brave man. That creature at least should never go from here alive.

In a little while the inner door opened, and Harry came out between his guards. Very neat and trim he looked in his best, washed and shaven and combed to perfection, hardly Harry at all. He was as pale as his clean linen shirt, but very calm. Something was left even of that light, incalculable smile in his disconcerting eyes, the same look with which he used to meet her flashes of laughter at the ceremonious life of Parfois.

'Good morning, Father! I hope we have not kept you waiting?'

'We might withdraw into the cell for a few minutes more,' said Father Hubert. 'They are not yet here, you have time to ease your soul.'

'My soul is at ease, I thank you, Father. It's my body that feels itself something less than easy. Come,' said Harry, 'I made my confession only last night. I'm fallible, but I don't soil as quickly as all that.'

He knew very well, of course, what the old man had in mind. He met her eye, and the flash of wicked joy passed between them like a spark of warmth in a world of frost. If Father Hubert wanted to shrive him of his supposed grievous sin, he would have to name it in good round terms; and that was an indiscretion he would not dream of committing, in case she should miraculously be still in favour. His dilemma was comic; indeed, she had often found him so, and was more than grateful for it now.

'Will you kneel with me?' said Harry, the laughter gone. He held out his hand to her, and they knelt together on the stone floor while the old man performed his last office. The bright, impetuous profile beside her was grave; the closed lids and joined hands gave him the hieratic dignity of a figure on a tomb. When they rose the escort of men-at-arms was already at the door.

It was Langholme who came for him. He looked sick and unhappy, she thought, and warmed to him. De Guichet would never have turned a hair; he had done the same office too often.

'I am ready,' said Harry, and turning, held out a hand to either of his gaolers. 'Lads, you've been good company. I've never wished you ill, and wish you none now. If it had lasted a while longer I'd have made steeple-jacks of you both.'

'I wish every man as good a heart as yours,' said Guillaume in a grudging growl, and winced at the indiscretion of using the word 'heart' on this of all mornings. And Harry laughed and clapped him reassuringly on the shoulder. How much of his remaining strength did every laugh cost him now? He turned to her, and before them all took her by the shoulders and held her to his heart. His cheek was cold against hers, and the steadiness of his breath faltered for a moment. Then he kissed her on the mouth.

'Goodbye, Benedetta.'

'Goodbye, Harry. But if I say it now it is only to have it said in quietness. I am coming with you.'

He looked at her in wonder and doubt, but half assured now that she had some foreknowledge which he must not and need not question.

'Madam,' said Langholme hesitantly. 'I have no orders concerning you.'

'Then you will not be contravening them in allowing me to walk as far as the field by Harry's side. That is all I am proposing.'

She knew she would get her way, because no one could be sure that it was safe to flout her. Evidently Isambard could not yet bear even to speak her name, or they would have known how to use her.

They went out from the cell and climbed the stone stairway to emerge into the outer ward. The purple shadow of the curtain wall lay unbroken across the courtyard, but the sky was pale blue without a cloud, and on the western merlons the sunlight lay sharp and bright. Harry looked up, sniffing the air, and the longing for life shone like flame though his pale face. To be dying in May!

She took his hand, so that no one could thrust between. The outer ward was silent and deserted. Only an old blind man sat on one of the blocks outside the mews, and followed their passing with his tilted, listening head. No point in driving him out to the spectacle, since he could not appreciate it. One column of men-at-arms went before, six men walking in twos, then Father Hubert clasping his breviary, then Harry and she, hand in hand, and after them the remaining six of the escort, and Langholme bringing up the rear. It could have been a marriage procession, and she in her cloth of gold was splendid enough for a bride. She clung to Harry's cold hand and prayed.

They entered the dark passage of the gate-house; at the end of the tunnel the dawn sun was radiant. A bubbling murmur came to them from the crowd on the plateau, and the light before them seemed to shimmer and coruscate with reflections of colours and movements, like a tremor of sick excitement shuddering on the air. They stepped on to the bridge. She checked her pace, so that the interval between the escort and the prisoner might be enlarged. The plateau opened before them as they emerged from between the low towers. From their left the great sighing murmur of pity and horror and anticipation blew upon them like a rough wind; but before them, alone and beautiful and sufficing, the church soared in the dawn.

'Look up!' she said. 'The tree is in flower.'

She fell back from him a pace, drawing her hand from his. The first ranks of the escort had wheeled to the left, towards the gallows; there was nothing, no one, close enough to separate him from his masterpiece. He halted, looking up from the shadowy ground, up the delicate tapering lines of the buttresses, up the loftly sweep of the wall, to the tower. The light from the east touched the cool grey stone and it blazed into gold. Every pinnacle was an ascending flame. Stage upon stage, the tower drew upwards its gleaming walls, its taut, true, pure brush-strokes of light and shadow, until the golden stem burst into the pale, shining flower of the sky.

He stood with uplifted face, dazzled with delight, worshipping the work of his hands. Death had loosed its hold on him; he withdrew from it by a tower of gold, a staircase of amber, a shaft of crystal filled with the spirit.

Out of the ray of light a ray of darkness, plunging invisibly, cried and shuddered through the air with a note like the vibration of gigantic wings. It struck him true, full in the left breast, and hurled him backwards into her waiting arms. She heard the hard, thudding impact; it seemed to her that she heard even the severing of his flesh as the arrow split the disputed heart; and she gave one cry for the instant of his agony, though he made never a sound. His weight falling against her breast bore her down under him, and she let herself sink to her knees on the grass, breaking his fall so that he came to rest as on a bed, cradled in her arms. The convulsion of pain was already past; she braced herself still, that there might be no second, smiling and weeping over him, and dropping broken words among the tears, though she never knew she had spoken.

'My love, my little one, my heart's dear – !'

The sea-green eyes, gold-flecked with the sun, saluted her with the last fleeting glitter of triumph and laughter, and wandered beyond her, amazed and enchanted, into the radiant spaces of eternity that blossomed from the golden stem. Bending her head, with terrible care not to touch or disturb the arrow, she kissed his brow and cheek, and the smiling, startled mouth. When she drew off and looked at him again the light was fading from his eyes, and the hand that clutched at the shaft protruding from his breast had slackened its hold. Hand and wrist slid down into the grass and lay at ease. She held him dead on her breast.

The arrow, passing through his body, had pierced through her sleeve between arm and side as she sprang to hold him, tearing her gown and grazing her arm. She plucked free the torn shreds of velvet, and her blood and his spattered the grass. Now that he was safe for ever from being hurt she drew him more securely into her arms, and rocked him gently, her cheek against his hair. The world came back to her slowly and grotesquely, its manifestations without meaning for her. The escort closed round her confusedly, at a loss what to do; Father Hubert was dementedly praying, Langholme was shaking her by the shoulder. Across the sunlit field people were running and shrieking, and guards were thrusting them back. There was shouting and confusion and haste as they cast about to see from which quarter the shot had come. Where she crouched in the grass was the heart of the whirlwind, and there all was still and silent and at rest.

Only when the long, single shadow fell across Harry's body, and all the insignificant people who had been battering at the doors of her tower of silence drew off in awe, did she look up. Under the streaming fire of her hair the pale face was fierce and bright with triumph. She looked up over her dead, and demanded in a loud, exultant cry: 'Give me his body! It is mine!'

Isambard stood looking down in silence, his eyes lingering upon the dead face, still fixed in the eagerness and wonder of life. He marked the riven breast oozing a thin dark circle of blood about the shaft, and the pale flesh of her arm shining through the tatters of her sleeve.

'You shall have it,' he said softly, 'since this is what you want. You shall have his body and hold it, hold it fast for the rest of your life.'

They cut off the arrow-head, blunted and bloody and fringed with a few tiny splinters of bone, and drew out the shaft. An effusion of blood followed it, and the lips of the slit wound gaped for a moment, and closed again, sealing in the pierced heart.

They handled him gently, as though they went in awe of him, for someone in the crowd had already whispered 'miracle'. Was it a man who drew the bow? They had found no man in the church or among the trees, and there were not wanting voices to swear that the shaft had been loosed from some vantage-point higher than the tower. Not until they had numbered all the household and determined whether any man was missing would they be sure that God had not reached out a hand and taken his master-mason to him, out of the very noose of his enemies.

They wrapped the body in a cloak and flung it over a horse, and set the woman on another, and so brought them down after Isambard to Severn side. The spring rains had been heavy, and the river was running high and brown, dappled with eddies and full of torn bushes rolled under and over with the stream. On the half-dismantled jetty where the stone had been landed Isambard stood and looked down into the flood. It ran less than a yard below him, tugging at the piles of the stage until the planking quivered. The shrunken green meadows on either hand had the vivid colouring of bog, and sparkled here and there in the hollows with lingering pools. Downstream, where the forest poured down the steep flank of the Long Mountain, all the English bank was hidden beneath overhanging trees.

He turned and came ashore along the tremulous planking, and

looked long at the dead man, where they had laid him in the grass. The flesh was at his mercy still, but he had no quarrel with the flesh. He was a bird of prey, perhaps, but not a carrion crow. He had never seen Harry in stillness before; the waking face had been as mobile as light, and only once had he watched his sleep, there at the edge of the wood by Erington, with the boy in the crook of his arm. They had closed his eyes, but still this had not the look of sleep. The recovered childhood was there, the unruffled innocence, but not the helplessness. He was invulnerable now; the face bore the print of it.

'Strip them!' said Isambard.

No one moved. They looked at him with frightened, reluctant faces, unwilling to believe they had heard aright.

'You heard me? Strip this carrion. The woman, too.'

They fell on their knees and began to unfasten Harry's cotte, and to slit the bloody shirt from his body, which submitted to their touch with an unmoved face. But they still hesitated to touch Benedetta. She stood waiting, with a slight, mocking smile, and the sun gleamed on her finery, and darkened the tarnish of blood on her breast.

'Are you afraid of her?' said Isambard with a curling lip. He set his hand to the neck of her cotte, and wrenched at it, and the velvet tore with a sound like parting sinews, but the cloth of gold over it was too strong for him. He drew his dagger, and setting the point of it in the cup of her throat, slit all her clothing to the waist, and dragged linen and velvet together down over her shoulders. She stood like a white birch tree shaken and mishandled by the wind, and accepted it with the like indifference. There was nothing he could do to her that could move her now. Sheathing the dagger, he filled his two hands with the slit cloth at her hips, and tore it almost to the hem, and all her garments fell together about her feet. She smiled still, stepping out of the ruins, and herself kicked off her soft leather shoes. It was himself he humiliated. She was clothed magnificently in her triumph and her indifference, and these he could not strip from her.

'Bind them together, face to face. They shall lie in each other's arms till they rot.'

Stricken into silence, but afraid to disobey, they lifted Harry's naked body upright, and raised the limp arms to draw them about her neck. Two of them would have taken her by the wrists, too, though they shrank from her whiteness, but she started forward with a wild tenderness in her face, and took into her arms gladly the slender trunk on which last summer's brown was not yet quite faded. Close, close she held him, breast to breast with her and thigh to thigh, and before the cords were drawn tight about them she settled him at ease, his right cheek pillowed on her shoulder. They held up his dead weight from falling all upon her, but he was so slight that she could almost have supported him alone. She spread her hands against his back and pressed him to her, and the two vertical wounds were hidden, the frontal one against her breast, the other beneath her palms. His forearms were drawn together behind her shoulders and bound fast; knee was lashed to knee and ankle to ankle, until they stood like a pillar of marble, held upright by guards as pale as they.

'Throw them in,' said Isambard, 'let them sink or swim together.'

To the end she thought of nothing but Harry. As they were dragged along the stage he saw her, all trussed and helpless as she was, hunch her shoulder and incline her cheek to steady the lolling head from the uncomfortable motion; and when they were held upright for a moment at the end of the quay she turned her head and looked at Isambard with a kind of distant pity, and laughed, before she kissed the curve of the sharp young jawbone that was all her lips could reach.

She did not lift her eyes again. She watched her darling's last sleep, and cared nothing for cold or violence or shame or death or the unassuageable anguish of hate and love that made all the air about her bitter. Neither living nor dead could he ever get her back. If he crawled after her on his knees to the water's edge, and implored her to have pity on him and fear him and weep, and live, she would not do it.

'In with them! Make an end!' he cried in a suffocating voice, and striding along the quay tore them from the hands that clung irresolutely still, and flung them out into the stream.

The rapid water hardly cast up a fringe of spray from their fall, but took them hungrily and sucked them under, and darting eddies followed their submerged passage downstream. Beneath the leaden surface he saw the pallor of their bodies like a great silver fish for a moment, then they broke surface already thirty yards away, and fast being tugged down towards Breidden. The long red hair, streaming about them, coiled round them both as they were rolled over and over in the uneasy currents.

In the shelter of the encroaching forest another pale shape slid unseen down the bank into the water, and stood breast-deep, braced against the impetus of the stream, watching the floating crimson sweep towards the shadow of the trees.

Isambard stood motionless, following their hapless passage, until they were lost to sight. Then he turned and walked slowly back to the shore. His men fell back before him with pale faces and frightened eyes, but he looked at none of them. His face was fixed and grey. He crossed the greensward as though he felt himself to be alone, mounted, and wheeled his horse towards the rising path to Parfois. They followed, but he was not aware of them. He rode in a desolation without limit in space or time; he had depopulated his world.

CHAPTER SIXTEEN

Pain came back to her first, and in the pain a sense of helplessness that was not all unpleasant. She was taken up in great hands that hurt her sides and forced her to draw in anguished breaths to the inmost deeps of her body, breaths that stabbed like knives and burned like flames. Later there was warmth about her, and a drowsy comfort, and the touch of some rough texture that pricked her body. And after, sleep.

She opened her eyes upon a bearded face that hung over her anxiously, and seeing faint colour in her cheeks and awareness in her wondering stare, shed unexpected tears upon her. There was a warm brown gloom, smelling of wood and smoke and humankind, and the flicker of firelight in the beams of a low wooden ceiling. The hands that had racked her drew up the skin coverings more closely over her naked breast.

'John!' she said.

'Thanks be to God!' said John the Fletcher. 'Rest quiet, mistress, till I bring you a drink of milk. I thought we'd never fetch you back.' He brought a pitcher of milk warm from the cow, and raised her in his arms to drink from it.

'What is this place?' she asked, looking round the small, bare hut.

'An assart in the wood, close under Parfois.'

'You took me out of the river,' she said, lying back against his shoulder; and again, in a stronger voice: 'Where is he?'

'Here, safe.' A pale smile touched her lips at the word, but she found no fault with it. Safe he was, inviolate, inviolable. 'He's lying in my cloak, below in the undercroft, and my bow with him, and the horse you gave me. The goodman here helped me to bring the pair of you up from the water, and his wife's about finding some clothes for you when she's done with the cow.'

'I can't repay her,' said Benedetta.

'I can. I have the money you gave me.'

'For your own escape,' she said and frowned. Life was flowing back into her mind and will. There were yet things she had to do, since it seemed she must still be doing. 'I bade you get out of the shire. Why did you not go?'

'And leave you in his power, and I not knowing how he meant to use you? No, mistress, I am your man as long as I live, I'll go nowhere without I'm sure all's well with you. I made my plans to lie up in the woods here and wait for word of you, but he brought you down to the shore before my very eyes, and did the thing I'll slit his throat for some day if God's good to me. Praise be, I grew up beside a river, and learned to swim as I learned to walk. Lie down and rest now, and keep covered up warm. Her man's off bargaining for another horse for us.'

'You'll be as destitute as I am, if you spend on two.'

She lay silent for a while, and presently he saw that heavy tears were spilling over from her wide-open eyes and running down her cheeks. He knelt beside her and took her head between his rough hands, and to be held so was a luxury like the return of innocence, and to have him wipe away the tears was a comfort that touched her to the heart.

'Was it well done?' he asked gruffly. He knew how well, for he had seen the body, but he wanted her word to satisfy him.

'Well done, John. Quick and clean. No man could have bettered it.' She lay looking up into the smoke-blackened beams, and purpose and will and mastery came back gradually into her face. 'It remains to bury him honourably,' she said, 'before we go seek the living.'

With her own hands she washed him clean of blood and of the stains of the river, and combed out the tangles from his thick brown hair, and with John's help she dressed and composed his body for burial. They laid him in the boat from the mill downstream, and rowed him over to Strata Marcella on the Welsh bank. When the brothers came down at midnight to Matins they found a dead man, closely swathed in a coarse cloak, laid at the foot of the chancel steps, and two in worn homespun clothes who kneeled over him in prayer, one at his head, one at his feet. He at the feet was in the middle years, a bearded countryman. He at the head was young and pale and comely beneath the shadow of his hood. The prior was about to order him sharply to uncover when he saw in the descending light the swell of breasts below the hem of the capuchon.

She joined her hands before him in supplication. 'Father, for

God's charity give quiet lodging to this child of God, untimely dead, until he can lie in the church which he himself built. And of your grace mark the place where you lay him, that we may find him again even after years. I will not rise from my knees until you receive him from me.'

The prior looked long upon the dead, and saw how slight and young he was. The marble serenity of death had not quenched the ardour and energy of the face, but only charmed it into stillness. It seemed that if they raised their voices he might awake and open his eyes.

'Daughter,' said the prior, 'how may I take in one who died, as I see, by violence, and of whose manner of life I know nothing?'

'He was noble,' said Benedetta, 'by birth and in the manner of his life. His work was noble, and he died nobly in place of another, whose life he saved. Is it enough?'

It was enough; nevertheless, for his own reasons he asked for a name.

'His name is Harry Talvace, master-mason.'

The prior drew a long breath. 'Well, well!' he said; and after a moment: 'He is welcome to our house. He shall have honourable usage and a worthy grave.'

She did not wonder at finding the name known; it would have seemed to her matter for astonishment if she had spoken it aloud anywhere in Christendom and failed to start golden echoes. He so filled her world, living or dead, that this recognition seemed only his due.

She spoke her thanks simply, and bending over the dead tenderly kissed the cold brow. 'Rest tranquilly, my soul,' she said, 'until or she or I come to bring you home.'

When she was gone they took up the body reverently and laid it upon a bier before the altar; and after Lauds they kept vigil for Harry Talvace all the night through. At first light a lay servant rode hotfoot to Aber, to Llewellyn; but he came too late with his news, for the Prince of Gwynedd was already on the march.

The portress was up with the child at first light, clucking to him sleepily and walking the tiny round of her cell. The muffled thudding of hooves on the turf of the valley track came to her sharp old ears clearly, though it was rather a vibration than a sound. She reared up her head and froze where she stood.

Who rode this way at such an hour? The recluse sisters of Saint

Winifrede, clustered about their tiny wooden chapel here in the wilderness, had little to fear even from masterless men at ordinary times; the virgin martyr was as forward in blasting those who behaved disrespectfully to her as she was to favour the devout. But these were no ordinary times. The king was in arms in the south, and most of his barons compounded in a great alliance against him, with the archbishop in the van. Shrewsbury, which had profited by John's want of money in the past to enlarge its civil liberties by charter after charter, stood by its bargains and declared for John; but in North Wales the men of Gwynedd were massing to the banner of Prince Llewellyn, who had joined hands with the rebels. Rumour had it that the insurgents had entered London. A rider here in the dawn might be the messenger bringing the alarm of Welsh raiders already over the border.

Then she heard the knocking at the gate, counted the raps and marked the intervals and knew who came. She went to the gate in the wattle fence with the baby on her arm, lifted the pin and let them into the enclosure.

At sight of two men she drew back in momentary alarm, but the elder was certainly John the Fletcher, whom she knew well, and the younger pushed back the capuchon from his head and let fall on his shoulders the red hair of Madonna Benedetta. She had put on chausses and tunic like a countryman, rough, threadbare brown weeds that turned her into a franklin's boy, but for that milkwhite skin of hers on which the sun and the wind seemed to have no power.

She saw the child, and stood with her hands at her heart, the greeting struck from her lips before she could utter it. She reached out her arms and took him gently to her breast, and looked down at him with a pale, wondering smile. He had a fluff of soft black hair like his mother's, and eyes as yet of an indeterminate colour, that might well clear into sea-green flecked with gold.

'When was he born?' she asked, hanging over him like one dazed.

'Four days ago, about Prime.'

At much the same hour his father had died.

'And Gilleis?'

'She had a hard time of it, but she came through it well. You'll have news for her – ' There she stopped. By the set of the pale face she saw that Benedetta's news would be of little comfort to Gilleis. 'He's gone?'

'He's gone. Thank God she has his true-minted coin left!' She looked down at the two tiny fists doubled under the baby's chin; she had never held so new a human creature before, it seemed impossible that he should compress within that infinitesimal measure all the potentialities of a man. They come into the world perfect, she thought. A hand no bigger than a primrose, and as fragile, and yet there are the lines, the joints, the finger-nails, all the marvellous machinery that will raise cathedrals some day, and play on the lute, and handle tools and arms, and write songs to melt the winter ice, and take women by the heart-strings and draw them after him through the world.

'I must talk to Gilleis. We must get her away from here with the boy, somewhere safe, if there is such a place. There's fire and sword out along the borders of Powis already. And I am not easy in my mind while she stays in the same shire with Isambard. Even yet, if he knew there was a child – '

'He'd never touch such an innocent,' protested the portress incredulously.

'So some charitable soul must have said of Herod. There is not much he would not do, except break his word. We'll not leave temptation in his way. If I could get her to Shrewsbury we could make shift well enough. But is she fit to ride?'

'Not yet, not alone. John might manage her if you could carry the child. She's not much more than child-size herself. But she ought to rest two or three days longer, even so. Shall I see if she's waking? You'd as well tell her soon as late.'

'Ay, do, but if she's sleeping, leave her be. No!' she said jealously when the portress made to take back the child. 'Leave him with me! You see he's content, he isn't crying.'

She was still carrying him when she was admitted to the cell where Gilleis lay. The great black eyes, dark-circled, stared up at her from the pillow their unspoken question. Benedetta stood beside the bed, and what she had to tell seemed to her to have no possible beginning.

'He's dead, then,' said Gilleis, not questioning any longer.

'He's dead,' she said, so low that it was difficult to hear the words.

'I was sure,' said Gilleis. 'I felt him go from me.' She turned her head upon the pillow, her face to the wall.

'He sent you his undying love. And bade me kiss his son for him.'

The faintest of smiles plucked for a moment at the full, soft mouth. 'How like him, to be so sure it would be a son!' Her fingers, spread on the covers of the bed, clenched slowly until the nails dug into her palms. 'Was he – cruelly hurt? Was he shamed?' It was not that she cared for herself about that last, but only that it would have wounded him to the very soul to be less than magnificent.

'No, never! He was the victor. He never lowered his head, never bent his knee. He went in God's good time, not in Isambard's, and it was quick and clean and like a bolt from heaven in their faces. One instant, and he was gone. The executioners never laid hand on him.'

The averted face was still, faintly flushed, listening and wondering. 'Tell me!'

Benedetta told her all, even the full horror of the death he had escaped, since his victory was thereby so much the greater, and the death which had overtaken him so much the easier to bear. Only what had passed between Harry and herself she kept in her heart unspoken. It was enough for Gilleis to know that he had asked for speech with her so that he might send and receive the last messages of love.

'If I might have seen him once more!' whispered Gilleis, voice and heart aching past bearing.

She lay like one dead, her face still turned away. Benedetta leaned over and laid the child in her arm, and by instinct her hands came up and settled him easily against her breast. In a while her drawn brows smoothed a little, feeling his weight and warmth on her heart.

'If you knew,' said Benedetta, 'how I envy you!'

She sank to her knees beside the bed and laid her head on her arms. In a moment a hand stole across the coverlet and gently touched her cheek, and looking up she saw that the black head on the pillow had turned its face towards her, and that the great eyes were kind and full of tears.

A messenger came on the second day seeking John the Fletcher, who in his turn made haste to Benedetta with the news.

'The lad's from close by Parfois, I made it good with him before I left that if there was rumour of search still being made for Mistress Gilleis he should come and leave word here. For I knew you'd come to fetch her away, her and the child, if it was in your power. He says they've told over the whole household to find who loosed the shot that robbed that Gascon crow of his dinner, and the whole stable to know if a horse is missing. And the upshot is, they know now both the one and the other, and are scouring the countryside for me and the grey. The lad says they've picked up his traces as near as the alehouse at Walkmill, and are bound this way.'

Benedetta was on her feet before he had told the half of it. 'By Walkmill? Then before they draw near here we could be down into the valley road and head for Shrewsbury, and they'd have to ride clean round Longmynd or clean over it before they'd be able to sight us.'

'They would. It should give us a fair start. But the grey will be carrying two.'

'No help for it! Saddle up, John, while I warn Gilleis.'

'And cover your hair, lady. In this light they'd see it a mile away and more from the top of the ridge.'

'They think me dead,' she said. 'It's not red hair they're looking for, but a grey horse.'

'Nevertheless, hide it. They have but to glimpse that and well they'll know you're living, for there's no second such head in Britain.'

She hid it within the capuchon she had from the goodman in the assart under Parfois, and pulled on again the coarse chausses and tunic. They had no such concealment for Gilleis, but she took John's dun cloak about her, the same in which Harry had lain shrouded as they rowed him to the abbey. Their farewells were hasty and brief. John mounted first, and Benedetta offered a knee to help Gilleis to the saddle before him. She had protested that she was strong enough to ride pillion and ease him of the burden of holding her, but they mistrusted if her strength was equal yet to her spirit. The baby was handed up to Benedetta and settled securely within the folds of the cloak the sisters had given her. In this fashion they rode out by the green track and wound their way down from between the hills to take the direct road to Shrewsbury.

Benedetta set a fast pace. The valley was open here, and the great ridge of the Longmynd overhung them on the left hand. Several times she cast anxious glances along the smooth slope, straining to see as high as the crest, where ran the old, old road. There was a brisk wind blowing, and when she turned her head it tugged at her capuchon, which was overlarge for her, but she had no hand to spare for clutching at it.

They were almost abreast of the last folds of the ridge when she heard the baying of a dog, high on the crest, and recognising the note only too well, looked up in consternation. The wind filled her hood and tore it backwards from her head, and her hair streamed out in the fitful sunlight. She freed one hand to cover her betraying splendour again, but late. A shout echoed down distantly but clearly from the hill. She saw a tiny dark figure launch itself over the edge of the slope, a second, a third and fourth, six at least, and a tawny thing that flashed before them like an arrow down the green sheep-track.

'Soliman!' she cried, and drove in her heels and put her horse to a gallop. At least if they were to be ridden down it should be by the hound only, for he could outrun most horses. She was not afraid of the beast himself; this great creature had lain with his head in her lap too often now to be turned against her. But his power to bring the huntsmen down upon their quarry she did fear.

'A mile to the ford,' cried John, close behind her. 'We can take to the water there.'

He knew this country as she did not, and she was willing to be guided. She cast one glance down at the child; he was asleep, as serenely as in a guarded bed. Who would believe there was so much resilience in such a tiny creature?

Soliman gave tongue behind them, startlingly close. Over the rough descent he had had the advantage of the horses, and surely outstripped them by a long distance. And here the Roman road plunged into the woodlands, and from men they might be safely hidden, but not from him. The next time he belled the cry seemed hard on their heels.

'I'll take him at the ford,' cried John, and loosened his dagger in its sheath.

'No!' She knew which of them would be the more likely to die, and wished harm to neither. She plunged down to the brook and swung left-handed from the track into the water as he directed her, and there she reined in and cried to him to take the child from her.

'He'll not touch me. He's lived familiar with me for six years and been taught to know me as his mistress. Not even for Isambard would he harm me. I'll try if I can send him home. Take them ahead! I'll follow.'

'No, it's my part – '

'Take them!' she cried, and thrust the baby into Gilleis' outstretched arms. 'I'll come after!' and she wheeled in a shallow flurry of spray back to the ford. She heard the ripple of hooves recede downstream until a curve of the bushy bank cut them off sharply. Then there was silence. She strained her ears for voices or hoofbeats on the road, but heard nothing. The dog did not give tongue again. He came out of the filigree shadow and light like a tremor of the branches, stretched out low to the ground in his long, smooth gait, his vast head down. She called his name softly, and the folded ears pricked high and the amber eyes were raised, though he did not lift his muzzle from the trail he was following. At the waterside he checked, quested a little this way and that, and stood at gaze, waving his tail at her doubtfully.

'No, Soliman! Home!' she said, and lighted down to him, splashing through the water to take the tawny head, broad and heavy as a war-helm, in her hands. 'Hear me! Leave it now! Enough!'

The yellow eyes stared back at her dubiously, acknowledging her right to give him orders, but loath to leave a pursuit on which another voice and another authority had launched him. 'No more, Soliman, it's finished. Finished! Go home!'

She pointed, not back along the track but due westward, towards Parfois. He turned slowly, looking back at her over a rippling shoulder, and when she motioned to him again turned his head also, and began to lope easily back along the road.

'No, Soliman! Not back! Home!'

The silken ears signalled disappointment and reluctance, but he complied, turning off among the trees; and having made up his mind at last, stretched out into a leisurely run, and laid his nose towards Parfois. When he had vanished she mounted and rode after John the Fletcher down the bed of the Cound brook, picking her way delicately among the stones.

'He's gone. Not back to them, they'd only have set him on again. Straight for home. Unless he falls into confusion now they'll not find him again this side of Parfois. But the creature has a conscience, he hates to give up. We'd best stay in the water a while.'

They pushed on as fast as they could, leaving the water only where the brook's complicated windings lost them ground. After two miles of this they thought it better to take to the open track again, and made good speed through Condover.

They had seen and heard no more of the party which had ridden down at them from the Longmynd, but at Bayston they all but rode into them before they were aware. Outside the alehouse a number of people were gathered, looking towards Shrewsbury and making a great clamour with their talk, and Benedetta would have ridden innocently into their council to find out what the excitement was if John had not clutched her suddenly by the arm, and drawn her hastily aside with him into an alley between the houses.

'De Guichet!' she whispered, seeing in the middle of the group the massive shoulders and the tall skewbald horse John had seen, and the Greek, useless now without his hound, turning his narrow, weatherbeaten face from one person to another with the blind look of one who follows speech in a language only half understood.

They were all there, and all between her and Shrewsbury. While the hunted were laboriously covering their traces by keeping to the water the hunters, abandoned by their guide, must have held to the road and ridden it hard, to reach this point ahead of their quarry, though it seemed they did not realise they were beforehand.

John the Fletcher tightened his arm about Gilleis, and looked down at her with an anxious face as he walked his horse along the beaten earth of the alley. 'She's flagging, poor lady. Take the little one again, we'd best be ready to run for it.'

Gilleis opened her eyes to say faintly that she was well enough, but she gave up the baby without complaint, and Benedetta made him secure within her cloak and tightened the belt that held the folds of his cradle together. He began a thin wailing, no louder than a blind kitten's cry, but it wrung her heart. He should not fall into Isambard's hands, to be done to death, or more likely raised up in cold blood as Isambard's creature, in ignorance of his father; never, while she lived.

They circled the village by way of the fields, and drew in to the road some way beyond, and there took a gallop again on the grass verge, where the turf was lush and deep. If the crowd outside the alehouse had not been casting such constant and strained glances towards Shrewsbury they would have got clear away; but every moment someone was turning to point that way, and the dappled horse, so pale as to show white against the May greenness, caught the eye all too easily. When Benedetta looked back, she saw the dust of the pursuit rolling purposefully after them along the road.

There was smoke on the skyline, they saw it now as a rising column against the blue, disseminated by the wind in the upper air into a tenuous cloud which lay floating above Shrewsbury. In Meole, too, people were out before their houses, babbling and pointing, and when John the Fletcher would have bellowed his way through them in haste, one of the men ran and caught at his bridle.

'Turn here, master, if you're in your wits. Shrewsbury's afire, do you not see the smoke? The Welsh have fired the mill, and the abbey storehouses are ablaze.'

'Better brave a Welsh raid than go back,' said Benedetta, kneeing her way forward.

'This is no raid, lad. They're bent on taking the town, and there's no one this side of Gloucester who could stop them. They circled the river to come at the eastern side, where they were not looked for. There was a rider through here half an hour ago who told us the Prince of Gwynedd is on the bridge already and battering at the gate.'

'The Prince of Gwynedd?' She cried it aloud in a shout of joy. 'Thanks for your warning, friend! Be sure to repeat it to those who come after us.' She thrust forward resolutely, and they fell back from her and let her through, though no doubt they thought her mad.

The smoke had thickened over Shrewsbury, she watched it as she galloped. Only once did she look back for a moment, before Meole fell out of sight. De Guichet had ridden past the barrier of excited people, only to halt by the roadside irresolute. They were unwilling to follow him farther; they were six men, and had no orders to ride into a Welsh army. Yet there was more than a mile of road left before the fugitives would reach the bridge, and they might yet be overtaken. He was waving his men on furiously, and they were coming, some of them at least, two more figures, three – that meant all, for the last two would never dare go back to Parfois if they set themselves apart now. She fixed her eyes on the unrolling ribbon of road, and urged the tiring horse with knee and voice and hand.

Down the long slope now towards the great silver coil of the Severn; and already rising into sight beyond, clouded with the hovering pall of smoke, the moated hill, crowned with its turreted wall. The track bore round right-handed to circle with the river, and the town revolved like a wheel on its plateau, slowly bringing into view tower after tower like the terminals of the spokes, and taking tower after tower away. The gate-towers rolled round towards them, first as one, then dual, with the dark inlet between, and on the bridge below a mass of men heaving faintly with movement and flashing fitfully with steel. The smoke had no stem to earth within the wall, it drifted on the wind from the near side of the river, where the abbey and all its attendant buildings lay, and the almshouses, the dwellings of the devout pensioners who had made over all their goods to the abbey in return for this little pittance of board and bed. The church itself stood inviolate, the great boundary wall preserving all within; but the mill was sending up tall flames, and a tower of smoke, and the granaries and the gabled timber houses clustered between abbey and river were all ablaze.

A crossbow quarrel thudded into the grassy verge. Benedetta hunched her body about the child, and drove in her heels and plunged on. If they were shooting now, it was because they were about to draw off. She heard the full, hard impact of a second bolt, fallen short, before the smoke wrapped itself about her, filling her throat and stinging her eyes. She caught the edge of the cloak in her teeth to cover the child's face, and rode on half-blind into the turmoil at the end of the bridge.

There were men all round her, clawing at her bridle, shouting in English and in Welsh. Faces loomed out of the smoke and vanished again, distorted by her streaming tears. She looked round once to be sure John was at her back, and then fought her way forward through the press, kicking off hands that clutched at her, wrenching herself out of their hold. Someone caught at the liripipe of her capuchon, and dragged it backwards from her head, and the tangled masses of her hair gushed down about her shoulders and streamed in the wind of her frantic passage.

'Where is the Prince of Gwynedd? Where is Prince Llewellyn?'

She was on the bridge now. The press of men hemmed her in, dark, darting clansmen, most of them afoot, some on wiry, strong hill ponies. The wind from off the water ripped a clear passage through the murk, and she caught a glimpse of the gate of Shrewsbury between its towers, and a cluster of tall horses and mailed riders, and a young squire clasping a broad war-helm circled with a thin coronet of gold. She tossed back her hair from her eyes and shouted again hoarsely above the clattering of hooves and the babel of voices: 'Bring me to the Prince of Gwynedd! Where is Prince Llewellyn?'

'Who's that calls so loudly on Llewellyn?'

The ranks parted before him and she saw him, darkly bright in the flush of his triumph. His head was bared and his sword sheathed, for the town lay open to him with hardly a blow struck. Smoke had soiled the shoulders of the white surcoat that covered his banded mail hauberk, but the outline of the red dragon on his breast stood clear. His black horse was tall and great-boned like the rider, and set him a head above most of those who rode with him. The vivid, falcon's face, all shadow and light about the darting, intelligent eyes, was flushed with exertion and the heat of his helm. He was laughing; laughter, anger, generosity, pity, all that was quick and warm would come readily to this face. He stripped off his mail gauntlets and let them hang from his wrists, and even that small movement had a fiery liveliness about it.

'Who is it cries on Llewellyn?'

'One who has a life's claim on him,' she said, reining in at his knee. 'His name is Harry Talvace.'

The prince's eyes swept over her in astonishment, marking the coarse, countryman's garments, the soiled, weary, lovely woman's face, the long red hair darkened to crimson purple with sweat. By that hair he knew her; it was not difficult to describe Benedetta so that there should be no mistaking her.

'Talvace is here?' He looked beyond her eagerly, searching for one of whom he had heard so much already from two who praised and loved him; but seeing only a grizzled serving-man with a young woman in his arms, looked back bewildered into Benedetta's face. 'Where is he? Bring him to me, and more than welcome! We were coming to Parfois to fetch him, but by God's help it seems he's come to us, and I am still his debtor.'

She gently loosed the belted folds of the cloak, and held out to him the child, confidently asleep again in the middle of turmoil. He looked down in wonder at the tiny head of black hair and the minute, folded fists, and the shadow of understanding came down upon his face.

'Here is Harry Talvace, son of Harry Talvace,' she said, 'and this is Gilleis, his mother. They have great need of your protection, and I ask it for them in his name.'

Behind the clear grey of her eyes Llewellyn saw an aching emptiness, a void no other, not even the child, would ever be able to fill.

'Dead?' he asked.

'Dead. Seven days gone.'

He looked down at the child with a sombre face. 'From my heart I am sorry. We counted on having longer, or I would not have waited for FitzWalter to reach London. There's his foster-brother yonder among my men will be sorrier yet, and a gosling at home will cry bitterly when he hears it.' He shook his head, and the dark, curling locks, disordered from his helm, fell damply about his forehead. 'We counted on having longer,' he said again, with angry sorrow. 'We meant to have him out of hold by force, or bargain Shrewsbury for his ransom.'

From the gate of the town, wide open to receive the conqueror, his knights looked back in wonder and curiosity at the stranger woman with the baby on her arm, and the horses, impatient, stamped and shook their harness. The castellan stood within the shadow of the gateway, the provosts and the keepers of the crown pleas at his back, waiting nervously to deliver up the keys.

'We're keeping the good burgesses waiting,' said Llewellyn, looking back over his shoulder with a quick, wild toss of his head. 'Come, at least let's get his lady safe to her bed. Follow close after me till we bring her to the castle.' He looked with great gentleness at Gilleis, pallid on John's shoulder, her eyes closed. 'Talvace's widow is my kinswoman,' he said, and putting out his hand, touched with a broad forefinger the child's flushed forehead. 'And his son is my son!'

He wheeled his horse, and cried to his men in Welsh, and the ranks drew in about them, and moved slowly forward towards the gate, and there halted to let their prince ride first and alone into the town, but he reached an imperious hand to Benedetta's bridle.

'Ride by me with the boy. For his father's sake he shall make a prince's entry, and lie in a royal bed tonight.'

The black horse paced forward with a high, disdainful step over the threshold, beneath the raised portcullis. The confined breeze between the towers lifted Llewellyn's trailing silken moustaches and short dark curls, and fluttered Benedetta's long hair in a cloak of shadowy imperial purple about the child she carried, as prince and fosterling rode together into the captured town.